CRAZY QUILT

Borgo Press Books by Ardath Mayhar

The Absolutely Perfect Horse: A Novel of East Texas (with Marylois Dunn)
The Body in the Swamp: An Occult Mystery
Carrots and Miggle: A Novel of East Texas
The Clarrington Heritage
Closely Knit in Scarlatt
Crazy Quilt: The Best Short Stories of Ardath Mayhar, Intro. by Joe R. Lansdale
Deadly Memoir: A Novel of Suspense
Death in the Square
The Door in the Hill: A Tale of the Turnipins
The Dropouts: A Tale of Growing Up in East Texas
Feud at Sweetwater Creek: A Novel of the Old West
The Fugitives: A Tale of Prehistoric Times
The Heirs of Three Oaks: A Novel of the Old West
High Mountain Winter: A Novel of the Old West
How the Gods Wove in Kyrannon: Tales of the Triple Moons
Hunters of the Plains: A Novel of Prehistoric America
Island in the Lake: A Novel of Native America
Khi to Freedom: A Science Fiction Novel
The Lintons of Skillet Bend: A Novel of East Texas
Lone Runner: A Novel of the Old West
Lords of the Triple Moons: A Science Fantasy Novel: Tales of the Triple Moons
Makra Choria: A Novel of High Fantasy
Medicine Dream: Being the Further Adventures of Burr Henderson
Messengers in White: A Science Fantasy Novel
Monkey Station: A Novel of the Future (Macaque Cycle #1; with Ron Fortier)
People of the Mesa: A Novel of Native America
A Planet Called Heaven: A Science Fiction Novel
Prescription for Danger: A Novel of the Old West
Reflections; & Journey to an Ending: Collected Poems
A Road of Stars: A Fantasy of Life, Death, Love, and Art
Runes of the Lyre: A Science Fantasy Novel
The Saga of Grittel Sundotha: A Science Fantasy Novel
The Seekers of Shar-Nuhn: Tales of the Triple Moons
Shock Treatment: An Account of Granary's War
Slewfoot Sally and the Flying Mule: Tall Tales from Cotton County, Texas
Soul-Singer of Tyrnos: A Fantasy Novel
Strange Doings in the Pine Hills: Stories
Through a Stone Wall: Lessons from Thirty Years of Writing
Timber Pirates: A Novel of East Texas (with Marylois Dunn)
Towers of the Earth: A Novel of Native America
Trail of the Seahawks: A Novel of the Future (Macaque Cycle #2; with R. Fortier)
The Tulpa: A Novel of Fantasy
Two-Moons and the Black Tower: A Novel of Fantasy
Vendetta
Warlock's Gift: Tales of the Triple Moons
The World Ends in Hickory Hollow: A Novel of the Future
A World of Weirdities: Tales to Shiver By

CRAZY QUILT

The Best Short Stories of

ARDATH MAYHAR

by

Ardath Mayhar

Introduction by Joe R. Lansdale

THE BORGO PRESS

An Imprint of Wildside Press LLC

MMIX

CONTENTS

INTRODUCTION

ARDATH MAYHAR, EAST TEXAS MAGICIAN

Ardath Mayhar is a neglected writer, and that is criminal. She is one of those born storytellers and natural writers who has done so much so well, that it is easy to take her for granted. It's like assuming the Statue of Liberty will always stand and that we can see it at anytime. The problem is, there is no statue to Ardath. Until now. This book is her statue. Cherish it.

She can write anything, and she can write it with great panache. She is one of my favorite writers of all time, and I'm especially fond of her short stories, which is the point of this collection, to introduce her to new readers, and to give already established fans a chance to reacquaint themselves with old favorites, to reunite with the magic that is Ardath Mayhar's work; to visit a Statue of Liberty of fine storytelling and to come away with good memories of the visit. And with this book now in existence, it's a site to which we can return again and again, taking in all of its wonder and magical goodness.

Ardath reminds me a bit of Mark Twain, or of more modern ilk, Manly Wade Wellman. She is perhaps most noted for her SF in the long form (please find *The World Ends at Hickory Hollow*—it's great!) and in the short form for her horror stories. But these recognitions, though nice, do not do her justice. Like all labels they leave out a lot of the things she has written, and try to box up everything else into a couple of small containers. They do not take into account the genre-bending work, the articles and essays and opinion pieces she has written. There aren't enough boxes to cover what she had written, and if there were enough boxes, I can assure you, they would be overfilled and leaking out from under the lids.

Ardath is also an excellent writer of western and suspense and crime and mystery tales, and one of my favorite kinds of stories, the East Texas story. These are stories that can be considered tall tales about our region, or she may take another avenue where the stories are about everyday life in East Texas, then and now. Sometimes the two types of stories are pretty darn close to the same thing.

If ever there was a place that gave birth and housed a group of bigger-than-life individuals, it would be East Texas, sometimes referred to by the more timid Texans of the heartland and the southern and western and northern parts of Texas, as being "Behind the Pine Curtain."

This is true. Ardath is here to tell you about it. If you have not read her, then might I say that this collection of her varied works, many of which I had the privilege of hearing read at our East Texas writer's meetings that took place just about every month for twenty years or more, is here to enlighten you.

The writer's group has faded into obscurity now, many of the participants having moved off or grown old, a few dead and long gone, but once upon a time, in those great days of East Texas Camelot, it was aces, my friends. A meeting place for all kinds of ideas and criss-crossing worlds, much of it Deep Fried, Baptized, Crucified and Sanctified, rat-killed, dog-bit, and just plain old odd.

Many of its members were published writers of fiction or non-fiction, or they wrote poetry. Ardath and I were, to the best of my memory, the only full-time writers in the group, and I can tell you, when Ardath brought a story to read, we all listened with enthusiasm.

You never knew what she was going to do.

Her stories, like the best of the stories I enjoy, came out of left field, and my favorites of her work came from beyond the stadium, flying in on dark wings. There was often a folksy angle to her work that I greatly enjoyed, she and I having grown up years apart, but, really, in not too different times and circumstances.

Her stories generally have an East Texas taste, or after-taste, even if she's writing about places and people far removed from here, but even then, I can sense East Texas in her stories about other places and other worlds. It writhes snake-like under the blankets of her prose. She brings the unique character of our region to her work, and has been long neglected for her contributions to Texas writings.

She has certainly been an influence on me, and it is mostly due to one story.

Once upon a time my wife and I were truck croppers in Starrville, Texas, and I was a would-be writer. I had actually written and sold some non-fiction, but fiction was my love, and my dream of being a full-time writer had been with me almost since my arrival from the womb; well, I was aware of it by the time I discovered crayons and pencils—soon as I had those in my hands, I wanted to write. Fact was, I couldn't contain myself. I didn't pick it, it picked me, and my muse is a brutal lady, and for many years she chased me up one hill and down another, cracking a whip.

I guess most dedicated writers feel that way.

The bottom line was, I had to write.

I tried writing the kinds of stories I read in magazines, and certainly I learned much from the effort, but one day I was looking through a collection of stories in an anthology of offbeat crime tales, one of those many volumes of *Alfred Hitchcock Presents* that were so popular in the nineteen seventies, and I came across a short story by a writer I had never heard of. Because the name, Ardath, was unusual, it stuck with me, and because the last name, Mayhar, reminded me of the villainous winged reptiles in Edgar Rice Burroughs's Pellucidar series, I was driven to read the story.

It may be funny reasoning, but, there you have it.

I also, perhaps because the name was not one I associated with the feminine, assumed the writer was male; could be that was male chauvinism on my part, though I like to think not. But somehow I didn't associate Ardath with a female name anymore than I originally associated Flannery O'Conner with a female or Harper Lee with a female or Carson McCullers with a female.

Anyway, I read her story in the anthology, "Crawfish," and it was about this man who had committed a murder and was haunted by what the crawfish might be doing to the discarded body he had placed in the water. It had a kind of Robert Bloch feel to it (another favorite writer of mine), but it had something Bloch's work did not, something no genre writer I was reading had. She was writing about the world I knew: East Texas. I remember almost letting out a whoop as I realized where the story was taking place, and feeling even more satisfied when I realized the voice in the story was authentic, that she knew of what she wrote. This was my world, my little spot in the universe, and she had nailed it. And now that the nail was in the wall, I hung my pictures on it.

Yes, dear readers. Reading that one story changed my life.

It is still a favorite of mine.

And another thing: I knew upon reading this little gem that I could write about my own world then. I had been given permission and the truth had set me free. I knew, because of Ardath Mayhar, that I could and would bring the elements of my life into my fiction and that it would be the better for it.

A little later my wife, Karen, and I moved to Nacogdoches, Texas. One of the first people I met there was, you guessed it, Ardath Mayhar. We hit it off immediately and have been fast friends ever since. She's like an aunt to me, and I love her dearly. But if I did not, if I didn't know her at all, I would write a glowing introduction to her work, would shout to you from the rooftops:

READ ARDATH MAYHAR

Trust me, as the spider said to the fly: read Ardath's work. Enter into her world, and understand that it has many alternate universes into which you will travel. Be captivated by her worlds. They will never let you go, and you will never ask to be released.
Promise.

—Joe R. Lansdale
October 2007

I love to turn fairy tales inside out and upside down. Asking myself, "What would happen if...?" I've done this to more than one basic fairy tale concept. I had fun with this one.

FIDO IS A LOVING BEAST

The clanging of metal upon metal brought Florelle to the edge of the forest. "God's boots and buckler!" she said aloud, reveling in her irreverence. "What can that signify?"

She listened, her golden head cocked on one side, the better to hear.

It was not the urgent yammering of the great iron bell that her father was so proud of. Besides, that only signaled war, and all the neighboring principalities had made peace long since. A couple of her father's peers were, even now, working in the hayfields with him and all the serfs they could spare from necessary tasks.

No, that sounded like—she sighed. Another noble lackwit, come to make his name by slaying the last dragon in all the known lands. Drat! He was hammering with his sword-hilt upon the metal-studded gate of the keep, even though the thing stood wide in time of haying.

She pulled her oldest gown above her knees and sped back the way she had come. Poor Fido! He was such a loving beast. It always upset him when this happened. And she! It made her wince to think of all the far from noble dodges she had been put to in order to protect her unlikely pet.

But she had reared him from a tiny creature, hardly eight feet long. Just from the egg, he had been, when his mother had fallen victim to just such a one as now stood at the castle gate. Florelle had been wandering the forest, as her habit had been since she was tiny, and had found him, lying all but starved in her path.

For months, nobody had been able to explain the disappearance of hens and eggs from the poultry runs. Then he had graduated to live game, which had relieved her of much unpleasant scrambling about after disturbed hens in the most distant of the runs.

It was too bad the forester had sighted him. By then, of course, he was at least half grown and a very respectable dragon indeed, with lengthy coils and scarlet wings. The word had gone out at once. Another dragon for the slaying! Wonderful!

And all the idiots with nothing better to do had donned their armor to come and do battle with him. As if Fido knew how to fight armed men! Only his mother could have taught him that. All Florelle could do was to teach him to trick them, and that she had done with a will.

Of course her father had been forced by tradition (and her mother, who felt herself to be tradition's mainstay) to offer his daughter's hand to the one who would deliver his principality from the fearsome beast. That was the way it was done, notwithstanding the fact that the aforesaid beast had never harmed a creature under his protection, unless you might count those early hens. Prince Paulus's forest was singularly free of predators and of large rats, as well, though nobody could account for that, except for Florelle.

Now she ran among the huge boles of oaks and beeches, and her thoughts were as unprincesslike as her gait. The charcoal—was there enough? Yes, she had seen to that after the last attacker, back in the late fall. And the cauldron of dye as red as blood? It was full. She had checked only a week ago. Still, she must warn her pet, for he was entirely too trusting for one of his species.

Pausing before an outcropping of rock that had tumbled down the steep cliff at the edge of the wood, she whistled sharply. There came a grumbling roar in reply—a very soft one, she was glad to note. Fido had learned not to give full voice after shaking the ground all the way to the nearest cathedral town and setting the bells to ringing at midnight. That had given her a fright, indeed, though the scholars and theologians luckily decided that the Devil had been unusually active in Hell on that night.

Fortunately, men were mainly fools, she had decided long ago.

A large head with liquid green eyes and golden whiskers came slithering out of a cranny in the rock-slide. The eyes went soft when they saw her, and a burbling purr came from the cart-wide span of his mouth.

She smiled in spite of herself. He was so loving! But entirely too trusting. She scrambled into the cavern and sat on a rock. The great creature arranged his coils among the stones that furnished his home and laid his chin—or what served as such—at her feet.

12 * *CRAZY QUILT*, BY ARDATH MAYHAR

"There is another one at the gate this moment," she told Fido. "Metal from head to heels, and likely a helmful of purest granite. He will probably dine and sleep the night before coming out to find you, but I want you well hidden, just in case he is in a hurry. I shall slip away before the house wakes in the morning and stoke up the fires at the back of the cave.

"You go into the deepest places and keep very still. Go to sleep—you do that so well, dear. I'll make a dragon for him, smokes and flames and all, and if he is like the rest he will claim to have slain you and nobly renounce all reward before he leaves. Heaven knows what I should do if one came who had no honor at all and tried to claim me. I might well bring him here for a dalliance. Yet I would hesitate to give you a taste for humanity. That might become awkward."

The big creature burbled softly, and she patted the scaly head. "We shall worry about that when there is cause," she said. "Until then, go quickly and hide. I shall visit you after we have put this newcomer to flight."

Fido arranged his coils and glided away over the stony floor, his scales rustling in a shivery fashion. His friend and mistress watched him go with a fond smile.

Florelle arrived home a bit late and more than a bit untidy from her exertions. She was met by her mother, who was more indignant than usual at her daughter's unladylike ways.

"Here's a fine young man, come all the way from Bar-Bludgeon to fight the dragon and claim your hand, and you are poking about in that dirty wood, getting insects in your hair and dirt on your dress. If only I had produced a proper daughter! But you are too like your Aunt Alzabel. Entirely too like! I wonder why I consented, when your father asked me to wed. I knew Alzabel. I should have been warned!"

Florelle was too used to such tirades to listen. She washed and changed and went meekly down to dinner, where she was all a young girl should be, quiet, meek, agreeable. So much so that her mother glanced suspiciously at her more than once.

The knight, once he peeled off his crust of armor, was very young. Almost, indeed, as young as Florelle. All of the others had been hard-bitten sportsmen with nothing in their heads but spoor and tracking techniques. They had wanted her as little as she did them, for all their lust had been for poor Fido. Until, of course, they came within sight of the cave, with its billows of smoke and its scarlet flames shooting out of the cavern-mouth.

Once they established in their minds that a real...live...dragon lived there, it was a matter of much simplicity to send them flying. A bellow from Fido, rumbling up from the depths where she hid him, always had done the job quite well.

She rather hated to do that with this one. He looked too ill-at-ease, too unsure of himself to play such a trick on him. After dinner, for the first time in her life, she consented to sit at one side of the fireplace with him while her mother sewed on the other, within sight but out of easy earshot.

"Why do you come hunting our dragon?" Florelle asked him, pretending to poke back a stray coal into the fire. "From your look, I should say you would take naturally to farming, as my father does."

His hand stole from his side and found hers, where she had carefully left it waiting under a fold of her skirt. Florelle felt something that had not occurred to her before.

A most interesting sensation, indeed. She looked questioningly at him, then at her mother.

A grin touched her lips. "Edred, do you like to get up early? Very, very early? There is something I might show you, before dawn tomorrow, if you would meet me at the postern gate." She watched his face closely.

A smile touched his own lips. He shot a glance at the old Princess, but her eyes were fixed on her work. "I'll be there," he breathed.

* * * * * * *

Fido liked Edred at once. When he overcame his surprise, Edred found the big beast every bit as affectionate and interesting as did Florelle. Before the sun rose, the two young people had gone deeper along the cliffs to find another cavern, better hidden and less accessible than the first.

Getting Fido there was not as chancy as it would have been later in the morning. Once he was well hidden they poured the cauldron of "blood" on the floor, whacked about with Edred's blade to scar a few rocks, and made it look as if a terrible battle had taken place there.

The Prince came, when they called him to view the place where the dragon had been slain. Though no body was found, everyone agreed that not even a Worm could withstand the loss of so much blood without dying, sooner or later.

"He flew away," said Edred, gesturing upward. "I would guess that he fell in the mountains beyond the cliffs. He could hardly fly at all, and he wavered in the air."

The Prince sighed, partly with relief that such foolishness was over, at long last, and partly with regret at what he must say next. "And now I must, by my word, offer you my daughter's hand in marriage. What say you? Though I admit that she will be sorely missed."

Edred's face reddened, but he stood squarely before the older man. "Sir, I will accept her hand, gladly, if she is willing. Not otherwise. And if it please you and your lady wife, perhaps we might live here with you. It seems you have need for another pair of strong hands about your fields. Farming is my interest and my love, after your beautiful daughter. My father has many sons and you have none. Would that be agreeable?"

So the two were wed. Amid much rejoicing, they rode away for a fortnight of privacy, as was proper. They never told anyone they spent the weeks in Fido's cavern, visited often by the big beast.

And no one ever understood why they and their children spent so many fair summer days wandering in the forest at the foot of the cliff near the mountains.

Years ago a friend who studied in Wales send me a set of Welsh folktales, which contained a wealth of fantasy ideas. This is not the only story to develop as a result.

A HARPING OF WATERS

A CELTIC MYTH RETOLD

It was a long walk across the hills, long and hard and perilous, and few found business to take them there. None went for their pleasure.

So it was that Gheros stared with astonishment at the shape striding down the low hill toward his stone hut. Not only astonishment touched his heart—more than a bit of foreboding accompanied the approach of the man—or boy, as he turned out to be—to the small dwelling. Just so had that other messenger come, all those years ago.

A hail cut into his thought, and he saw the newcomer was a stripling clad in the green and purple of Lord Ambro's livery. A bitter taste rose into Gheros's mouth, but he forced a civil reply.

"Who comes seeking Gheros, so far from the haunts of other people?"

The lad stopped at the doorstone and wiped his sweating brow. "A messenger from our Lord," he said. "You are commanded to return to the Palace in the Vale, bringing with you your harp and all your accoutrements. Every harper and dancer and piper in all the Four Dukedoms is ordered to attend, for a great entertainment is planned. You will be expected to come at once."

The boy was hot and weary, Gheros could see. Swallowing his feelings, the harper set a stool in front of the hut and brought water and bread. "Here, now. Drink and eat. Rest before you go about your work. It is a long and wearing way from here to the Palace in the Vale."

He stood looking down at the boy. "When I was younger than you by a bit, my own father went that path and never returned to this hut or my mother or me. Only his harp came back to us, in the hands of a peddler who knew Gher the Harper. He bought the instrument from the lackey who took it from Gher's dead hand, before the face of Lord Ambro's father. For love of my father, he brought the harp to me."

The lad rose to his feet. "A pity. More than one has died untimely at one of the Lord's feasts." Then he looked frightened at his own words. "Good day to you, Gheros the Harper. I must go with all haste."

Watching him hurry away, Gheros thought again of the messenger who came for his father. That was not so civil a person as this, by far. He haled Gher away as if he were a criminal going to gaol, rather than a master harper summoned to a feast.

The harper turned into his hut. He had to stoop, though he was not over-tall, to clear the door-beam. As he straightened, a bird fluttered to his shoulder and perched there.

"Ssirroo?" That trill was a language, as anyone could have recognized. It was also a question.

"Indeed, Shura. I am summoned at last. To harp for a great entertainment, which means, I have no doubt, that another of the line of Ambro has been born to carry forward the cruelties of his sires. You shall go with me, if you like. After long years of waiting, my mother's dream will be realized at last."

"Llirras!" said the bid, hopping excitedly on its crimson feet. Its black and white feathers ruffled and smoothed on his back.

Gheros smiled grimly. "You are right," he replied.

He did not wait for another day. In the late afternoon, with the pale summer sun slanting across the hills and casting lavender shadow around his feet, he started out. His harp was on one shoulder, his pack balancing it on the other. The bird darted ahead or waited perched on bush or bramble, sometimes even returning to ride on the top of his hat.

He traveled far into the night, until he could hear the sea and see its shining line beyond the last of the hills, which glimmered uneasily in the starlight. Then Gheros turned south, passing into the foothills of the mountain range holding the Palace in the Vale. In the edge of the forest, he camped, but he slept poorly and rose early.

He arrived in two days at that beautiful Vale where the first Ambro had built his house. Yet Gheros did not go down at once to present himself at the gate allotted to tradesmen. He lingered amid the trees, watching for a time. Then he tuned his harp with great care.

The bird watched, its bright eyes following every motion of his hands. Now and again it gave a quiet "Ssrrp!" It was not quite a comment, not quite a plea. When that happened, Gheros turned and smiled.

"I do not expect to return to our home alive, Shura. Feel free to go, if that is your desire. You may find a mate, though your kind has become scarce. Live a long life, for my quarrel is not yours."

The bird ruffled and subsided, while the harper finished his tuning and took the instrument into his arm. He touched a note, and it went singing away into the reaches of the wood. A chord joined it, and another, forming no melody ever heard before by a human ear. The bird shivered its feathers, and even Gheros was pale beneath his tan.

When the tune died away, he packed his harp into its wrappings and took up his bundle. "Time, Shura. Do you come, or do you fly free? I will not blame you, if that is your choice."

The bird flew to his hat brim and settled. Gheros sighed and turned his steps toward the ornate house below. He was admitted with two other musicians, just arrived for the celebration.

One day more would see the feast begin. The musicians' quarters were crowded and noisy, for every sort of instrument was being cleaned, tuned, restrung, and practiced upon. Singers vocalized, lutanists strummed. To one used to silence, it was a chaos, and Gheros fled to the kitchens, where he listened to the gossip of the ill-conditioned servants.

A son had been born to Ambro's pale wife. She still languished, half between life and death, but Ambro gave no thought to her. He was bursting with pride in his son, the heir who would quiet those who had begun eyeing the Four Dukedoms with acquisitive gazes. Ambro's great-grandsire had acquired his oversized holdings by seizing them from heirless estates or childish heirs. Now, Ambro boasted, there was an heir to his holdings with a father young enough to rule until he was full grown.

Gheros offered a helping hand to the harried cooks and serving wenches. He found himself accepted into the kingdom below stairs, and he heard much that sickened him and nothing that made him glad.

Ambro was an even crueler lord than his father. The line seemed set upon growing worse with every generation. There had been times when Gheros wondered if his mother had been justified in her hatred, in her summoning of potencies and teaching them to him, giving him some power over the elements. As he watched the hierophants nod and smile, the guests smirk and sneer, he lost any doubt he might have known. There was no virtue here, from the temple to the tomb.

On the morning of the feast, pale Cheras died in her tower room. No one mourned. She had been the vessel for bringing a new Ambro into being. Her body was taken to a chapel in the forest, and the guests were not informed of her death. None would, Gheros thought, have spared her a prayer, if they had known.

The night of the feasting came. All the nervous musicians, singers, bell-ringers, mimics, jesters, and dancers jostled in a curtained room adjoining the hall. Gheros was among them, his bird on his red velvet cap that had been his grandfather's. One by one (or however they performed), he saw his companions go out through the draperies. None returned, for they exited into another chamber, where they had been told their payment would await them.

Gheros listened with a knowing ear to songs, dance music, jests. He tuned his harp, while he and the slender dancer and her musicians waited together. There came a round of applause, and the hand of the Director twitched aside the curtain.

"Gheros the Harper," he said.

No one applauded as the musician stepped into the hall, though a twitter of laughter greeted the bird atop his head. He bowed, straightened, and turned to gaze toward Ambro, who was sitting in the half-empty double throne at the end of the room.

"Twenty years ago, my father harped here, in this chamber," he said. "Now I intend to perform for my Lord Ambro, giving him his due."

His hand swept across the strings. A chime of notes filled the air, and at the cue the bird flew to the edge of the table. It opened its beak and began to sing in tune with the harp.

Such music had never been heard, everyone knew, by any listener before. The intricate pattern of notes enspelled the listeners, as great waters seemed to move inside the music. Waves and tides rushed in from some infinite sea. Storm and calm were there, the cries of gulls meshed with a subtle trill, which died away as if into a great distance. Bird and harper muted the note to silence and waited for a moment.

Shura went to Gheros's cap again, but there was no sound in the hall. Each listener seemed to hear that music still, to think about it inside his spirit. Gheros turned back through the curtain and went into the room from which he had come. The dancer was standing there, entranced.

He touched her arm. "Come with me, child. Those who went to that other room for their reward will not be seen again, I think. Bring your musicians, before it is too late."

The musicians refused. "We need no dancer to complete our performance," they insisted. "We intend to have the gold we were promised."

The dancer looked up at Gheros, wide-eyed. "I will go."

Shura swooped into the room. "Hurry!" he said in the tongue of Man. "The others are dead and being dragged away, while servants spread rushes to hide their blood. And the waters...."

"Ah, the waters," said Gheros. "Come or die," he said to the musicians. But they would not come, and the man, the dancer, and the bird went out into the courtyard and thence through the musicians' gate onto the slope. As they went, the sound of running water filled the air. They hurried as they climbed, and behind them they could hear the quiet river flowing through the Vale become a torrent, rising and grumbling in its bed.

They reached a high spot, and there Gheros stopped and looked back toward the Vale. Beside him, the dancer gasped. Where the Vale had been, a lake was settling into new-formed banks. Only a shadow beneath the moonlit waters showed where the Palace had stood. The sound of the river was quieting, and the star-kissed expanse of water lapped peacefully at the trees trapped in its verges.

"Llirras!" chimed the bird.

The harper smiled. "Vengeance, indeed, little Shura. For my father and my mother and all those who have perished unjustly in those walls at the behest of the line of Ambro. And for the poor little mother, dead and unmourned."

The dancer was trembling beside him, and she caught at his sleeve for comfort. He gently disengaged her grasp and slipped the harp from its strap.

"I must make a gift. Wait here and I will return soon."

He went down the wooded slope, harp in hand. Unwrapped, it hummed faintly as the breeze touched its strings. When he reached the lake, he bent and laid the instrument on the star-sparked wavelets.

"For you, Father. For those who aided my mother so that I could do this task. Ease of spirit, Gher. Go forth with a bright heart." The harp bobbed on the water, floating away from the shore.

He climbed again, and with his companions he watched the small shape as it moved away into the darkness. When it was gone, Gheros turned to the dancer.

"Where would you go now?" he asked her.

She looked at him, her eyes wide and shy. Her finger touched his sleeve. "With you," she said.

As they moved away, Shura dipped and swooped above them. "Laughter will sound in your house," he trilled. "A new harp, untainted with grief! Perhaps a child to teach to play it!"

"Go and find a mate," said Gheros, finding the dancer's hand warm in his. "Old bachelors make dour companions. I would see some of your own young nesting in the thatch."

With a twitter of glee, the bird dipped its wing and turned toward the forest. Gheros smiled, and the dancer tightened her grasp on his arm and smiled too. Behind them, the lake glittered beneath the stars and the moon, smoothing away all trace of ancient wrongs and vengeful acts.

This is my twist on the concept M. R. James used in his wonderful horror story, "The Mezzotint." Art is a sort of magic, and it might well work in many strange ways.

A PAINTERLY EFFECT

JUDITH'S JOURNAL: OCTOBER

Grief does strange things to you, I have found. For the past month I have been painting frantically, as if by envisioning alien worlds and putting them on canvas I might create some context in which my children would still be alive.

Joshua, on the other hand, grieves by retreating into some distant place, inaccessible to anyone. He has taken guilt to his heart, as if even the most devoted father could prevent spinal meningitis from attacking his young. Nothing I can say reaches him. I would be lonely, if I were not so busy.

Our isolation, formerly treasured by all of us, has become a prison from which neither Joshua nor I expect (or want) to escape. Trapped here with our memories and our separate griefs, we have ignored the approach of winter. No wood is stacked beneath the deck to feed the hungry fireplace.

We will depend upon the oil furnace, this season, to keep from freezing when the deep snows come. I remembered to order the furnace tank filled, even in my state of shock. Joshua would never have done that, even if he began to stiffen in his chair.

In my studio, the extra oil heater fuming as it warms the place, I will be safe from self-indulgent agony. I will continue to hold death away by the power of my brush. For I find myself able to put into those fantastic landscapes the shapes of my children, distant as yet, but recognizable. As long as I envision them so clearly they are not dead.

I tried to explain this to Joshua, but he stared at me as if he thought I might be mad. Perhaps I am, but at least I am not living as a mummy, immovable, inscrutable, shut away from everything and everyone. Even his mother, wracked with her own grief, could not stir him from his apathy.

I was glad when she left. Not that I do not admire and respect my mother-in-law, but as long as her pain was added to our own, in this house where our children lived, the burden was more than I could bear. My own loss is all I can deal with. She knew, I think, for when she found she could not wake her son from his withdrawal, she returned home to her invalid daughter.

Now only Joshua and I live on the mountain, each of us encapsulated in a different shell of suffering. He does nothing except sit in his study, only leaving it to prepare a bit of food when he is hungry. I do the same; when I tried cooking for him he ignored the meals until they were ruined. So we move, most separately, quite silently, through the increasingly chilly days.

NOVEMBER

Although my work was always realistic before—landscapes, portraits, mental visions that I managed to convey to a painted surface—it is growing stranger. I have created gardens filled with flowers so alien that I doubt any could exist on earth. Landscapes have grown beneath my brush that might be found on some world with a sun of a different color, soil of very different qualities, and two shadowy moons that are visible by day.

Always, in the background, two children lurk, distant but coming closer with each painting. I knew from the beginning they were Julie and Eric, but now I can recognize their faces, peering through huge purple ferns or peeping from behind scarlet and ocher-streaked boulders. Both are solemn, but I believe I can see a hint of familiar mischief in both sets of gray eyes.

This should be incredibly painful, and yet it is not. Each morning when I rise from my tumbled bed, where sleep was interrupted by continuing nightmares, I am not weary but refreshed. The smell of linseed oil and turpentine, the feel of each brush between my fingers, welcomes me into a universe where all is well and no pain lingers.

As long as I paint, I am happy. Only when I clean the brushes, cover the palette, back away to examine my day's work do I begin to feel that terrible emptiness.

My agent, by the way, loves the new style, the new subjects, everything about my completely uncharacteristic work. The paintings are selling as quickly as I can complete them.

How can I bear to sell them? I wonder. Yet when I have done with each, I do not turn back to it, even for a glimpse. It is in the past, and every new beginning is a future that I cannot guess, a discovery I must make.

The snow has come, great drifts of it very early in the season. Our road has to be plowed regularly for the mail man to make his rounds. Soon the snow will be too deep, and we will not have mail until the next thaw.

I have no regrets. Enclosed here, with Julie and Eric emerging from those alien backgrounds, I can hardly wait for morning and the beginning of a new experience. Something strange and marvelous is going to happen!

DECEMBER

We have been cut off for a week now. The thaw in late November was followed by a blizzard worse than any I can recall since we moved to the mountain. Now the snow is piled to the eaves, only my shoveled path from the back door allowing me to see out over the cliff. Below, the valley is blindingly white, the drooping firs so heavily laden that you can hardly see hints of dark green needles beneath their hoods of snow.

The painting on my easel is also filled with snow. This is pale blue, and the strangely shaped monoliths pushing up through its layers are dark red, bruised gold, and purple-gray against that background. Two wool-capped and jacketed shapes in the middle ground seem to be building a snowman.

I am watching my hand closely, for it seems to be moving independently of my mind. Will this snowman have a wide, goofy grin made of black buttons? Julie and Eric invented their own "trademark" in the snowman field. In a drawer of my desk those very buttons wait for a snowman that will never be formed again in this world.

Will they find black buttons in this new place? Or am I truly mad, as poor Joshua believes?

* * * * * * *

I completed the painting at noon. Outside, the wind has picked up again, hiding the valley in a swirl of blowing snow. The light is thin and grayish, but the painting seems to glow with a blue-white incandescence. The figures on either side of the snowman now face each other, their small profiles acutely sharp. Julie's stubby nose is red with the cold, and Eric's blond cowlick has escaped from his woolly cap and hangs, as usual, over his left eye.

The snowman grins at me with a curving row of black buttons, his expression incredibly smug and knowing.

If I am mad, then so be it. They are there, well and happy and still alive in some unknown time and place. I never believed in the rigid heaven that my mother tried to teach me, but I can believe in a world with two pale shadow-moons low in the sky, blue snow, red rocks, and black buttons for snowman noses.

I must go and tell Joshua.

* * * * * * *

I have just locked the door behind me, shutting away the still house, the low mutter of the furnace, and the memory of Joshua, sitting in his study beside the open window, frozen blue and stiff. He did it purposely, of course, unable to deal with our loss. I can sympathize, for if I were the kind to stop dead in my tracks and die of grief, I would have done something like it.

There is nothing to do until the roads open again, though I have used the ham radio to get in touch with the sheriff's department. They say to leave him where he is, window open to preserve his body. They are most concerned, but with the blizzard raging outside not even a helicopter can get to me. I would not risk a man's life on a snowmobile in such a storm, for I am in no danger.

The finished painting faces me, and suddenly I realize that it is still incomplete. My fingers are digging for brushes, uncovering the palette, dipping into dark blue before I can catch up with them.

My hand moves quickly, smoothing strokes against the pale stuff of the snow behind the snowman. A big shape, wearing a familiar Navy peacoat and a scarlet scarf, stands between my children, one mittened hand on each small shoulder. The thick blond curls blow in a stiff breeze, and Joshua's face is ruddy and happy.

All four, including the snowman, grin at me across intervening dimensions of time and space.

Their father is there, caring for his children as always. They are secure in that strange world, never to be harmed again by anything Earth holds.

Perhaps they will be there when I come, however long it may take. When the thaw comes, I shall go down the mountain and find a place in a sheltered valley. There I will paint and paint and paint, looking through oil and canvas into that distant world.

My agent will be gratified. There will be no worry about money, if the paintings continue to sell as they have until now. I will stay busy, despite my losses.

When I die, I hope I, too, will go to a world with twin moons, blue snow, red rocks, and three people whom I love very much.

If not, I will have had this much, and it is more than I ever expected.

Years ago, Ed Kramer asked me for a story to consider for his anthology of stories about Excalibur. This one sprang to mind instantly and in detail. All I had to do was write it down.

THE WEAPON

The buried weapon slept, for nothing had disturbed it for almost a millennium, and its powers had been withdrawn into the depths of time. The earth surrounding it was quiet and damp. Not since a grieving knight flung it into a forgotten lake, there to be hidden away, had the sword tingled with its charge of unlimited potential.

Those hidden potencies had become less-than-memory, unlikely ever to wake again. Perhaps, if greed had not disturbed the thing, it might never have roused.

* * * * * * *

The local people stood about grumbling, watching the clearing of the site with avid interest. Bringing in an American construction company to build this complex was one in the eye for them, with work so slow. Henry Carnes could tell that the thought of the fat wages those strangers earned was slow torture to men whose families were living on the dole.

Jordan Harp's arrival shifted their attention to a flat space where ancient forest had stood a week ago. "No one but an American would visit a building site in a bloody helicopter," one leathery fellow muttered. Even though they said nothing, it was obvious that his companions agreed.

But Henry hurried to greet his employer, hoping that he would be satisfied with this beginning. The shopping complex he intended to build here in this picturesque area promised to add even more millions to his astonishing hoard. It was only one of dozens scattered about the globe, every one set in the middle of what had been a remnant of natural beauty and now had become asphalt parking lots.

Harp was staring about, checking the damp, bare-scraped soil that had once been a bog, and the leveled forest, now reduced to sticks and stubble. This was what he loved to see, Henry thought for the thousandth time, nature subjected to his will. That seemed to be the man's real goal, rather than more useless millions.

Harp absently twirled his raw-gold medallion, twisting it about his forefinger as he examined the site. That, too, was a symbol of his power.

"Here are the plans, sir." Henry took the roll of blueprints from the foreman. "Would you like for me to show you where everything will be?"

"No." The voice was high-pitched, rather old-maidish, though the man had the reputation of being a womanizer from his youth. "It is about to begin. That is all I need. You're employed to design and oversee the building of the damned thing. Get to it!"

He turned his back rudely and moved toward the knot of English laborers. They glared back at him balefully over the fence enclosing the construction area, and Henry felt a sudden qualm.

He hurried after Harp and touched his elbow. "It might be best not to get too near those fellows, sir. They're bent out of shape because they've not been hired to do the work. We've had some minor vandalism, and I suspect some of those very men may be responsible. We wouldn't want you to have a problem with them, now would we?"

Harp turned and stared at him, as if unable to understand. "Have a problem? With those...."—he waved a contemptuous hand toward the glowering crew beyond the fence.

"Surely you're kidding!"

But to Henry's relief he turned away, walked the perimeter of the first building site, and got into the chopper again. Not until he was safely aloft did Henry relax and return to his duties. Designing a shopping center of this size was hard enough without having to nursemaid that egotistical—but he caught himself. Not for him to criticize the one who paid him so handsomely for his services.

The bulldozers were ready to dig the foundation holes. In such heavy, wet soil you had to do that right, or there would be settling and all kinds of problems down the road.

Even in the wet British climate, surely he could get that done by midsummer, foundation down, maybe even the interior dried in. It was only early May, after all.

The first dozer was going down fast. The driver's head was disappearing at the bottom of his trench now, and the other machines were busy in their own areas. Henry strolled to the edge of the cut and looked down, watching the peaty soil pile up ahead of the heavy blade.

George gunned the engine and started across the bottom. There was a sudden painful screech of metal on stone, and the bulldozer came to a halt. Henry jumped down into the cut, concerned.

There wasn't supposed to be any rock at this level. This could be something moved in long ago when the ancient Britons were putting up their stone circles. If this was such a matter, they might be hung up for months, fighting it out with the antiquities people.

But Henry had figured out ways of getting around such things. What wasn't officially found never became a problem. If he located some antique-looking stone and smashed it to flinders, it would become just more gravel to be hauled away.

George backed the dozer away from the obstacle, his blade shrilling along the obstruction. The dirt fell in behind it, but Henry glimpsed a pale gray length before it was covered.

"Come on, George, and bring your shovel. Let's see what's hanging you up," he called, his voice pitched to reach no farther than the driver.

Together they scraped the damp clumps of soil away from the coffin-sized stone. Henry frowned. That was a hard son-of-a-bitch. He'd never break it with what he had. Then he wondered if it was as thick as it looked.

"Let's dig down beside it," he said.

They found, once they used the spade vigorously, that the thing was only some ten inches thick. Henry grinned. "We can pry it up, roll it onto its side, and break it with the blade," he said.

They heaved, and it sucked free to stand on edge. It was a handsome thing, Henry noted regretfully. Carved with twining vines that framed a lion in one loop and a sword in another, it had to be extremely old. This area had been bog for as long as any local account could recall.

For an instant Henry hesitated. He loved old things, even when his work demanded that he destroy them. The ancient trees that had already fallen grieved him, but he had hitched his destiny to that of Jordan Harp. That meant he had to become a destroyer, building altars to wealth instead of creating structures of beauty.

But George was raising the dozer blade, shaking off the dirt, getting it positioned above the edge of the stone coffer. Henry stepped back, and George brought the heavy metal down onto the thing.

There was a grinding crack, a flash of light, and George screamed. Henry saw the metal of the bulldozer begin to glow, red to yellow to white, blindingly brilliant. George jerked spasmodically, and for an instant his skeleton was a shadow beneath his dissolving flesh.

Henry felt himself pushed backward to land against the wall of the cut, his face singed by the holocaust that enveloped the bulldozer. As the light began to turn red again, dying away, he shook his head. Where are the men? Haven't they heard or seen what happened down here? he wondered.

He staggered forward, his shoes heating against the smoldering earth. Beneath the blade of the dozer lay segments of gray stone, cracked apart in regular sections as if they had been assembled so. A glint of brightness shone amid the parts, and, compelled by some unknown power, Henry bent and touched it.

His fingers touched icy metal, there in the middle of that steaming pile. Without thinking about poor George or the ruined dozer, he lifted it free.

A sword. Long, exquisitely worked yet clean of line, it fitted into his hand as if designed for it. He watched, dazed, as the steel blade rose high, moving his hand rather than being moved by it. He struggled to control it, but still it moved, turning him to face the ruined bulldozer. The thing sank forward to touch, very gently, the fire-blackened blade.

Metal whispered on metal, as the entire mechanism crumbled into dust, which mingled with the ashes of its unhappy driver. In a heartbeat, nothing remained that might be identified as man or machine.

The sword tingled with a strange electrical charge, which now was dwindling. Henry managed to set it aside at last, his arm and hand numb, his mind overloaded with unanswerable questions.

Then the water began to come in. Henry grabbed the blade and climbed out of the ditch, frantically trying to outrace the flow. When he reached the top, he found that no worker was in sight, no bulldozer, no distant piles of girders.

Forest, ancient and unbroken, lay beyond the verges of a lake, now filling to its old measure. As Henry waded out of the lake, he saw with disbelief that he wore rags wrapped about his feet, a coarse tunic, and he could tell with ease that he wore no underwear.

He staggered into the shade of a great oak and dropped to the ground. The sword, still clutched in his hand, rang softly against one of the gnarled roots, and the sound seemed to still the breeze that had whispered through the leaves.

For one moment the birdsong that had filled the place went silent. Henry stared, stunned, at the lake, now filled with dark, peaty water, and the village that lay beyond it. Wattle huts were clumped awkwardly about a pole that held an oddly shaped symbol on the top. A woman sat on a bench before a door, holding up a tunic much like his own and shaking her head over its ragged holes. Two men came out of the forest carrying a deer slung to a pole.

What had happened to him in that moment when the blade struck the coffer? Was he dead? Mad? Or had he returned to a time before the England he had come to know?

He shifted his weight, and something rolled beneath his foot. He dug into the turf and uncovered a rounded shape, which he cleaned against the grimy tunic. Then he stared, appalled and confused.

He held in his hand a crystal sphere. He had seen it many times, for Claude, the foreman, carried it as a good-luck charm. Inside the crystal was a bit of fossil fern that he had found on some job in his youth. There was probably not another luck-piece anywhere like Claude's. That meant that all the men, Claude, the machinery, everything had been reduced to dust, as George and the bulldozer had been. But the forest had been felled! How had it returned, in a matter of minutes, to its ancient glory? What power was contained in this long-buried sword?

Henry staggered to his feet. He must learn how far this alteration went. There had to be some limit to the change, and he would walk until he found it. Taking up the sword, which now was a heavy burden, he moved toward the east, where the sun climbed an unpolluted sky.

He was soon completely lost in the tangle of ancient boles and grasping roots. Stumbling, almost sobbing, he kept moving, afraid that he might be circling, for the sun was invisible through the thick canopy of branches.

Again the metal tingled with life, his fingers clenching harder about it. The sword moved, rose to point a direction. Henry had no other guide. He must follow its guidance.

For a long, long while he moved through the forest, and as it grew dark the sword itself began to glow, a faint glimmer that was only a little better than no light at all.

He wondered why he never tired or grew hungry. It could only be some property of the sword, he thought, before his mind went numb. After that, his legs moved, his feet walked, his hand held the sword as if he were some robot, moving to the will of another.

Nights passed, and days, as he trudged through the forest. From time to time he came to a skimpy clearing, where huts held people who tilled small fields with crude wooden tools. Always the trees closed in again, and he began to understand why old texts referred to ancient England as a single forest from end to end.

His mind waked from its rest and began worrying with the questions that tormented him. Was there no end to this? Would he never emerge into the modern world of cleared lands, crowded cities, clogged skies?

When the sword rested, he forged ahead blindly. When it roused to life, he followed its pointing tip. And after many days of walking, he came to a spot where a ray of sunlight struck through a rent in the canopy. It sparkled on something dangling at arm's reach above the path.

Henry reached up and caught the golden bauble. Then he caught his breath in wonder and despair. He held Jordan Harp's medallion, which the man always wore: a golden harp on a golden chain with the initials J.H. engraved at the lower edge.

Had the helicopter dissolved as the bulldozer did, along with its riders? Was this all that was left of the empire of chrome and steel and stone that Jordan Harp had created in a world that seemingly no longer existed? Had the strange effect of the sword moved outward like a ripple in a pond, changing all in its path?

He lifted the chain, settled the harp onto his chest, and sighed. The sword was not done with him yet. There was something left for him to do, it was clear, for the haft tugged at his hand, and the point quested eagerly forward, pulling him along as if it were a hunting dog after game.

When he came out of the forest into clear sunlight and broad meadows, he blinked rapidly. It had been days since he had seen such brightness, and now it almost blinded him.

When he adjusted to the clarity of light and air, he realized that he was looking across a vast lake toward a city—a real city, though not a modern one. The tallest building was a tower inside the crenellated walls. Roofs of dull gray slate and red tiles rose higher than the walls, but were none of them of any great height above the ground.

For the first time since the strange quest began, Henry felt a flicker of excitement. He was looking at a medieval city, at least, perhaps one from the Dark Ages. As an architect, he found himself fascinated. Artists' conceptions and photographs of restored buildings were not, he saw at once, enough to show how one really looked.

He tried to move toward the lake. There must be some path or road that ran along its shore to that distant vision. But the sword would not yield its dominance. Instead, it jerked him, resisting and complaining, along the edge of the forest, toward a gap where a road cut through the trees.

At last he surrendered and followed, regretting the lost opportunity. In some strange way, his fate was compelled by the sword, and he knew that he must submit.

The road was only a cart-track, two worn marks winding through the forest, avoiding big trees or rocks or bad places to ford streams. After some distance, the land began to slope upward, and the trees became smaller, less tangled. And then, rounding a bend, Henry found himself staring up at a castle out of some book of fairy-tales: golden towers, battlements, gay flags snapping in the breeze from the sea below the cliff on which it stood.

The sword, which had been exerting a steady pull, began to pulsate, like an eager dog that sighted its master. Henry found himself running to keep up with his own hand and the blade that now sliced forward toward a gate in the wall. Its gleam had become a blaze and grew even brighter as Henry came near the moat that surrounded the wall.

Must I swim? Henry wondered.

But the sword did not hesitate. It swept into a figure eight, and pulleys began to creak as the drawbridge descended slowly to bridge the moat. Pulled along helplessly, Henry sprang onto the near edge, before the bridge was entirely down. Pell-mell, he hurtled toward the heavy gates, the blade leading the way. When it touched the iron-banded oak, the great gates shivered into splinters.

Henry felt his arm sink beneath the weight of the weapon. For the first time since he had started, the sword was entirely quiet, though his fingers still clasped it, unable to loose their grip. He had to raise it to keep the blade from trailing in the dust as he entered and looked about. This was a place built for serious defense, he saw at once. Inside the gate was a small chamber with walkways about the top. Anyone breaching the gate in war would find himself trapped here while archers above poured arrows into his men. But the gates that should have closed it off stood open, letting the soft air of May sweep through into the space beyond.

Four men in chain mail turned at his approach, staring at Henry with stunned gazes. Two women skittered across the cobbles and into open doors, which slammed behind them.

Henry held up the sword. Now it took on life again, began to tingle, then to throb. As two of the men drew swords and a third bellowed to the archers on the battlements, a tall man came down the steps of the inner keep and strode toward them.

Henry felt his knees move. He had never knelt to anyone in his life, but now he went down onto the cobbles and dust, holding out the sword to this lordly man who now stood gazing down at him through quizzical hazel eyes.

"I have brought this...to you," he gasped. It was the first time he had spoken since George disappeared, along with his bulldozer.

The man spoke but, strain as he might, Henry could not understand his words. Still, the gloved hand stretched toward him and took the sword, which began to glow, its fires rising to new heights. A delicate humming filled the air, and Henry felt it inside his bones, which now seemed attuned to the weapon.

"Artorius Rex!" the guardsmen shouted. "Excalibur!"

Those hazel eyes met Henry's brown ones. Henry rose slowly, feeling himself compelled now by the power within the man. He felt the chain about his neck, lifted it over his head, and held it out to the King.

"It belonged to another king," Henry said. "Now it is yours, and you will be a force for good. Why else should all this have happened?"

The long face smiled down at him. The King held the harp high, sparkling in the sunlight. "This is a symbol of power that is dark," he said, and though Henry did not understand the words he heard the meaning clearly.

The King climbed a stone stairway to stand on the seaward battlement and look down at the curling waves. He spun the golden harp around his head and let it go. The bright sparkle whirled over the edge of the cliff and was quenched in the water below.

Then Arthur turned, his face blazing with joy. Again he spoke in that archaic tongue that now Henry could understand clearly. "The world is renewed. Not again will we see the dark days come. Men will be freed. Land will be tilled to richness, but the forests will not be destroyed. Cities will rise, but cleanly, without poisoning their people.

"Come, my friends. We must go out into this restored England and tell our people that the evil times have ended and the past has returned in better form and more hopeful guise."

Henry felt his heart thudding. Was the entire world changing as England had? Would he have the opportunity to see Arthur, returned to life as the old prophecy had predicted, take up his sword again and create a new and better life for mankind?

Smiling, he strode after the King and his men. Something inside him, long dormant, began to flower. This was going to be a life worth living!

Having become old and somewhat near-sighted myself, I wondered what would happen IF....

GRYPHON'S NEST

Griselle flapped irritably through the fog, peering downward from time to time in search of her nest. Short-sighted as she was, it was hard enough to see when the weather was clear, and now, after casting about for hours in this mucky weather, she was totally confused. Not a single mountain peak loomed through the mist to give her guidance toward her nesting place, which was neatly situated in a sheltered valley among the Drachenberg Mountains.

Not that she was terribly happy with nesting. A Gryphon was simply not designed for sitting on eggs, and that was a fact. The lion's body wasn't designed for it, though the wings did a fairly good job of keeping the dratted things covered warmly and the mist off them.

It was not an easy life, being a female Gryphon, and Griselle was not naturally maternal. Young griffins were nasty tempered and their beaks were painful when they tried to suckle. That was another mistake of nature that she resented rather bitterly.

She hoped that the present batch would be her last clutch of eggs. She was getting too old for this, not to mention entirely too blind. Keeping track of the young monsters was no easy task, once the boring job of hatching was done with.

She tangled with a small tree and found her wings flailing desperately at flexible branches and wet leaves. Was this the rhododendron growing on the ledge just above her nest? She pecked at a leaf, decided it must be, and dropped through the damp foliage to land springily on her lion legs.

Her tail switched with impatience as she made her way among stones that were like any others anywhere. She never had made a study of them, and whether they were granite or sandstone she couldn't truly say.

There were, however, rocks around her nest, so she must be headed in the right direction. And after a half hour of stumbling and bumping and thrashing around in the fog, she found a huddle of jagged boulders in the midst of which lay three pale eggs. They seemed a bit smaller than she remembered, but her memory wasn't very good any more either. It was a nest, and that was good enough for her.

With a whistling sigh the Gryphon settled painfully onto the rock pile and scuffled her legs to arrange the eggs so her leg-bones wouldn't break them. Strange—they felt comfortable for a change. Instead of having slick shells, they seemed to have become leathery and slightly soft. They didn't seem quite as large either. A nice change! There were too few pleasant surprises these days.

The night-mist lifted, but Griselle was sleeping, her whistling snores echoing among the distant heights. When the sun topped the eastern mountains the Gryphon opened one eye and looked about. She raised her head and peered short-sightedly toward the blue peaks. Their shapes swam dizzily before her, not exactly like those she remembered but not exactly unlike, either. Near enough.

Warmed by the sun, she dozed away the summer days, waiting for hatching time to arrive. Garamond, her mate, did not visit her, which was not surprising. She had left him sitting on their nest while she went to find a sheep or a man or some other tasty bit to keep her from getting hungry while she sat, and she had found it unattended when she returned. He knew better than to face her after such slack behavior.

The visit of the Manticore almost caught her unaware. Deceived by his lion body, too blind to note the lack of wings and the leering man's face, she moved lazily at first, thinking it was that laggard Garamond. She opened her beak to dress him down before she caught the gleam of those human-like eyes.

She sprang into the air with a desperate flap of her powerful wings and a surge of energy to her furry legs. The Manticore lunged, but she was out of reach and the thing squirmed out of the nest and backed away, its triple rows of teeth grinding together in fury. Nasty things, Manticores!

Griselle might not be maternal, but this was her nest; he was threatening her property. She settled back, her wings covering the nest jealously, her razor sharp beak ready to amputate any part of the creature that came near.

The Manticore paced to the right, and her sinuous neck followed its movements. It moved to the left, and again Griselle kept her clouded gaze fixed upon its blurred shape.

When it sprang toward her, with the terrible speed and distance of its kind, she was ready.

Her beak dug into its tender underside, and the thing gave a shrill shriek as she tossed it aside. The beast's voice fluted a challenge, and she rose to her full height, wings ready to buffet, beak prepared to strike again.

This time the creature did not dare to spring. Instead it turned and leaped toward the mountains, disappearing in a few bounds beyond the first line of peaks with incredible agility, as that kind was wont to do. They were speedy creatures, and they could jump almost as high as she could fly.

Her blood racing nicely after the workout, Griselle rearranged the eggs and prepared to sit again. It should be time, and past time, for them to hatch. But eggs were eggs, and they always kept to their own schedule, no matter what their mother might prefer.

Even as she drew her legs up and sighed, she felt a quiver beneath the fur of her stomach. Was something happening? Was it time at last? She rose again and put her beak close to the nearest egg, trying to see with one dim eye if it was cracking.

At first she doubted what she saw. Her vision was all but gone, anyway, and surely she couldn't be seeing the shell of a Gryphon egg rippling as if it were made of skin. Even as she watched, the covering tore, and something poked through the hole.

This was no child of hers! A Gryphon pecked out respectably with its beak, and its damp, furry body followed it out of the shell. This...creature!...had a pointed head, its shiny eyes visible even to Griselle. As the thing slithered out of the soft egg-leather, a sinuous body followed the head, and the dumbfounded Gryphon realized that she was staring at a young Basilisk.

The shock was terrible. That night when she last fed—the fog— she must have lost her way and found herself by accident to this Basilisk nest. Where was the parent of this small creature?

It was too late to ask that question, for the little serpent wriggled to her side and curled about her leg for warmth, its small body quivering with contentment. In time two more joined it. She knew that it was too late. They had seen her and claimed her for their own.

I am the mother of three Basilisks! Griselle thought, her heart pounding. But what has happened to my own eggs? Is poor Gara-mond still sitting there, waiting for me to return? And to think that I blamed him for deserting our nest, when it was I—I!—who never came back!

Now, however, she had other things to think of. If young griffins were difficult and painful to feed, how much more difficult it was going to be to keep three infant Basilisks alive. What did they eat? Serpents did not suckle their young, that was one thing she knew without doubt.

Eagles, who were in a way her distant half-kin, brought meat to their ravenous young. She had seen that. But when she put her head down near those of her foster children, their mouths were totally unsuitable for chewing. What on earth should she feed the creatures?

One put its snaky face near her eye and opened its mouth as if hungry. Fangs—yes, there they were, set well back but definitely there. No. she would NOT allow them to suckle, even if they showed signs of wanting to. She had no desire to test the potency of Basilisk poison.

She spent futile hours catching bugs, which she couldn't see but had to listen for and squash with her awkward paws. The young cared nothing for squashed bugs.

She left them squirming in the nest and went toward the stream that ran down from the mountains. There she hunted painfully for fish, for rabbits, for caterpillars, for anything at all that might tempt their unknown appetites.

The blood of the rabbit proved to be the one thing they relished, and in the next weeks the population of rodents around the nest diminished remarkably. Given suitable nourishment, the young Basilisks grew with terrible speed—almost as quickly as young Griffins, in fact. Before Fall, they were coiling around the rocks, catching curious birds and animals that thought to den against the cliff.

Although they returned at night to warm their sluggish blood against her furry body, Griselle realized that these were young who took their own way at an early age. She hunted her own food now, leaving theirs to them, and often she thought about her stressful months of suckling her own kind, pulling her weight down to nothing, having to eat every week instead of once in three or four months.

Given the choice, she realized that she much preferred being foster mother to Basilisks. But she often wondered what had happened to their own parent before she had arrived on the scene. Surely the creature must have died in battle or accident, or she would have come back to tend her eggs.

When the sun had moved to the south and cold winds swept down from the mountains, the brood grew quiet. Even Griselle knew that they must hibernate during the cold months, and she watched with interest as the three hunted among the boulders for snug dens in which to sleep away the winter.

Once they were settled, she stretched her wings and sighed. It had been an interesting summer, but she had best seek out her own family before the clouds and storms again dimmed her vision. Garamond would have given her up, she was sure, and her children would not know her at all.

She sprang into the sky, feeling her old muscles ache with effort as her wings strained for altitude. Surely she must have come too far and crossed a second range of mountains on her way back to the nest, all those months ago.

She soared, riding a thermal draft up and over the heights. She could smell fresh snow, still distant in the north but on its way to add depth to the white fields below her. Garamond would have withdrawn from the summer nest into the high cave against the cliff where they always wintered with a new brood. The small ones would be flying on their own, by now, though still dependent upon their parents for food until next summer.

Griselle swooped down the slope of the range now, scanning the dim distances hopelessly. Where was that peak that so resembled the one near her Basilisk nest? It had seemed such a fine landmark, with its broken tip and the hump on one side—and then she saw it, looming against a snow-laden sky.

She wheeled, seeking the dark spot against the sheer wall that would be the cave. When she found it at last she found her heart beating rapidly. It had been so long—would Garamond be happy to see her? Would the young be afraid of her?

She cupped her wings and settled onto the ledge outside the cave. From inside came the whistling roar that was the challenge of a Gryphon, but she shrilled her name into the echoing tunnel. There was silence for a moment, and then Garamond came sidling from the darkness to peer at her.

"Griselle?" he piped. "Alive?"

"Lost, but alive," she agreed. "Did the young hatch? I thought I was sitting upon them until the Basilisks hatched and I realized my mistake."

Garamond made a strange sound, something between another roar and as near to a chuckle as one can come using a beak. "Basilisks!" He lay on the cold stone and whipped his lion's tail wildly against the cliff.

Griselle looked down, alarmed at his behavior. "Of course, Basilisks. What is wrong with you, Garamond?"

Then there came a hissing voice from the darkness of the tunnel. A long shape slithered into view, its face familiar even to Griselle's dim eyes.

"Why are you not asleep, with the rest of your kind?" she asked the intruder.

"I have found furred and hot-blooded creatures to keep me warm and awake," said the Basilisk. "You sat, I think, upon my abandoned nest. My thanks to you, but do not think to push me from this place. Your eggs hatched and the young Gryphons accepted me as mother."

Garamond looked sheepish, as much as could be done with his birdlike face. He rose to his feet and stiffened his tail. "You were gone. I was alone, sitting on eggs that you left to me. This one assisted me, and she has found a place among us."

For a moment Griselle felt a hot rage building in her bosom. Then she realized that this was just what she would have chosen if asked.

No more egg-laying! No more suckling young with eagle beaks! No more soothing Garamond, whose temper grew worse every season. She felt a great sense of relief.

"Allow me to rest for the winter in our warm cavern," she said to the Basilisk, ignoring her former mate. "I will leave with the spring to find other Basilisks who desire relief from nest-sitting. I shall become a foster-mother to the young of your kind, now that I know how to manage them."

The Serpent hissed agreement, withdrawing into the deepest chambers of the cavern. Garamond glanced apologetically at Griselle before stalking away behind her, his tail twitching nervously.

As well it should! thought Griselle. If he tries to mate with that one, he will end up dead, but I know better than to speak of that.

She found a convenient chamber, small enough to be kept warm by a single Gryphon, and curled her tail around her paws. Settling her beak on a convenient stone, she closed her eyes and thought of those comfortable leather eggs, the affectionate young Basilisks, their early independence.

She had found the calling for her old age, she knew, and when she slept, she dreamed of pleasant things. Next summer...ahhh! Next summer!

In the very old days, the skills of a blacksmith were considered magical—if not demonic.

THE FORGING OF FEAR

My father sold me to Gillam for two pennies and a good plow. It was a far better price than he had had for Arn, my older brother, and, as well, I could be in the same village and see my parents at times. Arn had gone to the collieries in Wales, and we knew we'd never see him again.

I was happy in my new life. Gillam was the gentlest of men, for all his size and strength. And he was rich, compared to those who lived on the scrap of ground allotted by Lord Roderick to his commons. A smith's skills are so rare and valuable that even nobles give him some leeway in his life and work. And not only for his skills—there is an edge of fear clinging always about his almost magical craft.

This being a new fiefdom, recently granted by King Ethelred to Roderick's family, there was much work to be done. Though Gillam was no armorer, he shod the steeds of the nobles, and he forged the tools used in breaking and clearing the land. So strong was his art that he was chosen to forge the iron bands that bound together the oaken door-leaves of the Lord's new keep. I arrived in time to help with that.

I was not allowed to touch one scrap of the Lord's metal. I only cleaned and put away the hammers and tongs and punches and rasps used in the work. But I pumped mightily on the bellows, forcing the charcoal to white-heat at the center of the forge. I watched closely, even while pumping, as the straps took shape. They were formed into graceful curves, with the heavy lily-crest of Roderick centered upon each. I was fascinated by the boring of the bolt-holes, the shaping of the hinges, the finishing of the edges. Though it was obvious how each matter was done, still I felt the magic of the smith's skill.

And I vowed to become a smith, too—a frivolous dream for one born to my circumstances, but it kept me pumping enthusiastically.

Even better than the work was my treatment by Gillam's family. He and his wife had no child of their own, to their sorrow, and his wife seemed to extend toward me some of the affection that she would otherwise have given to her children. Gillam's niece also lived with them, having been orphaned very young, and the two of us, both in our early teens, settled amicably together almost as if children of the family.

There was altogether enough to eat! That always astonished me—my father would never have sold his children if he could have fed them by his efforts in the Lord's fields. But those efforts always fell far short, once the grain was divided, and starvation stood beside his door every day of his life. He knew that we could only be better elsewhere. I cannot know of Arn, but for myself I was more than happy with the life he contrived for me. Instead of toiling in the fields from dawn to dusk, ill-fed and more inadequately clothed and housed, I was full and warm, and could watch the miracles that took place at forge and anvil.

Gillam never struck me—few lads might say so much, I know. Yet even when my master was angered (and he had cause to be more than once), he withheld the sweep of his huge hand that might well have taken me out of this world entirely. It was not only his need for my services. He also had affection for me. When I was burned by flying sparks or fiery bits of metal, his broad face would furrow as if my pain were his own.

But the thing that convinced me of his regard most firmly was the fact that he talked with me as if I were a man, a man with the education and wit to understand his words. This was the bond that kept me by him more solidly than my servitude.

He was no peasant, was Gillam. He had been trained by the clergy—at Avebury, no less—his father having been bailiff for a powerful Lord. Gillam could read, either in Latin or in our pithy Saxon. He could set quill to parchment with a hand finer than our Lord's own priest could manage. He understood many things of which others in our village never dreamed.

He talked of the past to me as we worked together filing punches or adjusting the jaws of tongs. "It was in many ways a good life," he said, his big hands moving lovingly over the shape of a maul. "And there were writings in the abbey—I would dearly have loved to have had the time to read through the entire lot of those. But it was not to be. I could not accept many matters that were articles of faith—and there was one at which I laughed. When added to the list of my sins of omission and my interest in the Old Religion, that was the last matter needed to expel me. So I became a smith."

I was no fool, young as I was. I knew that a good story must lurk behind that statement. I asked, "What was that? The last thing you could not accept?"

He laughed, pitching a bolt into a bucket and taking up another to check the fit of it into the Lord's chariot-tongue. "Now that was humorous! Sheer folly, you understand, on all parts, from the abbot down to the lay brothers. You have heard the name Donnestoun?"

I gaped. "Him that was Abbot of Glastonbury and adviser to kings? Indeed, even here we know his name. They speak of him now as a holy one—"

"That great ninny! And now they do, indeed, call him Holy One, when he was and remained a self-seeker—or a deluded fool, which is worse. He was a smith when the need arose, the brothers told me. And one day at his forge, he looked up to see the face of the Dark One in the window at his side. Filled with holy wrath that the demon might try tempting him, he heated his pincers to red-heat and caught the fiend by his long nose, pinching and burning him until he shrieked for mercy and swore never to trouble the pious fraud again."

Despite myself, I laughed.

Gillam laughed with me, though a hint of anger curved his grizzled brows down over his eyes. "Laughable enough. Even a child can see that. Either the holy Donnestoun was a liar or a fool, as I said before, but the brothers swallowed that great tale as if it were a custard. Never a one seemed to contract a bellyache trying to digest it. I was not of such tough stuff. I threw it up into the face of the master of novices, and he, in turn, cast me away from my intended goal."

I thought long about that conversation. It seemed to me that a man who was less honest than Gillam might have aped his fellows and pretended to believe, in order to save his place. But I learned, as I lived with the smith, that his honesty went, like the roots of an oak, right down to the streams that fed his being. Every soul in our village knew that, as did even the Lord and his sons and those lesser nobles who served the Lord and lived in the keep that was rising, every day, to loftier heights above the village.

A day came when the Lord's youngest son, Ranald, brought his favorite mare to be shod. As the red metal clanged beneath the hammer which curved it to fit the anvil, the young man looked about him, his nose in the air. There being none of his own kind with whom to talk, he deigned to speak to me as I rested from my bellows work.

"A low place!" he sniffed, drawing away from the pile of fresh dung that his own steed had dropped near his boot. "A veritable Hell, in fact. Stenches and sweating serfs! Not suitable for me to wait in, I swear. Call me when all is done, boy." And he strolled into the yard separating the shop from Gillam's house.

Something made me follow him to peer through the doorway. Lilibet, unfortunately, was just hanging the newly washed underclothes upon the barberry bushes to dry in the sun. Gillam's niece had grown, along with me, so gradually that I had not realized how much a woman she could appear. But when she stretched up to spread a length of stuff across the stone wall that faced the road, the sight was not lost upon Ranald, I could see. Something cold thumped, just once, in my chest.

I returned to Gillam's side, trying to hurry the task along in any way I could. I mistrusted the arrogant young man as much as I hated his sneering face, and I feared for Lilibet. There had been that in his look—I spat into the dust and crossed myself....

Gillam shod the horse in jig time and let the beast out into the yard and assisted the youth to mount. Not even a small coin was forthcoming as he wheeled the mount and sped away.

My master looked about the yard, but Lilibet had gone into the house again, and I hesitated to tell him the thing that I had feared. Yet he knew that something was troubling me, so he led me back into the shop and sat upon a billet of wood.

"It is hard, young Pell," he said, "when you are young to swallow the like of that young sprout. Yet he is not what he thinks himself to be, as his father is not the great and earthshaking Lord he pretends that he is."

I looked up at him from my seat on a sack of charcoal. My eyes widened. "How not?" I asked. "Both have the power of life and death over such as us."

"As does a greater Lord, back to the east, over our Lord upon the hill. And above that Lord, the King, far away on the coast. And over the King—why the Deity Himself. Not one is without one greater than himself. And not one of those fine men, puffed up with self-esteem as they are, can do this—"

He reached down and lifted a bar of metal that waited to be turned into shoes or shafts or bolts. With his two hands, he curved it into a bow. His face was a bit red, though the remainder of the glow from the charcoal in the forge might have been to thank for that.

Before I could think what to say, he frowned, his brows meeting above his deep, gray-green eyes. "There are many kinds of power, Pell. The power in my hands is one kind. The power upon yonder hill is another. That of the Abbot is still a third. And there is a fourth."

My heart thudded in my side. I knew what he meant, though we had never spoken of it. We both knew that there were those who disappeared from their hearths around the time of All-Hallows and Midsummer Eve. We had both heard tales of dark doings that stank of brimstone.

"But you have never...," I began.

He raised his hand. "That is a child's power, out there among the standing stones. Capering in the night is for those without the wit to seek for true strength of will and of thought. When they sent me from the Abbey, I did not turn from the Light—but I did not turn away from other matters either. There are other magics than those of the Dark, never doubt it. Those I have looked into...a bit."

We went home to our supper in silence. The Dame and Lilibet looked questioningly at us both, but what might we have said? Nothing that they would have understood, it was certain. Yet each time my eyes met Lilibet's, a shiver went down me. She was so fair, so sweet in her young innocence. In time, Gillam would petition the Lord to wed her to the miller's son, and it would be a match that was good for her and for him. Stan, the miller, was in full agreement.

Yet there in the rushlight, before a board laid with food in plenty and in the company of those I loved and served, I felt a chill of foreboding come over me.

Would a warning of mine have averted the thing to come? I doubt it. Ranald lost no lime. Less than a sennight later, he abducted Lilibet while Gillam was away dealing with the charcoal burners. Two of his brothers came with the young noble, along with several of the young spurs who tenanted the keep. They struck down the Dame and then laid me low with the flat of a blade.

When my wits came to me again, I was lying with my head in Dame Marga's lap, and she was sponging the blood from my face. Tears were tracking her pale face. When I struggled to sit, she pushed me back with a firm hand.

"Oh, Pell. Lie still until your head is quiet. A clap to the skull such as that can be dangerous if you do not care for it." Her tone was matter-of-fact, belying the tears that still streamed.

"Lilibet?" I whispered, dreading her answer.

She bent her head. A tear dropped onto my face from her cheeks.

Then I sat up. "I shall take Gillam's staff and go after them," I cried.

"They have gone into the keep. You cannot follow there, Pell. Gillam will be here soon—the sun is almost down. Then he will know what is best to do. The Lord has ever dealt justly with us—but. Ranald is his son...."

I could see that she had scant hope of justice this time. No more than had I.

Gillam returned before nightfall. When the news was told, he turned terribly pale, even through the ruddy flush set upon his skin by the heat of the forge.

"I shall go at once to my Lord," he said. Without another word he did just that. It was midnight when he returned. His thump upon the door brought both of us running to open the latch and slip away the bar.

He had brought Lilibet. Her slight shape barely weighted his arms at all, and her fair hair trailed in a tousle from the crook of his elbow. For a moment I thought that he had succeeded, that the Lord had granted her return. Then I saw the blood upon her sleeve, the limp way her wrist swung, her lax hand.

The Dame gave a little moan. "Dead?"

He nodded, entered, and laid my foster sister upon her narrow couch. Weeping, I barred the door again and turned to face my master.

"What happened...to her?" I choked, though I greatly feared his answer.

"They had no time to ravish her, Pell," he said, and there were tears in his own eyes. "She found a knife in a fruit bowl and used it well." He sobbed one great, strangling sob, then was silent.

"I'll kill them!" I shouted, turning blindly toward the door. His great hand caught me.

"No. We will do...something else. We will imprison them in fear. We will drown them in their own panic. They will know more than the things they made our little one feel, before they are done. Come with me, Pell. There is much to do before midnight."

We set pitch torches about the shop until it blazed with light. While I set the charcoal into the forge and began bringing the heat up, Gillam made a pile of stones that looked something like the new keep that was the Lord's pride and home. By the time the forge was glowing, he had the model of the great house completed.

We knew the approach of midnight, as did the animals, by the feel of lateness in the night air, the set of the stars. As iron heated, we felt the time draw near. Gillam drew a long breath. Then he took a lengthy strap of red-hot metal from its fiery bed and laid it upon the anvil.

"Doom! Doom! Doom!" said the hammer, ringing against the anvil.

He forged the straps together, setting the lily-crest at the join. He did not make them beautiful, as he had done those others. He made them terribly strong. I could see his lips working as he hammered and shaped the metal, but what words came from him I could not hear above the clangor of his labor. He seemed bigger than before, taller, more threatening than I had ever dreamed that he could be. A strange tingle filled the workshop as he tempered the straps in cool water and drew them, still glowing dully, forth again.

We slipped them, with the aid of tongs, over the modeled keep that filled the space braced by the oaken beams from which we suspended heavy work. As the straps cooled, they tightened until not even a blade could fit between metal and stone.

I stared, awed. "What magic is this?" I whispered, and Gillam heard.

He bent upon me a gaze so withdrawn and terrible that I cringed. "Those who practice the Old Religion call it sympathetic magic," he said. "As fares this small keep, so will the great one. The strength of the very soil and stone will hold it captive!" New words came from his lips as his eyes turned from me, but I stopped my cars and would not listen. By the time the second band was cramped about the keep, I was filled with terror.

Yet anger kept me going. Whatever Gillam was doing, whatever force, Dark or Light, that he called upon, this was justified. Lilibet had been all that was good and pure. Men who could cause her death in such fashion had no right to be called men, far less virtuous ones. If the Dark One had appeared at that instant and warned that my continued work at the bellows would mean instant translation into Hades, I would have pumped on. But the work was done, at last. The darkness faded from Gillam's face.

The old kindly smile shaped his lips. "We have done well, Pell. Dawn is upon us. Come into the yard and look up."

The breeze was freshening when we stepped into the open. A hint of dawn glowed in the sky behind the black bulk of the keep. It seemed as usual. The cry of the sentry on the tower came to our cars, dimmed with distance.

"I can see nothing amiss," I said, disappointed.

"We will rest awhile. You will see the result of our labors when the tenants of yonder house begin to stir." He turned to the house, and when inside, he fell into his bed beside the quietly weeping Dame.

We woke to screams and curses. I sat, and Gillam sprang to his feet.

"Pack up the things we must have, Marga," he said to the wondering Dame. "We will leave this place almost immediately, and there will be none to question our going. Pell and I must tend the forge before we go."

She asked no question but began bustling about at once. I could see that she had no objection to leaving this spot behind her forever.

We entered the smithy with the first rays of the sun. Someone hammered upon our door a moment afterward, crying, "Gillam! There is need at the keep! All are trapped there, inside the walls, and none can even so much as leap down from the parapet!"

Gillam grinned, his face ghastly. "Tell Lord Roderick that I will not come!" he shouted. "And be damned to him."

We emptied out the bits of charcoal and packed the forge-bowl into the cart. The anvil strained us both, but it went in too. All the tools, those precious things, were wrapped in leather and placed neatly in a big chest. When we had that in place, and the shop was stripped of everything useful, Gillam backed the old horse that had hauled so many loads of charcoal and metal for us between the cart-shafts. We hitched him, and he drew the cart out into the new sunlight.

I waited in the now-familiar smithy. In a bit Gillam returned with Lilibet in his arms. Where the anvil had stood, he laid her tenderly upon a sheepskin from her bed. At her head was the banded keep. At her feet he set into the dirt floor an iron cross that he had forged for the gate of the Lord's chapel.

Then he showed me where to dig, where to pry. We worked in a frenzy, loosing stones at key points in the structure. The stones began creaking about us.

He bent and kissed his niece on the forehead. I touched her hand. Then we left her there, went outside, and brought the entire building down over her. No noble Lady ever had a finer tomb. None that would ever dig through that rubble to find her—or that ensorcelled model of the castle above the village. It would remain there, secure and undisturbed, while serfs and freemen struggled to free their Lord from his own house.

The last of the dust had not settled when we pulled away from our own home, out of the low gateway, into the dusty road. The cries of those trapped in the keep filled all the air. The Dame looked quizzically at her husband.

"Will they ever escape?" she asked. Her eyes told me that she had a notion of the thing that we had done that night.

Gillam's face was as grim as the stone of the crag as he whipped up the horse. "Not until they go forth as ghosts," he said.

The Dame reached behind and patted my arm. "Good. Let them rot!" she murmured. The road wound ahead, exciting to me who had never traveled past the fields. There was always work for a smith... and his helper. Wherever we might go. we would prosper, I felt certain. It would have been better if Lilibet had gone, too, bubbling with laughter at everything new, but she was, at least, safe from harm now.

I looked up at the crag, the castle shining in the morning brightness. No eye could see the spell that bound it round, yet my knowing seemed to visualize the bands of metal centered with lily-crests that imprisoned those within.

I crossed myself. They were in Fate's hands now. The Dark One had nothing to do with it.

Did you ever read the Malleus Maleficarum? *This was the Inquisitors' handbook for dealing with witches. Talk about ridiculous. And why did those cretins think that if witchcraft had been real the practitioners wouldn't have wrought vengeance against those persecuting them?*

WHO ACCUSES THIS WOMAN?

Though it was still very muddy from the torrential rains of the night before, Tenacity Cobble was out and about. Others, younger than she by far, kept to their hearthsides on cool, damp mornings like this, but the straight carriage and firm gait of the old woman spoke of an almost supernatural lack of rheumatism.

Her bead turned back and forth, as she scanned the sides of the pathway with sharp black eyes. The basket on her arm was already half-full of new dandelions and other herbs, and now and again she would dart aside and dig energetically with her trowel or snip with her small scissors and stow away another treasure.

All the while, she talked. "There's Mistress Blakeby hanging out her wash, Aristotle," she commented as they passed that harsh-tongued lady's house. "I wonder if her goodman came home last night—he's seeing the chambermaid at the inn, you know."

Aristotle grunted noncommittally. He had lived with Tenacity long enough to know that her intuitions outran other folk's certainties. His yellow eyes were carefully neutral, as he stopped to bite the top out of a thistle. As he munched and waited for his mistress to dig another root from the wayside, he could see Mistress Blakeby staring after them. This was another thing that he was used to, though it made him obscurely uneasy. Goat though he was, he was fond of his strange companion, and he felt that many of those who stared after the two of them felt far differently. Reaching about for another bite of thistle, he found himself looking down the path at the person who made him more uneasy than any other. The goat raised his head and moved across the path to nudge his mistress with his nose. She looked up and frowned.

"Oh, perish and drat!" she muttered. "I could lack for Thomas Watley with much resignation, Aristotle. Forever he's cajoling me for money, knowing full well that I promised his Uncle Hezekiah, even as he lay dying, that not one penny would I provide to that young scoundrel while breath remained in my body. Hush! Here he comes!"

Aristotle obediently hushed, though he felt that any comment he might make upon Tenacity's nephew would be better made with a good butt from his hard head. There was something about Thomas Watley that made his hair feel prickly along his backbone.

Perhaps it was his attempt to look taller than he was. A short, stocky man cannot appear long and lean, however much he tries to, and the effort gave him a strange air. It might have been the avid look in his watery gray eyes. Then perhaps it was his voice, which alternated between overly-jovial bellows and pleading whines, at least when he approached his uncle's widow. Aristotle found him crude and offensive, and he suspected that his mistress felt likewise, though she was always civil to the young man.

"Dear Aunt, what a pleasant chance! I had thought to visit you today, but I find you out, bright and cheerful, on this wet morning." He was bellowing, as usual.

"Dear Thomas, if you were thinking to find me changed, it is as well that you were spared the full journey to my house," Tenacity answered. "My word, once given, can only be released by him to whom I gave it. Your uncle, may he rest in peace, is beyond asking for such release, so I must regretfully refuse you. It may soothe your feelings to know that I have made a will, since last I saw you. I did not promise your uncle not to bequeath the property and the money to you, and I have decided to do so. Judge Barlow prepared the papers for me a week agone, and I have signed them."

Thomas grew red, then pale. "It is a gracious gesture, Aunt," he said, "but that very Judge Barlow is the cause of my need. He demands payment, or he will foreclose upon my farm. My wife and my children will be left destitute."

"If that is so, then bring them to me, and I will shelter them until you can find work. But I cannot break my promise. I have done as best I can with the only thing left to me, Thomas. You will simply have to resign yourself to the loss of your land, or else to arrange otherwise with the judge. I am going into the hills after spring herbs, and unless you are eager for a long walk, you had best go home and consider."

Her nephew stepped aside, and the old woman moved past and turned up the steeper track that led to the hill that bastioned the eastward side of the village. Aristotle brushed against the man as he went by, and Thomas found himself staring into those yellow eyes that seemed to know more of his innermost thoughts than was seemly for a beast.

All the way up the hill, Aristotle kept looking back to watch Thomas. Something troubled the goat, something about Thomas Watley. But the man went down the path steadily, turning into the wider road that led through the village. The only thing that seemed strange to the watcher was the fact that the man stopped for a long while when he reached the gallows that had been raised beside the track.

The hills were full of burgeoning growth, however, and the two who searched there soon forgot about their encounter. The basket filled rapidly, and Aristotle filled even faster, enjoying the young leaves that were just beginning to appear on the hawthorns and the berry vines. By noon, the old woman and her goat were back at her home, and a batch of dandelion greens was simmering in her pot, while bread baked on the hearthstone.

Tenacity took her egg basket in hand and went out toward the hen-run, leaving Aristotle dozing on the doorstep. His sleep was interrupted by a step on the flags of the walk, and he opened one wicked yellow eye to see Mistress Cradshaw coming. If Mistress Blakeby was a gossip and a scold, Mistress Cradshaw was the troublemaker who fed her habit. Aristotle knew them both well, both from his own and from Tenacity's observations. At their last encounter, the woman had fed him a tidbit, pretending friendship. He had trustingly accepted a leaf that had been coated in something that burned his sensitive throat like coals of fire.

She was burdened with a bundle from which peeped scraps of colored cloth, and Aristotle knew that she was there to ask his mistress to draw her a pattern on the bit of paper she held in her hand. With a sigh of regret for his lost nap, the goat rose to his feet and watched her approach. With the steep, wet path behind her, her hands full, and her mind on other things, she was in his power, at long last.

The thump of his head into her middle was sheer delight. He stepped back and peered down at his victim, as she sat in a puddle, stunned for a moment. When she rose to flee, he thumped her again, from behind. This sent her into a galloping, staggering run down the path, as she tried to keep her balance without losing her grip on the bundle of precious quilt-scraps. Her voice raised in a cry of mingled rage and terror, the woman fled toward the village, leaving a thin trail of colored bits behind her.

Aristotle lay back down on the stone of the doorstep, but he was too much filled with unholy glee to sleep again. Tenacity found him there, looking innocent, when she came with her basket of eggs.

It was raining again, as Tenacity settled to her afternoon of sorting through her harvest of herbs, setting aside those to be dried in the sun, those to be pounded and sealed into jars, and those to be infused immediately. Aristotle had taken himself off to his shed, leaving the door stone to the mercy of the rain. After a snack of old hay, he settled himself to resume his interrupted nap.

An uproar from downhill woke him, just before sundown. He arrived in the yard just in time to see a small group of villagers, led by the puffing judge, whose bulk was not easy to carry up so steep a hill, pound on the door of Tenacity's tidy cottage. It opened, and he could see by her expression that his mistress was not pleased.

"How, now, Judge Barlow! 'Tis an untoward time of day to be battering at the doors of honest folk! Your business had best be of the most urgent, else I will be most annoyed."

"Here is a warrant," he panted, waving a sheet of parchment in her face. "Just this past hour I have indicted it, at the plea of those who have reason to abhor you. You are accused as witch, Mistress Cobble. Two several people have raised the cry, and by the law of our land I must take you to be tried."

"And hanged, I'll warrant," the little woman snapped. "Just as they're doing now in Salem, harrying poor old folk who have neither wealth nor kin to stand between themselves and a wicked judge. Cotton Mather hath much to answer for.

"You will find, however, that I am neither poor nor friendless. Have a care, you who accuse me. Those who tread on the unfortunate may find themselves trodden in turn."

But those behind the judge raised outcry, and Aristotle could see in the failing light that Mistress Cradshaw and Mistress Blakeby were among their number, together with three men from the town. There was the apothecary, whose business was much infringed by Tenacity's trade in healing herbs; the schoolmaster, with whom she had crossed wits more than once, to his chagrin; and the parson. Tenacity's infrequent attendance at meeting had doubtless ripened his mind against her.

In the last of the sodden daylight, Tenacity was hurried from her house, bundled in her cloak against the growing chill of the evening. Aristotle could see that beneath the cloak she held her reticule, and he was comforted. In that shapeless handbag she kept a bit of almost everything she might need under any circumstances.

Taking advantage of the darkness that now hemmed the sky, making useful shadows about the countryside, Aristotle followed the procession. He was not astonished to see Thomas Watley join the judge at the edge of the village. That pause at the gallows had given Aristotle much food for thought, and even be knew the tales of witch-hangings that even now were taking place in other parts of Massachusetts.

Being so small, the village of Rideover had no lockup. When such a thing was found to be necessary, Judge Barlow's woodshed was forced into service, and there they took Tenacity and flung her into its chill and comfortless darkness. To that place of incarceration Aristotle followed faithfully, keeping always out of sight, though he was certain that his mistress knew him to be nearby.

There was no window in the shed, but he huddled against the rough log wall and bleated very softly. A wisp of a whistled tune answered him, and he sighed so gustily that it blew out his whiskers. Then, reassured, he dozed against the shed until the first light of dawn woke him.

Too late! The judge's manservant, coming to bring the prisoner some food, surprised the goat before he could escape. Feeling much assured at the justification of the charges against the old woman, the man thrust her goat into the shed with her.

"Belike, we'll see a double hanging," he hissed as he closed the door behind him. "It do be said that goats are the cattle of the Devil."

It was noon before the two captives were brought from the shed. Tenacity was given opportunity to wash herself and tidy her hair and clothing. Aristotle was watched with disturbed attention, and his watchers were not reassured by the amusement in his vertically pupilled yellow eyes.

Trial was held in the schoolhouse, which did triple duty as school, church, and courtroom. The place was crowded, and in that throng there was hardly one who had not taken some ill of flesh or spirit up the hill to Tenacity Cobble and returned comforted with poultice, physick, or sympathy. Now they waited with relish for the entertainment to begin, little caring that the victim was one who had done them nothing but good.

Tenacity and Aristotle sat quietly on the bench provided for them, watching the villagers gape and whisper and smirk. It was plain that they thought a witch-trial of their own brought them nearer to the prominence of greater and more populous places than Rideover. And when the judge entered, resplendent in robe and wig, it was also plain that there was no hope of justice to be found in that crowded room. "Hang...hang...hang....," went about the room in a breathy whisper.

The testimony would have been comic, had it not been so venomously false. The two women who accused her set into words all the jealousy and suspicion that the old woman had waked in their tight-pinched hearts. Tenacity's nephew attested that he had seen her engaged in satanic rituals. And two young children, well-coached by their fond parents, went into convincing fits when Tenacity passed by them on her way to the witness-box.

"Is it not true that...?"

"Do you not admit...?"

"Can you possibly deny...?"

It was quite plain that the questions, not her answers, were the words taken to heart by the hastily assembled jury. Tenacity looked over the judge, the jurors, the folk who were now set avidly forward in their places.

"Have you anything to say on your own behalf?" asked the judge at last.

"I have," she answered. Quite tranquilly. "Every soul within this chamber knows that I have dealt justly by all, that none who came to me for aid was ever denied, and that I asked no payment. All know that never once has any being suffered because of me.

"If frivolity and greed can thus overset the works of a good life, then I see that I have embraced the wrong part of my art. However, I am not ignorant of other arts, though I have never practiced them.

"I warned you that those who tread harshly may, in their turn, be trodden. Now you will see proof of that." And she began to whistle. In total silence, the old lady and her goat vanished from the sight of the stupefied group. One who sat by the open door looked about outside, then called out in dismay. "They stand upon the hill! Witchery!"

From the sky, which had seemed to be clearing in the forenoon, came a clap of thunder fit to shake the earth. Rain poured down in sudden fury, and a rumbling could be felt, more than heard, in the earth and the air.

From the vantage-point to which his mistress had taken them, Aristotle could see white water roaring in a wall down the small river that circled the farther edge of Rideover. Reaching the flat spot on which the village had been built, the water spread out fanwise, rising with terrible rapidity. The houses nearest the river vanished in a cloud of spray. The road disappeared. The schoolhouse dissolved into a jumble of logs and clapboard. The waters swept clean the place where the village had been, and when they subsided there was no trace that might have indicated the presence of Man.

Aristotle looked up at Tenacity. Just below them, snug on its little hill, their house and sheds, their cattle and sheep, their poultry and dovecote waited. The goat was unsurprised. Who but a familiar can know better the powers of a witch?

Reading ancient history and archaeology and anthropology can provide wonderful material for stories. This might have taken place on Santorini, if some visitor from the future had been doing on-the-spot research.

A SHIMMER OF BLACKNESS

I gripped my stylus tightly to stop my hand's shaking. If this was indeed the ending of everything we knew, giving in to hysteria would not help. And I might as well keep my dignity—for what good that would do.

The Philosopher stood quietly, waiting for us to complete our copying of his words. The last, it might be, that would ever fall from his lips. The thought made tears form in my eyes, but I held them back and shaped the script carefully. Who would read the words? Perhaps none ever would, but I would finish my task with all due care.

The marble pave trembled, causing the old man to sway and to catch at a pillar. The volcano rumbled, deep in its throat. Ash filled the air, stinging the eyes and making it hard to breathe, but not one of us rose from his bench or even looked up, except in a covert fashion. Our island home was doomed. The last of the ships had gone, and even the pleasure boats were now far across the Middle Sea. Only we remained to record the death of a country and a culture.

I blinked hard. Not only ash was burning my eyes. The wasting of so much beauty, so much joy was a sorrowful thing. As the Philosopher paused, I looked up at him and saw that tears were staining his face and his garment, making tracks down his ashy face. Reassured, I let my own flow also.

Perhaps our observations and records would help no one. Yet we had felt, each one of us, that a careful record of every phase of the ending of our world might help our kinsmen, far across the sea on the mother-island. Crete, too, was subject to tremors.

I looked down at the graceful angularities of my script. A concise description indeed. It only remained to wait until the last possible moment, writing all the while before casting the precious wax tablet into the waters, sealed in its floating case.

Glancing up again, I saw that the Philosopher was staring at something behind the row of benches that held us, his helpers and disciples. I turned my head that I might also see. A finger of chill ran up my backbone.

At the back of the lecture-terrace was a platform of white stone. It was used in acting out plays composed by those of our number who indulged in such things. Now, a shimmer of blackness was forming in the center of the pale stone. Something was...growing... there.

The discipline held us rigid until he bent his head, indicating that we might rise and turn to see. He walked through our ranks, as we turned, touching first one, then another, with gentle fingers. But his eyes were set upon the squarish shape that was becoming, there on the terrace where he had taught us so many things.

We crowded after him, up to the edge of the knee-high ledge. In the exact center of the stage, the shimmer was solidifying into a tangible thing, black as the chitin of a beetle, with the same iridescent glints in its dark coloration. It was shaped like a woman. A woman who lay on her back, legs folded, feet tucked into the backs of knees, forming two angles of a triangle blunted at her waist to meet another formed by her arms, which bent above her head, hands crossed precisely above her, elbows making another pair of angles.

The glow that had accompanied its formation died away, leaving the thing dull. Infinitely detailed, it followed the contours of the woman faithfully, yet we knew that it must be a casing of some kind, for its texture was extremely hard. Yet there was no indication of an opening.

The Philosopher stepped up onto the platform and bent over the casing, touching it delicately.

"It is warm, not hot," he said, and we came to our senses and began describing this strange occurrence, each in our own words, ending with his observation upon the temperature of the thing. We had no more than completed that task than our teacher gasped with surprise.

We looked, and he pointed downward. A pale cone of flame was forming above the brow of the black figure. He dared a quick pass of his hand through it, flinching as the light touched his skin.

"It is cold—burningly cold. Painful to touch." We wrote that down, too.

The flame concentrated into a blade of whiteness. With precision, it moved down the shape, brow to nose to chin. Down the torso, bisecting the hips, it moved, and over the sunken space between the knees. When it reached the end of the black casing, it winked out.

There was a moment of silence, as we waited for the thing all knew must come. With a slight crack, a hissing, the tip of the thing split into halves and hinged back to lie on the stone. Even the Philosopher was reluctant to look inside, and our positions were too low to see clearly what was contained within. As we hesitated, there came a sigh, and a woman sat up, then stood to turn toward us.

She was black, also, yet a lustrous, sheeny black that invited the eye. Between her brows was a pale gem that glowed with fires similar to those that had freed her. She was naked, without even a jewel for concealment. Our women wore only skirts, but the glimpse of even an ankle was enough to set other men panting. Even we, faced with a view of those long legs, the neat ankles, the rounded thighs, felt a tingling that only our long disciplines held in check. When our eyes met hers, that tingle died aborning.

They were the eyes of one who held knowledge to make even our Philosopher pale by comparison. She looked at us, one by one, ending with him who stood so near to her, frozen into attention. Once she had assessed us, she bent with the flexibility of a bulldancer and brought something from the casing at her feet. It was small, black, shiny. She held it to the gem between her eyes, and her gaze drew inward, concentrated.

Not one of us breathed, I think. If I were already bereft of flesh, I could not have been less conscious of myself as a living being. Even the Philosopher, wisest of all who had ever lived upon Thera, seemed stunned and abashed.

When she removed the thing from her forehead, she looked at us again, and this time her eyes were bright and compelling. "Speak to me," she said. "Tell me what you call this place, in this time. I wished to arrive just before the eruption, the cataclysm that destroyed this island and shattered the power of Crete. I can hear the noise of the mountain. Speak!"

The Philosopher bowed his head. "We call this island, our home, Thera. Long past, our fathers came here from that other, greater land you call Crete. And we are, in very deed, awaiting the end of all. The volcano is shaking everything, now. It will not, I think, be long."

She bent her dark gaze upon him and scanned him, head to foot, with much interest. "You are?" she asked.

"I have been called the Philosopher for many years. But I was born Kyros, the son of Pylli. My school has trained thinkers who have gone out over the civilized world, bringing the gift of precise observation and clear thought to lands where such disciplines were unknown. Now we wait to die with our homeland—but not without recording for those who come after us the things that we learn from the catastrophe." He raised his head and looked into her shining ebony face. There was no lack of confidence in him now.

She nodded slowly. "A laudable task, though not precisely everyone's sort, I should think. Is the island cleared, then, of people, except for yourselves?"

He swept his hands wide. "In all of Thera, only we remain. Everything afloat was commandeered by the Governor for the saving of his people. He remonstrated long with me and with my adherents when he learned of our decision to remain here. It pained his heart. Yet he promised, if he survived, to scan the waters for at least a year, searching for our floating writing-cases that will hold our notes upon the matter. To those who think, Lady, death holds no fear."

We stood straighter, proud of him and of ourselves. None other, not even the soldiery, had the discipline to choose our road, we felt. To hear our teacher speak of the decision made us realize that fact more acutely than ever before. Who, indeed, would choose to die in the embrace of an eruption, given the chance to escape?

"Are you...?" It was the voice of Kapyl, the youngest of us all. "Are you, then, the Earth Mother, come to see to the ending of your own?"

I held my breath. The question had arisen in my own mind as well. Who else might arrive in such a strange fashion? Though in no tale I had ever heard had the Earth Mother been described as she now stood before us.

"At least—at the very least—I am one of her daughters," the woman said. She stepped high to clear the edge of the case and now stood upon the stone floor of the platform. Her feet alone were not bare. Narrow golden straps held a thin sole of some scarlet stuff upon them.

From the platform one could see across the terrace, the vineyards that now lay gray and dead beneath a layering of ash, to the Mountain itself. It spewed a stream of ash and steam high into the air, hiding the sun. A bright streak of lava was drooling from a crack partway up its side. We turned to follow her gaze, though we knew all too well what would meet our eyes.

She drew in her breath sharply. "A frightening sight," she said to Kyros, who stood at her elbow. "One well worth traveling so long and so far to see. It will be recorded, never fear, in all its horror and glory for a generation far removed from this to study and to appreciate."

The Philosopher's white brows rose to the edge of his hair. His eyes kindled. "You come from—where? Almost, from your words, I might think it to be the future, some era yet to come. Explain, if you will, your words."

"The future." She smiled, the whitest of teeth glinting in her shining black face. "A future that I am forbidden to explain or describe, Kyros. And that is a pity, for I believe that you would fit well there. A scientist of your devotion might well teach an old lesson anew to those of my generation."

She studied his face for a long moment, while the terrace heaved so drastically that a long crack split the marble and the stone, making an ugly scar down its length. She rode the tremor lightly, as a sailor rides a heaving deck, though she reached a dark hand to steady Kyros.

"I have the authority—there is no doubt of that. When I volunteered for this duty, Anders told me...." Her voice wavered away, as she thought deeply. Then she spoke again. "Kyros, I have the power to transfer you to my own time and place. It is so different from this—so utterly divided by intervening history and social evolution that it might well dismay you. Even send you into madness. Yet if you could survive that stress, there are valuable things that you might bring back into your race. The discipline that you exhibit— and that you were able to instill into your adherents—is all but lost to the world of the future. Will you come with me?"

He looked down at the dark case behind her. "There is hardly room for another there," he said. A smile grew inside me, though I felt my face to be still stern and seemly. For there was rejection in his tone, unmistakable and inflexible.

She turned from the volcano to look at him again. "You will reject the chance of life? Of a vision of the future offered to no other in all of history, so far?"

"I have already rejected the chance of life," he said mildly. "If I had been anxious to continue my existence, I would not have decided upon recording the death of my world. Even to the end. As for the future—it sounds to be a place where I would find no disciples worthy of my teaching. If discipline is, indeed, lost there, it cannot be brought back by one lone teacher resurrected from a past that is forgotten."

"But we need you!" she said impetuously. "We have lost so much, even while gaining mastery of material things. Surely you will come!"

He stepped down from the platform to stand in our rank. "These men and women have given their lives into my hands. They have dedicated their very spirits to the task I set for them. Shall I leave them to die in my place and flee to some wonderful time, betraying my own teachings? No, Lady. I will not go."

As if to emphasize his words, the volcano belched a gout of flame and smoke that turned the day into twilight. Two of the pillars that were set about the terrace rocked drunkenly, then fell away to break on the stone below.

"It is not useful to master material things," Kyros cried above the rumbling of the Mountain, "unless you have first mastered the flesh you stand in and the spirit that lives inside it. Without that mastery, you are like children playing with chips and stones. Without focus and without restraint. Record my words, Lady, for your future."

"Be certain of this: I have already recorded all that has happened since I appeared," she said.

"Then say this also, to the ones who come after. A readiness to die for knowledge should be nothing to amaze those who seek after it. Unwillingness to betray Truth in order to empower oneself or to bolster up a theory should be more integral to the seeker than the very blood in his body. If, in that unguessable time, those who are teachers and philosophers have forgotten this—or never learned it—then our race has gone back, not forward, and I do not wish to look upon such a time or such people."

It was very dark now, yet the shimmer of her blackness was quite visible against the pale stone and ash. She seemed to have drawn herself up, almost quivering with some emotion that we could not assess. She was beautiful, strange, frightening—as the Mother Goddess indeed.

I went to my knees at the edge of the platform. "Surely you are She!" I cried, above the rumbling and hissing of the Mountain. "Only the Earth Mother would come at this time to comfort our passing, to see to the working of her world! Tell us; oh, tell us!"

Ash was swirling in the air, half hiding her. Yet we could see the smile that dawned in her eyes. I felt a feather-touch inside my head, and she looked down at me.

"Lakit, my Son, you must be correct. Surely the Mother of your world would not leave such devotion unacknowledged. Be comforted. Your sacrifice will not be forgotten forever. Those who stand here will be heroes in another age, as well as in this. Time will praise you, Children of Thera!"

She reached down and down and took my tablet from my hands. "Your writing will go back with me to my own place. Those of the others must be cast into the bay quickly! Quickly, or you have wasted your lives. Run!"

My fellows sealed their cases of writings. Then they ran to the far edge of the terrace that rose above the bay and cast their burdens as far across the choppy waters as possible.

Hardly had they regained their positions near the Goddess when there came a roar to beggar all those that went before. We turned to see the top half of the Mountain rise into the air, parting slowly as it rose, moving outward above a hellish glow that must be all the lava of the deep, set free into the world of day.

Kyros knelt among us, as we looked up at the woman, the Goddess, whoever she might be. She stretched out her hands as if to ward away the debris that was almost upon us. Then she stepped back, back, into her casing.

"I wish that I might die with you. Death in battle is easy, amid the excitement of the moment. It requires only the discipline of hot blood and desperation. This is another thing, cold and disciplined and purposeful. It is a great thing. You will be remembered. Go with that in your hearts and minds. You will be remembered!"

A rush of over-hot air blew me flat on my face, but I pushed upward, feeling my robe smolder on my shoulders. Beside me Kyros stirred feebly and I put out my hand to comfort him. But I couldn't breathe. My eyes seemed to be bursting from my head, my lungs heaving with effort. I knew that I was dying.

Yet even then I saw the cold flame move again—up the casing of the woman who had come. And a shimmer. A shimmer of blackness that was the last thing that I knew.

There are so many potential futures, and if we make bad choices they may well include some horrible ones. We seem to be very busy preparing those right now.

THE NEXT GENERATION

The infant never breathed.

Noura, tensed over her control board in the observation station, bent forward, her fingers ready over the keyboard.

The staff in the birth cubicle was superbly competent, their electronic nervous systems incredibly swift, their pseudo-flesh fingers agile. There was a Nan on duty, her padded shape warmed to comfort the child, if it should breathe on its own.

Yet Noura, in her role as observer and representative human being, knew that at times only flesh-and-blood intelligence could step in with necessary insights.

Golden hands, made of an amalgam of plastic and metal, drew the child from its mother's body; the eyes opened in the blood-streaked face. For one instant they stared into the monitor, seeming to look directly into Noura's. Then the umbilicus was snipped and tied, and at the instant of severing the eyes went dull. The tiny lungs never fluttered. No blip on the monitors offered any hope.

Noura pressed the SALVAGE key, her fingers going down too hard, too fast. One of the staff slid the gurney on which the sweating, exhausted mother lay into the tube leading to Post-Delivery, and the others closed in about the table on which the child had been placed.

Noura touched another key, sending the Skull-System down from its position in the oval top of the cubicle. Golden figures moved, placing the infant beneath the cupped protrusion, which opened like a flower to reveal petals of keen metal. It moved down onto the small head, closing the features, still streaked with birth fluids, from Noura's view. She winced, knowing that the blades were slicing away the soft skull like the peel of a fruit, exposing the mass of the brain to those ready to link the life-support systems.

While the machine was cautiously severing the brain's connections to the dead body of the infant, Noura's fingers were racing, ordering up the components of the body for this newly salvaged child. By the time the leads and the tubes of nourishing fluids were in place, the tiny, shining body came sliding down the delivery tube into the hands of the attendants.

Her part was done now. It would be some time before the child would be secured in his new environment, and Noura found that she could not sit there, watching, waiting, until that was completed. No, she would go and observe the School. It would make her, perhaps, feel a bit more cheerful.

She rose, her old joints creaking and painful, and turned to the Slip, which carried those who lived in the Laboratory Complex wherever they wanted to go. All were almost as old as she, and they were grateful for that effortless manner of getting about.

She touched a button on a map of the interior of the Lab, and the strip began to move, smoothly, slowly, along the dim hallways. She could remember when all this had been sparkling new, shiny-clean with steel and paint.

She could recall when human children were born with the ability to breathe on their own, to live with pleasure and pain in the bodies they should have, instead of plasmoid and metal shells. The woman now recovering from childbirth was the last one of fertile years in all the small remaining enclave of their kind, and she was forty-three.

The birth had been hard, and there would be no more pregnancies for Lisha. This was almost to be considered a wasted effort, except for the fact that there was one more human mind available to their dwindling complement.

Noura came to a corner and touched another point on the map, riding the Slip smoothly around and down another angled branch. She wondered, for the thousandth time, what error her species had made, here in its third millennium of technology, that had doomed its children. Was it the artificial manipulation of viruses? Was it the experimental use of radiation to spur growth and intelligence?

The Slip came to a halt beside a long rank of windows. Noura stepped off and moved to lean against the glass. No matter how alien the School might be, the sight of all those small bodies, playing, learning, creating, always made her feel less despairing.

The human brain being conditioned over the generations to exist at each step in its development in a body of a certain size, the robot bodies into which the salvaged brains went were made in various dimensions, from infant to adult.

The oldest Salvaged child was now twenty, and it was now a teacher of its younger kindred. Noura saw Estil bending over a youngster who was manipulating shapes and colors into intricate patterns, its gleaming metallic skull reflecting the clean pinkish light.

Estil would have been a woman now. Instead, she was a sexless creature cased in a body without sensation. There had been a great deal of hesitation before the Elders had agreed to put Salvaged brains into mechanical bodies. Some feared the resulting intelligent and emotionless personality. Some felt that it was better for their species to die out entirely, instead of creating what might become a race of monstrous semi-robots.

One of the smaller children glanced up and noticed her face at the window. The face, of course, was a smooth curve with only the eye-cells breaking its symmetry, so it could not smile, but one hand went up in a shy wave.

Noura felt a surge of pain rise in her chest. She remembered the warm, heavy feel of a baby in her arms, the milky smell, the mutual comfort of physical contact with her own flesh and blood. Even diapers and spit-ups had been worth it, she now knew.

The light in the Schoolroom turned blue. The dozen children, all sizes from toddler to teenager, stopped immediately, shutting off computers, closing down holo-generators, putting away tapes and viewers. Bodiless children had no feelings. They did not object to stopping their play or to going to bed, though once there they lay wakeful, needing no sleep.

What did they think, in those long reaches of the night while their parents slept? Noura was grateful, sometimes, that she didn't know.

Now the line of parents, here to take away their young for the evening, was slipping smoothly into the hall beside her. She smiled at Lotta and Wim, who came to stand beside her at the window, watching their nine-year-old, identified by an orange dot on the upper front of the metal skull, pick its way out of the room.

One of the toddlers tripped and fell, and Orange-dot bent and set it gently onto its feet. Noura recalled with sudden intensity a time, eighty years in the past, when she had tripped in the schoolroom and a larger boy had taken great delight in stepping onto her outflung hand. There had been no gentleness there.

Had there ever been that sort of caring among her flesh-and-blood schoolmates? She tried to think, but her memories of childhood were a long, cold corridor of misery and competition.

She and her peers had been taught to excel, and those teaching them had lost sight, she now knew, of the thing that made the species work best. Cooperation, tenderness, mutual understanding, and effort had not been a part of the human condition for centuries before her birth.

She had often watched the Schoolroom here in the Labs. She had never seen one of the children assault or tease another or otherwise disrupt the even tenor of life there.

In their chilly, unfeeling bodies, did the human brains, nourished with uncontaminated and perfectly formulated nutrients, fed exactly the correct amount of oxygen, cleansed of waste with mechanical efficiency, still long for contact? For love?

Noura shivered. The parents, holding small metal hands in their own, were leading their young away, sliding effortlessly along the corridor amid a light hum of conversation. The small one who had waved, a Blue-dot, passed her, and she heard the speaker that was its voice say, "Goodbye, Ma'am Noura."

"Goodbye," she said, straining to recall the name. "Goodbye, Petro. Perhaps I shall see you tomorrow." Then it was gone, and she knew that the time had come to return to her terrible task.

In the main corridor again, she found herself moving along beside Andre, who once had been her mate. He was bent—more than she, she noted with satisfaction—and his wrinkled hands were spotted with brown. He glanced aside and his narrow mouth thinned in a smile.

"The child—it is born?" he asked her, keeping his gaze away from her face. "It is...normal?"

"Normal for the present," she said. "They are making the transfer now. It should be finished by the time I return. Lisha is alive, though her vital signs were alarming during the delivery. But she will recover, though never again will I ask her to undergo this. And she—she was the last woman capable of conceiving."

Andre's fingers clenched on his loose robe. He had paled, his face going gray. "No. There is no point in going on. Those back there in the Schoolroom will carry on, when their time comes." She could see his pain in the set of his frail body.

"How?" The question came almost as a cry. "For what? And how could they ever carry on the species, without bodies, without even hormones and ova?" She caught his robe as he prepared to step off at his own workspace.

"Andre, tell me. Have we done a terrible thing to these children? They would be safely dead, out of the stress, the demands, the unmapped wilderness of the future that must lie before them. When Lisha and those of her age-group are gone, the little ones will be on their own.

"What sort of world can they shape, if they manage to survive? Have we sentenced them to a hopeless future that will end in intolerable loneliness and death?"

He pulled the cloth gently from her fingers and stepped free of the Slip. "Whatever their bodies may be like, the minds are human. They are not distracted by the matters that have made our kind self-centered and aggressive and brutish. Perhaps they may create a better world, however long they can make it last, than our sort ever did." Then he was left behind, as Noura slid on toward her own place.

She left the Slip at her door and stood staring into space for a moment. A memory, sharp as a cameo, came.

She stood in an open field, the grass as high as her waist, staring about at this untamed world outside the Labs. No plow had broken its soil in many centuries. No hunter had invaded the forest beyond it; no fisherman had dropped his lures into the stream wandering through it for so long that those things might never have happened on this world at all.

Her father, holding her hand and leading her through this unimagined world outside their protecting walls, was speaking to her. "Soon we will close the portals permanently. Now that we can create our own sustenance, using the reactors, there is no necessity for us to come out into the wild, but I wanted you to see it before it is shut away forever.

"It is dangerous here now. Animals we had thought gone forever, a few generations ago, now hunt the wood, prowl in the fields, fly across that unpolluted sky. We no longer know how to deal with them, and there is no need for us to learn. But remember, Noura. Remember, and tell your children about this, for it is the world to which our kind was born."

The vision fled; but she had, indeed, taught her daughter about that invisible world beyond the barriers, the ventilators, the exhaust chutes. Was it possible that the young ones in the Schoolroom might one day unseal the portals, iris their round locks open, and walk out into the wonder of a planet healed of its wounds and free of the poisons her species had loosed there?

She turned, feeling a lifting in her heart. These children cared. She could see it in their interactions in the Schoolroom.

Perhaps they would revel in the freedom, after their long captivity. Surely they would not work the damage upon it that their ancestors had done.

She touched her door, and it slid into the frame. Even as she moved toward her keyboard and the waiting chair, there came a sound from the door connecting her post to the Birth Cubicle.

The Nan, her warm padding wasted on the chilly shape in her hands, stood there. "Ma'am Noura," said her somewhat metallic voice, "Here is the child."

Noura drew a deep breath. Then she turned and opened her arms, allowing the robot to set into them the body of her newborn grandchild.

The day may come when the most wonderful luxury possible will be the world we have right here in our hands but do not appreciate or protect.

INDULGENCES

She sat in a lotus position at the very edge of the free-flowing brook. The ripples purled about her hips and her angled knees; the rounded pebbles, green and pale blue and ochre, made the moving water sing in a muted series of tones.

Her eyes were closed, for the Seller of Indulgences was forbidden to look into the faces of those who came to buy. And Jonah, just off the shuttle, found himself awed at the calm clarity of her expression as he inched forward.

Indeed, all of those who approached her seemed wide-eyed, their gazes sliding from the overarching green of the immense trees that bowed above the stream to the miraculous brook itself. Nothing in all their constricted lives had prepared them for the vibrant livingness of this forest. They came, all of them, from the Colonies; this was Jonah's first glimpse of the world that had given birth to his grandparents.

He followed the Guide to the brook with the line of holiday-makers. He found himself wondering, as he waited his turn, why he had felt so compelled to make a pilgrimage back to the home world, when he had everything he could possibly need was there on the Station.

If there was no sky, blue or otherwise, there was always the constant reassurance of the pressurized hull. If there were no trees, there were always the plants in the hydroponics gardens. He felt a sudden surge of agoraphobia. His head spun, and his heart began pounding.

The Guide seemed to sense any problem among his charges; he was beside Jonah at once. The prick of the injector fed tranquilizer directly into Jonah's bloodstream, and he felt himself settle into his usual calm. Yet that sudden and unexpected panic unsettled him.

"Don't let this worry you," the Guide was saying. "Almost every visitor from the Colony Satellites feels this, sooner or later. The transition from a Station to the open world is a shock. Breathe deeply and turn up your flow of oxygen."

The filter-mask that protected those without immunity to this rampant jungle of organisms began to hiss, as the Guide opened the oxygen tube a bit more. Jonah nodded his gratitude and turned again toward the Seller of Indulgences.

Her long brown arm reached for a metal box sitting upon a stone beside her in the water. She turned a knob, and something clicked loudly.

"Have your credits ready," said a mechanical voice. "It is required that all visitors to Terra purchase Indulgences in the amount of all possible damages that they might inflict upon this planet while visiting here. The rates are now being posted."

The voice paused, and a hologram formed in the air above the box. The symbols that had replaced the clumsy written language centuries ago began to become visible. Jonah studied them carefully.

POLLUTION FROM NATURAL PHYSICAL FUNCTIONS
One hundred credits, mandatory, non-refundable

CONSUMPTION OF FOODSTUFFS AND POTABLE WATER,
WINE, AND OTHER BEVERAGES
One thousand credits, mandatory and nonrefundable

DESTRUCTION OF FLORA/FAUNA
Fifty thousand credits, refundable if not used,
to be prorated if not used in full

INJURY TO NATIVE INHABITANT

FATAL: Five hundred thousand credits
INCAPACITATING: One hundred thousand credits
TEMPORARILY PAINFUL: One thousand credits
Refundable if not used

* * * * * *

Jonah felt his waist-pouch, which was fat with hoarded credits that had been saved for this once-in-a-lifetime adventure. He calculated the total on his watch/calculator, and he had the proper amount in his hand when the Guide moved him up beside the Seller of Indulgences.

She extended a packet of plastic slips, as he passed her the payment. She smiled, so automatically and meaninglessly that he knew she had to be an automaton.

When Jonah turned away from her, he was fully authorized to move about this world, which was no longer the birthright of his own variant of the human species. His ancestors had ceded all rights in their native world to those remaining behind.

Jonah had to admit that those hardy holdouts, remaining on a world that was stifling in the aftereffects of over-industrialization, had done a remarkable job of restoring things to their pristine condition. The sky was unstained except with natural clouds, and the air was intoxicating, even through the filters.

He emerged from the forest, still at the end of the line, into the edge of a meadow on which stood a circle of pavilions. Those were gaily colored and made, he thought, of silk. The effect was that of a field of flowers in the sunlight, and he was immediately charmed. Beauty was not a priority on the Stations.

He examined his packet. The topmost slip assigned him to a bright blue pavilion with pale green stripes. He went carefully, trying not to dislodge the grass or to tread on the small yellow blossoms growing in the meadow. The remarkable business minds that had made a tourist haven of a world given up as ruined would, he felt certain, would charge him for every bruised sprig.

Jonah stepped around an earthworm and a dung beetle, rolling its egg-filled ball along a tiny path amid the grass stems. He had studied for years in preparation for this trip, and he felt some satisfaction at his ability to identify such minor creatures. But by the time he reached his tent he was exhausted with his efforts to avoid damaging anything.

If earlier generations had taken such care, he thought wryly, they might not have pushed their world to the verge of systems failure. They might not have overbred and reached the point at which it was leave or die. It was apparent that those remaining behind were not the cowards that Station history made them seem. They were heroes who stayed behind on a sinking ship and kept her afloat.

Once inside the tent, Jonah paused, his eyes widening. On a white wicker table lay a snowy cloth edged with lace. Fruit was piled in a glass dish, and a carafe of purple juice sat beside a tumbler that refracted the sunlight into rainbows of light and color.

He sank into a wicker chair and poured cool liquid into the glass. It was as refreshing as it looked. A plum and a peach sent his taste buds, used to bland Station fare, into shocked ecstasy. He leaned back and put up his feet on the embroidered cushion evidently there for that purpose.

This could not possibly be the standard of living for those who lived on Earth all the time. That would seem unreasonable. But he had never dreamed even of such color. And this kind of flavor and comfort were outside anything he had ever considered in all his forty years.

From the shuttle he had seen clusters of bright domes nestled into woodland, and the Guide had said those were the homes of the native population. Those had looked, from above, very neat and well arranged. Jonah found himself contrasting his life, which had seemed perfectly orderly and satisfactory, with that of the earthlings who now owned the home world.

Did they walk, every day, in halls painted gray and vibrating with the voices of the machines that made life possible? No, they walked beneath flowering trees and picked fruit off the branches. They moved on grass and picked flowers and saw, probably, living animals in the meadows and the forests.

Jonah's eyes closed, and he drifted half into sleep. The juice had not seemed alcoholic, but he felt somewhat removed from himself.

Someone entered the tent, and he was lifted carefully from the chair and laid on a couch. His clothing came off smoothly and he felt himself being bathed in scented water. A robe so silken that it was an erotic experience was wrapped around him.

He kept trying to open his eyes, but they seemed to be glued shut. He listened hard, but only the sounds of quiet movement came to him. Not a whisper, not a word—until....

"Now he is ready," someone breathed, at the very limit of his perceptions.

The robe was slipped aside, and a warm body moved against him. This had to be a dream! But if it were one, it was the most satisfactory dream ever known to man.

He let himself go, sinking into an experience that he knew, even in this exalted state, would warm his memory for the rest of his life. There came a peak, higher than anything to which he had dreamed his flesh could go. Then he sank into total relaxation and sleep.

Jonah awoke feeling incredibly fit. There was a lightness to his bones, but he did not at once recall the dream. He ate, when food was brought, and even the snack of the night before did not compare with this for flavor.

The day was fascinating, spent at the heels of the Guide marveling at the antiquities in museums, the glories in the arboretum and the gardens. Art works, ancient and modern, astonished him. On Station, there was no time for such personal expressions of creativity. He had been fortunate that his beloved theoretical mathematics was a technically viable creative outlet.

Day flowed into day, and the week passed smoothly, filled with interest but never allowed to become exhausting. The group was whisked deftly from meals to points of interest, to amusement and to rest in a well-conceived round. Jonah found himself dreading the day that would take him away from this enchanted world, returning him to Station IV, which now seemed sterile and confining by contrast.

Of course that day came at last. He had no idea which, if any, of the indulgences he might have used as he waited, with some trepidation, at the terminal computer for his transgressions to be tallied. Now that the holiday was over, he was again the thrifty and practical person he had always been.

The computer did not provide the same exotic atmosphere that the Seller of Indulgences had done. He had already been separated from his money, and this was a simple business transaction. The return of refunds was strictly mechanical.

A packet spat from the rectangular mouth of the machine, and he took it, releasing the packet of plastic slips. Those were whisked away instantly.

He stepped back to let the next comer approach the machine, as he looked down at the packet. It seemed very thick—as thick as it had been when he handed the credits to the Seller of Indulgences, in the beginning.

Curious, he opened the thin film enclosing the packet and flipped through the stack. All of it was there, even those amounts that had been listed as nonrefundable!

There was a strip of symbols printed on the film, which he had been about to discard. He flattened the strip and read it once, then again. And then he began to chuckle.

ALL CHARGES WAIVED as payment for GENETIC DONATION RECEIVED: Mechanical abilities, mathematical skills, logical thought processes, calm nature, creative ability.

DNA SCAN POSITIVE TO 999.9

THANK YOU for your contribution to the genetic health of our population.

* * * * * *

Jonah boarded the shuttle filled with a warm sense of well-being. It had indeed been a holiday worth waiting for.

Occasionally the Humane Society has been known to go overboard. This is what might happen, if pushed to the extreme.

HUNTING TRUCE

The Cagodot warrior tensed. His blue cranial plume came erect, warning the rest of the party that game had been sighted .The other blue-feathered warriors melted into the tall tan grasses, leaving the honor of the first run to the finder of the game. He, Tado, stood proudly erect, waving his plumed arms in the traditional patterns, in order to attract the beast's attention.

The zdin moved his horned and tusked head uneasily, as he sought with short-sighted eyes for the source of the scent which troubled him. When the form of the slight blue warrior came into his field of vision, he snorted, and his neck bristles rose threateningly. Then, ponderously, he began to move his great bulk toward the Cagodot, who stood unmoved as the huge beast thundered toward him.

Tado waited until the zdin was almost upon him before beginning his flight across the broad savannah. The beast veered after him, pounding along like a mountain gone mad. The Cagodot led his prey in an immense circle, returning almost to his starting place. There, one of his comrades took up the race, and Tado disappeared into the grass to rest.

In a small copse at the edge of the savannah waited the Blgat, their great, orange-haired forms blending so well with the tawny grass and foliage that they were almost invisible, as they waited their move in the drama of the hunt. With the infinite patience of the primitive, they watched the marathon in the meadow, gripping their broad-bladed spears and blowing out their lips in puffs of anticipation. Once or twice, when it appeared that the fleeing Cagodot would be caught and trampled, their eyes blazed red with glee, for they never forgot their traditional hatred for the feathered ones, even during the great fall truce. It would be great sport to see an enemy smashed beneath those tremendous hooves. So long as enough Cagodot survived to run the zdin into exhaustion, their temporary hunting partners would have enjoyed seeing one of them die on every lap.

Grkh, the leader of the Blgat, grinned savagely at the thought of the impending battle with the zdin. His broad, four-fingered hand caressed the haft of his spear. His shrewd little eyes flickered after the relays of Cagodot, without the spark of hatred that was common to his kind. A little more intelligent and a great deal older than the others, he had seen enough of the feathered people, during his twenty hunts, to realize that they were a brave and resourceful race. He grunted, thinking of the Blgat who would have had to die in order to kill even one zdin, had the Cagodot not run him to the ragged edge of exhaustion first. No Blgat could ever move fast enough to do the work that Tado and his friends were doing, and the old chief was fully aware of the fact. The zdin was slowing perceptibly now, and Locot, the present runner, seemed to float effortlessly before him, leading him nearer and nearer to the copse where the Blgat waited.

With a grunt of command, Grkh lifted his heavy weapon, and his companions, moving very quietly for such large creatures, grouped themselves about him, their waiting nearly at an end. Grunting again, Grkh slid, crawling, into the grass, and soon there was not a single orange-haired Blgat to be seen.

* * * * * *

"There!" Miss Pirtle-Smith's skinny finger snaked past Gambel's large shoulder, quivering with triumph.

Gambel said nothing, noted everything, and brought the observation car gently to rest on the savannah, some half mile from the hunt, settling on a hillock, so that he could see above the grasses. The zdin had taken refuge on another such hillock, and now stood snorting heavily and heaving with fatigue, while the Cagodot runners faded into the grass and a great circle of Blgat spearmen rose, like magic, about him.

The woman's mosquito-like voice whined past Gambel's ear, and he flinched. "You see, Observer! They are going to kill that unfortunate animal. You must stop them at once!"

Gambel's broad face turned a shade darker than its usual sunburnt hue. His voice, when he answered, was under careful control. "My dear lady. Your function—prescribed by your own society—is that of protecting native fauna from undue persecution by US. They explained that to you. I have explained that to you. Why won't you understand that it is not our purpose to interfere *in any way* with the native people? Our only purpose is to observe, to contact, if it may be done without upsetting them overmuch, and to report our findings to the Intergalactic Service. Only that." But his tone was hopeless.

"I am here, Mr. Gambel, to protect animals." Her voice rose frenziedly, *"All animals*—from persecution and death. If you don't stop that revolting massacre, I will!" Her thin, empurpled nose twitched determinedly, and she reached for the door-release.

"Dammit, woman, get your hand off that door!" roared Gambel, reaching across her and slamming down the lock. He secured the safety-lock beside his control panel and took a gulp of air, then turned to his flabbergasted passenger.

"Miss Pirtle-Smith. Your Society forced you upon us, through that ridiculous law they lobbied through the Universal Congress. We have borne you quietly, even though your presence, on a six-person craft, meant that we had to make do with my first-aid and emergency medical training, instead of having a medical officer. I am willing to endure your blather, but I refuse to die in a hopeless attempt to save the life of a mangy boar-ox."

Miss Pirtle-Smith's long face grew scornful. "Cowardice," she began, smugly.

"Cowardice, my foot!" exploded the Observer. "You saw the Cagodot hide in the grass. They're still there, between you and the zdin. And those big, orange-haired creatures are carrying spears." His words slowed and simplified, as though he were speaking to an unintelligent child. "Spears will kill almost anything. Even if it is from Earth and its name is Samantha Pirtle-Smith. I couldn't allow them to kill you without attempting to save you. Then they would kill me too. Because, if you will recall your indoctrination lectures, we are not allowed to kill or injure any alien intelligence, even to save our own lives."

He paused with a heavy sigh. "Those people may not be wearing the latest in fashions nor carrying the most modem weapons, but they are hunting for food to keep their families from starving during the 'time of cold winds'. They hunt each other all the rest of the year, but now, in order to survive at all, they make common cause in the fall hunt. They won't let you stand in their way."

The woman said nothing, but he knew that her shell was impervious to logic. Experience had taught him how hopeless it was to try to get through to her. He sighed again and turned to see how the hunt was going.

The zdin was turning slowly in his tracks, trying to keep his enemies in front of him, but the Blgat had encircled him and were pressing him closely. Gathering his energy desperately, the animal made a lunge at the nearest warrior. Old Grkh, seeing his chance, rushed in upon the left flank, driving his spear beneath the heavy rib-cage, thrusting with all his mighty strength. The reddish hide was dappled with a darker red, and still Grkh strained at his task, his orange pelt reddening with the blood of the beast. For a long moment, they were still, then the breath went from the zdin, and he gave a groan and died. Grkh, panting, withdrew his spear from the creature's heart and raised a dripping hand. The Cagodot rose gracefully from the grass and moved toward the giant corpse, their skinning-knives ready in their hands. Like bright vultures, the two peoples descended upon their fallen prey, to prepare it for the preservers.

Gambel thumbed a button on the control panel, and the car rose quietly from the plain and moved away over the countryside, He hoped that his passenger would preserve her silence. His difficult task had been made considerably harder by her unreasonable attitude, and he found himself thinking wistfully of the report he could have written: "Our SPAF representative was unfortunately killed while trying to preserve the life of one of the local fauna, a zdin...."

A period of two years was little enough time to try and observe a whole planet, geophysically, climatically, ecologically. When you added a factor like the almost year-round enmity of the two dominant races, who could only be observed during the yearly hunting truce, you doubled the difficulty.

The car buzzed swiftly and quietly onward, its cameras noiselessly recording everything within eye-range, its beeper keeping the Station constantly informed of its position. Crossing a broad area of stunted tree-like growth, they entered another of the great savannahs, cruising low, in order to check the vegetation closely.

To one side of the savannah, there was a group of natives, busy at skinning and carving up a zdin. Immediately in front of the observation car, a small group of Cagodot hovered over one of their brethren, who was lying on the grass, covered with his own purplish blood.

Miss Pirtle-Smith's nose wrinkled with distaste, but she nodded with brisk satisfaction. Gambel, sensing an opportunity for contact, eased the car to a landing. "If you get out of this car, I'll wring your neck," he said to his passenger who, for once, believed him.

Reaching into a compartment, he took out his emergency medical kit. Securing the door behind him, he walked toward the Cagodot, holding his arms out from his sides and trying to look friendly. The Cagodot perceived his approach with astonishment. mingled with alarm. They drew into a tight circle about their injured brother, but made no motion to throw their light spears.

Gambel walked slowly and steadily, making no sudden motions, until he was within a few feet of the nearest warrior. Consulting his memory, he located therein the proper Cagodot greeting for two hours before noon on a warm but cloudy fall day. "Lodog we-gota," he said pleasantly.

The Cagodot stirred as if a breeze had passed over them, but it was only their crest-plumes and arm-feathers stirring with surprise.

Pleased with the result of his first use of the Cagodot tongue, he blessed his first officer, who was the semantics man and linguist. Trying to recall every intonation precisely as Burke had recorded, he essayed another comment. "Doti selo? Doti bodot? (Is he hurt? Is he suffering?)"

The leader of the group spread his hands in the gesture of assent, his feathers rippling as he moved from his recumbent companion. At his gesture the others also moved, and Gambel knelt beside the injured native. Its light body scarcely crushed the grass it lay on, and its blue plumage was torn and splattered with blood.

With gentle fingers, Gambel examined him for injury, but his body was unhurt. Evidently, the torn feathers had sustained the injury. Making a mental note to record the odd fact that the creatures' plumage was supplied with blood vessels and nerve endings, he opened his kit and took out a jar of the soothing antibiotic which his biochemist had recommended for use on the natives, should the need arise.

Anointing all the injured places he could find, he closed the jar and stood up, observing his patient closely. The Cagodot had closed its great purplish eyes at his approach, but now it opened them and gazed up at him. Moving its head, then its arms, it gestured to its companions, who helped it to its feet. Though its feathers were rumpled and stained, the salve had evidently eased its pain considerably. It laid its hand to its cheek, in the gesture of gratitude, and Gambel spread his hands, regretting his lack of feathers to give the gesture true elegance. Gathering up his kit, he handed the jar of ointment to the leader of the group, who also indicated gratitude.

His return to the car was observed with acute interest by the Cagodot. His passenger, though, was unimpressed. He was greeted by a contemptuous sniff and cold silence. He was grateful for the silence.

Completing the last leg of their observation pattern, Gambel pressed the homing button, and the little car made a neat ninety-degree turn and moved off toward the Station, still continuing its low-level camera work.

Landing in the tightly fenced enclosure which encircled the Station and the ship, they were met by Rolf Burke, the aforementioned first officer, who helped Gambel to unload the film packs from the cameras.

"What happened to the Great Stone Face?" he inquired, nodding at Miss Pirtle-Smith's retreating figure. "She looked like fury, when she passed me."

"Tried to make me stop a hunt," grunted the Observer . "Fool woman's going to get someone killed, if she doesn't learn some sense."

Burke grinned, but suppressed his mirth quickly. He had a mental picture of the event, which, if not entirely accurate, was true enough to the characters involved to be amusing.

Gambel looked up, as he finished reloading the last camera and caught the last remnant of a grin, as it slid off Burke's face. "Glad you can find it amusing," he remarked. "She tickles me about as much as a spear in the gut.... A Blgat spear," he added thoughtfully.

"Come on and have a cup of coffee. Mardi's almost through in the lab, and the rest of them are waiting for lunch. It's zdin steak," he added, glancing sidewise at his superior. "The last batch of warriors that came by left us a haunch, in return for some salt and a carton of chocolate bars."

Gambel stopped in his tracks and raised his face prayerfully. A wide grin became a subdued rumble of laughter. He stood there laughing for a few seconds, then said to Burke, "Don't tell her! Don't anyone tell her—until after lunch." He choked again, but waved his hand commandingly in the direction of the mess hall, and Burke, understanding immediately, went quickly ahead to warn the rest of the Terrans not to spoil the joke.

Gambel went to his quarters and cleaned up, then, surprisingly easy at heart, headed for the mess hall. Miss Pirtle-Smith reached the tent at the same time, and he stood politely aside to allow her to enter.

Mardi Lindsay, the biochemist, had finished her morning's work in the laboratory and sat, dark eyes alert, beside Burke, whose solemn face hid the spark of mischief in his eyes. Jan Huffstedt, ecologist and zoologist, had placed his square form at the far end of the table, and his pale eyes surveyed the newcomers with angelic innocence.

"Come in," he wheezed, "and sit down. You seem to have had a long morning of it. But we have a good lunch for you, eh, Prue?" And he turned to their tall brown geophysicist, Prue Lynes, who smiled easily back. "I didn't scorch the steak, if that's what you mean," she answered. "Fall to, people."

And they did.

When they had finished eating, they settled back in their chairs for their customary recapitulation of the morning. As they had expected, Miss Pirtle-Smith's was the first voice heard.

"I must ask to enter a protest in the report," she said icily. "You people try to frustrate every effort I make on behalf of the animals here. This morning Mr. Gambel refused—utterly refused—to prevent the slaughter of a boar-ox. I was forced to sit there...."—Her voice broke—"...and watch its death."

Gambel's grey eyes lost their devilish twinkle. With a regretful shrug he shook his head slightly at Burke, and that young officer gave a sigh and turned to speak to Mardi Lindsay, who had missed none of the byplay.

Gambel, meanwhile, had pulled his chair close to that of Miss Pirtle-Smith.

"You may enter whatever you wish in the report," he said gently. "That is your right, just as it is my right to enter my reasons for refusing to help you this morning. I think we haven't made our purpose clear to you, Miss Pirtle-Smith. We are not here to alter anything. The Intergalactic Service has no interest save one, and that is to find out all it can about the planets in every sector under their jurisdiction. They want to know which can be colonized and should be, which can be but shouldn't, and which can't be. They have no intention of disrupting the ways and lives of the native peoples they encounter during the process of observation. Surely you can see that we can't go about trying to draft these beings into the Society for the Preservation of Alien Fauna, when their lives depend upon their success in hunting the very creatures you are trying to protect."

Huffstedt leaned across the table. "I think you can have no objection to the way we treat the beasts we examine in the lab, eh, Miss Smith? We are not heartless, I assure you, either in our work or privately."

But the light of compassion in the eyes of the two men was not mirrored in those of the thin woman. Uncomprehending hostility wrapped her about, as she rose and said, "Don't think to persuade me to alter my report, Gentlemen. I see through you quite well."

Prue Lynes grimaced as the door banged behind the woman. "You lost your laugh for nothing," she said to Gambel, who shook his head slowly.

"No," he said, "I'm not sorry we let her go without teasing her. The poor woman's really insane on the subject of animals, I think. I suppose she's just the cross we'll have to bear, until we get back to port. Try to bear her kindly! She seems so unhappy, poor soul." He rose, handling his big body easily. "Your turn with the observation car, Prue. See if you can cover the pattern from a good height. I'm afraid your passenger will try to jump out and run to the rescue of any hunted animal you may see."

Prue chuckled wryly. "I'm quite likely to let her," she teased. "If the Cagodot and the Blgat didn't get her, the zdin would, and she'd be out of her misery—and our hair."

Nevertheless, as the car pulled out, Gambel was pleased to note that Prue was holding a good altitude, swinging into the pattern which she was assigned to search.

The afternoon passed busily. Gambel's daily report was ready for the final entries, when he leaned back and stretched luxuriously. Rubbing the back of his neck, he rose and stepped to the door, gazing into the purpling sky. A sharp exclamation from the radio shack drew his attention. Running a brown hand through his cowlick, he ambled with deceptive speed over to the building and asked, "What now? Sugar beetles in the transistors?"

"Look at the blip!" Rolf answered tersely.

The speck of light which was the tell-tale of the air-car had veered sharply from the search pattern and was dancing wildly across the screen. Suddenly it halted, hesitated for several minutes, then turned and fled madly in the direction of the home camp.

"Uh, oh," grunted Gambel. But his face was anxious, as the two men watched the car's progress across the screen.

* * * * * * *

Night was drawing in as the heavily laden warriors toiled through the tear-grass. Though the Cagodot had taken their fair half of the kill, there was still much meat for the Blgat to bear home to their village. Old Grkh, bringing up the rear, as was fitting, surveyed the dripping haunches and ribs with approval. The time of cold winds would find his folk well prepared this year. The head of the zdin, borne upon a litter before him, seemed to glare more savagely than in life, fixing the patriarch with a glazed and scornful eye.

Annoyed, both by the beast's dead gaze and by the buzzing of some strange insect close behind him, Grkh raised his spear and gave the severed head a great whack with the flat of the blade, then turned to lay low the daring gnat buzzing behind his ear.

Much to his astonishment, an anguished shriek pierced his ear, and the huge and oddly shaped insect dropped a bundle, which turned into an angular creature with long arms. The creature bore down upon the dumbfounded Grkh and began to belabor him with a stick. Her insane frenzy enabled her to give him a puffed lip, a bruised eye, and several sore ribs, before he got his huge hands on her brittle arms. The warriors before him dropped their burdens and hurried back to their chief, but he had subdued the creature and was standing on her, as she was being tied.

Ulh, the shaman of the tribe, raised his hands toward the setting sun. "This demon came from the sky and sought to injure Grkh. It is fitting that it should suffer the Torture."

A grunt of assent came from the assembled warriors, and Grkh nodded, prodding his prisoner with a great toe. At this instant, the insect, which had been hanging motionless, buzzed off at great speed across the savannah. The shaman made an excessively insulting sign, and the procession got under way again, ignoring the dwindling speck in the sky.

* * * * * * *

The air car rocketed into its berth, and the two officers dashed to meet it. They were met by a white and shaken Prue.

"Oh, Dan!"

Gambel nodded, patted the girl on the shoulder, and said, "Take it slow and easy, Prue. Let's go into the mess hall and get some coffee, then you can tell us all about it."

Rolf Burke, who had been opening the passenger door of the air-car, in order to help Miss Pirtle-Smith to descend, gave a low whistle, as his efforts disclosed a cab which was entirely innocent of that lady's presence. Gambel looked back over his shoulder and shook his head warningly. Burke nodded and followed them to the mess-hall.

The others were already there, drawn by the sound of the air-ear's landing. When Gambel, Prue, and Burke entered without Miss Pirtle-Smith, Huffstedt's pale eyes widened and Mardi Lindsay opened her mouth to speak, then thought better of it, but moved to pour coffee from the ever-ready pot.

Prue took a long sip and sighed.

"Can you tell us what happened now?" asked Gambel.

"Yes, Dan, but it seems more like a fantastic dream than the real happening. We had almost completed the pattern and were entering the last leg, when that crazy woman saw a line of Blgat moving across the flat to our left. She wanted to see what they were doing. I hesitated at first, but I knew that it was too late in the day for them to be hunting, and I thought no harm could come of going over to observe them.

"I had the control lock on the passenger door, remember that, please. You had warned me, and I was careful to secure it the first thing. Well, we went in low enough to see details. They were evidently returning from a successful hunt, for they were loaded with fresh meat. At the tail of the procession, a huge warrior was swaggering along behind the group that carried the zdin's head.

"There were some odd air currents along there, and I was pretty busy holding the car steady and keeping a little altitude, but I was still watching them as well as I could. Anyway, the big bruiser suddenly banged the zdin's head across the snout with his spear. That woman gave a screech like a wounded toucan and wrenched the door open with her bare hands. She did." Prue repeated, to their incredulous stares. "Just examine that door, if you don't believe me. It was built for keeping things out, not for keeping people in. Anyway, she bailed out of the car and went for that tough old warrior with a stick. She gave him a rough couple of seconds, too, before he got hold of her. I was sort of proud of her, in a way." She laughed, but sobered quickly.

"I just hung there. I couldn't for the life of me figure out anything to do for her, so I let the cameras get everything they could pick up, then I scatted for home." The girl picked up her cup with a hand that was slightly unsteady.

Burke was on his feet at once. "I'll get those film packs."

Mardi and Prue went to their quarters, leaving Gambel and Huffstedt at the table, staring silently into cups of cooling coffee, while the red sun went down in unobserved glory. .

"Will they kill her, Dan?" Huffstedt's voice was oddly hopeful.

"It's likely," Gambel grunted. "Probably with frills; from what the Cagodot say, I gather that they have a pretty gory record for torturing their captives." He drained his coffee cup and stood up.

"We're pretty well stymied, Jan. We can't go in there and take her out. Those Blgat don't put up with such things. We'd have to kill about half of them. Which is utterly against everything we and the Service stand for. Oh, hell! I've known from the beginning that Pirtle-Smith...."—He grimaced at the taste of the name—"...was going to foul us up, somehow, before she got through. Let's go look at the films. Maybe they'll give us an idea of some sort."

The two men met Rolf at the door of the projection room, and they soon had the record of the trip unreeling before them. Their amazing cameras had tremendous range and versatility. Color was true to the nth degree. Sound was imprinted in the tape, along with long and short-range detail which was considerably more complete than the human eye can encompass.

The file of warriors stood before them, in all but living flesh. The direction finder, in the upper left corner of each frame, gave an accurate fix on their destination, as well as their position at the time. The camera moved closer, as the air-car drew near and hovered. Old Grkh showed up brightly, with his brilliant coat of hair still dappled with dried blood. The head of the boar-ox gazed ferociously, and it was easy to see why, in a moment or two, the old warrior should give it a blow on the snout. At that moment, the action grew blurred, as the air-car swung with the movements of its departing passenger. Then it steadied to show their animal lover charging down upon the astonished Grkh. His bellows of rage, as she caught him across the face with her flailing stick, nearly deafened the watchers. The words of the shaman were clearly audible, though their meaning would have to be deciphered later. As the car moved away, Rolf switched off the projector and turned up the lights.

"The old girl did sort of go at the thing like a heroine, didn't she?" he asked.

Huffstedt grinned. "Notwithstanding the fact that she has us squarely in an impossible position, I must admit that, given her peculiar set of ideals, she acted heroically to uphold them."

"It's much easier to admire her, when the Blgat have to put up with her," said Gambel, dourly. "Come on, boys, and get to work. Rolf, find out what the old witch doctor was saying, while Jan and I service the ground car. I don't know what earthly good we can do, but we'll get as close as we can to their village and then play it by ear."

* * * * * * *

There was rejoicing in the village. Even now, the preservers were filling the last storehouse with meat. All the warriors had returned, unhurt, from the hunt. And, best of all, there was a captive to torture to death. Young and old were filled with a spirit of frolic, and the village resounded with Blgat equivalent of laughter and song.

To their captive, the sounds denoted utter ferocity, but she sat, erect and disapproving, in the dingy hut into which she had been cast. A stalwart beldame removed a part of her bonds and offered her a portion of rather high-smelling stew. This she tried to eat, observing to herself that, come what might, she would need all her strength to face it.

The three warriors who had been detailed to watch her were struck with admiration at her composure. The Cagodot, those high-strung beings, though brave as lions at hunting and war, were usually demoralized when faced with imprisonment and torture. But this creature sat there, eating deliberately, and never once tore the somewhat scraggly plumage atop her head, and never once flung herself upon the floor in despair.

One of the warriors approached her and, grinning at the others, fetched her a medium-hard blow across the face. She stood up, in a flash, and flung the contents of the bowl into his eyes, then cracked the bowl across his orange-haired head. He stumbled back, grunting, and his companions, convulsed, pantomimed his misfortune.

At this moment, the chief entered the door-flap, and the warriors instantly ceased their horse-play. The old female cringed into a comer, trying to efface herself completely. Only the out-worlder was undaunted.

Samantha stood erect, her nostrils pinched, her eyes snapping. Old Grkh regarded her cautiously. Her character, her speech, even her sex were mysteries to him. Her manner of appearance seemed to indicate some sort of supernatural origin, but Grkh was a profound skeptic. Besides which, he remembered having seen the strange "bugs" flitting about the sky several times.

Advancing halfway across the room, he raised his hand and, in the intricate sign language which was the invention of the Cagodot, he informed her that her fate had been decided. She must suffer the torture immediately.

"You can just stop waving your hands about," Samantha said coldly. "I've nothing to say to a lot of murderers like you."

Neither, of course, understood anything that the other was trying to communicate, but the chief was beginning to admire his captive's lack of fear. However, he gestured to the warriors, who seized her by the arms and marched her out of the hut into the glare of fire-light.

The shaman looked almost like a shaft of fire, himself, as he stood waiting for his victim. Four stakes had been set in a rough square. To these they hustled their captive and tied her, hand and foot, at a slant like the pitch of a rather steep roof, hands high above her head. As the thongs tightened about her wrists and ankles, a look of discomposure crossed her disapproving face, but she quickly replaced it with one of disdain.

The flame of six great fires lit the village, throwing the shaggy forms of the Blgat into bright relief against the twilit foliage and the gray bark huts. They were gathered in a wide semicircle behind the victim, the warriors and women standing quietly and their young chattering, darting, and scratching behind and between the parents. Their orange coats reflected darting gleams of gold, but their flat, hairy faces showed neither exultation nor pity, as they waited for the evening's entertainment.

Taking up a short-hafted spear, the shaman passed it five times before the nearest of the fires. The Blgat stirred and began to intone a deep-throated chant, "Ca-Goom, Ca-Goom!" which went booming away over the low hills and across the savannah.

* * * * * * *

Far out on the grasslands, a faint echo of the chant vibrated in the ears of Gambel, who, with Rolf Burke, was pushing the ground-car much faster than it should have been pushed across unfamiliar territory.

"What does that sound like?" grunted Gambel, slowing to a crawl, then switching off.

Burke opened the door and stepped out onto the camera platform at the front. The distant rumbling chant went on. He listened for a moment, then got back in and closed the door.

"That sounds like something my Cagodot friends have tried to describe," he said. "And, if it is, we'd better hurry, for that is the song the Blgat sing when they torture a Cagodot to death."

The ground-car spurted forward, tearing a swath through the tall tan grasses.

"I don't know what they'll do to our fanatical friend, but whatever it is won't be pleasant," Burke gasped, between jolts, as the car bucked over the uneven terrain.

The chanting grew in intensity, quickening with excitement, with each step of the ritual torture. Each practiced motion of the shaman brought an increase in the tempo, a surge of excitement, yet there was a difference. As the climax neared, the chant died away and an expectant hush descended. At this point, the whimpering wreck of a Cagodot always succumbed, killed by loss of blood, as well as intense mental and physical anguish. This strange being, however, showed no dismay. Not one scream had been forced from its tight lips, during even the most agonizing parts of the ritual. The shaman finished his work and stood, bowed and shaken, in the firelight.

Old Grkh raised his broad hands above the victim. His deep voice boomed out, "Creature, go back to the gnat that bore you! Strange as you are, you have the gift of awful courage, and it fills our bellies with a strange feeling. Go back, out of our hills, and come to us no more!"

Samantha Pirtle-Smith stood rubbing her wrists, from which the cut thongs still dangled. Though she understood nothing of what the old chief had said, she realized that she was free to go. One thing she still had to say, however. "I understand now," she snapped. "You are only animals yourselves. If that fool Gambel had told me that, things would have been different." Then she strode, snorting delicately, through the village and down the trail that led to the savannahs.

The ground-car met her, just as she reached the grasslands. By the light of the triple moons they saw her, and their shouts of greeting died in their throats.

"Turn your back and get me the spare coveralls!" she said. "Those animals ripped my clothes to pieces, bit by bit, then burnt the edges off and wound up by taking them entirely off me. They must have thought the clothes were part of me, like the Cagodots' feathers. What can you expect of a bunch of dumb brutes, though?"

Shaking with a reaction composed of equal parts of relief and mirth, the men found the clothing and tossed it to her, keeping their backs carefully turned to her angular and unlovely nudity.

"Gambel," she said severely, clambering into the ground car, "you are a fool."

The Observer dared a quick glance at his passenger, avoiding Rolf's eye. "In many ways, Miss Pirtle-Smith," he said. "Which particular one did you have in mind?"

"You interfere too much with the beasts of this world," she snapped. "I am certain that it must disturb them when you hover so closely above their hunting grounds, while they are engaged in their normal pursuits. The Blgat and the Cagodot are most unusual animals—I shall write to the SPAF immediately concerning them. They must be listed in the Master-Roll and then studied carefully. *VERY* carefully," she emphasized, fixing him with a stem eye. "And you must NOT upset them unduly."

Gambel set his gaze upon the invisible horizon. Oh, God, he thought.

"Yes, Ma'am," he said.

For a student's guidance, I wrote an example of a way to get into an alien world. Then, of course, I had to go ahead and write the story to find out what happened.

FUNGI

Jonathan drew a deep breath, tainted, as usual, by the smell of recycled air. His space suit was awkward and it still rubbed his left knee, though the techs had worked on it again. He hated the suit, the domed station, and the world on which it sat. Almost airless, barren, holding only fungi and rock, the place was a disaster from the viewpoint of an ecologist.

He was thinking about that when the purple fungus spoke to him.

Damn! Contaminants in the air supply again, he thought, heading back for the airlock. He'd always had a sensitivity—the mold spores that often invaded the interiors of the breather units gave him hallucinations.

"You! Silver fungus! Have you no manners? I spoke to you!"

It wasn't a voice in his ear, but one inside his head. He'd never had anything quite like that before. Jonathan stopped and popped the top of his helmet with his gloved fist. Sometimes that put things back into place.

Not this time. A stream of images entered his mind, along with words. Real human words, not spoken but thought with great vigor. He stopped in his tracks and turned slowly, staring back at the clump of purple fuzz on top of a grim gray stone.

He increased magnification in his eye-plate, staring closely at the fungus. Each of the filaments that formed it was tipped with a speck of black so shiny it glittered in the unfiltered sunlight. As he stared, the entire group curved with synchronized choreography to point straight toward him—and stared back.

Eyes?

"Was that you?" he asked aloud, though he knew the helmet swallowed sound almost entirely.

There was no audible reply, but he knew the answer anyway. "Of course. I have been perceiving you and the other silver fungi for several black-times now. I have learned how you communicate, though the vibrations you make are painful. Where did your spores originate? You appeared so quickly—no other intruder fungus has ever grown so large in such a short span."

Jonathan backed up a step and found himself against another stony shelf, this one almost as high as his shoulders. Another silent voice said, "Watch it! Do you want to crush me?"

When he turned to look, a gray-green clump was staring back at him. He felt the hairs rise on his neck beneath the helmet, and sweat popped out on his chest inside the air conditioned suit.

"You must understand," the purple fungus continued, "that this world does not contain sustenance for more life forms than it now contains. No stone here can support more than a single organism, and all are occupied. You will have to encapsulate and send your spores elsewhere."

"But...but we are not fungi. We travel in other ways, and we don't live on rocks. I assure you...."—he caught himself and stopped in mid-sentence. Apologize and explain to a clump of fuzz? Ridiculous!

Something very like a sigh, though soundless, wisped through his head. "Very large specimens always feel they are above the laws of survival. We have noted that in the past, on other worlds. We have, however, invented techniques with which to defend our habitats, over the millennia of our travels between worlds. Be warned, silver fungus. Leave our planet or suffer the consequences."

Jonathan opened his mouth, but he could find no words. He knew he had gone mad. He had to get inside the dome, clear himself of the mold spores, and get the medication Dr. Tait kept for such situations.

He hated to think what Commander Robb was going to say when he made his report. Robb was a military man of the old school. His reply to any challenge to human authority was a blast of laser fire, and he had no use for "slackers," as he called those who developed psychological problems on alien worlds.

Although Jonathan was a civilian, Robb had a way of making him feel lower than the fungi back there among the rocks. Flinching at the thought, the ecologist made his way carefully toward the dome, avoiding the boulders with great care as he went. Only when the lock cycled shut behind him did he relax.

At last he stepped out into the dome, finding himself face to face with the Commander. "Eckles! What are you doing back so quickly? You were to examine Sector 16 of the North Quadrant. Surely you cannot be done with that already!"

"Medication," Jonathan gasped. "Spores in breather hallucinations."

Robb frowned ferociously, but he stepped aside. "When you finish with Dr. Tait," he said in a warning tone, "come directly to my quarters. I want a complete report from you, Eckles. I will not tolerate slackers!"

The doctor was interested in Jonathan's description of his aberration while outside the dome. "Not your usual reaction," he mused as he shot the medication into Jonathan's skin. "I would like to examine your breathing equipment before the techs clean it up. Have them bring it to my laboratory with your recording computer."

On his way to Robb's quarters, Jonathan left word for that to be done, but he was so worried about the coming interview that he didn't think much about it. His push on the Commander's may-I-enter button was timid, but the port popped open at once.

Robb sat at his desk, looking stern. "Sit down," he snapped. "Now give me a complete report of your very brief activities while outside the dome."

Feeling both foolish and terrified, Jonathan obeyed. When he was done, Robb's coarse white eyebrows were meeting above his craggy nose, and his thin lips had disappeared into a straight line.

"You expect me to believe that a fungus spoke to you?" His tone was dangerous.

"No, no. Not at all. That is only what seemed to happen. I am sensitive to the mold that sometimes grows in the breathers. The stuff makes me hallucinate. This was simply the strangest hallucination I have ever had. Dr. Tait is examining the equipment now to find what sort of mold it might be."

The Commander pressed his com button. "Tait! Have you completed your examination of Eckles's equipment?"

"Yes, Sir," came the smooth reply.

"Report to my quarters at once. I want this cleared up without delay." He glared at Jonathan as they waited for the doctor.

When Tait arrived, he was not nervous, not breathless, not terrified. Jonathan envied him his lack of fear around the Commander. No, Tait seemed amused, if anything. He trundled behind him a wheeled table on which lay the breather and Jonathan's recording computer.

Robb stared at the table, then at Dr. Tait. "What's all this?" he asked.

"Proof," said Tait, his tone crisp. "You will find the result of my scan on the mini-comp."

Robb took the memo-pad in hand and said, "Report on Eckles's breathing equipment."

The sexy voice, that of every computer sent into space, said, "No trace of mold spores was found in either oxygen tank or breather. No trace of hallucinogen of any kind, either on interior or exterior surfaces."

"Aha!" Robb stared at Jonathan. "So what do you have to say for yourself?"

Jonathan found no words, but Tait interrupted smoothly, "You need to hear the report on the material contained in the recording equipment. Before you make accusations, Commander, I recommend that you listen to the next report."

"Report on Eckles's record of mission begun at 21:35:10 this date." He sounded dubious, Jonathan thought.

"Overhead screen on, link to office com complete," the mini-com began. "If you will watch the progress of subject, you will see that he was on course and taking notes to point A-6." The overhead showed the boring terrain through which Jonathan was moving, and an overlay showed the mapped grid of his assigned sector.

"At that point, subject's verbal report is interrupted. Unusual auditory effects are recorded." A buzz, almost subsonic, sounded as the com replayed the record. "Subject turns, surveys terrain, focuses on fungus located on boulder. Note magnification." There the picture enlarged as Jonathan magnified his eye-plate, and the clump of purple fuzz came into sharp focus.

"Note behavior of fungus. Entire clump swings toward subject as if examining him visually."

Now the com replayed both visual and auditory recordings, only Jonathan's side of the conversation being comprehensible. As the report proceeded, Robb became very still, and his face reddened.

When the com clicked off, the Commander turned to Jonathan. "This...this thing dared to threaten us? A fungus wants us to leave this world we are assigned to survey and has the gall to suggest we might suffer consequences?" He looked as if he might explode at the slightest provocation.

He rose, and the other two jumped to their feet. "We will go back out there now. I want to...talk to this upstart mushroom. Prepare for external mission."

* * * * * * *

It was with considerable trepidation that Jonathan followed the Commander out of the airlock. Dr. Tait seemed excited, but he hadn't communicated with the fungus directly. There was something terribly self assured about that clump of fuzz, and references to millennia of travel between worlds hinted at knowledge that even a fungus might have acquired.

They reached the area more quickly than before. After all, he had been making verbal notes into his computer, pausing to examine anything the least bit unusual. Now they stood before the big gray rock, looking at the purple fuzz, which seemed to be dozing in the sunlight.

Even as he watched, Jonathan saw the fuzzy tendrils stiffen, curve toward the three men, those shiny black eyes focusing upon them. He felt a shiver down his back, and he hoped the Commander did, too.

"You return? After our warning? Silver fungi, you have no manners!"

The Commander clapped both hands to his helmet, and Dr. Tait shook his head as if trying to locate the source of the communication.

Jonathan said, "No, it's not a voice you hear, but it gets inside your head anyway. Listen to what it says. I think we maybe should consider...."

"You cowardly slacker! Be silent!"

Jonathan could see the fungus quiver as the Commander's roar penetrated the helmet. It focused upon him now, and Jonathan could not hear what it said, but whatever it was the Commander was clearly becoming more and more agitated.

Hopping mad, he would have put it, concerning anyone else.

Then Jonathan remembered that other one, the gray-green clump behind them. He turned cautiously to see what it was doing, and he found it, too, directing its attention toward Commander Robb. Something about the glint of those distant beads of black made him feel suddenly cold.

He backed away. Dr. Tait came into view, also backing away. By unspoken consent, they took shelter behind a slab of rock atop which a pinkish fuzz was also turned toward their commanding officer. Jonathan didn't know what to expect, but whatever it was he wanted to be out of the way when it happened.

"I believe Robb has met his match," the doctor whispered over the suit-to-suit radio. "Look at him!"

Now Robb was quivering with rage, his feet leaving the ground as he literally bounced up and down. Something very tense and powerful filled the air, felt even through the protection of Jonathan's suit.

He was about to ask Tait if he felt it when Robb's suit popped open and expelled the Commander upward. If there had been more air or more gravity he might have fallen to the ground again. As it was, he zoomed up under what was obviously great pressure and disappeared into the glare of the sun. The remnants of his suit lay crumpled beside the rock where the purple fuzz was now relaxing.

Jonathan turned to stare at Dr. Tait. Through the face-plate, the doctor looked greenish-pale, the way he felt himself.

Then, using courage he did not know he had, Jonathan rose and moved toward the purple fungus. "What did you do to him?" he asked. "Did you intend to kill him?"

The fuzz stirred lazily. "Of course not. Life is rare and valuable. We have learned to concentrate our energies and force alien fungi to expel their spores prematurely, sending them on toward other worlds. In this way, they pose no threat to us while continuing their life cycles."

Jonathan almost explained what had really happened to Robb, but he realized that this thing would never understand. Spores and fungi were all it knew, and it dealt with its problems on those terms.

Tait touched his shoulder with a bulky glove. "Let's go," he said. "I'll list this as a world containing toxic materials that are too dangerous to deal with. I think that will be accurate, don't you agree? Those bits of fluff could have exploded the dome, I suspect, as they did the Commander's suit."

Jonathan nodded, and the two turned toward the distant dome. They would be ready to leave in three days, he knew from old experience. In the meanwhile, no one else would leave the shelter until time to take the shuttle up to the orbiting ship.

He hoped the purple fuzz and its companions never met another human being. The doctor, he was sure, would make certain of that.

Some years ago a columnist for the newspaper for which I worked wrote a piece about his visit to Las Vegas. He speculated that the entire city's power needs could have been supplied by the intensity and persistence of one little old lady working a slot machine with incredible vigor. What a NEAT idea!

THE POWER THAT PRESERVES

I bounced into the Gamblecom gritting my teeth. I wore the set smile demanded of the Director, but it was an effort, as the door-bot's eyes lit up (literally). The thing whisked my paperfile into its storage unit as it said, "Good morning, Sir or Madame" in a second-hand voice.

I always ignored the thing, a cheapo model relegated to such minor stations as mine. Stepping up to the Dispenser, I held my palm on the Sensor. The fifty-unit gambling allowance rattled into the tray below, for even the Director of Gamblecom has to put in the obligatory minimum of twenty minutes of Powerplay, every cycle. Even though gambling seems a waste of time and money for one paid by the second, as I am, I must set a good example.

As usual, my luck was terrible. I dropped one-unit pieces into the machine, pulled handles, worked treadmills, hearing the tiny pulses of power added to the big generators far below in the center of the planetoid. Around me, citizens were working treadmills and pulling handles with glittery-eyed fervor. Now and again there would be the jangle of coins pouring into machine trays. Those were greeted with whoops of triumph from the winners and cries of encouragement from fellow gamblers.

As usual I lost, though a good quarter of the others there left with more than they had been given. I got back just enough to replace the fifty units I'd been given in the doorbot's tray. Everyone got back that much. The machines were rigged for that. I dropped the handful back into the slot and watched the square brown coins slide into the storage compartment.

The doorbot said, "Thank you, Sir or Madame," and flipped my paperfile into my hand with pneumatic speed, almost before I could remove my fingers from the Sensor.

Still bouncing and gritting, I reached the stair and made three effortless hops to reach the floor where my office lay in wait. I hoped that I wasn't so old as to be inflexible in my habits, but the minimal gravity of the Colony played hob with both my internal organs and my disposition. The effortlessness of everything made me feel under-exercised, and the frustrations of dealing with the matters awaiting my attention made me feel ill.

Sure enough, my computary clicked onto "voice" as I entered the office. It said, "Skidmore, William M., Director, Sir: Your office is tenanted by elderly ladies who want to play the gambling machines. Microfiles are available under keys K, J, and M. Your antacid is on the tray with your refreshment pitcher."

With another click, it switched off, though I knew its lines were still connected with terminals throughout Gamblecom, the Colony, and the subetheric system. Those connections stayed busy all the time, shuttling information, requests, and commands that kept the colony working.

Once the door slid back into its slot, I heard the cackle of many shrill voices. Still smiling (teeth gritted even more tightly), I took a tablet from the refreshment tray and swallowed it. Then I said, "Ladies, please sit down and tell me what I may do for you." As if I didn't know.

A tiny woman moved up to what would have been nose-to-nose, if her nose hadn't come barely to the insignia on my tunic. Her smartly coiffed hair was goose-down white, her face deeply lined, but her eyes were black and sharp and young.

"Young man, do you have any idea why this colony was placed here?" she asked. She cocked her head like a small bird, staring up at my face.

"Of course, Ma'am." I looked at her in bewilderment. "This is a geriatric colony, developed for the use of those who can no longer live comfortably with the normal gravity of their home worlds. But it is also a mining colony, offering R-and-R for the miners developing the potential of the asteroid cluster, which our orbit trails around Pliny II. I don't understand your question."

She fixed me with a birdlike eye. "I didn't think so. We are not basket cases, Director. Nor are we mental defectives. Most of us were active and useful before our loving relatives decided our hearts or our bones couldn't survive normal planetary conditions. We are supposed to find useful years of living here that would be lost at home. We are supposed to live USEFUL lives."

I gulped and nodded.

"This has now degenerated into a chrome-plated rest home. We are not allowed to exert ourselves at all, to do any sort of useful work. We are not even allowed to PLAY, unless you count Scrabble and knitting.

"I know you will touch some buttons and show us films on the strain that gambling puts on the human heart. Not to mention all sorts of charts and graphs showing the difficulty of operating your Gamblecom machinery. We know all that. We want you to understand clearly that WE DON'T CARE. Life is a bore. We have no grandchildren to liven things up, at least not here. So what if we drop dead in the Gamblecom?" She glared at me. I closed my gaping mouth.

She glanced around at the others, and they sighed and moved to the door. "Talk to the Medical Director," she snapped.

I nodded. The door slid shut, and I heaved a deep breath, looking longingly at the tube of happy pills on the tray beside the pitcher. Still, I had real problems to deal with, and euphoria just couldn't do the job.

The first communication flashed onto my monitor. Settling back, I read, ASTERMINECOM TO GAMBLECOMDIR: Compulsory gambling requirements cutting into work time of personnel. Suggest you find others to man machines, or urge Colony Director to find other sources of power.

The second communication was no more encouraging. POWERPLEX TO GAMBLECOMDIR: Suggested supplementing of solar power units nonfeasible, due to distance from Pliny II, lack of qualified personnel and materials for constructing expanded reflectors.

The third was the worst. COLDIR TO GAMBLECOM DIR: Power requirements to increase by one-third in next sixty cycles. Additional machines incoming, to be installed within next ten cycles. Suggest you increase minimum gambling requirements to forty minutes per day.

I didn't even read the fourth. As the happy pill took hold I sank back into the feather-puff chair and let a pleasant fog roll over me. A plague on them all, I thought, as dreams took over my mind.

I did not dream my usual bevy of sleekly clad beauties holding trays of real fruit. Instead I found myself back on Earth. In Las Vegas, where I had trained, watching the slot machines. I groaned. I had too much of that where I was!

I was near the machines, and as I listened to their clatter, I heard a tiny bell go ting! inside my head. Of the antique slot machines I watched, each was confronted by an elderly woman. The nearest was engaged in a monumental battle with a lady who might have weighed eighty pounds with a pocket full of lead.

I went to stand behind her. Coins clinked, lights winked, the handle was pulled again and again. Her skinny arm seemed too frail to work the thing, but she stood there for an hour and ten minutes by my chronometer and never raised so much as a dew of perspiration. She gained a bit and lost a bit. I succumbed to nervous exhaustion at last and left, but she had not yet come to the end of her coins or her strength. This was no dream induced by happy pills. This was a memory dredged from long-past years.

I drifted into sleep. When I awoke, I knew I had a solution to a number of problems, IF! It entailed one large, all but insurmountable problem named Anna Schwartzstein, the Medical Director. She was beautiful, hard-headed, and she intended to coddle those old people within an inch of their lives, even if it made them miserable.

When I came out of the happy pill fog, I used the computary. MEMOS: ASTERMINECOM, POWERPLEX, COLDIR, FROM GAMBLECOMDIR: MEDDIR suggests consideration request of geriatric citizens for use of Gamblecom facilities.

Such activity can free mining personnel from gamble duty, eliminate need for solar power augmentation, and increase power output as requested by COLDIR. Solution seems logical. Suggest implementation.

I thumbed the privately coded override and made certain that in no way could the Medical Director gain access to that memo from any memory bank. Then I obtained a list of those who had visited me that morning and looked up their residence units.

Elvira Vashon, spokeswoman of the group, lived with three of the others in a cluster suite not far from Anna Schwartzstein's rooms. I found her at home, sitting with three others around a table and playing a game of markers. She looked up as I entered the room.

"When you chimed, I thought it was one of the girls," she said, looking surprised. "What can we do for you, Director?"

I sank, as she indicated, onto a float, which adjusted at once to my longer leg-length. "I want you to help me to gain the M.D.'s approval for you to use the Gamblecom," I said. "It won't be easy. It is going to be personally painful for me, as you may well imagine."

They nodded. Everyone in the Colony knew of the relationship I had with Anna. It had endured for several years, and I now knew better than anyone the determination with which the lady held onto her opinions.

"She will think that you're all going to kill yourselves in short order. I happen to think you're a much tougher bunch of cookies than she gives you credit for being. I'm no doctor, of course." I sighed.

"However, I think I've come up with a really sneaky plan. It will take several of you to help me with my plot, and I'll lay my job on the line, but I am so bored I'm almost ready to jump off this colony anyway.

"They're making demands on me that cannot be met, using just the physically able members of the colony. You can make the difference between a viable, self-sustaining colony and another parasite clinging to the supply system. I've worked compulsory Gambling Complexes all over this sector, and I never before have had such interdepartmental confusion and lack of cooperation.

"Here is what I want you to do...."

That night (night being an arbitrary division of semi-darkness for sleeping purposes), I led a strange group into Anna's bedroom. I had, of course, access to her lock coding. We had no trouble at all in gaining entry.

My determination failed me when I saw her. She lay asleep in her foampack, and I maintain that anyone who can manage to look sublimely beautiful when she's asleep with her mouth open is a rare and precious asset to the universe. My cohort were not so sentimental.

A squirt of sleep-gas insured that our victim would remain asleep as Elvira, Lucille, and Nadine bundled her into a warm coverall and soft boots. I lifted her to my shoulder and led the way to the nearest lift to the surface of the planetoid.

The Observation bubble had been built and supplied according to specs for an outpost of this nature. There being nothing to observe, it was seldom used. I had spent a cycle or two there, looking into the depths of the sparsely populated sky, simply in order to get away from the close-knit, all-knowing population of the colony. Others had done the same. But since we had settled down to routine, nobody ever came there any more.

It was a perfect place in which to effect a bit of behavior modification. My three fellow conspirators had spent the past day in smuggling up to the bubble the non-regulation items they would need. When we arrived, they were prepared for a long siege.

Lettie, the fourth occupant of their cluster, had been rehearsed in her part to cover up their absence. They had decided upon a really intricate series of high-stakes markers games as their excuse for non-appearance in the common room of the geriatric quarter.

Once they were settled into the bubble, they assured me that they understood they were to treat Anna with all the tender concern with which she treated them. She was to have no opportunity to do any sort of work or to indulge in anything that was of consuming interest to her.

Elvira smiled and touched my elbow. "Dr. Skidmore, we'd never harm the girl. She really means us well; she just doesn't realize that old age isn't imbecility. Go along and hold down the fort. Leave her education to us."

I went down the cushion chute and skulked through the corridors to Anna's office. Though it adjoined her living rooms, it had a different locking system. I had a bit of difficulty in recalling the intricate codes to open it, but I succeeded at last. I went in, making certain that the seals were in place once I was inside.

Anna's office looked like a fine place for a robot to work. A stainless steel robot. Not a single non-reg item sat on her desk. No photograph of parents or loved ones (not even of me!) adorned the top of her paperfile container. Her computary was a soulless thing that would never have dreamed of providing antacid with its morning greeting. The office had no touch to make it human, and the computary had no voice-differentiation mode. That was all to the good. Ä human voice was a human voice, with no distinctions to the thing.

I dictated, "MEMO MEDDIR TO ALL PLEXES: Engaged vitally important project concerning geriatric patients. Will not be available six cycles. Should extreme emergency arise, direct through GAMBLECOMDIR until further notice." Then I fed into her computary a closed-loop problem that would keep it busy and inaccessible until our game was played out.

And that was that. If I had been a spy from one of the antique novels, I could have disrupted the entire colony as simply as that.

Six cycles passes very slowly when you are waiting. Though my work was as overwhelming and frustrating as ever, I could not stretch it to fill a day. Three nights a week, as specified by Anna, I went to her apartment and spent the night...sleeplessly.

I missed her frantically. More than once I kicked myself for hatching up such an insane plot.

When I returned, at last, to the bubble, I found my three hench-women attired in the spacesuits allotted to the bubble and bouncing with great abandon across the surface of the planetoid. Anna, attached to her chair with the soft restraints she favored for confining those elders who insisted on unsuitable activities, sat staring out the reinforced plasti-glas window. Tears rolled down her cheeks. She looked beautiful that way too.

I had her free almost before she knew that I was there. She turned to me. For the first time since I had known her, she put her head onto my shoulder and cried.

When I was able to make out the muffled words, mixed with hiccups and sobs, she was saying, "and I was cruel to them, all the time. You know, Will, that I really did intend to help them. Why didn't you tell me?"

I had tried, more than once, but I charitably did not mention it. Instead I mopped her eyes with a dispoz and said, "Well, Sweeting. now you do know. Will you let the poor old darlings gamble and play hopscotch and break their bones, if they feel like it? Will you let them run the machines that make the power that keeps us all alive? That will keep them alive much longer than all your coddlings and medications? They need to feel useful. You, of all people, should realize that to immobilize a compulsive achiever is to kill him...or her."

She nodded, subdued for the first (and probably last) time in her life. "I see, now, what they've been trying to tell me. It took living the life I prescribed for them to make it come clear. I'll...."—she choked on the words, then grinned with the unexpected humor that has kept me with her for so long—"...emancipate them!"

These days there is plenty of power. Miners have no more compulsory gambling time, which means that now many of them WANT to gamble. There is a waiting list for every machine in my Plex. I haven't dropped a coin into a slot for a long time, but I do go to watch.

You would think that some fiend was behind each of those old dears with a whip. They move with all the speed they can muster, pulling handles, walking treadmills, until the generators almost overload.

COLDIR has given Anna a commendation for her brilliant idea. The heat is off my department. And all our superannuated gamblers are in topnotch physical condition, as opposed to those who stick to the old regimen.

But I never mention that to Anna.

This tale was rejected by an editor who swore that journalists would never do such a thing. The next week there was a news story about reporters in Northern Ireland paying street children to throw bricks at British soldiers.

RATINGS WAR

New Britannia went up like a bonfire of rockets. There hadn't been a real dust-up in several years, and the holocasters were almost as depressed as their ratings. The populace was well and truly hooked on true-life blood and guts, and stories about natural disasters and human nature just didn't fill the bill anymore.

Of course I'm not saying—not out in the open—that the shindy in N.B. was contrived by the satellite syndicates to boost ratings. There had been rumbles in that part of the world ever since England had used Australia for a dumping-ground for felons, long generations ago. Once that continent made common cause with New Zealand, Tasmania, New Guinea, and the southern parts of Indonesia, it was just a matter of time. The mix of races and interests was almost as interesting as the assortment of grievances against old-world entrepreneurs operating concessions in that area.

They claimed their lands and resources were being funneled away into the worked-out, bombed-out, devastated areas of Europe and America. And they were. I've been down there a lot, and I've seen what goes on. But the Whole Earth Federation is a political organization, let no one fool you into thinking otherwise. Their complaints, over decades, were filed away and never heard from again. So the Associated States of New Britannia blew up in our faces, as anyone of my fellow 'casters could have told you it was going to do.

I had begun to build up a following by then. The name Tam Wills brought some recognition in the spot checks the systems run, now and again. I was young, too, and spry, which some of my more famous peers were beginning not to be. So Global let herself forget about my frequent mutinies against policy. I got the plummy assignment. Read that—crummy.

England's population-recruitment program had been pretty successful. A great many tenth- and eleventh-generation Aussies and New Zealanders had taken advantage of the generous allowances made to those who would return to the old country to help restore it to viability, after its last flare-up. That left Aborigines and Maoris to run their own countries at last. What they found, when they assessed their record books, left them unhappy with any unarguably white face they saw. And mine was whiter, even, than most, for my mother was a Swede.

I was hassled from the word go. The drop took place in a violent rainstorm, and things went downhill from there. The battle I was supposed to be covering didn't seem to be where they thought it would be. I found myself staggering around in the dark in my Glow-Suit, lugging my personal belongings and the wrist-cam through boggy ground that would make the Slough of Despond look like a freeway.

There wasn't a sound except the slash of the rain and the whistling of wind. No light in any direction. No evidence that any skirmish had ever taken place anywhere around. I dug my short-range communicator from one of the Suit's sealpockets and thumbed the switch.

"Tamerlane Wills, First-In Holocast for Global Systems, coordinates z-slash-3, h-slash-9. Pickup requested. Error in drop-site."

The little bugger crackled and sputtered for a moment; then a loud beep vibrated my hand, and I flicked the incoming switch. "Remain exactly where you are. Remain exactly where you are. Major engagement took place your site 900 hours. Unexpended charges all around you. Make no light; you are under enemy observation and in range."

I stood, believe it, like a statue. Antipersonnel charges were nasty little things that are set off by the electrical field of a human body. Whoever gets within range meets his end in one of the stickier ways I know of. They are seldom used these days, for the military has lost its taste for bleeding indiscriminately. I guessed that those from the Indonesian splinter groups might well have sowed them, as they had large stockpiles of obsolete weaponry that they had scrounged from the devastated powers after the last big blowup in Europe.

Standing there, I knew that I would stand out like a bonfire to the UVs of whatever bunch "the enemy" was—if they were keeping close watch on an unused battlefield. I devoutly hoped that they were not, for I had a notion that they might well be a detachment of the NeoPrimitives, a far-right-wing Abo bunch. They didn't believe in anything modern except weapons. Those they used with a ferocity bordering on fanaticism. Even my Glow-Suit, supposed to protect me in any area of civilized warfare, might well make me a welcome target on this drenched plain. So far, since the coalition broke up into chaos, this action was anything but civilized, according to early reports.

It seemed at least a millennium before I heard the gentle swish of a hover-car making its way toward me across the invisible landscape. For a second, I was doused with rain coming down from the sky and up from the puddle the car landed in; then a hand touched me, and a voice said, "Get in fast, be quiet, and let's go."

That was fine with me. We were out of there, with all my impedimenta, in half a shake, slipping through the sheeting rain. I was full of questions, but something about the gruff voice had impressed me. I sat silent while we crossed the invisible landscape.

It must have been a British-made car. They made the best before they were hit, and this one moved with the quiet speed that argued a really fine machine. When daylight began to pale the wet sky, I was able to see numbers on the panel before me, and that confirmed my guess. It also showed me my companion.

She was a surprise. Dark, of course, but with that beautiful Maori color and the tall and slender build of her race. Even the combat fatigues couldn't hide her figure. Her face, however, was the striking thing about her. I have seen strong faces—a few. Hers was that and more. There was an air of leashed power in her expression, and her eyes that would have sat well upon the president of the Whole Earth Federation. Her long hands maneuvered the car through what I now saw to be an entanglement of gum forest with such skill that I had not been aware that we were avoiding obstacles all the way.

"Is it all right to talk now?" I asked, extremely softly.

She turned her black eyes on me speculatively. There was hostility there to some extent, but I felt that she was too much of a person to accept canned prejudices. In a moment she nodded, one quick dip of her head.

I sighed. "I'm literally in the dark. They dropped me where a battle had been hours before. They didn't tell me which side, if any, was going to cooperate with us—just tuned the short-range to the proper frequency. I don't know what faction you are with. I don't, for that matter, know what faction I'm with. Or where we're going.

Or what I'm going to do when we get there. Is your group open for interviews?"

Her hands flicked backward and sideways, and a huge tree skittered away into the half-light. "New Zealand stands as one," she said. "Only we, of all the divergent racial and interest-groups, make common cause with all those of our land—white, Maori, and half-blood alike. North Island and South Island. The moderate Abos are with us, with those whites who still remain emotionally stable. Some few of the Indonesians and New Guineans also have joined with us to try to keep some sort of system going. The rest of the Associated States are at each other's throats—and at ours. From what I hear, the rest of the world hasn't yet comprehended what is going on down here. I think your system might well be useful."

I didn't press my luck. She had answered, and her tone said that that was all she was going to say. But it was nothing unusual for 'cast subjects to use the system to get their viewpoints across to the rest of the world. Like it or not, we do a pretty poor job of communication. Sensationalism and propaganda are, as I suppose they always have been, the principal output of the media.

The morning was growing lighter—and wetter. We were now on a roadway, and I could see a complex of some kind ahead, though it quite definitely was not a town. Sensor-netting was up all over the place, its glittering strands of filament shining, even amid the rain.

"Command post?" I asked.

"For now," the driver answered. "We move often. Even with the netting, the satellite sensors will find us, after a time. But you will not remain here for long."

"What about my assignment?" I asked her. "I'm supposed to get some battles on tape, interview generals on different sides of the squabble. How can I get perspective on your problem down here unless I can move freely?"

"Move freely where?" she asked. "We don't even have a morgue anymore. It was blown away three days ago. And that's where you'd end, if you went wandering around this area. This is no civilized warfare with rules and gentlemen's agreements. The Primitives have reverted, all the way. Your white face would be an immediate death sentence if you came across any of the three factions that oppose us in this war. But with us, you can serve a useful purpose and get a story that will shake the Whole Earth Fed to its boot-heels. If, of course, your system will let you get it through."

I picked up my ears. "You sound as if you have something specific in mind."

She shut down the fans, and the car settled into the mud beside the timber and tarp structure. We're going to New Zealand, as soon as you check in with my superior. Of course, if you insist, we'll turn you loose. You can walk away into that...."—and she gestured toward the sodden grassland that stretched, empty as a plate, in all directions.

I thought of all those frantic casts about in the flooded battlefield and shook my head. "Just give me your word that you don't expect any major action in the next day or so."

She laughed. She was still laughing as she anchored the car to its post and ushered me into the semi-tent that housed the Command of this odd group. As I struggled out of my Glow-Suit and dumped it into a corner with my scanty gear, she sobered a bit.

"Tamerlane Wills, you are used to another sort of war entirely. Nobody knows when or where or even if there will be a battle. We hit each other as unexpectedly as possible. There's none of this idiocy of scheduling action to suit light conditions and the convenience of the holocast system. This is WAR, the old-fashioned kind, full of hatred and blood-thirst and guts. We mean it; can you understand that?"

I looked at her, and something of my confusion must have shown in my face. She went off into another peal of laughter. It stopped in mid-peal when an inner flap opened and a tall old fellow in combat-fatigues entered the room.

"Moana Fao, with the holocaster," she said, straightening, though she offered no salute.

The newcomer bore no insignia of rank, but his bearing in itself was enough to tell me that here I faced the head man of the Moderates. I met his shrewd black eyes, and a shock ran through me. I'd been meeting generals for years, but never before had I met one whose intelligence seemed to laser through my mind in an instant, winnowing out everything of importance. Before I opened my mouth, he was nodding to Moana.

"You have done well. It seems that he is one of those few who might be able and willing to help us. Have you explained the situation?"

She frowned. "I thought it better to allow you to do that. Some of his kind only believe what they hear from the topmost officer. It might save a reiteration of the tale."

"I think you misjudge this one," he mused, motioning to me to a the camp table by the wall, where I sat in a folding chair and looked across at him.

"We have a prisoner," he said. Then he smiled at my incomprehension. "This is no ordinary prisoner of war. He is, indeed, not even a participant in the war. He is the instigator of it. Or at least one of the prominent instigators. He is totally confused at this moment. He is used to fomenting wars and leaving them to boil away. He told us as much, before he realized that in this instance he had set off a conflict that had been merely awaiting a fuse. Once he knew that this was a serious, gut-level war, he stopped talking. We need someone who will get him started again. That being your profession, it could well be you. We suspect his identity, but I will not tell you what we think it is. That might prejudice you for or against him."

"But why do you think he'll talk to me?" I asked. "A man in a cell isn't going to take kindly to an interview that might get him into deeper trouble."

"Oh, you will be in the cell also," the tall officer said. "No wrist-cam, no Glow-Suit. Just you, a fellow captive caught in the performance of your duties. If the situation is what we think it is, you will come out of the cell with the story that will either make or break your career. Have you the courage to take that chance?"

I thought for a minute. The overly cautious don't make first-in reporters. And I was a tad less cautious than most. That little tingle that wakes in the back of my mind when I scent a topnotch story began to vibrate, and I looked over at him and nodded.

They were fast. I was fed while a VTO was being fueled for the long hop across a thousand miles of ocean to New Zealand. In thirty minutes, we were over the Pacific, heading eastward. Moana Fao was still my...captor? Companion? Guide? Whatever. Once she had set the automatic controls, she leaned her seat back and said, "It would be well to rest. We have just over an hour. One never knows when there will be another opportunity."

I'd have liked to talk, but she closed her eyes so determinedly that I did the same. I opened them again to a fervent beeping from the chronometer on the panel before us.

The hour had flown already, and I could see the double-shape of New Zealand showing through a thin haze of cloud below and ahead of us.

* * * * * * *

They mussed me up good. I looked as if I had been caught and manhandled by a bunch of gorillas when I was shoved into my waiting cell. The insults and threats that followed were a bit too convincing to be entirely acting, I thought, as I bounced off a dampish wall and sank to my haunches in the semi-darkness.

If this had been a real arrest and imprisonment, I'd have already activated the implant in my skull that signaled Global that I was in trouble. As it was, I let it ride until I saw how the situation shaped up. I wasn't quite convinced that I hadn't been skillfully maneuvered into something I didn't understand and couldn't control. But I wasn't quite sure the situation wasn't just as represented, either.

I heard a grunt in the corner to my right. I started (a nice effect, I thought) and asked, "Is somebody here? Say something!"

He had been wearing a tan suit when they caught him. It was now splotched and grimed with numbers of things better left nameless. His hair had been mussed until it could have doubled for a straw-stack. A light growth of beard stubbled his face. Above it, shrewd gray eyes looked me over.

"And who might you be?" he asked. Something about the way he turned his words told me he was Irish, or had been.

The Moderates had given me a cover story, fearing that my proper persona might make him suspicious, so I said, "Tom Willis. Buyer for Amalgamated Minerals—or I was. I don't know what I am right now. I came in from South Island in a small boat. A bunch of gorillas met me at the dock and gave me a working-over. I'm lucky I still have my teeth. What in hell has happened in the last week? I've been knocking around the Fiji Islands and Noumea for months."

He came over and hunkered down beside me. "I've been in here for three days, but the best I can figure, the gooks have fallen out among themselves. There seems to be a full-scale war going on. And I haven't been able to get anyone to call the Irish Consul. I seem to be stuck here for a while."

He seemed to have said his say, and I was quiet too, as if considering his words. Either he was the innocent he seemed, or he was playing it very close to his vest. I decided that it was going to take a while to build up the sort of rapport that leads to prison confidences.

"Damn!" I said. "I was almost through with my assignment. They were going to send me to South America next. Just my luck to miss that. I'd like to see, just once again, some place that hasn't been knocked to bits and patched back together." That earned no reply at all from my cellmate.

CRAZY QUILT, BY ARDATH MAYHAR * 111

It was a long day and a longer night. My nap on the VTO was a mistake too, for it left me too wakeful to relax on the pile of straw they thrust into the cell for my use. By the time a supper of thin gruel, moldy bread, and unidentifiable meat made its appearance, I was thoroughly sorry for my bargain with Moana's boss.

I got sorrier. Two days went by in grim boredom and desultory conversation. My companion, though he seemed to take me at face value, kept his own counsel. Whoever he was supposed to be working for must have trained him well, I thought. Then the guard came after me and dragged me away yelling at the top of my lungs. That wasn't all acting either. I'd no idea what was about to happen.

Moana met me in a small steel chamber that I thought must be underground, from the feel of it. When I gave her my report, she shook her head. "It is taking too much time," she said. "What if we gave you a beating? Would that make him trust you more?"

I stared at her, and she chuckled. "Not a real beating, you nitwit. Just a lot of noise and moans. Maybe a bruise or two."

I reached into my mouth and removed the bridge that was a souvenir of an early assignment. "Maybe knock out some of my teeth?" I asked.

She took them. "Remind me to give you something to make your mouth look bloody. Good idea"

I'd no idea that I was so much an actor. The very real-sounding thwacks of a rod against a stuffed bolster brought forth from me a performance I wouldn't have believed.

Stifled moans, uncontrollable whimpers, shrieks cut off in mid-wail by gritted teeth. No wild histrionics, you understand. Moana orchestrated and directed the thing, and I felt a chilly certainty that she had presided over the real thing more than once.

They carried me back and dumped me onto the straw. I seemed to be only semiconscious. After a while, I felt a hand on my forehead, then a wet handkerchief was applied, evidently engaged in wiping away the blood. (Real blood, too, from a pig.)

I grunted, then opened my mouth and felt about where the bridge had been. "Teef gone,' I breathed. "All right, though."

The man sighed and sat down beside my head. "I didn't know until they carried you away how much it had helped just having someone nearby," he said. "I've been a real rotter, I know, but you must forgive me. My name is Jeffrey Elliston. While I regret that you must be in this predicament, I am glad you are here, if you see what I mean."

From there on in, it was a cinch. Not in one day or in two did the story come out, but as I pieced together the bits of information he let slip, I realized that Moana and her superior had not exaggerated. This was a story of major proportions—if only I could get it broadcast. It was entirely too hot for that to be an easy thing to do.

On the fourth day since my beating, they came for me again. This time I did not return, but I got Moana's assurance that they didn't intend anything terrible for Elliston. He had, after all, only been doing his job. But that job!

Moana met me in the same steel cell. This time, her superior was with her, dressed in a no-frills uniform that sported a modest general's "wing" insignia on the collar. His dark eyes lit with interest as I entered, and he rose and extended his hand. "Mr. Wills. So glad. I did not introduce myself, simply as a precaution, before. I am General Karamea. Sit down and tell us what you have learned. We could not put sensors into your cell, for your cellmate had a telltale implanted in his skull to detect such things. You have something similar, I think?"

"All first-ins do, General," I said. "Not, however, bug detectors. Might be handy at that." I sat and looked across the small room toward the General and Moana.

"You were right, you know. This is a very big, very difficult, very nasty story. I may lay my neck on the line and get it cut off. If so, I want your word—both of you—that you will bring the truth before the Whole Earth Federation, if I am silenced, or killed, or simply disappear without a trace."

They both nodded, their eyes serious in their oval faces. Then I saw the resemblance. It sidetracked me for a moment.

"You—you're his daughter!" I said to Moana, and she smiled.

"Who else could he trust with a thing of this nature?" she asked. "Now, do go on with your story—"

"It isn't easy," I began. "I've worked in holocasting my entire adult life, and before that I dreamed of working in it. I've bucked policy, don't doubt it, but I never had any real suspicion that Global or her sisters were doing anything really unethical. Now I've got to grit my teeth and admit that the system is rotten to the core." I paused and looked about, found a glass, and poured water.

"Elliston is an agent provocateur. I thought those went out with the twentieth century, but evidently I was wrong. He has spent his working life going around the world, when things got too dull for his bosses' ratings, and stirring up grassfire wars. Planting false evidence, framing innocent officials—at least officials who were innocent of whatever he framed them for. He was the one, as I guess you suspected, who inflamed the Neo-Primitive Aborigines to the point at which they went to war against the other three factions in the N.B. setup. He assassinated their most important religious leader, in case you didn't know. That brought things to a boil much faster than he had intended.

"His employers, it seems, didn't do their homework very well. They didn't reckon with the built-in tensions and resentments down here. Or, indeed, with the legacy of hatred and suspicion the whites left behind when they went. Now you are stuck with a full-scale war of unguessable length, and the world can only look to its own frivolous desire for entertainment for its cause. Global and Trans-Terra and CIC, through their mutual 'public relations' set-up, are guilty of fomenting war."

Karamea sighed and looked down at his thin, strong hands, which were clenched together in his lap. "We feared as much. It would be terrible if we were merely stupid enough to fly at each other's throats like beasts. It is infinitely worse if we have been maneuvered into it for the entertainment of those who sit continents away and watch us die in full color and three dimensions."

I grinned at him. "You know, his sensor didn't pick up the recorder in my shoe heel. I got every word on indestructible tape. And now I'm going to get you to give me my gear, so I can key in the satellite transmission code."

In half a minute, I had the code on its way. I waited a second, until the steady hum told me the way was open, then I coded "Imperative and immediate override of editing," for the first time in my own experience or that of anyone else I knew. When I began to run the tape on my player, it went out uncensored to every receiving set tuned to Global at that time.

* * * * * *

The systems would have shot me, make no mistake. My hosts, however, hid me out until the Whole Earth Fed had time to take things in hand and curtail the activities of the media. That took a bit of time—but I didn't mind. Moana and I found that we had more in common than just steady nerves. I was really a little sad when the all-clear sounded, and I had to return to New Boston to face my employers.

Moana, of course, had years of work ahead of her. The war went on for six or seven years—I can't remember which, for the Middle East broke loose before the end of the New Britannia affair.

I thought of her, though, every time I caught a 'cast of the nasty little pitched battles and ambushes that went on there for so long.

Global, to say the least, was not happy with me. I had been sent to cover a flare-up and had nailed them with a major infraction of international law. They would have nailed my hide to the wail, except for the fact that I returned to New Boston a bona fide hero. In the face of public opinion, they had to swallow their ire and keep me working.

People, you know, aren't callous or cruel. Not intentionally. They like a lot of excitement and interest, but they want it to be spontaneous. All you have to do to prove that is to call something like the mess Elliston caused to their attention. A lot of heads rolled, to be sure, but mine wasn't one of them.

So I was still a first-in, and because of the strange twists and the personality factors in the story I had covered, I was now prominent among my peers.

War is a crazy business, and holocasting is even crazier.

Perhaps the most self destructive thing a culture can do is to try to dictate the course of the arts. To do that for political correctness is even worse.

SOLO PERFORMANCE

Lerovik sat with the instrument in his lap, his fingers precise on the keys. Mozart purled away over the tops of the pine trees, down the declivity to the small lake below the cabin. Beyond the lake, the music was lost among the conifers that ringed his hiding place. He was careful not to open the volume stop too far—you couldn't be too careful.

He was all but lost among the intricacies of the work when his alarm rang, bringing him out of his hidden world with a jerk. He felt shocked, disoriented, as he unplugged the precision amplifier and slid the minipiano into its waiting case. This was, in turn, lowered into its cavity in the deck of the cabin. He replaced the worn planking carefully, backing away to make sure no unevenness revealed the opening from any angle. Only then did he disconnect the alarm and engage the scanner that would show him who was invading his privacy.

He was shaking, and that disgusted him, for he had no real fear of THEM any longer. The seven years he had spent in the solo cells of Artistic Control had burned out all his capacity for terror and anguish. Now his mind was at ease, and only his body shook with remembered stress.

Years in that sterile box, battered by the brutal cadences of the Anatonic School of Proletariat Music, appalled him still, but he had learned to shut off his senses. He repeated to himself the words of an early critic on the "new music" (the man had vanished into those same cells, after the Conformist takeover): "One can experience a comparable aesthetic impression by visiting a boiler factory while munching on uncooked spaghetti," Alor Vespi had said. Lerovik never, in his years of trying, bettered that description.

Though he was less qualified to judge the impact of the Movement on the other arts, he felt Artistic Control probably managed to remove any possibility of human pleasure or enlightenment from them all. The human dimension was not admitted by Conformists, which explained, no doubt, the multitude of problems that arose to plague the system over the past fifteen years.

Though the system sterilized the news media, it hadn't eliminated intelligence, try as it might. Word circulated among closet intellectuals, and he knew, along with a few confidants, that Earth's government was on the edge of ruin. Unrealistic policies in politics and agriculture, business, and education were bringing down the regime. Unless the newly formed Alien Trade Commission made some miraculous deal with one or more of the worlds in the Intergalactic Consortium, the situation on Terra would reach a flashpoint soon.

Shaking his head, he stared into the scanner, arranged to read sensors set along the approach to his cabin. Ah. There was the intruder!

A dung-colored hover-car made its way up his overgrown track. Within the clear passenger bubble, he could see three figures. No weapons—but he didn't trust that impression. Those were Conformity Monitors, for at least two wore spinach-green uniforms proclaiming that service.

He folded the scanner into hiding and drew straw matting across its hiding place. He was still shaking, but he stretched, shook himself, then straightened and dropped into a Meditation. Internal harmonies flowed through him, and he relaxed.

He had learned to do this during his long years in the cell. Despite the recorded chaos with which they tried to subdue his nature, he retreated into a soundproof spot in his soul that contained nothing except the logical precision of Mozart or Haydn or Vivaldi, Telemann, Brahms, or Chopin. He rethought his interpretations of the music, discovering in those strange circumstances potentials for expression that he might never have found, left to his old life.

His hands flexed in his lap, running soundlessly through the music playing inside his head, as it had done throughout his confinement. When he was released he went to a colleague who owned a piano, treasured despite the illegality of possessing it.

By then, Lerovik's hands had gained a life of their own. The years of concentration on the inmost meaning of music made them capable of rendering it without thought, only emotion. He had made a long run of it, playing concerts in abandoned buildings, isolated parks, sometimes the homes of the music-starved. All dared much even to attend, and many helped to transport the instrument in secret, passing word of the event to those interested. Defying the controlling Conformists, they put their lives in jeopardy.

He listened as the hover-car sat with a tired thump on the unkempt grass below his deck. The grass itself was anathema to the regime, who had tried, Lerovik thought, to cover the world with asphalt and concrete.

He stood, pleased to find himself fully in control. These people could prove nothing against him. He was no longer concertizing, and no one had ever revealed the fact that he had done so since his release. The officials might suspect, but there was literally no evidence, and even a Sniffer couldn't penetrate the hiding place of his mini.

He erased expression from his face and moved to the edge of the deck. Below, a lumpy woman in a baggy uniform struggled out of the car and stared up at him. His heart thudded violently, but only once. When it calmed, it tapped counterpoint to the harmonies filling his mind.

"Monitor Sverdla," he said, his voice coldly correct, though he would have liked to throttle her then and there. It had been her persistent nosing into his career, her discovery of his aberrant use of classical music, her testimony that sent him to the cells.

Rudely arrogant, she gestured to her companions to climb, uninvited, to his deck. When she mounted it herself, her square face was flushed and mottled. It was not, he thought, exertion that caused her high color, for there was a strange expression in her slaty eyes. Frustration? Resentment, certainly, but also anger.

He motioned for the newcomers to sit, took his place, and looked them over. He didn't recognize the others. One was small, fair, and thirtyish. His uniform, though green, was a different shade, and his insignia looked like that of the Alien Trade Commission. It was a new agency, but Lerovik was almost sure.

The other was about Lerovik's age, fortyish. Stolid and silent, he was much like all Sverdla's other assistants, uncommunicative as a stump, though the younger man kept looking sidelong at the musician.

Sverdla cleared her throat, her unease apparent. The pianist felt curiosity building in him—what duty had brought her to his door? A disagreeable one, he knew, for arresting him would not have made her uncomfortable. What, then?

"Musician Lerovik," she began, in that impossible tone they all used, "there is need for you in a matter of extreme urgency. Though you have not always conducted yourself as a loyal citizen of the Conformity, there has never been a question of your devotion to our world. Now it needs you...your talents. Your..."— she struggled as if the words strangled her—"...classical repertoire." She looked as if she had uttered an obscenity.

Lerovik felt blank with astonishment.

Sverdla stared at him, her obsidian eyes angry and ill-at-ease. "Ambassador Sissingham has a vital request. Control has agreed that specific circumstances warrant relaxation of the letter of the law. Though we still oppose your prior activities, we find your expertise necessary. Ambassador, will you explain?"

The younger man straightened on his hard stool. His face, as was proper with a good Conformist, was expressionless, but his coal-black eyes sparked with interest. "In this isolated spot," he began, "you probably have not learned about unrest in some areas of our world. Even among our most ardent supporters there are schismatic tendencies, some even sliding back into Humanism."

He glanced nervously at Sverdla. "Restrictions on grace and harmony are being eased, and some composers and artists are beginning to indulge in...harmony." His voice lowered as if he, too, found a word obscene. "There is economic dislocation as well. The public seems unwilling to produce for the common good. Suicide is becoming a problem. Of course, these are symptoms of a lack of dedication to Conformist ideals, yet understanding does not solve the problem."

Lerovik smiled. "An unusual confession for one of your beliefs. A thing defined is a thing controlled was, I thought, your dogma."

Sissingham continued, "My agency is charged with dealing with extraterrestrial beings. We found a world producing a substance that, suitably refined and used, could easily subdue all resistance on this planet. This species has a moon on which they grow animals for food. The substance, dispersed into the atmosphere there, creates euphoria, but it does not affect the health of those who inhale it. It controls their livestock without constant supervision. We have tested it, and our subjects become completely passive and suggestible."

"How can this possibly involve music?" Lerovik interrupted.

"The dominant species is unusual, its individuals totally self-directed. Worse, they are romantic in their tastes. They scorn our own artifacts, our arts, our techniques. After examining every product of our world, they found only one thing they desire. This was smuggled to their world by outlaws, giving them access to an art outlawed here."

"And what is that?" the pianist asked.

The man looked ill. "Mozart. A molecular recording of your rendition of all his piano works reached them. They want more, in living performance. They want you."

"Surely there is someone else who refused to recant the classics," Lerovik objected.

Sissingham shifted and blushed. "Unfortunately...." Sverdla caught his eye, and he changed his words. "Fortunately, Artistic Control succeeded in curing such aberrations. You are the only classicist left alive and functioning. We ask you to go to Agarica for the good of your world. They will honor you, for they assure us you will be their most valued asset.

"Your work excited them unaccountably. The offer of all existing tapes of our Anatonic Music was refused—rudely. Only you will satisfy them." He coughed. "In case you might think to inform them of the use to which we intend to put their 'agricultural product', you will be fitted with a device to release toxins into your blood the instant you speak or write any message concerning our intentions."

Lerovik clasped long fingers about skinny knees and regarded the trio on his deck. However reluctantly, they brought him the opportunity to live freely, practicing his art to appreciative audiences. He could not refuse.

"I will need the finest obtainable minipiano, for use in transit, even though that requires only ten days. I cannot allow my hands to grow stiff, and this requires daily practice. I will also need, shipped to Agarica, a grand piano. The Steinway at the museum, if put into order by an expert, would do. A computer can tune it, once it is in place."

Sverdla's mouth twisted, but she said, "It can be done."

"In addition," Lerovik said, staring straight into her eyes, "Carelia Hoehner must be released from detention. Her hands must be re-broken and repaired, so she can work them into playing condition. Whether she is now sane or mad, she must go with me to Agarica."

There—it was at last in the open, the thing that made him shake when he thought of Artistic Control. Those broken hands, Carelia's face, astonished, then agonized, then shattered, like her hands. Their interrupted duet could never be resumed, and he had hidden that agony through all the years of his confinement. Now he opened the floodgates and the old wrath returned.

Sverdla swallowed hard, her official face almost showing expression. She suppressed it with iron control. "It...will be done." Her voice rasped in her throat. "You will come with us. Your house will be closed. Anything you need must come now."

"I need very little," he said truthfully. Perhaps other fugitives would find his cabin, even the instrument beneath the deck. Someone might find sanity here, as he had done.

* * * * * * *

The transit passed in practice, as well as in working to bring Carelia's hands back to usefulness and her mind out of the depths to which it had retreated. He massaged her fingers, worked them with his own, flexing, stretching. When she realized what had been done, she looked at him at last, past years of blocks and guards she had set inside herself.

That happened on the fourth day, and on the ninth she held the mini in her lap and tapped out a little tune. On the tenth she knew him completely, and it almost sent him into tears as she began to play, somewhat stiffly but with improving flexibility in her fingers.

Holding those battered fingers, he said, "We are going to a safe place, Carelia. Free to make music! I brought all they could find in the files, as well as all I have memorized. You know as much as I, and between us we will satisfy our audiences. While the people we play for may look strange, their spirits, I believe, will be matches for ours."

Her wide brown eyes regarded him doubtfully. The coppery halo of her hair was soft beneath his hand as he stroked it. "We must go. The Agaricans are waiting. Take heart, Love. We are free."

A reception committee was waiting. Sverdla, Sissingham, and the silent aide went with the musicians to the staging area, their clunking steps following as Lerovik approached the waiting beings.

The Agaricans were watching, and for a moment he felt like some beast, inspected for sale. Then the tallest of the wispy people drifted to his side and took his hand.

"So most grateful, revered musician. None have we of your sort. You being of most beneficial to us. Be welcome." The voice was musical and soft.

Lerovik bowed. "My wife and I are happy to be here. We have music for people of discernment and will make it for you with much joy. But my wife is ill and must go to a place where you treat the sick."

The slender creature waved a filmy hand. Another offered an arm to Carelia, who took it, looked searchingly at Lerovik, and was reassured. The Agarican led her to a waiting vehicle. Now, Lerovik thought, she was entirely safe.

Sverdla grasped Lerovik's elbow firmly. Staring suspiciously at the remaining Agaricans, she said, "Before you take possession, we must have the formula for your agricultural product. That is the price of this musician!"

The Agarican to whom she spoke fluttered as if caught in a breeze, evidently its gesture of agreement. "Of most certain, Lady Monitor. Yet to we is necessary to hear. Must be certain is needful for we. You agree?"

Lerovik grinned. These shrewd people were buying no pig in a poke, and he didn't blame them. Sverdla did not inspire confidence.

She nodded. They went into a nearby building, which had been converted to a concert hall. The Steinway, glowing with antique power, stood in the center of the room on a circular platform. Lerovik touched the keys, finding the instrument perfectly tuned.

He looked up at the Agarican spokesman. "You have heard only Mozart? Do you want that or something different?"

"There is other?" the being asked. "Other, indeed!"

Lerovik moved his hands on the keys, and Bach's "Sheep May Safely Graze" stole into the room. Then he played the Grieg A-Minor Sonata, a movement of Beethoven's *Appassionata*, and climaxed it with Mozart. His audience was almost reeling with delight.

"Yes," fluted the Agarican. "Most precious! Will trade, indeed!"

Lerovik said, "My wife will be able to play those and more, once she is well. Protect her from all harm." Then, using all the control he had learned in the cell, he said, "But you must not give my kind your formula. They will use it to enslave our own people."

Something burned down his veins. The light dimmed. As darkness swept him away, he rejoiced aloud, "Carelia is safe!"

Blackness shattered into a million golden notes, and he traveled with them, outward into timeless space.

Driving to a writer's conference once I was delayed by the resurfac-ing of a highway. By the time I could proceed a small furry animal had been laminated into the asphalt by a passing car—the sacrifice had been made!

THE CHILDREN BENEATH THE STONES

The first was purest accident. Flavius was as shocked as the slaves, who were in the process of dropping the stone into place, when the child lost her footing and slid, screaming, into the leveled roadbed. The wet crunch of the falling pavestone was echoed in his own belly, as he signaled a halt to the work.

The other children lowered their water bags and cups, their pale faces and their gray eyes blank, as they stared at the spot where their companion had died. That look—it still made Flavius uneasy as he thought about it. The men and women who had been inching for-ward, one stadium at a time, building this road in the gods-forgotten north of Britannia, looked the same, their eyes going blank, their bodies freezing into position. Even the whips had been hard put to get them into motion again—leveling roadbed, cutting and hauling stones, setting them into place according to the specifications of the engineer.

He shivered and rose from his blanket. The season for road building was over now. Soon the snows would join this chill rain, covering the ground. The season had freed him from this distasteful task. Battle was a thing he savored, but this slow and disgusting process of road building was not acceptable to one with his ambi-tions. Surely the Decurion would relent! Surely he would be re-turned to the maniple, where he belonged!

He had not become a Legionary willingly, but his father had succeeded in buying a place for him suitable to his station. He had distinguished himself in battle, and it was only the worst of luck that the wrong person found him sporting in the bushes with the wench the general favored. That, of course, caused his removal to the road-building detachment and to his eventual distasteful duty as official child-catcher.

And that was the fault of the engineer. After that first accident, the weather had miraculously turned fair. The conscripts, though they glowered and said nothing, had worked to better purpose. The gods seemed to smile on this toilsome road, and the engineer did not fail to notice that.

When they finished some ten stadia and the weather turned foul again, Praecipius had called in Flavius. "Go and find another child. We cannot afford to use another of ours, for their parents would object, but if you can catch a wild one in the hills, that should suffice."

Flavius still felt the shock that burned through him, as he stared into the engineer's small eyes. They glittered at him like bits of coal, and the ugly face wrinkled into a smile that would have shaken a Gaul. "You intend...you deliberately plan to murder a child, just to find if that will improve the weather?" he had asked, feeling a hollow space inside his spirit that told him the madman did, indeed, intend just that.

The smile grew wider, the wrinkles forming a mask that might have been the face of one of the old gods of nastier habits and inclinations. Without another word, Flavius had turned and gone out to catch a child.

That had been the first of many, for it had worked. Strange as it might seem to one who had polished his logical faculties upon the words of Socrates, every time a Celtic child was dropped into the roadbed and crushed flat by the next stone, matters improved dramatically for something like ten stadia. After that—Flavius sighed, staring out into the gray morning—the entire thing was to do over again.

Except, of course, for the Celts. The slaves, naturally, were watched and guarded too closely to allow any rebellion, but those wild men in the hills were another matter. There was battle enough to suit the most bloodthirsty, as the guardian Legionaries patrolled the countryside around the building site. Ambushes of the most exquisite subtlety were made, taking several of the best soldiers of the lot through wounds or death.

Stragglers were shot from cover, arrows skewering them like hedgehogs, as they lay kicking in their blood. It became unsafe for any Roman, or even for a Celt enslaved by them, to go far from the campus, and the latrines had to be dug too near the main camp for even the least sensitive noses. Even then, a sufferer from diarrhea sometimes fell in the night, quilled like a pheasant from incredible distances.

His work of child-catching had become not only sickening and difficult but actively dangerous. He had gone armed, with a guard of ten, just to keep him alive. Even then, he often returned with only a handful of those who went out with him, the others having disappeared, screaming, as they rummaged through bushes or down ravines.

Some had been found, flayed and dripping. Others had never been seen again, though their voices had sung evil songs in the darkness. The parents of those sacrificed children were unhappy, he knew. He would have been unhappy himself. Their mothers and fathers were stalking the Roman builders, and he wondered where this insane adventure would end.

Now, however, the weather had closed in for winter. The day dragged past, and the night of the bonfires was beginning, and fires were already lit on the tops of the surrounding hills; sounds of dim drumming could be felt in the bones as much as heard by the ears. He shivered.

The thing was done. By spring, surely, he could talk the Decurion into returning him to duty fit for a soldier! He would never again have to carry a wriggling, screaming child in his arms to its death.

As evening drew in, the drums grew louder.

The engineer came into the tent and shook the damp from his cloak. "The barbarians are chanting up there. I can hear their voices, though not the words. We should never have let the slaves go. They have joined their brothers, or I know nothing of such animals."

"We could never feed them and the troops too, through the winter," Flavius objected, his tone milder than it would have been with one who was his junior. "We have stripped the fields of grain and the hills of game. We will be on short rations ourselves before spring."

"We will retreat southward now," the engineer admitted. "The winters are harsh in this place, and we will join the troops in their winter camp soon. Perhaps it is as well that we do not take those stubborn Celts with us." He grunted, as a wail called thinly through the gathering gloom.

Flavius went, for the hundredth time, to peer out through the door flap. Now the fires above were showing up brightly against the cloud-darkened sky. He was glad that a cohort guarded the road-building crew, for those bright-haired people on the hills were fighters to be feared. Three hundred and sixty men were not too many for the task. Even the blue-painted Picts feared the tall, fierce people of the hills.

Even as he thought that, there came a shriek from the direction of the stream beyond the guard post. Another rose from the opposite direction, as he seized his short sword and pulled his cloak about him.

"There is an attack!" he told the engineer, who was already addled with the wine he drank steadily from day's end to day's end.

The man took a step and fell over the stool he kept beside his sleeping place. He was grinning, too drunk to know or to care that the barbarians might soon be roasting his bones over their Samhain fires.

The watchfire at the end of his row of tents lit a scene of furious activity. Shapes moved abruptly into and out of sight, struggling, stabbing. Flavius ran to help someone in armor—but when the man turned, he saw the flash of pale eyes under the metal helmet, and before he could stop he found himself caught between three men, all taller than he, all stronger and smelling of rage.

Then something struck the back of his head, and everything went completely dark.

* * * * * * *

Flavius woke abruptly, his eyelids springing wide and his body attempting to sit. That, however, was impossible, for he found himself bound securely to a complicated structure made, he thought, of tree branches.

He could see nothing. It was still night—or another night. He could not be certain.

In the darkness, he heard a groan, and the voice was familiar. "Praecipius?" he whispered. "Is it you, Engineer?"

"Ummm," came the moan in reply.

Flavius struggled with the bindings about his hands, but the leather thongs were tight. His hands, in fact, felt swollen and numb. Even if they had been free, he was sure that he could not have untied the rest of him, without working life back into his recalcitrant fingers first.

The drums were louder. Much louder. He realized that he must now be up on one of those forbidding hills, separated from his fellows and beyond the protection of mighty Rome. He and the engineer, it came to him in a sickening flash of understanding, were about to pay for all those Celtic children they had crushed beneath the stones of the road.

The freed slaves had told their fellows in the wild of course. Among all the alien people down in that encampment, with its rigidly straight lines of tents and its praetorium set on a slight knoll commanding the entire complex, there could have been no way for these people to pick out so unerringly just whom to blame for the loss of their young ones.

"Praecipius!" he said into the darkness. "They are about to serve us as we did them. What do you think of that?"

There was the sound of rough breathing beside him, and the noise of a struggle. He laughed silently. He knew the security of those bonds, and Praecipius would no more succeed in loosing them than he had done.

Rank smoke came to his nostrils through the openings in the rough shelter that he could now see looming about him. The light of a fire striped the wall above his head, where it trickled through the slatted sides. His skin was ridged with gooseflesh, from fear as much as from the cold.

He would not live to see the great work completed, the road connecting the strong points, the wall holding out the wild men from the north. He would not see Lavinia again, or his father's villa overlooking Mare Adriaticus.

He believed in no gods, Roman or others. He certainly did not believe in the ancient and primitive deities that these people worshiped. He only believed in pleasure and pain—and death. He felt that he was about to make the acquaintance of that last, very soon.

Praecipius groaned again. "Flavius?"

"Yes."

"They have us then?"

"They do."

"You were right, you know. We should never have killed the children. Some of the slaves, perhaps, might have been better."

Flavius almost laughed. "If you truly believe that, you are even more stupid than I thought. We are about to die, Engineer. Think about that." He closed his eyes and listened to the chanting in that alien tongue. It mingled with the sound of wind whistling evilly between the slats and the pelting of the rain. How did the fires burn in all that rain?

A sound at the door brought him to instant alertness. He could see faces, striped with ash and shadow. Hands seized him roughly, hauling him upright, as a cold blade cut the ties holding him to the litter.

When they were outside, he could see the faces, pale blots amid wildly blowing hair that ranged from white-gold to almost crimson. Men and women alike, regardless of the cold, wore only loincloths and short cloaks. All carried knives, some of stone, some metal ones stolen from his own kind. His belly cramped, and he bent over and vomited in the mud at his feet.

They tugged him to the fire, where he saw a tall stone of the kind that seemed to stud this countryside. It stood with two more in a rough triangle, in the middle of which burned the fire. The stones sheltered the spot, so that when he stood near the flames he hardly felt the wind and the damp.

A howl made him turn his head. Praecipius sagged between two Celts, a man and a woman. Both were painted with stripes of ash, and Flavius thought they might be the grieving parents of the last stolen child.

At the back of the stone toward which he faced was a dark well of shadow, deeper than it should have been. He realized, even as the engineer was dragged to the edge of the spot, that it was a trench, dug into the muddy soil at the foot of the megalith.

The woman worked about Praecipius for a moment, binding him fast from neck to heels. Then she and the man held him over the hole, extending their burdened arms as if he weighed nothing, and let him drop. He hit with a thump and a wail.

As Flavius watched, his stomach heaving again, yet empty of anything more to lose, two more of the barbarians began levering the bottom of the stone beside the grave. It had, he saw now, been excavated to some depth, and the levers were making the tall shape totter already. It moved, the soft mud letting it lean slowly, then more swiftly, and at last it began to fall.

It seemed to take forever. The angled top wavered in the fitful light as the wind moaned about it, and at last it moved downward, the foot kicking up a bit of soil as the thing fell with a thump that shook the hill. Any cry Praecipius might have made was smothered beneath the noise and the weight of the thing.

Flavius tried to swallow, but his mouth was dry. Would he be served the same?

Now the fire was dying, and those standing about it did not renew its fuel. Instead, they turned shining eyes toward the Roman, and he felt his bladder release its burden, wetting his legs and his tunic. What would they do to him, who had carried their weeping children away to be killed?

The ash-striped woman approached, her hair glinting like copper in the dying firelight. Wind swirled strands of it about his face, as she pushed him against the stone at his back. With deft speed, the others wrapped bindings of leather about him, tying him securely to the enigmatic stone.

The woman looked into his eyes, and she spoke in his native tongue. "Flavius Decius, you will speak to the old god you have helped to wake. This is not the Mother, who nourishes the land. It is not one of your tame Roman gods who want only to drink and to wench. This is one of those old ones who had gone to sleep with time.

"We have made sacrifice to it. The children's blood gave it an appetite for more, and your friend should satisfy it for years to come. But you we leave to speak to it. Tell it, Flavius Decius, to sleep again. To dream again!"

She turned away, and he croaked after her, "But why should it listen to me? I am an outlander and an alien. I believe in no gods at all!"

She turned back, her gray eyes shining with a reddish light. Her lips curled wryly, as she said, "But you will, Flavius Decius. You will believe, before you go free from this stone."

Then they were gone into the shadows, leaving him to stare into the coals, which were being quenched quickly, now that there was no fresh fuel added. Tears ran down his face, mingled with the cold rain, and he felt snowflakes beginning as well.

He would freeze soon. That was, he had heard, an easy death. He might have lain on his back, watching that monolith crush down onto his unprotected body, as Praecipius had done. He was fortunate....

And then he heard the laughter, mocking and wicked, rising from the ashes. Something swirled there, evil and hungry, turning toward the sacrifice that had been made.

"Oh, god of the ancients!" Flavius cried, "spare me! I am ignorant of your ways. I have done nothing but good for you, providing you with the blood of infants...."

But that was the wrong thing to say. Eyes that were eddies of mist turned toward him, examining him, and a bulging head of fog nodded softly, once.

Fear filled him. Belief grew in his heart, as the thing neared his helpless body. He cried aloud to the gods his dead mother had revered—but that did him no good at all.

The hunger he had helped to create in that ancient sleeping thing found him, now, to be a satisfying offering. Neither his cries nor his prayers affected it at all, for it believed in no god but itself, and now it was freed into the world again, to feed as it would on Celt and Roman alike.

Coming from a family of musicians, I have great interest in music and its creation. So I added in a "what if?" and this is what I got.

CONCERTO

When you are trussed up in braces and prosthetics, confined to a wheelchair, life is never easy. When, in addition, you need to find an apartment in which you can get around in your chair, with room for a piano and neighbors of more than human patience to endure a resident composer, it makes things even harder.

Once I got out of the hospital, I rather expected that my friends and acquaintances would drop me pretty quickly. A concert pianist whose hands have been damaged too badly to stand up to the demands of practice and concertizing is pretty much a dead issue, even when he has had some success as a composer.

But, aside from my fiancée and my professional friends, my Aunt Gwen took over, deciding to coddle me. She couldn't understand, after a while, that she was smothering me. A concerto that I had begun just before the plane crash was struggling into life, and coddling didn't help anything.

I was, after all, twenty-eight years old and nobody's infant. I needed my own place, though there was no way I could go out and look for it, as things stood. But I found that friends filled the gap, rallying around instead of backing away. My agent did even more than the rest. He assured me that David Eichermann the composer was worth as much or more as Eichermann the pianist. Among the bunch, they managed to find a suitable place for me, to Gwen's dismay.

I hated to upset her, but when a call came from Ted, I was ready.

"Listen, Dave," my agent said, "I think we've found the very place. Ground floor—it's a sound old building being renovated. Side entrance, near your own door, with a ramp for your chair. No other tenants above you yet, but the place is so solid that you probably wouldn't bother anyone who lived above you. The super—you are not going to believe this!—is a classical music nut. Has all your recordings. In an emergency, he'll be there like a shot."

My heart thumped beneath the crosshatched metal and leather that held me together. "If there is room for the piano, I'll sign the lease right now."

He laughed. "I'll bring it, and my secretary will witness it. Callahan, the super, says the paint will be dry by Monday, and you can move right in. I'll call the movers and get your stuff out of storage. We'll all get together and get you moved."

I leaned back in my wheelchair amid a creaking of braces. "Ted, that's above and beyond the call of duty. How will I ever thank you?" I looked down at the tangle of metallic exoskeleton that held my shattered body in order. "You know I'm not in any shape to do much."

"I'm going to work your ass off," he chuckled. "I knew before the crash that you had more in you than simply playing. *Sinfonia, with Roses* made a real splash when Bernstein used it as his season opener. I knew then you had found your real strength. You're going to make us both rich."

I laughed. "Okay. I'll tote dat bar, lif' dat bale. Go hire your van and get me out of jail!"

Which was neither kind nor fair. Gwen had been glad to take me anyplace I was able to go, had done everything she could to make me comfortable. But I still felt like a prisoner whose parole was coming up.

* * * * * *

When Millie, Ted's secretary-cum-strong arm-cum surrogate Mom, together with my aunt, finished unpacking, arranging, and getting rid of cartons, the apartment was already licked into shape. They had even vacuumed the nice Aubusson-reproduction rug. We looked around at the white painted wainscoting, the satin-stripe paper, the high ceilings. My antique piano, which had been my mother's, looked right at home.

Once my helpers had worn themselves out and gone, I was alone for the first time in almost a year. Independent at last, thanks to the elaborate equipment Ted kept finding that would help me with things like taking baths and getting into and out of bed. It felt wonderful.

I turned out the lights with some regret, for I would have loved to pitch into the concerto then and there. When I woke, it was with a surge of energy that I thought had been lost forever. It was a joy to hoist myself into my chair, scoot on my own to bath and kitchen. Gwen had equipped the kitchen for my convenience, and I cooked and ate a huge breakfast. That done, I didn't even take time to dress.

I wheeled to the piano, where Ted had left a table at hand, holding music paper, pens, and the harmonica I sometimes used to work out my frustrations. I let down the movable arms of the chair and touched the keys.

Music flowed into my mind, the joyful early theme composed before the accident rising to a crescendo, then dying away into a simpler, sadder melody. Shifting to a minor key, it became a blend of melancholy and nostalgia. The months of pain and depression had touched it, but all of it fitted together.

The morning passed in a mist of music, though to a casual visitor it would not have sounded like music at all. The process of composition is not pleasant to hear. Yet the thing was coming into focus, getting onto paper at long last.

* * * * * * *

I settled into a schedule. Every morning either Ted or Ev, who would have been my wife by now, if not for the accident, came by to check on me. Sometimes Ted brought papers from the insurance company for the airline. I would be taken care of for the rest of my life financially, but that didn't stop me from working steadily every afternoon.

I stopped by five, when I began listening for Ev's steps in the corridor. It hurt to think about her—she still wanted to marry me. I couldn't let her do that, for it would be a travesty of a marriage, and we both knew that. Still, that didn't stop us from loving each other. Nothing could keep her away, and if she managed to do that I would probably have withered up like a dried bug.

She was tall and cool and quiet, and she soon made a habit of bringing supper with her, from one of the ethnic places near her office. Then we'd pretend we were old married folks with years of happiness behind us and a comfortable old age ahead of us. Silly, *n'est-ce pas*?

After a few weeks, I felt as if I'd lived there for years. Callahan was my good right hand. Anything I couldn't manage, he was willing to tackle. Built like an economy-sized King Kong, he had the face of an amiable bulldog, and behind that battered mug lived a mind that reveled in the precise mathematics of Mozart and Gabrieli and Bach.

When tenants moved upstairs at last, I wondered if they might object to the sound of the piano. I tried to compose only by day, but sometimes the concerto possessed me by night as well. But no protest came. At last I asked Callahan about the newcomers.

He squinted as he talked. "Oddballs. Never see 'em in the halls or the elevator. Pay in cash the first of the month. Not a word of complaint from them in three months they've been there. They don't go out to work, but they seem rich enough."

I was intrigued. "What sort of family?"

"Andrei Haslip is the father of the family. Pretty old, too, but big and strong. White hair. Palest eyes you ever saw and a big deep voice like a bass viol. Wife's name is Hazel, but it doesn't fit her. Skinny dame. Good legs, great big teeth in a little dried-up face. Dresses in caftans that'd knock your eye out at a hundred paces. The girl's about fifteen, boy's seventeen or so. Nothin' special about 'em, except they never go out. And that's weird."

"They never make a sound," I put in. "I'd almost welcome a loud party, just to know they're alive."

He grinned. "That's the house. When this baby went up, they build solid. You'd have to hammer hard on the floor up there, to make it heard down here. A scream wouldn't make it."

Oddball neighbors were fine, as long as they didn't object to music at all hours. I forgot about them, for the climax of the concerto was building. Something eerie was stealing into the themes, too—some of the harmonies made my skin goose-pimple, but it all felt right. I was making something unique.

Then came the Braseltons. They were on the other side of the house, fourth story, but they complained to Callahan about everything they could think of. And when someone told them there was a musician downstairs, they started complaining about music they couldn't possibly hear.

That made me wonder again about the Haslips. Surely they heard me when the windows were open! I asked Ev, one day when she stopped by at lunchtime, to go up and ask them, for I couldn't bear to think of people suffering through the hellacious sounds of composition, because they were sorry for a poor cripple.

She came back and shrugged. "They're not there. I knocked and rang, both, but there was no answer."

I had to be satisfied that I had done what I could. I forgot about them in the throes of the concerto. I was in a fever—a physical one, as well as a creative one. I was allergic, it turned out, to the metal of the braces, to the stuff they used as an alternative, and only when I invested in solid silver did the itching and sweating stop so I could complete my work.

At noon on July tenth, I finished the last note, wrote in *da capo al fine*, and leaned back. A mixture of triumph and regret filled me. I felt at once exultant and antsy.

Callahan photocopied the sheets and mailed a set off to Ted. I settled down to wait the hours until Ev would come, but I couldn't relax. I hadn't yet played the thing in full.

Without the orchestra, it would sound a bit thin, but I flexed my painful hands and tore into it.

I listened as I played. It was good. Damn good. It was neither classical nor atonal. It went its own way, creating new sounds, new harmonies, new rhythmic patterns. I would probably get as much flak as Beethoven had from the critics, but I knew that this thing broke new ground and would last and set new trends.

My hands felt like murder before I was done, but I didn't pause to ease them. I went through the tolling depths of the last movement, the final motif. Eerie and strange, it sang itself to silence.

There came a tap above my head. Someone was rapping hard on the floor, trying to get my attention!

I looked at the clock. Ev was going to be a bit late tonight. Callahan had some errands. Nobody could see what the Haslips might need, unless I could manage.

I snapped on the light, for twilight had crept into the room as I played. I maneuvered the chair to the door and saw the elevator waiting, doors open. It was wide enough for the chair, and I realized that I could make the trip upstairs for myself. Filled with daring, I wheeled into the cubicle and pushed the second floor button.

That floor was just like the first. I found the door above my own and pushed the bell. A voice, forbiddingly deep, asked, "Who?"

"David Eichermann, from downstairs. I heard a thump on the floor, and I wondered if someone needs help."

The door opened. Haslip was just as Callahan had described him, and his eyes shone as he saw me. "Ah, but come in! We have so enjoyed your music over the past months. We do not say, for we are recluses, even the young ones. But we listen with wonder to your composition. Now it is done, we must thank you. Come and meet my family...."—he wheeled me into the room.

Suddenly, I didn't want to go. The chamber was filled with the odor of incense, through which Mrs. Haslip's tight little face appeared, split into a toothy grin. Two more faces swam into view in the subaqueous light.

I touched the reverse to back the chair. "I don't want to intrude," I began, but the chair didn't move. Something was braced behind a wheel.

"Nonsense! We want to tell you about our admiration for your work. Our family were musicians long ago. Erica! Dohrn!"

The young ones sat on a huge sofa, beside their parents. They looked like a row of—not crows—vultures. I shivered inside my barricade of braces. "I was worried that the music might bother you," I croaked.

Mrs. Haslip reached to take my hand into fingers as clammy as dead fish. "Indeed, no. Our joy in your work fills us with gratitude. What have you titled it?"

Before I could reply, Erica smiled, her teeth bright in the dimness. "We have the recording of *Sinfonia, with Roses*. This new one—a concerto, I think?—needs an equally intriguing title."

"It is untitled, as yet." I wondered how many kids her age could recognize a concerto when played without orchestra. Or even with one.

Mrs. Haslip's cold hands tightened. "It should make a pair with the first. Possibly...*Concerto, with Vampires*?"

They laughed, and what blood I had left chilled. That was no joke!

I jerked my hand free and backed the chair, but they were standing now, moving to either side of me. Their smiles were impossibly wide. I strained my arms, pushing the wheels to augment the chair's capacities.

Haslip bent over me. "You will not suffer. You will compose forever—at night, of course." He leaned toward my throat, and I jerked convulsively.

He screamed with agony.

His wife tore away my shirt, revealing my withered chest, meshed in a webwork of silver crosses from throat to waist. His fangs had scored my skin only lightly, but his lips seemed seared, as if burned. Eight bright eyes focused on my blood. Those accidental crosses could not possibly hold off these creatures!

There was a firm rap at the door. The Haslips froze, trying to put their faces into order, but Ev had touched the panel; it swung open, revealing the strange tableau.

She took one swift look, darted in, pivoted my chair and tore away down the hall in a heartbeat of time. The elevator was waiting, but the doors were beginning to close. I jammed an elbow between their padded lips, and she wrestled the doors open again. As the rubber gaskets lipped together, something bumped outside. But we were on our way down.

She stared down at me. "Were those really...?"

I nodded. She was examining my shirt and bleeding neck when the doors opened. Callahan was turning into the corridor, and he stopped, staring at us. Ev grabbed him and hustled him into my apartment. They patched me up while I told them my tale.

They glanced at each other, from time to time, and I wondered what they were thinking. But Ev pushed me to the piano. "Play!" she commanded. "Something quiet, classical, religious. NOT the concerto. And don't worry."

Callahan turned toward the door. "I'll go talk to the priest. He has what we need, and he trusts me."

When the two left the apartment, twenty minutes late, their arms were filled with paraphernalia. I couldn't stop them, no matter how I argued.

"You are supposed to disable them by day!" I shouted after them, but they didn't pause. The elevator whined upward.

I could hear hurried sounds from above, thick though the floor might be. Furniture scraped and things thudded on the hardwood floors. Someone was packing up in a rush, I thought.

Ev and Callahan should be getting there just about now. There's the knock—it would have been inaudible to ears less anxious than my own. I am beginning to play 'Jesu, Joy of Man's Desiring' as I try to recall the prayers I was taught as a child.

Why knock at a vampire's door, when you are going to destroy him? Ridiculous. I play a bit louder.

There is a crash—Callahan must have kicked in the door. Why didn't he use his key? Not as dramatic, I suppose. I play louder, still.

God!

Who said you couldn't hear screams through those solid floors?

In an archeology book, I found the photograph of this mummy, and it literally haunted me until I told its story (or at least my take on its story).

THE DIG

The bones came to light almost too easily. Even in the dimness of the cavern they shone with that unmistakable calcareous gleam. Tennant's heart jumped with the old excitement, and Peridot's eyes were sparking behind his thick glasses. Tennant pushed the Indian gently aside and went to his knees, brush in hand, to remove the loose powdering of dust from the ancient skeleton.

The floor of the cave was uneven with old falls of earth from the roof, as well as with the remains of middens and anonymous heaps from the debris of those whose old dwelling this had been. It was only luck that had set Azilio digging in this particular spot of hummocked dirt. Now the loose layer that had underlaid the hardened top layer seemed to slide away from the skeleton.

The man had been set into a hole dug into harder soil. The bony hands had first come into view, then the skull, still cupped in their clasp. Breathless, Tennant wielded his brush and trowel, feeling the suppressed excitement of those who stood behind him as he worked. Azilio quietly drew away the extra soil he was dislodging, struck a light blow with his pick when the harder layer got in the way, and passed Tennant the tools he needed with the accuracy of a surgical nurse.

Now the figure was coming into view. It was sitting, legs drawn against the chest. It had probably been bound into position, Tennant thought, for the hole wasn't tight enough to have squeezed the legs so close against the torso. It was obviously the body of a grown man—a big one. Long bones, big feet, long-fingered hands indicated as much.

It had also been a terrified man. The attitude, now that the shape was free of the concealing soil, was something between that of the "see no evil" monkey and a terror-stricken child. Those hands were shutting away from the empty eye-sockets some vision too frightening to admit.

The body was almost mummified. Large patches of leathery skin still adhered. The backs of the hands were partially covered with it, the finger-bones thrusting through like fingers through worn-out gloves. It was so nearly a man, still, that the living men fell back a step or two, shaken by the fear implicit in the pose.

Even Tennant moved out of the shallow hole and stood away. There was a moldy smell—too faint now to hold the taint of death, yet unpleasant enough. He brushed the dust from his hands and breathed deeply of the musty cavern air.

Turning to Dr. Peridot, he asked, "Well, what do you make of him, Ted? We'd hoped for some bones, and here we've found an entire specimen. Something rare too. Did you ever see anything like this before?"

Peridot gazed into the pit, his glasses twinkling in the torch-light. "I find him frightening," he said. "Fetal position is not un-usual—but this isn't quite that. Not precisely. I would say that the man was alive when he was placed in the hole. Partially tied, possibly, but his hands were free. Dead hands never gripped anything as tightly as those still hold that skull. He was seeing something when he died. Something that he couldn't bear to see."

"A torturer? I can't see any marks on what skin's left."

"I think not. These people were not hung up on things like that, as you Americans say. Pain was a natural part of their lives—with death itself. I don't think he was hiding from a hot iron or even is own death. Something else. Something not nearly so human and un-derstandable." Peridot shivered.

Tennant looked at him, surprised. Ted's getting old, he thought. I've never seen him so affected by anything.

But Peridot had stepped into the hole and was brushing at some-thing on the stone that formed a wall behind the crouching figure. Something like an inverted v came into sight. Beside it something else, big-eyed and round-faced, with two small—horns?

"What in the world is that?" Tennant bent to see. "An owl?"

"I think it was originally a carving of Tlazolteotl," said the older man. "The stone was soft. It has crumbled quite a lot. But I think, yes, Tlazolteotl. Which might explain the poor man's terror."

"Tla...the Mexican witch-goddess?"

"You were there when I gave the class in ancient Mexican witch cults. You saw the cuttings in the stones. There...."—he touched the v—"...is her pointed hat that so puzzled the archaeologists. And her owl. Perhaps her little house, with its dangling herbs, was originally cut into this, as it was into that other rock-face."

"But that is thousands of miles north! A cult wouldn't have come so far!"

Peridot stood and stepped from the pit. "You think not? It traveled to Europe—or from Europe westward. Pointed hat, broom-riding and all. Why not southward, down its own continent? If it crossed the Atlantic, why not a few thousand miles of dry land?"

Tennant looked at the shape in the hole. Something *outré* had happened. It was implicit in the frozen posture. The teeth, bared by time, had most likely been bared by terror in the beginning. In his turn, he shuddered.

Azilio touched his shoulder from behind, and he jumped before he could control it.

"Sun going down," said the Indian. His face, usually a study in taciturn brown, held a deep crease between the brows. "Time to go from here. Not good here at night."

Tennant reached down to set the torch in its case at his belt. He realized that every afternoon about this time the Indians had gently but firmly brought their work to a halt, cleaned their tools, and steered the two white men toward their waiting suppers. Nothing had been said, and he had thought these people to have inflexible work habits. Now he wondered.

A red glow entered the westward-facing mouth of the cavern. The sun, setting behind the forest far below, was catching the hillside opening, sending the beams into the depths of the tunnel. It caught the head of the skeletal man, tingeing his hands with a bloody color, staining the skull with red.

Azilio sucked in his breath. *"¡Manos rojas!"* he muttered, almost inaudibly. "We go now." He turned and set his tools into place, lifted his pack onto his back, and set the strap across his forehead. His companions did the same, leaving the white men to follow as they would.

Tennant found himself unaccountably restless that evening. Uneasy and dissatisfied with himself; he had reacted almost as strongly to the find as the superstitious Indians. He couldn't account for Peridot's attitude either. The man had seemed almost frightened, though he had found skeletons and parts of them by the dozens in his long career. That irrational unease had affected even Tennant's objectivity. It disturbed him.

The moon was high. He wasn't at all sleepy. He looked about the sleeping camp. Peridot's lamp was burning, his silhouette staining the side of his tent as he wrote up his notes for the day. The Indians were recumbent shadows. Tennant went into his own tent and took his pocket pistol, a fresh hand light, and his notebook. He went quietly up the slope in the moonlight. Toward the dig.

The cave was totally dark, the moonlight blocked by the boulder that interrupted its angle. He kindled a couple of the pitch torches and switched on his hand light, then moved into the big cavern. Setting the torches into their notches in the wall, he took his own light and stepped into the hole.

Inch by inch he examined the new find, making notes as he worked. He touched the bony figure as lightly as possible, making measurements with calipers, noting the number of teeth remaining in the skull. He knew that Ted would be pleased. With the preliminaries out of the way, they could take the *in situ* photographs and begin arranging to remove the body for shipment to Ted's museum.

He was whistling softly between his teeth, busy and happy, when he heard it. Something was whistling along with him. Softly, then louder. Louder. Until it seemed that the rocky walls vibrated with the shrilling. It was strident, frightening.

He laid his torch on the edge of the hole and looked toward the entrance. The torchlight, added to the beam of his flash, lit the alcove inside the opening. He stepped from the hole and took up his hand light, moving toward the entrance. The whistling knifed through him, making his head hurt, piercing his head. Addling his wits. He put his left hand to his head, pressing against the pain, and turning his flash back toward the alcove. Something was coming... into the cavern.

He reeled back, dropping the light onto the rocky floor. Both hands went to his ears, trying to stop out the keening whistle that was stabbing directly into his brain. Staggering, he backed toward the rear wall. Suddenly there was nothing beneath his heel, and he fell into the pit, jostling its other tenant aside. The whistling grew louder.

The newcomer was inside the cave. It was loud enough to daze him—to unsettle his vision.

He shrieked and cowered against the wall, shoulder to shoulder with the skeleton. The old woman in the peaked hat moved toward him, making the air tremble with the force of the shrilling that seemed to surround her.

Tennant pressed against the stone, feet drawn tightly to his buttocks, hands gripping his ears with all their might. Eyes wide, staring at that wavering shape in the torchlight, he waited. Her gray lips were motionless. Her bottomless eyes were without light. Her hands were moving. Beckoning.

He screamed. His flesh shrank upon his bones—all his vitality was draining from his body as he cringed in the hole. The bony shoulder against his was shuddering—or was it his own, shivering?

Something tugged insistently at his mind, drawing him out... out....

Then the light went out.

This story is just a symptom of my innate pure meanness.

A NIGHT IN POSSUM HOLLER

It took eight years to pay off all our debt. It took another seven to save enough for a down payment on the house we'd wanted for years And then inflation took a hand, and we realized that we were like the frog in the well—crawl up two feet, and fall back three. That's when we decided that instead of doing the sensible thing and holding on to our jobs in Houston, we were going to take that sum and buy us a place up in Poor Man's Country, which is the accurate name of East Texas, when folks are feeling honest.

We knew we'd be broke and stay that way, but what the hell—it was better than knocking ourselves out playing Russian roulette with Houston traffic every morning and evening, breathing carbon monoxide and the effluents from the petroleum plants in Pasadena, as well as things less easily identified. We'd been poor before. There wasn't any great trick to that, and we'd learned all the dodges by the time we were weaned.

We spent a spring traveling up into the woodsy hills and poking around, both with and without real estate agents. We wanted a bit of ground, which came well within the capabilities of the cash we had. Land in East Texas costs a fraction of what it costs in Houston, believe me. A house we could fix up would suit us very well. We found, once we got to looking hard, that we could pay cash for a place that our little hoard wouldn't even make a down payment on where we were.

Maudie almost laughed herself sick when she saw the name on the road sign the first time we went into Possum Holler. But she quit laughing when she was looking at the place we went to see. It was a little gem—to us, at least. Ten acres on a hill slope, with an all-season creek branch running across the low end. Lots of big hickories and a few oaks and a ring of huge pines circling the knoll where the house stood. And the house was nice. Shabby, yes. Run down for years without paint. But the tin roof had saved it from leaks.

It was an old dog-run house—two halves separated by a wide hallway running from front to back, open to the air. But that had been enclosed some time in the past, a kitchen built across the rear of it, and a nice screened porch across the front. The rooms had ten-foot ceilings and were big and square and solid. The thing was built of cypress and there's just no decay in that stuff.

Because it was old-fashioned and would take a lot of work or money or both to get into shape, we bought it for a pittance. Also because it was in Possum Holler, which was a bit behind the back of beyond. Also for other reasons, but we didn't know about them at the time, and it's too late to worry about them now.

We moved up in a borrowed camping trailer and set it up down by the road. There wasn't a really flat spot to put it anyplace else, and that was handy for getting in and out, as we had to run into the Holler for nails and barbed wire and all the things it was so easy to forget when you do things like fixing up a place that's been neglected for twenty years.

Maudie and I both grew up on shirt-tail farms. We knew how to work, and we made the fur fly. I rented a tractor first off, and cut all the weeds and persimmon sprouts and sassafras clumps that had been making free with the pasture land for umpteen years. Maudie scrubbed woodwork and slapped on paint and put up new screen wire on the windows and around the porch. By the time I had fences mended and the land in shape, she was ready for some help fixing the roof. Some of the tin was loose, and all of it needed a good thick coat of aluminum paint. Maudie's a willing old gal, but she had trick knees like you wouldn't believe, which made getting up on roofs nervous work for her.

We were getting pretty tired of that camp trailer by the time things were so that we could move into the house. Our stuff came out of storage on a Friday morning, and we hauled it out in four loads of a U-Haul trailer and parked it out on the front porch. Arranging it took most of Saturday. Sunday morning we headed back for Houston to return the trailer, Maudie following me in our '78 Ford station wagon. We got back to the Holler about eight in the evening.

It took us most of the summer to do all that fixing up, and it was late September. An early norther was blowing through the woods, and we were glad to get back home. Maudie had a fire all set in the living room fireplace, and we looked forward to lighting that and sitting in our own, by God, house, by our own fire and owing no man a thin dime.

We ate sandwiches by firelight and made coffee in an ancient granite pot we'd found at the General Merchandise store in the Holler. Pushed it right up into the coals, and it turned out the best cup of coffee I ever swallowed in my life. Then we just sat there, almost purring with satisfaction and smugness.

What did the Greeks call that? Hubris? The kind of pride that goeth before a fall....

And we got worse. All through September and October we kept working—there's always more to do when you take on a project like that. The tacky little job I got fifteen miles away at Nichols was a snap, and while I was working at it I was thinking about all the things I was going to do when I got home. Maudie was worse. She put an ad in a writer's magazine to do typing, and that let her stay at home all day. She'd type a while and work a while, and when I got home she'd be full of satisfaction.

You wouldn't think there'd be anything about that to bring a Wrath down on anybody, now would you? But what else could it be...? Well.

Anyway, the fall wore itself out, and winter came on stronger than usual in that part of the world. Northers chased each other through the pine country, one right after another, and we were mighty glad of our fireplace and the big woodpile that I'd accumulated while trimming and cleaning up our woodlot. Those thick cypress planks were good insulation by themselves, and we'd gone inside the floors and the walls and blown more insulation too. We were snug as bugs in a rug.

Other critters liked the setup too. At night we'd hear scrufflings and gruntings under the house. Armadillos, the neighbors told us. And probably skunks. Mort Feldon gave us a pointer pup he said would be good at scaring away varmints, and we fixed him up a burrow under the porch. Then we stopped up all around the foundation—but those noises kept right on. Digging sounds. Grunting and snuffling sounds.

"You think there's a bear wintering under there?" Maudie asked one night when things were unusually noisy.

"There's no bears left closer than the river," I said. "And precious few there. No, it's some tiny little old animal that can slip through the chinks. You can bet on that."

Funny thing, though: Pat, the pointer, didn't say a word, no matter how loud the critter got. He'd look up at me if I'd go out to check on him, and something in his eyes told me he knew exactly what that was digging away down there, and he hadn't the faintest intention of meddling with it.

We finally went to see Mr. Heaton at the store and laid our problem before him. He turned away and scrabbled among the packages of rat poison for a box of stuff he said would kill anything up to a rhinoceros. But I noticed all the time we were talking that he looked a little funny and shaky. He came out onto the porch of the store when we drove off. Waved goodbye, as if he didn't expect to see us again. Of course, I didn't put it together and realize that until later.

We followed directions to the dot, put out old tuna fish cans of the stuff mixed with everything from cornmeal to hamburger, all under the house as far as we could push it with poles. Then we tied Pat up short, so he couldn't get to any of it. And then we waited to see what would happen next.

Nothing did. The noise went on exactly as it had before, night after night. When a month went by without any results I went under and took out all that stuff and buried it deep and put a big flat rock over the hole so Pat couldn't dig it up.

Just after Christmas the hearth began to buckle. Did I tell you the house had two fireplaces? One for each of the original halves of the house, you see. One was in our living room, and that was the one we used. The other was in the room we took for our bedroom. When it was particularly cold we'd build a smudge in the fireplace to take the chill off the room, but we never had roaring fires there as we had on the other side of the house.

Maudie noticed the way the bricks were out of line one night when she was about to lay a fire there. When I came to her call, I could see that something had dug out under the hearth, so all the thicknesses of brick had sagged down into the hole. That was the only thing that could cause something like that—the hearth was a good three feet thick from top to bottom.

We knew that for certain, since we'd been so happy that someone had redone both fireplaces, filling in new brick from top to bottom beneath the firebox. It seemed as if whatever was giving us all the trouble at night had done it before now, digging out under fireplaces. Who knew how many times? And who could tell what it might be?

Well, there was nothing to be done that night. We didn't light a fire, for fear it might find a way to get a spark out through one of the cracks and into the old cypress walls. We just went to bed and snuggled close together until we warmed up some. Then we slept.

I woke with a jerk. Something had sounded—a sharp crack of noise. I reached to switch on the light, just as Maudie said, "Unh? Whassamatta?" in her usual sleep-drugged way.

Then it was on us.

The lamp was a little night-light affair, but even it was enough to show what came surging out of the hearth in a shower of mortar and bits of brick. It looked a little like a bear, at that. But it had no fur and it had no face, and it was slimy as a snail. I tried to roll out from under as it came down on the bed, but it was no use. I stuck to it like a fly to flypaper, and I knew Maudie was in the same fix.

I could barely breathe, and that only because I had turned my face to one side. If I'd been facing up like Maudie was...maybe I'd have been luckier. She must have suffocated pretty quickly. She was gone when the thing lifted itself off us.

It must have been hungry. It might have been hibernating, or whatever it did, for the whole twenty years the house hadn't been lived in. It ate Maudie almost entirely, right then and there. I could hear it champing her bones and grinding and slobbering away on that side of the bed.

Why didn't I run for it while the thing was busy? There's a good reason for that. While it was on top of me it glued me to the bed with that gunk that covered it. From the middle of my chest downward I seemed to be a part of the mattress. Nothing but my right arm and my left hand could move at all. It's a good thing I kept this pad beside the bed for making notes on supplies when I woke in the night and thought of them. At least I can keep my mind off what's happening.

Because when it finished Maudie it started in on me. But it's not as hungry now. It's been four days, and it's not much farther up than my knees. I figure tonight it'll get my right thigh, and tomorrow night the left one. It'd be better if I could bleed to death, but that slimy stuff seems to seal off the blood vessels, so that doesn't work.

If I can hang on without going stark crazy, in three more nights it'll get to a point where it'll chomp up something I can't live without. That'll be damn good. I'm almost out of tablet, now. Maybe I will go off my rocker—that would make it easier. Some. I hope.

God, when we moved here I thought the Holler part of the name meant Hollow. Now I know it doesn't. It means Holler. Like scream, you know?

I do a lot of that.

My mother finally gave up on solving this sort of problem. No mat-ter how hot the East Texas summer night, from the time I could sit alone I had to have a sheet over me. She'd spend ten minutes gently moving it off me, and I would sit up, eyes closed, and pull it back again. Luckily, no gray hand ever got me.

THE TUCK AT THE FOOT OF THE BED

"Mama!"

"What is it, dear?" This was spoken very innocently.

"Tuck sheet! P'eese!" Two round dark eyes peered accusingly over the top edge of the sheet.

With a sigh, the mother tucked the sheet tightly beneath the side of the lower end of the mattress. "Why in the world you have to have that top sheet tucked that way is beyond me." But it was done now, and the eyes had closed in sleep.

* * * * * * *

"Barbara, you know you want to go. All the rest of the girls are going—Doctor Jarvis's daughter, the judge's girl. All the best fami-lies, too. I just don't understand you!"

"I just don't feel comfortable. I don't like sleeping on the floor, and they talk all night. I don't particularly like any of them anyway. And you won't let Annie Wimple come spend the night with me."

"But her people are sharecroppers!"

Barbara sighed and pretended to busy herself with her lessons. Her mother would never understand. She had to sleep in a bed, an actual bed, with the sheet tucked tightly at the lower end. Otherwise there was no rest, no security for her in the dark hours of the night. Her mother, infuriated at the illogic of her actions, would have forced her to change, but for the intervention of her father.

"Everybody's got somethin' they're set on or afraid of," he had said. "This seems like a pretty small thing. Nothing unreasonable to take care of. You just let her tuck in her sheet like she wants to."

And that had been that.

* * * * * * *

"Jim, I...I have to tell you something. You'll think I'm silly. Mama always did. But before we marry I have to let you know, because it means a lot to me."

He looked down at her, his blue eyes quizzical. "You sleep with a teddy bear!" he teased. "No? Then you have a very large dog that's used to sharing your bed."

"Silly!" She stood on tiptoe and kissed his chin. "No. It's such a little thing. I have to have the top sheet tucked in tightly on my side of the bed. I have always had a terror...."—she looked about to make certain that her mother was still in the kitchen—"...of having my foot hang over the edge of the bed. Now I know! I know! It's childish. It's Freudian something-or-other. But I cannot go to sleep without that sheet tucked in good and tight."

He smiled. "I think we can manage that—at least for now. Eventually I think I'll be able to talk you into realizing what causes that particular need. Then you won't need it any more."

* * * * * * *

"You're right. I see it. It makes so much sense. Insecurity can do odd things to us, can't it? And to think I've spent all these years tucking in that sheet to keep my foot on the bed! It seems so silly now."

She sat on the bed and swung her feet onto the mattress. "It really is too hot for pulling up the top sheet too. I know you've suffered from the heat, even with the fan going. You're a nice, patient person, love."

He took his place beside her, stretching himself on the cool linen. He chuckled. "I have had many a patient who couldn't see cause and effect nearly as soon or as clearly as you have done. Now you're free of that little worry. I suppose I see myself actually as some sort of Great Emancipator, freeing everyone from their niggling little slaveries to fears and phobias."

The lamp snapped off. The sound of crickets from their large lawn filled the night, and Barbara thought sleepily how good it was to have married for love and to have found money too. She dozed, her foot edging near the side of the mattress.

It slipped over.

A long, thin hand, grayer than the moonlit room, snaked up from beneath the bed. The foot moved a bit, and the ankle drooped over the edge. The hand darted upward and fastened its grip about Barbara's leg.

She shrieked, struggling upward and clawing at Jim for stability.

"What? What's'amatter?" he mumbled groggily, as her hand gripped his pajamas at the shoulder.

"It got me!" she screamed, and the cloth in her hand tore as she was dragged away from him, toward the edge of the bed.

Jim grabbed her hands. "I've got you! It's just a nightmare!" But his words caught in his throat as he saw her pulled away from him, and he was forced forward in order to hold on.

She went over the edge. He heard no thump, and her hands grew cold in his. "Barbara!" He hurled himself toward her side of the bed and looked over the mattress. She was disappearing into a kind of hole that swirled at the edges. His hands, as if paralyzed, loosed their grip, and she was sucked away. The hole pulled inward after her, and he found himself staring at the pattern of the carpet.

He huddled on the bed, shaking. The top sheet, folded neatly at the foot of the bed, gleamed accusingly at him in the light of the waning moon.

When Bill Pronzini was requesting stories for his MUMMY! *anthology, I recalled the Plains Indian habit of putting their dead up on scaffolds, to be mummified by the arid western air.*

THE EAGLE CLAW RATTLE

It was a shackledy old scaffold. You'd never catch a white man doing such a sorry job, particularly if he was planning to stick the body of one of his great men on top of it. The Sioux, though...what can you expect from a bunch of heathen Injuns who think that's the only proper way to do the dead? Closer to the Great Spirit—hah! Any white man can tell you that the only place to put a dead man is in the ground. This scaffold business is just unsanitary, if not down-right sinful.

Anyway, it was the devil and all to climb. Particularly in the dark. Even out there in the back of beyond, you never knew if one of those red-tailed varmints was there in the rocks, watching. A cautious man doesn't rob Injun graves, mind you, but of those that do, the most wary live longest. I've been at it (and other things) all over the Dakota Territory for a long time, and I've still got my hair to prove it.

There was a tad of moon—just a toenail-trimming's worth. A low and lonesome wind was whishing along the ground, stirring up enough dust to fog up the landscape a bit, which suited me fine. If it was also moaning and hissing around the scaffold and its burden, well, that was fine too. I figured that the day had come and gone when old Thunder-on-the-Mountain could give me any hassle.

I could see the dark, oblong shape against the stars whenever I'd look up. Mighty long and thin.... Of course, he'd been a big cuss from what I'd heard. Likely the desert air had dried the juices out of him and thinned him down. Even with all the bundled wraps they'd put around him, he looked mighty narrow. Still. I'd never seen one yet that'd rotted away to bones, not in this climate. When I first started taking orders for "Indian artifacts," I unwrapped one or two, just to see what I was dealing with. They were just like old, still leather. Not much different from what the really old Injuns look like when they're alive.

This one was the top of the line though. The red devils think old Thunder helped hang the moon, from what you hear around the campfires at night. Said he could shake up storms out of the mountains with that painted rattle of his. Could make the ground shake so hard it split open and let whole rivers get lost and never come out again.

I laughed. Now here he hung, with the wind singing through his teeth, not even able to spit out a mouse-sized curse at the white man who was going to make off with his fourteen-karat, hundred-proof magic rattle. And sell it, what's more, to an Eastern fella who was fool enough to offer *two hundred dollars* for it.

The wind seemed to pick up the higher I got. Or maybe I was going above the shelter of the ridge of rocks that curved away to the east. I could see eagle feathers fluttering now, tied onto the scaffolding in untidy bunches. They were all but worn down to the nub by the wind and the dust, but they still spun 'round and 'round, or else flittered away at the ends of thongs.

Funny the way your imagination will rise to any occasion. I'd have sworn that I heard that corpse shift, just the way a man does when he's been lying down too long and needs to ease his bones. It was the wind moving the deer hide wrappings, of course, but it gave me an almighty start until I figured it out.

When I came out on the narrow platform, it seemed almost light, for the moon had pulled out from behind the thin mare's tails that were misted across the sky to the east. I could see the way the outer wrap was tied. It was buffalo hide, weathered to the toughness of wood, and the bindings had been knotted for so long that there was no way on God's green earth you could have untied them.

I got out my boot knife and began cutting. I knocked down a couple of pots and what must have been a bundle of lances while I was moving around the edge of the platform, trying to get everything cut before I opened it up. They made a godawful clatter and crash, and I stopped for a minute and listened. Injuns have an unchancy habit of going out to forsaken places like this to sit and meditate and wait for their heathen gods to talk to them.

Still and all, if there'd been one around, I'd know it by now, and I carefully pulled back the buffalo robe. It cracked in a long split, and the section I'd lifted caught the wind and went sailing away, That left a shell-shaped something like a long narrow boat, and in it was Thunder-on-the-Mountain in person.

They'd tanned deer hide so fine that it was silky. Even in the dark I could see the beadwork twinkling in the moonlight, as I unfolded the top layer. Underneath that was a pair of dark hands. They were so well-preserved that they still looked strong enough to strangle a bear. Big, tough, long-fingered hands, they were, and they were clasped like grim death around the handle of a big gourd rattle,

And that was what I'd come for. A gourd that old, mind you, can be brittle as paper, so I tried to ease it out of those hands. It was as if they'd been glued together. I stood up for a minute to ease my back, and as I did, I looked up at the end where the face would have been, if it hadn't been covered with deerskin.

The wind fluttered the layer of hide just a bit. Just enough so it looked like somebody was breathing underneath it. And I felt like two hot black eyes were blazing away under there, fit to burn twin holes in the pale skin.

I shook my head and laughed. Robbing graveyards—even heathen graveyards—was no business for a man who let himself get fanciful. I laughed again and went back to work.

Now, it's not that I'm squeamish. I've handled more than my share of dead bodies, both fresh and mummified, and I've never thought a thing of it. But those hands were another matter. First off, they looked alive. They looked as if, when I laid hand to them, they just might grab hold of my wrists and throw me down off the scaffold.

As I stood there considering, it suddenly dawned on me that he didn't *smell* right either. All the others had had a faint, musty, nasty odor, not strong but mighty noticeable.

This one didn't, and it wasn't just that the wind was carrying it off. The only smell there was tanned deer hide and old buffalo robe. Not the best of stinks, but better than mummified Injun.

The moon was way up by now, and I wasn't done with my job, so I shook my head to get the foolishness out of it and went about my business. If the hands wouldn't turn loose of the rattle, then, by George, they'd just have to go along with it, at least until I could figure out a way to get them off without busting my two hundred dollars all to flinders.

My boot-knife was just the ticket, and I had them off at the wrists in no time. Even then, they held onto that rattle as if they'd grown to it. And I couldn't see that fella buying a pair of dead hands. Easterners have weak stomachs.

CRAZY QUILT, BY ARDATH MAYHAR * 153

I cut off a bit of hide and tied it around the whole thing, rattle and all, making a loose bundle of it. As I lifted it, the eagle claws fastened to the rattle clicked sharply against its painted sides. It was shuddery—worse than a rattlesnake in a dark room.

I put things back as well as I could, for it's just as well to avoid any trouble you can. The piece of robe that had blown away was long gone, but I fixed the deer hide back together and tied some of the fringes to keep it in place. I'll admit that it was a relief to hide those dark wrist stumps too.

I went back down with the bundle slung over my shoulder, the rattle clashing gently away at every move. The wind was picking up too, whipping my coattails and pushing and prying at my bundle. As I reached the ground, the moon went under a cloud, and I looked up to see that the mare's tails had moved together into a black mat that covered half the sky.

My horse was dancing around, whinnying that wild way they do when a storm is coming, and it was all I could do to calm him down enough to get mounted. I hadn't more than got my feet settled into the stirrups when a wall of wind and dust and rain, all mixed up together, came whooping down on me.

I kneed Gray over against the rock outcrop to knock off part of the wind, and we just hunched down to wait it out. The lightning came then, sizzling down so close that I could hear the little pop that comes before the big crack. Thunder rolled down over us like a giant walking on drums, and I glanced out from under my hat brim to see if the rain was slacking off any.

It wasn't. It was, if anything, harder, and the continuous lightning lit it into silver sheets.

In the midst of it stood a big man. He was dressed in fine-tanned deerskin, and the rain hadn't wet an inch of it. He was standing four paces away, just looking at me, and his eyes were big dark holes in his face. The thunder boomed right above us, shaking the air and the ground and even the rock my elbow was touching.

The Injun didn't move. He stood there, waiting and watching, and I stared back, knowing what he wanted, but still too stubborn to admit that I had to do it.

The rain got harder; the lightning danced around us like mad fireworks, and the thunder sounded fit to shake down the sky. In a little bit, that Injun stepped forward one pace. I shrunk down into my coat, wet as it was, but I couldn't look away.

He raised his head toward the sky, and he held up his arms. His hands were gone, but as if he had called on further powers, the storm got worse. A lot worse.

So I slowly got down from my shivering horse and tied him securely to a knob of rock. I took the bundle and put it over my shoulder again. Then I waited. I wasn't going a bit closer to that big Injun than I was, and he sensed it right off. Between one wink of lightning and the next, he was gone.

I sighed; then I gritted my teeth. To think a white man, a Christian, could be maneuvered by a heathen Injun made my blood boil—but quietly.

I climbed the scaffold again, and the rain was ending as I reached the top. The long form lay there, and the wind hadn't stirred a fold of its wrappings. I untied the strings, then the bundle I carried. Carefully, I fitted the hands back to the stumps of the wrists. Before I could take my fingers away, I felt...I felt the damn things *flex*.

The lightning, dying away to westward, lit the place by flashes. The hands lay still and dark, grasping the rattle. I shook my head and looked at the bundled shape. Might as well do the thing right, I thought.

Sighing, I went down and got my buffalo robe from my bedroll. It was two jobs to get it back up, with the wind still blowing in gusts, but I managed. Then I lifted and shifted and maneuvered until I had it around old Thunder-on-the-Mountain, and I tied it down good and proper.

He lay there, quiet as death, but I still had the feeling that those eyes were wide open and seeing through to *my* bones. I went down the scaffold for the last time in one rush, got on my horse and lit out.

The lightning had stopped now, but I could hear some sort of low, grumbling sound that hadn't any direction that I could fix. Then, over the rumbling and pounding of Gray's hooves, I could hear the sharp, clear sound of that eagle-claw rattle.

Gray screamed and shuddered, rearing and turning as the ground opened in front of us. It unseated me, and I fell, my boots sliding out of the stirrups as if they were greased.

I seemed to fall forever, with the sound of that rattle clashing and laughing in my ears all the way down. I felt bones snap all over me when I hit bottom. My teeth were full of grit, and I think my jaw was busted. I went out for a long time.

When I came to, old Thunder was sitting there beside me. The rattle was shushing away in a soft rhythm, and the old bastard was saying something long and complicated in his heathenish lingo.

Now and again he'd stand up and shake his hands at the sky. They were back on, good and tight.

He's waiting for me to die. He's making Injun magic right now, and it'll trap me down here, with the walls of the crack already beginning to sag back together. As soon as I die, he's going to bury me, body, soul, and all, in all this rock and dirt, and I'll never get to heaven. I'll turn to old boot leather, just like he did, instead of rotting away, like a Christian corpse, to bones.

Damn him. He's going to make me a mummy too.

What would it be like to be a lunatic under seven moons?

THROUGH THE PADDED DOOR

I felt the pressure of their unseen gazes on me. The mutter of voices came to my ears, though the construction and the padding are supposed to prevent one in my circumstances from knowing that he is observed. This detention seems to have sharpened my senses to preternatural acuteness.

Or perhaps the shock treatments—could those terrible bouts of terror and pain have had some effect that the doctors never dreamed of? Possibly. I do know with certainty that the almost invisible flicker of lines across my vision slowed a great deal after the first series of those treatments. To the point at which I realized that such things are no mere aberration of the eyes, but actual dividing-lines between multiple dimensions that must coexist with ours.

After every shock, I could hear and feel and see more acutely. Words became perfectly audible, through the layered padding and the thick walls.

"He shows every sign of improvement, Doctor. Do you think that we can risk him in one of the secure rooms now? He seems very calm and quite docile, except for his struggles when we take him to therapy." A female voice. A face rises in my memory: eyes with the bulge of thyroid, spotty skin, hairline moustache. No charmer, to be sure, but not, all in all, unkind.

"Not yet, Thurgood. Things seem to be going well, but I have an uncanny hunch about Carver there. I've seen too many madmen put on a good show of being completely stable, only to run amok almost immediately upon being given the chance. No, we'll keep him in maximum security for another week. After all, we wouldn't want a recurrence of...of what sent him to us, now would we?"

I could see Durstine's heavy face as he spoke. It loomed in the eyes of my mind, and I hated it. Hated it in the way I had hated—but no. I mustn't think of that again. My only chance of escape is in cool, calm, balanced behavior. No one has *ever* left the walls of Clendenning Institution except by release given by the doctors or by death.

But how can one become sane under conditions guaranteed to drive any human being to insanity? They have taken away the straitjacket now, but even that small favor leaves me to stare at four pale-green padded walls, a darker green padded floor, a padded ceiling seven feet above the floor, and the padded interior of the door, with its six-inch-square inset of one-way glass. Enough to drive anyone out of his skull.

* * * * * *

Thank God for the flickering lines. It has reached a point at which I can slow them by an act of will. Slow them, actually, to a stop for a short time. And then I can see *into* those alien dimensions. Without that diversion, I might well have dropped into a melancholia from which nothing could rouse me.

My favorite is the one with seven moons. There is a strip of beach that glistens darkly in the moonlight, a troubled bay—or perhaps a sea—with sharp-topped waves whose edges are trimmed with pearly foam. Three of the moons range along the horizon at differing angles. Two are almost overhead. The complex light patterns indicate that at least two more are down in the sky opposite the visible horizon. I have always had a thing about the moon, and the notion of seven drives me almost giddy.

Of course, the pink world is charming. It gives me a very drowsy, peaceful feeling, and watching the odd little creatures wriggle their darkly pink bodies into and out of the huge bell-shaped flowers is almost hypnotic. I'd like to visit that one. Not to stay, just to find out why humanoid beings live, or nap, or forage, or whatever they do inside plants' blossoms.

There is a hard-edged dimension that makes me think of the way Africa must be—or must have been before the advent of Man. Desert abuts heavy forest lands, in which grim beasts prowl and prey and mate and die. Strange beasts, to be sure, but in their habits not unlike those of our own world. Yet I would not want even to visit there.

Oh, there are dozens—perhaps there might be hundreds, if I were expert enough to halt the flipping lines quickly enough. Worlds and spaces, peopled and unpeopled. Nighted and lighted, though by going back I can sometimes catch a familiar world by day instead of night, or vice versa. Going back—that is something that I can't quite comprehend. In some way I have become able to reverse the flickering pattern of lines, run them backward until I catch a distinctive color gradient. I have now seen my seven-moon world by day and night, by summer and winter. At times there are people on that beach. They construct intricate sculptures of some glassy substance on the flat rocks that seem to have been placed along the sands just for that purpose. I have, just once, been able to hold the dimension open for long enough to see the waters rush greedily inward to devour those fragile shapes and bear their fragments back into the deeps. The tides, I assume, are irregular and chaotic in the extreme there.

Every trip to therapy leaves me more enervated, more despairing. Yet those trips seem to be refining my abilities. I can find my seven-moon world at any time now. Those choppy waters soothe me, help me to maintain my counterfeit "sanity." They help me to forget my last moonlit night of freedom, here in my own world. To smooth away the memory of the thing I did, there in the moonlight.

But I am not able to continue as I am. Blackness looms behind me, threatening to inundate me in its moonless flood. A week here? I cannot bear another day here. Desperation flavors every motion, every thought, every message sent along every nerve.

As I thought that, I was staring into "my world," on just such a night as I best loved to see there. Four moons ranged up the visible sky, and the light from the others was "behind" me. The waves were slapping at the shore, almost audible, even across the dimensions. A single figure sat atop one of the stone slabs, staring out to sea. As if my desperation had found its way to touch him, he turned and looked directly into my eyes.

He saw me! I had no doubt of that. His eyes were puddles of shadow beneath a high forehead, and they widened visibly. His hand moved out toward me. His thin, inhuman lips moved, as if he were asking a question,

I knew that our languages could not be mutually comprehensible, so I didn't try to speak. Instead, I concentrated with every bit of strength at my command. *I* am *imprisoned,* my spirit screamed across unguessable depths. *I* am *tortured almost every day! They will never let me go free, no matter how well I behave, and I cannot endure it any longer. Darkness is coming to claim me, and I am unable to resist it.*

I was sweating, my shapeless overall damp with exertion, though I had moved no muscle. Yet how could that alien shape help me? Why would he help me? Not one of my own kind would lift a finger to do that. Tears rose in my eyes at the thought.

There was a clicking at my padded door. Another trip to therapy! I could not—*could not*—could not bear it!

The surge of raw emotion touched my friend in the seven-moon world. He lifted a rod made of the glassy stuff. His thin lips moved. As the gross shape of Thurgood came through the padded door, I dissolved, stretched, thinned, changed...something. And slipped sidewise through the line that held that beach, that sea, those moons.

I landed on my knees beside one of the slabs. Sand gritted under my palms as I heaved myself onto my feet, and I could hear, at last, the slapping of the waves. My joy lifted me, for an instant, to unimagined heights. I turned to thank my new friend.

And the mad forces of the moons caught me in their grasp! The strangeness that had overtaken me beneath Earth's single, though large, satellite was multiplied many times by the seven moons that spangled the beach and the sea with maddening patterns of light. My head spun, my senses struggling for balance in this terrible new system.

The creature who had brought me through had risen and was coming to meet me, thin hands outstretched. Its tinkling voice added to my distress. Overwhelmed by the strangeness, the alien pulls from the sky, I gestured for silence, but he did not understand. He came nearer, tinkling and tinkling his mind-piercing words. My hands moved, of their own volition. He broke into shards in their frenzied grasp and fell onto the sand, glittering in the moonlight.

Oh, God! It has happened again, and I am in a place too strange to comprehend!

I want to go back! Back through the padded door!

Sometimes writing a pastiche is great fun! I never did think Mrs. Hudson got her due; having Sherlock Holmes for a tenant must have been a pain!

THE AFFAIR OF THE MIDNIGHT MIDGET

221B, Baker Street
3 November

Dear Doctor Watson,

It is with some trepidation that I take pen in hand to interrupt your convalescence (I hope that you are now able to walk with more ease and comfort). My apologies to your good lady for the intrusion of my affairs into her regimen, and I hope that she will forgive me for it.

However, after observing Mr. Holmes's behavior for some time, I have determined that something very strange is taking place. As you know all too well, this is nothing new with Mr. Holmes, but so bizarre is this new matter that I feel you will agree that it needs some attention from one who understands and makes allowances for his eccentricities.

He has, for the past fortnight, been arriving home very late. Indeed, I might even say that on several occasions he has not come in at all. This would give me no occasion for uneasiness, except for the fact that he has suffered from a bronchial infection, and the weather has been notably chilly and damp. Remaining out at night seems rash, when one considers the risk.

In addition, the array of small boys has stopped coming altogether. For many years, I have been used to having street urchins cluttering my doorstep, and I must admit that I rather miss their shrill voices, if not their grimy feet on my hall carpet. But this, if nothing else, has alarmed me. If Mr. Holmes no longer needs the services of his Irregulars, either he is far more ill than he has shown or admitted to me, or he has some venture on hand that is too desperate for risking the persons of his young colleagues.

Having kept a cool head over the years of his tenancy, under, I believe that you will agree, some extremely alarming circumstances, I feel that I am not showing undue concern, at this point. And in order to prove to you that this is true, I will list the oddities I have noticed lately in order of their seeming importance:

1. A well-dressed midget arrived four days ago, while Mr. Holmes was out. Knowing my lodger's habits, I scrutinized the man closely and decided that under no circumstances could Mr. Holmes have compressed his lanky height into such a minuscule form, and so I denied him entrance. He turned upon me a scurrilous attack, and that proved past question that it was not our friend, for he is invariably civil in his treatment of me. However, the midget left behind a packet, which I placed on the hall table.

2. Mr. Holmes must have come in without my hearing him, though I hardly see how that could be. However, I was awakened at three o'clock yesterday morning by a muffled explosion. Donning my dressing gown at once, I hurried downstairs, to find Mr. Holmes standing in the hallway, holding what seemed to be the remnant of wrapping from that same packet.

"Do not be alarmed, Mrs. Hudson," he said, as I approached, in some dismay. "Nothing is seriously damaged—not even the intended victim." Here he laughed in a rather bitter manner and turned back into his rooms, still holding the wrapping. Shortly afterward, I heard his violin start up, and it was a dreadfully dismal air that he played.

Now you know quite well that this is not the first violent occurrence in the chambers at 221B. I have never objected to such matters, for it seems clear that a detective's life is subject to this sort of happening, and the rental paid is more than enough to cover incidental damage. However, when I entered the chambers the next morning to lay out his breakfast, I found that the room, though tidier than usual, still reeked of something like gunpowder. There was, in addition, a bloodstain on the carpet, although it had been scrubbed almost clean.

I observed no wound upon Mr. Holmes's person, nor any blood, the night before, and it occurs to me that if the blood is not his, there is someone else hiding in his rooms. Would you have any notion as to who that might be?

3. This morning when I tapped on the door before entering with the tray, I received no reply, though there was indubitably the sound

of movement inside the room. I called out several times, asking if he might be ill, but, while I heard footsteps crossing the uncarpeted area of the floor, I still received no reply. The steps were brisk and did not drag, as one would expect those of a sick or injured man to do.

As you might suspect, I am extremely worried and upset. It is obvious that someone is posing a danger to my tenant. It seems obvious also that he is hiding someone (perhaps sheltering them from harm?) in his chambers.

Yet he is exhibiting none of his usual methods of dealing with such problems. Not one person has approached in weeks, with the single exception of that objectionable midget. He is, I believe, more often in than out, though I can no longer be certain of anything concerning his movements.

And, early this morning, his brother Mycroft sent around a note by the hand of one of the ushers at his club. I have not been able to receive an answer to my knocks, and I hesitate to slip it under the door, in the event that the person inside is one who should not know whatever message that note contains.

Dr. Watson, I badly need advice. If I should call at your home tomorrow, would you be so kind as to see and to advise your respectful

Martha Hudson

* * * * * * *

221B Baker Street
5 November

Dear Doctor Watson,

It was most gracious of you and your lady to receive me, as well as to advise me concerning the current problem. Indeed, I will gladly keep you abreast of the situation, as events come to my attention.

I have taken your advice and hired an extra cleaning-woman, who is charged with scouring every staircase in the house from top to bottom, taking her time and doing the thing properly. As this involves mops and pails, brooms and scrubbing brushes, which seem to be scattered along every length of steps in the house, it is quite probable that I will know if anyone tries to creep upstairs.

Mr. Holmes is definitely out at the moment. I saw him go myself not an hour past. He looked very drawn, with his throat muffled closely. I do worry about that bronchitis. He seems thinner than before, and he did not walk with his usual decisive tread. Something is worrying him.

Immediately after watching him from view, I climbed the steps, being careful to avoid every obstacle that Tilly left there, and listened at the door of the rooms. Someone was pacing back and forth, and I thought that I caught the hint of a whistled tune, though that was quickly discontinued.

And here comes Mr. Holmes, back already. I must put away my writing things and prepare his tea—he has taken none for several afternoons.

* * * * * * *

Later—

Dear Doctor Watson,

My plans were disrupted by the arrival of Inspector Lestrade of the London Police. Would you credit it? He arrived with a warrant and proceeded to search Mr. Holmes's chambers from top to bottom. He was searching, if you can believe this, for my tenant's nephew!

This was a great surprise to me. I have known that there was a brother, a recluse, I believe, and I would have thought him a misogynist as well. However, it seems that in his early youth, our Mr. Holmes's relation contracted a marriage with a young woman who died after producing an infant. This child was reared by a distant cousin and is now in his early twenties. He has been accused of murdering the father of a young person who, he claims, is his fiancée.

No trace of anyone other than my lawful tenant was found on the premises, which puzzled me a great deal for a time. And then I recalled the false ceiling that Mr. Holmes asked to have installed in his study. I suspect that the young man is, even as I write, cramped and dusty in the darkness of that narrow space between the new and the old.

This explains the person hiding in the rooms, true, but it leaves almost more questions unanswered. Who was that midget, and why was a bomb left for Mr. Holmes? Why is he keeping his usual contacts at a distance? And why is he hiding a person who is wanted by the law, when, if the boy is innocent, he might promptly prove that to be true?

As you may suppose, I am bewildered, but I will continue to report. I hope that your relapse is a short one, and that you will soon feel up to getting about.

With sincere regards,

Martha Hudson

* * * * * *

November 10

Dear Doctor Watson,

Although you may think me neglectful, I have not written simply because there has been nothing to report. Mr. Holmes seems content to remain indoors after receiving his brother's note, and has kept to his chambers for several days. The young man, his nephew, I am certain is still in the house, though there has been no further instance by means of which I could prove that.

However, this morning found matters altered. Mr. Holmes rang for breakfast a full two hours earlier than usual, and when I took up the tray, he was pale, and his cough shook him painfully. He was so ill that he asked me to remain while he drank a bit of tea and crumbled a piece of toast. When I insisted that he allow me to call a physician, he sighed and nodded.

"A pity that Watson is under the weather, but that seems advisable. Yes, Mrs. Hudson, call in your doctor. I believe that I am too ill to go on."

This astonished me, as you may well imagine. Never before have I heard him admit that he was not well, no matter how obvious that might be to the unaided eye. However, I called Tilly and sent her after Dr. Jermyn, whom you may recall as living two streets over and one down.

When that gentleman arrived, he insisted that Mr. Holmes be taken at once to hospital, as his bronchitis had become pneumonia. This left my tenant in a quandary, as you might think, for I was not supposed to know of the presence of the nephew. However, he took the opportunity, while the doctor sent for a carriage, to speak with me.

"Mrs. Hudson," he said, staring into my eyes as if to read my thoughts, "I need a favor. You have never failed me, and I trust that you will aid me now. My brother's son, Andrew, is staying with me. He is, as you probably gathered from the visit of our brilliant Lestrade, in a bit of trouble at the moment, and only this damnable illness has prevented my finding the true culprit and freeing him from this dangerous situation."

"I knew he was here," I assured him. "And I suspect that he hid in the overhead, while the police searched."

He looked surprised, though why that should be true I cannot think. But I went on, "I handed in that note from your brother, as well, and that told me something, though I have no idea what was written there."

"Mycroft has learned something vital. His own life may be in danger, for the father of that young woman was Lord Tenningsly, the Chancellor of the Exchequer. A plot has been afoot to discredit the British currency, and the Chancellor was murdered in order to conceal its existence. My unfortunate nephew was inadvertently caught in a web of international monetary manipulation, and if he is apprehended it will mean that the true culprits will never be brought to book."

Dr. Jermyn's steps approached along the hallway. Mr. Holmes laid a small envelope in my hand. "Care for him as you would for me. I will return, and those who intend to kill him, claiming that they acted in self defense, must not find him before that time comes."

Naturally, I trusted his words implicitly, for although he sometimes takes a devious route, I have never known Mr. Holmes to arrive at anything other than the truth. I tucked the envelope into my apron pocket and assisted the men as they carried the sick man down the stairs. I removed the brooms and mops as they passed, but before they were out of sight, I had them all replaced. Now, more than ever, we needed a functioning alarm system.

When Tilly left, that evening, I went upstairs and tapped on the door of 221B. "Mr. Holmes! Mr. Andrew Holmes! Your uncle has entrusted you to my care, and I need to talk with you. Will you open the door?"

After a long interval, during which I thought more than once that the young man was not going to risk unlocking the door, the key turned in the lock. A pale face, long in the bone like his uncle's, stared out at me. Along his cheek was a partially healed cut, which would, I was certain, have been caused by that bomb.

"You are Mrs. Hudson?" he asked. Even his voice was like, and when I entered the room and saw him in full I could see that the Holmes bone structure was there. His hands were long and thin, and they twitched, as Mr. Holmes's do sometimes when he wants to play his violin but is prevented by other affairs.

"It is a pity the illness came on him so quickly," I said. "He knows who killed your young lady's father, and he would prove it like a shot, if he were able."

He sighed. "I know too. Danvers, the secretary, was the key to the entire plot, and Lord Tenningsly caught him out. He told me, before he was killed, but little good will that do me. Everyone thinks that I killed him because he objected when I courted Millicent. And he didn't even object. Not really. He simply wants—wanted—us to wait until she is eighteen before we announce our engagement."

I believed him. I think that I would have, even had Mr. Holmes not told me the facts in the case.

I smiled at the boy. "Keep the blinds drawn closely," I said. "We want no light to show in the street, for the rooms are supposed to be empty. I will bring up your breakfast early, before the servants arrive, and your dinner will be served at about nine o'clock. I hope you will not become too hungry in the time between. Keep the door locked and the chain up. And remain in the back rooms, if you can manage to. Even if you pace, no one will hear you there."

He nodded. I felt it a pity that so likely a youngster must have so harsh an initiation into the world, but that comes when it comes, and nobody can alter that.

I was abed before midnight, and I slept deeply, after the excitements of the day. Yet when the first pail clanged down the steps and the array of mops and brooms began their clattering falls, I was up in a moment, wide awake. Lighting a lamp, I hurried down the stairs toward the landing at 221B. The disturbance came from farther down, however, and I continued on my way.

The door opened as I passed, and Andrew Holmes looked out. "Trouble?" he asked.

I nodded without speaking, for I was wondering how I could cope with those who seemed determined to climb my stair, no matter what clamor they set up. I seized a mop that leaned against the railing and charged downward into the darkness.

Behind me, I could hear Master Holmes's slippers flapping on the carpet. "Are you armed?" I asked, over my shoulder yet keeping my gaze fixed on the motion below.

"Now I am," he said, his voice grim. "You are not alone!"

Even armed only with mop handles, I found that comforting. I had given my word, and anyone coming up the steps to harm this young man was going to answer to Martha Hudson!

I stumbled over the midget. He rolled beneath my feet, and I saved myself by grabbing the railing. Another shape, much larger than the first, loomed against the dim light from the foyer lamp, and I aimed my mop handle and rammed it into his waistcoat. He grunted and folded over, giving me the opportunity to rap him smartly upon the head.

I could hear a scuffle behind me. Then there was a sharp smack, and the midget rolled back down beneath my feet. I stepped over him and pushed the other man off the expensive carpet runner that protected my foyer. Blood is most difficult to get out of wool!

"Are you all right, Mrs. Hudson?" asked the young man.

"Quite well, Mr. Holmes. If you will retire to the upstairs, out of sight, I will summon the constable on duty. I have a whistle that will have him here at once."

He moved out of sight, and I went into my lower rooms in order to find the whistle. As I rummaged about, I checked my apron pocket, and there was the envelope Mr. Holmes the elder had left in my hand. Surely he had intended that I open it!

I unfolded the crisp page, and another fell out of the protective wrapping. I stared down at it. Then I went to the door and blew the whistle shrilly into the damp night.

Of course, the envelope that Mycroft Holmes had sent was a note (how he put his hands onto it I probably do not wish to know) from Tenningsly to his secretary, asking him to come to the office in order to explain his recent activities with regard to the International Currency Market. While it did not directly accuse him of misdoing, the inference was plain, and the police saw that as quickly as I had done.

I can only assume that Danvers's attempts against Sherlock Holmes were caused by his uneasiness at the thought that the great detective might take a hand in proving the innocence of his nephew, and in so doing would uncover the plot and its participants. The police believe that as well, though Mr. Holmes only smiled when I mentioned my theory.

You have, no doubt, read the newspaper accounts of the affair. The police, of course, never apologized to Master Holmes, but that is something they seldom do.

I understand at last the irritation that Mr. Holmes must feel when his dangerous and difficult work is ignored, while the police

take all the credit. It was I who captured Danvers and his midget accomplice. But what did the *Times* headlines say?
LESTRADE SOLVES TINNINGSLY CASE
The very idea!

* * * * * * *

I hope that you are now well enough to visit Mr. Holmes, who is again in his rooms, though unable, as yet, to get about much. If I have rambled at some length, you must understand that it is seldom that a respectable female has the opportunity to participate in such exciting and interesting affairs, and this has been a most enlightening experience for

Your respectful friend,

Martha Hudson

Growing up in the East Texas woods and river country, I know all about crawfish!

CRAWFISH

It's chill down there in the river, I reckon. She don't know, though. Can't know. Them big innocent brown eyes are starin' away down there, unless the crawfish—God, I wish I didn't know nothin' about crawfish.

She's got this soft white skin, like to a baby rabbit or some baby animal, sort of. It shined, like, even through the muddy old river water. I could see her, shinin' and shinin', as she sank. Her hair moved all out loose on the water, dark and curling in the moonlight. It kept moving in the water, all the way down...them crawfish....

She was a tramp, I tell you. Everybody knowed it, I reckon. Smiling and smiling at everybody went by. I moved way down in the bottom-lands, 'count of that. No fancy traveling salesmen comes down here. No Avon women selling damnation. No men in cars and men in trucks that'd look at her when she worked out in the yard. Bending over, showing her legs! Tramp, just tramp!

Must of been born that way. She was just fourteen when I hitched up with her, and hadn't had time to learn nothing about men then. Just naturally bad, flirting when we went into town, smiling at them tellers in the bank, in their white shirts and city suits. Looking with eyes of lust and fornication at them. First time, when I got her home, I beaten the living daylights outen her.

Way she cried and took on, you'd of reckoned she was crazy. Her Pa never had no gumption with his women folks. Let 'em have their own way clear to ruination, seems like. His woman even had money to spend, when she felt like it. So I guess Mattie wasn't all the way to blame for her sinful ways.

Still, beating didn't do no good—not to last. She'd go 'round with her head down and her eyes on the ground, like is fitten, for a while, then she'd see something, maybe just a flower or a bird or some such sinful uselessness. All that decency would be gone in a minute, and she'd be laughin' to herself. And when she laughed, any man inside a mile would be starin' at her like they knowed her already.

I come home one evenin', and she was full of talk. Met me at the door, jabbering fit to make me deaf. I slapped her a couple of times and quieted her down, like as my Pa used to my Ma, iffen she said more than is fitten for a woman. She didn't say nothin' else, just slapped the supper on the table and went off in the back to the garden and started pullin' weeds. I looked 'round to make sure she wasn't meetin' nobody, afore I set down to eat.

Next day, Miz Rogers, down the road, met me at the end of the row and asked me, real sly like, who'd been visitin' Mattie yesterday. Seemed like I got hot all over—it just seemed to rise up from my feet clean to my head—and I was so mad I could of busted. Miz Rogers, she looked at me kind of scared-like and took off afore I could answer.

It was away before noon, but I took the mules in and unhitched. When I got to the house, she was gigglin' in the kitchen. I crept up, real sly like, and peeped in. They wasn't no one there. She was crazy. Clean crazy and a whore too.

I slammed the screen open till the spring busted. My head was like to bust too, with the blood poundin' and poundin'. She looked 'round and turned white and funny-lookin'. After she picked herself up from where I knocked her, I started tellin' her what she was. The Whore of Babylon was nice to what I called her.

I slapped all her lies back into her teeth. She was gabblin' about flat tires and women with thirsty children, but she quit that soon enough. She wasn't so all-fired pretty, after I got through with her. Her nose was all lopsided and her eyes was so swole you couldn't see what color they was. I figgered, Hell, I might as well of married a homely woman, iffen I was goin' to have to keep mine all bunged up to keep the men away from her.

Next day, I went down to see Pa. Didn't let on what was goin' on, but Pa, he's read the Bible and helled around some, so he guessed pretty close. He told me he knowed of some land that was for rent, down close to the river. Said iffen I wanted, he could find somebody to take over my place and finish my crop. It was still early in the spring, so's I had time to make a crop down there in the wet land.

So we moved. There was a fair cabin on the place. Not fancy— she started sayin' something about havin' to carry water so fur—but

I just had to look at her mean by then, and she shut right up. I broke a garden patch, and she put in a nice garden, but seemed like she didn't care iffen it growed or not. She didn't put no more flowers 'round the front, neither, so's I knowed she'd done it, t'other place, just to bend over and show her legs to the men on the road. She didn't fix up the cabin none, neither. Just went around like she was listenin' to somethin' inside her head. Her Maw come, a time or two, but I didn't care about havin' her come 'round givin' Mattie fancy notions, so I got rid of her quick as I could.

Got so I hated to come in, after finishin' work. I'd stay out till dark, near, or go night-fishin' with the niggers down the river. She kind of looked at me like I was somethin' scary. Give me funny feelings, the way she looked at me.

No, sir, when I took her where she couldn't go smilin' at the men and flirtin' all over town on Saturday no more, she kind of dried up. Never even tried to talk to me no more. I might even of let her, so's to liven up the quiet some, but she kept her lips tight shut over her broke tooth and let the mosquitoes buzz.

Her eyes got queerer and queerer. They was big to start with, but it got so that they was deep as the pool down at the river, and just as full of strange things. I'd go in at night and she'd watch me, starin' and starin' like I was a bug or a snake. She was crazy, I tell you.

Anyways, one evening, I come in dead tired. Crop was laid by and I'd been fishin' all day, but it was so hot it like to of took your breath. They wasn't no air down there, 'count of the woods just closed in all 'round like walls and kept it out.

While I was eatin' supper, she was standin' by the wash-pan, waitin' for the dishes. All of a sudden, she turned 'round with the meat knife in her hand and started for me. Iffen I hadn't of looked up, she'd of killed me where I set. Seems like, when she done that, everything just come together like. I took her 'round the neck and shut my hands tight and when I opened 'em up, she was dead.

My folks has always been mighty proud and upstandin' people, 'round here. And Pa, why it'd kill Pa iffen they hung me over a woman. So I took her through the woods down to the river.

I could hear the snakes slidin' off in front of me, while I carried her down the path. The 'gators was bellowin', and the moon was comin' up full. It was right hard, gettin' her down the bank to the deep water. She was right smart tall, if she was so slim. I got her down, though, and tied on some weights offen the nets we'd been settin' that day. They wasn't too heavy, but nobody never come there, no way. So I put her down in the water. And she sunk, slow, and the moon made her go down shinin' and shinin', real soft, like a dream.

Wasn't till the next day I started thinkin' about them crawfish. Iffen you never seen a body that's been et by crawfish, you don't want to. It's a sight to turn a goat's stomach, let alone a man's. I kept thinkin' about her, down there, with them things eatin' out her eyes, nibblin' on that soft skin. Seems like I couldn't rightly stand it. For two days I held myself down. I took out and went with the niggers down the river and never come back till the morning of the third day. This morning...seems like forever.

Something drug me down there to the big pool. It's like I couldn't help myself at all. And when I got there, I couldn't see nothin'. I would of thought she'd of riz some by then. Seems like I had to see what they'd done to her, though. Thinkin' was a lot worse than knowin'. I took a sweet-gum sapling and started dredgin' around in the deep water, wadin' out fur as I could. I didn't want to, couldn't hardly stand it, but something made me keep pokin' and feelin' around with that pole, till it caught her.

Must've been caught on a snag or something, cause when the pole hooked her, up she come, slow and easy, just like she gone down. And I throwed up in the water until my insides like to of come out my mouth. Then I had to go and git rocks and rope and sink her good, so's I couldn't never see what they'd done to her, never no more.

I guess I must've went off my head, like. I come to wanderin' 'round in the woods, all black and blue from bumpin' into things. I went back to the house, but it stared at me outen its windows till I couldn't even go nigh it. Then I went up to Pa's. Course, I didn't tell him nothin' about what had happened, but I could see him wonderin'. He loaned me a clean pair of khakis and five dollars, and I come on into town. Seems like I had to see people, be away from the woods.

First thing you know, Will Pollard come up and winked. "Got a jug hid out in the back of the hardware store," he says.

So I went with him. Guess he didn't get much of that jug. I must've drunk most of it. Next thing I remember, Will was lookin' at me with his eyes bugged out and his face fish-belly white.

And now you've got me locked up in here, and they're all down there right now, fixin' to drag her out. And you're lookin' at me like I was the one that was crazy and sinful. And they're goin' to see what I seen when she come up.

Damn them crawfish!

On reading in a book on writing the mystery story the statement that any time you begin a story with a feeble little old lady confined to her bed you automatically know what is going to happen, I chuckled. This time I bet you didn't *know what was going to happen.*

AUNT DOLLY

Outside the tightly closed window, the ivy leaves were beating against the small panes in the first real storm of winter. Even though the house was tight, the windows closely fitted, Dorothy shivered, feeling that the heavy draperies, only half drawn as yet in the last light, should be billowing in the fury of the wind.

Snug in her rose-shaded room, safe in the bed in which she had been born, Dorothy should have been content, but in the last month that had been lost to her. The hearty old woman who had broken wild horses, reared her three great-nephews to adulthood, if not to responsibility, and managed the horse farm she had built up from the tatty farm her father left her, seemed lost in the past.

Now she was an invalid, wrapped in plush blankets, confined to this room that had never fitted her personality. The pale rose blankets, the deep rose velvet of the draperies, the charming flower pattern of the sheets, those were matters that had appealed to her mother.

Dolly was a farmer, a horse breeder, a tough-minded, tough-bodied creature who had never been ill in all her sixty-seven years. This terrible thing that had happened to her frightened her for the first time she could recall.

A small stroke—what nonsense! You stroked a cat or the nose of a horse. This was more like a blow, aimed not only at her mind but at everything she had ever stood for.

Aimed, worst of all, at the independence she cherished above anything else.

There came a stir in the hallway outside her door. A timid tap told her that Cynthia, her third nephew's wife, stood outside with a cup of chocolate and the afternoon paper.

Dolly sighed. "Come on in," she grunted. "And close those damned drapes. That wind wants to come right through the glass, it seems like, and at my age I don't need that for a bedfellow."

Cyn set the tray just so, its legs straddling Dolly's lap, and moved to tug at the velvet rope that shut out the chill pewter of the evening. The delicacy of her motions, the finicky precision of everything she did grated on the old woman's nerves like diamond on glass. She suspected that in private, Cynthia was far less ladylike than she appeared now.

"Do sit down!" she commanded. "And don't fiddle! I like my room messy. Makes me feel at home."

She stirred the marshmallow into the steaming cup of chocolate and took a tentative sip. Ah! The warmth relaxed her a bit, and she settled back against the piled pillows behind her, holding down her irritation at the frills edging the cases.

"Tell me about the mare—did Dr. Winlow find out what ails her? She's too valuable to risk, let me tell you, and if we need another vet, we've got to get one. Winlow isn't bad, but he's an old fogy in a lot of ways."

"Oh, Auntie, don't worry yourself about the horses. Jerry is taking the most splendid care of everything...."

"Don't give me that! Jerry never took splendid care of anything but himself, and that includes taking care of you. He's checking out every salable item on the place with an eye toward sneaking it out to a pawnshop is more like it. He'll rob his brothers, if they're not careful." She watched the young woman closely, but Cynthia had learned to hide her feelings when Dolly went on a tear.

Rather disappointed, Dolly drank down the chocolate and poured another cup from the rosebud-sprigged pot. That was Haviland that she had bought to please her mother, once there was money for that sort of nonsense.

She wondered if any of the pieces had been sold, downstairs, by her rapacious kinsman. The stuff was worth a mint; the antiques dealer had told her when she made the purchase.

She always rolled her food and drink around her tongue, these days, trying them for any odd taste. She wouldn't put it past Jerry and his nasty nice wife to try poisoning her. Then they'd have a free run at everything while Ed and Charlie traveled the long miles from England and Africa to protect their interests.

Cynthia turned even paler than usual, but she held her peace. The old saying, "Wouldn't say boo to a goose," applied nicely to her, Dolly thought.

"Winlow," she said again, her tone stern. "Tell!"

"The mare was only bloated. He tended to it and gave her something to help. Jerry says he thinks she'll be fine tomorrow." The words came out slowly, precisely enunciated, spent grudgingly as if they were dollars instead of breath.

"Good." Dolly finished the cup, placed the thin china in its saucer with a decisive clink, and motioned toward the door. "Now go and do whatever it is you find to do all day and all night. I'd as soon talk to a parrot!"

When the door closed behind the thin behind and the sharp elbows of her great-niece-by-marriage, Dolly sighed. She had tried. She truly had!

But those boys were a handful, and no matter how she worked them and taught them and made them toe the mark, they kept breaking out wherever she wasn't expecting it. If she'd had a husband, it might have helped. A man would have understood them better.

But as it was, she was a better man than any of the three, and they all knew it. They all resented it too, which was why Ed had gone to London as soon as his paper had an assignment there. Charlie had taken himself off to Botswana or some such godforsaken place to write a book.

Jerry had been closest, and that only because the chemical firm for which he was a sales rep was based on the West Coast. They gave him leave and here he was, complete with baggage and wife, who was also a pretty fair baggage herself.

She listened sharply as the crisp steps descended the uncarpeted stair. The kitchen door gave its usual definitive thunk as it closed, and she smiled. Time to practice walking again.

She didn't intend to be a bedridden invalid for the rest of her years, that was certain. But every time she suggested that Jerry help her stand and walk, he fussed and worried and all but said that he wanted her flat on her back.

There was no way she was going to put up with that, and his refusal was motivation enough to drive her to secret exercises that by now had strengthened her legs considerably.

* * * * * * *

"How is the old...darling?" Jerry asked, as Cynthia entered the kitchen. "Bitchy as ever?"

She sighed, her thin face pinched. "I think she's a lot stronger than she was. It wouldn't surprise me if she got out of that bed one day and went back to running the farm."

Her husband turned pale. "That's impossible. At her age, with a stroke...."

"It was a minor one, with no permanent damage, Dr. Armworth said. Sixty-seven is not old. Not any more. I warned you to take your time and be certain, but no, you had to sell those two fillies when you had that offer from the breeder in Kentucky. If she takes hold again, you're going to have to buy them back, whatever it costs, and you know we haven't a dime between us."

She glared at him. "We could both go to jail, Jerry, if she gets back to normal."

The man dropped into the rocking chair behind the long table where the family had always eaten informal meals. His sallow face was still pale, and his dark hair drooped dispiritedly over his forehead.

"When Ed and Charlie come, the fat's going to be in the fire. You thought she was a lot worse off than she was, or you never would have risked going ahead with those sales. Now what do we do?"

"We think," he said, putting his head into his hands.

"Think!" she muttered, clanging pans together as she started supper. "With what, I'd like to know?"

"I can't get that money back. Arnie will turn his bruisers loose on me if I don't get another fifteen thousand within the next two weeks. The boys will be here next week as well. I've just got to sell the gray stallion and use that to clear my account."

She turned on him, red spots glowing in her cheeks. "That's my Jerry—just keep going ahead, even when you know you're going to fall over a cliff in the dark. The old woman's going to get well, you fool!"

"Maybe...not." He looked up from the rocker, a gleam dawning in his eyes. "Maybe not. Armworth is a lot like the vet—he doesn't keep up with the times, and he all but said that someone her age was likely to pop off at any time. He won't be surprised if she does, and he'll sign her death certificate without any question."

She, in her turn, went pale. She turned back to stir the pot on the stove, into which she had been slicing carrots, turnips, potatoes, and cold roast with vicious precision.

Back turned, she said, "You mean to kill her."

"No, no. Not strangle or anything violent. There's some stuff they prescribe for her that should do it. Just give her her regular dose and put a double-sized one in her supper. She's supposed to have it in her system anyway, and Armworth will never think to do an autopsy."

Cynthia's skinny shoulders sagged suddenly. It was the only way, and she knew it as well as Jerry did. She didn't like the old biddy anyway.

Jerry rose and went upstairs. She knew he was visiting the bath that connected their bedroom with that of Aunt Dolly. There was a new vial of medication there, along with a few tablets in the old one.

Like it or not, they were about to become murderers.

* * * * * * *

Dolly heard the heavy steps coming up the stairs. She had gained a lot of mobility in the past couple of days, and she managed a pretty fair sprint back into bed before they reached the top and came down the hall. To her relief, Jerry went into the bathroom, instead of looking in on her.

She picked up a mystery novel and turned a page, staring at the lines without reading them. She had, she felt, to pretend to be a coddled old lady, helpless, weak, unable to get about. Some instinct told her that her life might depend on it.

Water ran. The toilet flushed. There was a tap on her door, and she glanced about to make sure everything was normal before responding. Her slippers, shed in her flight back to the bed, lay in the middle of the floor. She reached for the cane she used in going to the bathroom and raked them close beside the bed.

"Come in," she said, in her most unoffending voice.

"Cyn's making her special stew tonight," he said. "You'll like it a lot, I think. Should be ready about six-thirty. How are you getting on, auntie?"

"As well as can be expected," she said, her tone dry. "I'm not twenty, Jerry, but I seem to be holding up pretty well, considering." She felt a sudden pang, recalling the thin, tanned little boy who had brought his troubles to her.

He had been the youngest of the three, hit hard by the loss of both parents to a virus infection while they were abroad. He had seemed wary of everyone, as if fearing that they, too, might go away and never return.

She sighed. "That's nice. I like a good stew. But I'm tired now, and I think I'll take a little nap before supper time."

He nodded and crept out, looking entirely too satisfied with himself. She knew him too well to believe that such a look could possibly be innocent.

When his steps had died away in the distance, she waited. Usually he walked around the place before supper, and when that was something that could be left to simmer, Cynthia went along. Perhaps the cold wind would keep them inside, but she hoped they might at least check on the animals in the barn some three hundred yards from the house.

When she had heard nothing from the lower floor for fifteen minutes, Dorothy swung her feet to the floor, slid them into her slippers, and rose unsteadily. The cane propped her nicely, as she donned her robe and headed for the closet.

This was a very old house, and rooms, stairs, even the floors had been altered time and again, over the years. There had been a back stair once, and her closet was the head of it, using the space between the inner and outer walls to make a walk-in space.

The steps were still there, leading down into blackness and emerging in the back entryway as a deep supply cupboard beside the kitchen door. The well was narrow enough to allow her to brace one hand against the wall while bracing the cane on the other side, securing her slow downward steps.

She paused from time to time, resting, listening for any sound from the kitchen, now just on the other side of the partition. But no hint of movement came to her ears other than the slap of wind-blown shrubbery against the outer wall.

Then her descending foot found no further steps. She was in the cupboard, her right shoulder brushing the shelves stacked with preserves and canned goods, some of them years old. She opened the door a crack and peered into the hallway, finding that after the darkness on the stair even this dim passage was visible.

Nobody.

She crept along the hall and into the kitchen, finding one light burning over the stove and the stewpot simmering obediently, its contents smelling delicious. She was tempted to take a taste before doing what she came to do, but she pushed the impulse away.

She took a vial, salvaged from her stash of medications for healing—and killing—animals, from the pocket of her robe and dumped its contents into the stew, stirring it vigorously with the spoon conveniently placed in the flower-shaped holder. When the last hint of oily liquid was gone, she turned away and made her painful trek back up into her room.

* * * * * * *

When she dropped into bed again, she was genuinely exhausted. Jerry, checking on her before bringing her supper, found himself wondering if he needed to trouble himself to doctor her food, but he knew it was better to be safe.

"She doesn't look good at all," he said with great satisfaction, as he helped Cynthia dish up the stew into rose-sprigged Haviland bowls. He piled crackers on the plate under the bowl, and his wife added a salad to the tray as he assembled his aunt's supper, complete with special seasoning.

Dorothy had to be helped into a sitting position, and he almost felt a qualm, remembering all the times she had nursed him through childhood illnesses. But he placed the tray across her lap, folded the napkin over her chest, and asked if she needed anything else.

"No, no, I'm quite all right. You go and eat your supper. I'll manage by myself. And when I'm done I'll set the tray on the table, here. This does smell good...." She inhaled greedily, and he smiled as he closed her door behind him.

Cynthia was waiting for him. She was very persnickety in many ways, he had to admit, but she was an excellent cook. They dug into their meal with good appetite, his enjoyment augmented by relief at the solution of his immediate problem.

* * * * * * *

Dolly set the tray aside on the bedside table, the stew untouched. That was bad—she had to get rid of it, and the best way was to flush it, if she could make it that far.

She didn't want to risk the Haviland, her footing being as unsteady as it was, so she dumped the stew into the emesis basin kept in the drawer and carried it cautiously into the bathroom. The stew went down without leaving untidy fragments in the bowl, and she rinsed out the basin and set it in the bathroom cabinet before turning toward her room again.

The cane hit a slick spot on the tiled floor and skidded. Dorothy flung out both hands to catch herself as she went forward toward the tub, but even before she hit the hard edge she felt that familiar blackness engulfing her again.

* * * * * * *

Dr. Winlow rapped on the door. "Miss Pelling? Mr. Danvers? Is anyone there?"

He rapped his heel irritably against the flagstone walk as he waited. Surely, so early in the morning, there would be someone stirring. He had taken the trouble to check again on that mare, and here they were lying slug-abed, neglecting their work.

He rapped again. "It's the vet! Come on, now, I'm a busy man."

He touched the knob and it turned. They hadn't locked the door last night? That was odd, in these days of vandalism and pilfering.

He pushed and went into the wide, inviting hall at the front of the house. Lights were on at its other end, in the kitchen, and he went that way, calling at intervals.

The Danverses were there, all right, convulsed, soiled, and quite dead beside the cold remnants of their meal. On the stove a scum of scorched stew smoked nastily on the low-set burner. There was an odd tang there, even amid the smell of burning.

He turned to find the phone, which he knew was in the hall. Then it occurred to him that the old lady might be upstairs, helpless, hungry, wondering what had happened. He called the sheriff and Dr. Armworth; then he climbed wearily up the dark walnut stair, clinging to the banister and feeling very old and tired.

There was a line of light below Dorothy's door. He tapped softly. "Miss Pelling? Miss Pelling? It's Dr. Winlow."

There was no reply, and he turned the knob and thrust his grizzled head into the room. The covers were tumbled back, but the bed was empty. The door into the bath was, however, open.

He felt something tighten in his throat. He stepped to the door and tapped again. "Do you need help, Miss Pelling?"

Still there was no sound.

He flipped the switch and light blazed from the old-fashioned white ceramic tiles. Dorothy lay sprawled, face down, against the tub, her cane caught beneath her hips, her legs at ungainly angles.

Dead? He touched her wrist, found it cool, but not with the chill of death. She was alive, he thought.

Catching her as gently as he could manage in the cramped space, he turned her onto her back, straightening her limbs and pulling her nightgown down over her knees. Her face was drawn down on the left side, the eyes wide, staring up into his, trying, he could feel, to convey something to him.

But this stroke was a major one, unlike the earlier. This time Dorothy Pelling would never ask the question or say the words that burned on her frozen lips.

Another slightly warped tale of East Texas.

THE CREEK, IT DONE RIZ

Only the Lord knows why I ever took the old road that day, particularly since the water was out all over the map from the big rains. I could have stuck a dozen times, coming across the bottom lands. It's a wonder in this world that none of the rickety little bridges were washed out—or that one of them didn't go out with me halfway across. Still, Pa's old 1939 Plymouth could mighty nearly swim, and we always took it out when we were going way down into the boondocks.

The whole thing was a lot of foolishness, anyway. I didn't get a degree from Texas A&M in order to go paddling around in the riverbottom in the middle of a flood to count hogs. But try telling the boss that. He sits in his air-conditioned office, thinking up dumb schemes, and never knows if it rains or shines. And he can come up with some of the gosh-awfulest ideas. A hog census! Now I ask you: how he thought that knowing where every hog in the county was located would help him sell his damn feed, I don't know.

Anyway, there I was in the river bottom in a car twice as old as I was, sloshing down a road that wasn't much more than a lane when I could see it, which wasn't often. The wet sweetgum saplings were bent way down and slapping across the windshield. I was crawling along, cussing some, when I saw something out in the woods.

I crept on until I could feel gravel under the wheels; then I stopped. I could have sworn I saw an old man sitting on a stump. I stuck my feet into the rubber boots I had learned to take along with me, being as most hog-pens can't be said to do shoes any good at all. Then I got out and started off into a thicket. And sure enough, there was a grizzly-headed old cuss, soaked to the bone, dripping water off his nose and his eyebrows. He never acted as if he saw me, just muttered to himself as if that's what he'd been doing for quite a while.

When I got close enough to hear, I stood there for a minute, admiring his style. You don't hear cussing like that any more, with real feeling and meaning to it. And he was cussing the weather, which deserved everything he gave it and then some. But it was wet as all get-out, and finally I went up and touched him on the shoulder.

"Sir, I beg your pardon," I said, "but would you like a ride someplace? Out of the wet?"

He gave a jerk and looked up at me for a minute, sizing me up. Then he gave me a couple of cusses too.

I shook my head admiringly. "It's a privilege to listen to a man who can handle the language the way you do," I said. "Even my Pa, and he's no slouch, can't touch you. But it does look like you're set to catch your death of cold, if you sit out here much longer."

Then he squinched up his eyes and looked me over, real carefully. "You look to be a Jenkins," he said, when he had gone from top to bottom. "Got that Jenkins jaw. Any kin to Ralph Jenkins?"

"That's my Pa," I said. It's the darndest thing—anyplace I go, people spot me for Pa's son right off. Even if they never laid eyes on me before.

He grunted and shifted on the stump. "Tell you, Son," he said, "I ain't got no place to go that you can take me to in no car. But bein' as you're Ralph's boy, why you might help me out a little bit."

Now that's where I should've said goodbye and been off to count hogs. But Pa raised us all to be polite and helpful to old folks, and I can't seem to break the habit. When an old geezer looks at you kind of slant-eyed, with his head cocked on one side like he's figuring out how far he can con you, it's time to take off. Not me, though. No brains, that's me.

So pretty soon I found myself slogging down a pig-trail through the woods, looking sharp for cottonmouth moccasins and stump-holes. He kept talking all the time, as if he was scared I'd change my mind and leave him. Nothing he said made me anxious to keep on.

"I've got a kind of boat a little piece further on, tied up along Eel Creek. If it's still there, we can take it and get up to my house. The house ain't washed away; it's just the damn creek's done riz so I can't get to the yard. With a strong young fellow like you to help me with the boat, I kin make it." He paused and panted a while. I could see that he wasn't in too good shape.

I turned around and said, "Why, Pa could put you up until the water goes down. He'd be glad to. Why don't you just go back to the car with me, and I'll take you straight on in and have you dry in no time at all."

He started shaking his head before I was done. Then he looked all around, really careful, as if anybody but a couple of fools would have been out in the woods with the river out of its banks.

"I guess I ought to tell you, Son, seein' as how you're helpin' me and all. I've got my life's savings buried in that yard. If the river backs the creek up too high, it'll likely wash it right away. It's all I've got to stand me through my old age. I just got to get back there and get it out before the water comes up any more."

Well, he did sound pitiful. I couldn't help but wonder why he didn't dig up his money before he left, but I guessed that you might be forgetful at his age. So we went on, and the water was mighty near the tops of my boots before we came to his boat. Then I saw why he called it a kind of a boat. The baling bucket was the only thing that didn't have a hole in it. A good, sound log would have been a lot safer to try to travel on.

"You sure you want to risk that thing?" I asked him.

"It's a sight better than it looks," he answered. "I been fishing in that boat for twenty years and never drowned yet."

I never was one to believe in miracles, but maybe such things happen, or else he was an uncommonly solid ghost. But I was pledged to help him, so I bailed out the water that was sloshing around in the bottom of the thing and heaved it out into the creek. I stood there and watched the little wiggles of water come through the holes and start moving down the sides.

He got right in and started bailing. "Reason I had to have help," he said, "is somebody has to bail while the other one rows. I always borrow one of Rupe Miller's kids to do the bailing, when I go fishing, but they left when the water got high. Get in, Boy. Let's get moving. That water's not going to wait on us."

So I said a prayer, which would have pleased Ma, and got in. Then I didn't have time to pray. That water was wild as a yearling colt. It took everything I could do to keep the boat from taking off in ten directions at once.

I fought with the paddle to fend us off floating logs and brushpiles. I guess I came nearer to poling it along than paddling. In the middle of all that, it came to me—I didn't know his name. I twisted my head 'round and yelled, "Hey, Mister, what's your name?"

He looked up from his bucket, kind of startled. "Why, I'm Abe Willitts. I thought everybody in the county knowed of old Abe."

Then I really started to sweat. Everybody knew about Abe Willitts, sure enough. When I was little, Ma'd hush me up with, "Crazy Abe'll get you, if you don't be good." When his wife died, all the women looked at each other and said, "He finally killed her. I knew he would, one day." And nobody could prove them wrong, because she was buried by the time he got around to letting anybody know she was dead.

Even Pa, who wouldn't hear a bad word about anyone, had to be still when that hunter disappeared. He'd told his wife that he was going to bird-hunt down in the bottoms, and he'd intended to get Abe and his setter to help him find the birds. Nobody ever saw nor heard from him again. They looked too. All over the place, with dogs and men. Abe claimed he never got there at all, and nobody could prove different.

So here I was in a leaky boat in the middle of a flood with a crazy man. A hog census looked mightily calm and peaceful, when I thought about it. Still, I hadn't time to worry overmuch just then. Working that crazy piece of junk around the bends in the creek took all my energy. By the time we came in sight of the house, I was done in, sure enough.

Abe jumped out onto the bank, only it was the yard fence, the bank being a hundred yards behind us in the middle of the flood, and tied his rope to a fencepost. "Here we are, Boy. You just wait right here, and I'll go 'round and dig up my savings and be right back." His eyes slid round at me and didn't look quite sane.

"I'm too tired to move, Sir," I said. "You just get your stuff, and I'll rest. It'll take all we both can do to get us back up that creek."

Soon as he was gone around the house, I slid out of the boat and eased up the slope. It took a while, and once he looked out around the corner of the porch to see if I was still in the boat. Luckily, I'd propped up the bucket so it looked like a head leaning against the edge, and he didn't go down to check. I stayed hidden in the bushes for a while to let my heart quit thumping, then I went on.

When I peeped around the porch, he was digging hard. You could hear his shovel going "Shloop! Shloop!" in the mud, because the water had got around to that side of the house too. He was in an almighty hurry. I scootched down and watched. I don't quite know why, but I just had to know what it was he was in such a hurry and a sweat about. He had to be living on Social Security, just like Pa and everybody else their age. I figured he couldn't have saved up enough to amount to anything.

When a shovelful of mud came out of that hole with something dark and solid on it, I perked up. It was a hunting jacket, as I could tell after it lay there a while and the rain washed off the mud. The kind with a bag in back for shot birds and shell-pockets across the front. Then Abe's hand came up with a shotgun in it and laid it on the ground.

I didn't wait to see more. All of a sudden, I figured I'd better be back at the boat—or further still—when Abe came around the corner of that house. I made it a lot quicker than I'd come and leaned back in the boat as if I'd been dozing. Then I got to thinking.

Whatever he was getting out of that hole, he'd likely send down the flood. Maybe he'd feel safe then. Maybe not—the more I thought about going back up that creek with him bailing behind me, the less I liked the notion. I had a little money in my pocket. Probably about what that hunter had had. And nobody knew where I was or what I was doing.

I eased out into the bushes and crept along until I found a likely log. It was half afloat, already, so I goosed it out into the current and held onto a stub of branch, with my head close under the side so it couldn't be seen. That log and I whirled and twirled and twiddled down the creek with the rest of the stuff floating there until we lodged way down on Bobcat Ridge. I guess Abe never did know what happened to me.

He must've tried to make it back in that boat, all by himself. We'll never know, though. They didn't look for him nearly as hard as they did for that hunter.

According to a newspaper account, many years ago, there was actually a serial killer who distributed bits of his victims widely across west Texas and Oklahoma. Who could resist making a story of that?

JIGSAW

They found his head in Grand River. It took a while, because I had spray painted it with marble-colored enamel and set it up in the town's only park, where most thought it was a bust of somebody important. Only when it began to stink did the park attendant check out the thing and discover what it really was.

Then the law and the papers and the politicians went into a flap that would have been funny if it hadn't been so ridiculous. Instead of checking with other places for painted pieces of a man, they just raved and roared and didn't get the point at all.

People are so damn dumb! That's why I can continue my life's work without much fear of discovery. Even after they identified that head, through the dental work, they didn't seem to understand that there had been a lot more parts to Ben Craddock. Not until the others began to show up, scattered to hell and gone across the country, did they understand just what I had done, and even then it took them months to put it all together, if you will pardon a bad pun.

I had created the world's first human jigsaw puzzle. Each piece could be fitted into its proper place, if anyone had the wit to check it out. And each piece was a different color, as a jigsaw puzzle piece ought to be.

When they got it assembled, they got a real shock when they saw the overall design, but of course it took them half a year to do that. By that time the colors had run and faded, and the flesh beneath the paint had shrunk and ruined the effect of my painting.

Being an artist can be frustrating, when those the art was meant for don't understand it. That has always been my problem; even my parents didn't appreciate it when I reassembled that cat into a more pleasing design and painted it blue. The child psychiatrists were worse, though being easier to deceive, they made it possible for me to go free when I was eighteen.

Now I can follow my artistic bent as I please. My job in the artists' supply shop gives me a living, as well as all the paints and brushes (at discount prices) that I could possibly want. All the customers love me. I understand, you see, just what they are trying to do, whether or not they have quite succeeded in getting the effect they intended.

Of course I leave them strictly alone. It wouldn't do to create art by using people you know. Aside from its being rude, even the police might trace them back, when identified, to a common denominator, which would be the shop, Painters' Prize, and its friendly clerk, me.

Ben Craddock has been by far my best work. The first few were experiments, and Lucas Granieri was a less ambitious project, for I merely decorated him and suspended him from the top of a pine tree in the Big Thicket. By the time he was found, the paint had washed to slime, and the glass Christmas tree balls had been blown away by the big storm last winter. What a waste of talent!

He was, the sheriff's department decided, a suicide. As I said before, people are incredibly stupid. How many suicides have streaks of purple paint under their skivvies? Or traces of tinsel and crumbs of blown glass caught about their persons, even after spending the winter out in the weather?

No, after that fiasco, I decided to stop piddling around with minor effects and go for a big one. Once the law got its act together, I succeeded beyond my expectations.

When the gray-painted buttock turned up amid the stone work in a wall in New Mexico, and the feds began to assemble the information about the pink forearm in Kansas and the golden thigh in Oklahoma, the penny finally dropped.

SERIAL KILLER AT WORK, the headlines screamed, at the mildest. "Psychologists claim color choices for body parts show unhealthy fixations." A good way to say nothing at all and still seem to know something.

Before I'm done, they will find that I will use every color of the rainbow. I wonder what THAT will tell them?

* * * * * * *

They located the last bits of Ben Craddock after nine months (ironic timing, that); they have put them together and buried them, with suitable ceremonies. Craddock's widow is quoted as saying that she will personally find and eliminate his killer. Her photo shows a dumpy little woman with a pile of fuzzy hair and a thin-lipped mouth. I would wager she is a shrew.

Her claim strikes me as hilariously funny. If the law enforcement agencies of five states, plus the feds, haven't been able to put together even so much as a psychological profile, how does this silly little woman expect to do it?

Still, her attitude has spurred me to action again. I have chosen another target—this will be my fifth, although four of the others were wasted efforts, principally because of the ineptitude of the officers and investigators involved. This one will be my *chef d'oeuvre*, the masterwork that will set the tone for whatever comes after it.

I will abduct Mrs. Craddock. This will tell everyone what is happening and who is doing it, without in any way endangering me in my true persona. To that end, I have begun studying her habits, which is not difficult, as she lives only a half hour distant, in a town readily accessible via the Interstate. I had familiarized myself with the place while stalking her husband.

My plans for her are vague, at the moment, although I am more and more inclined to gild her entire body, as Goldfinger did that bimbo in one of the James Bond movies. Watching her suffocate will be a pleasure that I have not, so far, enjoyed.

Both husband and wife being painted will create a certain symmetry, although I do not intend to dismember her. Scattering those bits and pieces about the map became a bit dangerous at times. I will not risk it again.

* * * * * * *

Celeste Craddock is a creature of habit. I would have guessed that, if I had taken the trouble. She is actually inviting her own destruction, it seems, going to work at seven-thirty, coming home punctually at five-thirty, visiting the grocery (always the same one) on Tuesday afternoons after work, never later than a quarter to six. Except for a visit to her married daughter on Sunday afternoons (predictable, as is everything she does), she has not varied her routine by more than five minutes in the two weeks I have watched her.

It has, as usual, worked out well for me. My vacation was due last month, but Mr. Kintell was sick and I had to delay it until now. Taking vacation time for the purpose meant that I could get the woman's schedule down pat, allowing me to complete my scheme without a problem.

As I work on Saturdays, I take Tuesdays off. Craddock will disappear from the grocery's parking lot next Tuesday evening. This late in the year, it is almost dark by a quarter to six. Simplicity makes for efficiency, I have found; nobody has ever seen anything when I took my other victims.

* * * * * * *

The parking lot is dark already, and the vapor lights are obscured by a light mist of rain. Just right for my purposes. Craddock's car is parked three down from mine, and beyond it there is a gap of four spaces. I hope no one drives up just as she comes out—no, there she comes, that pile of hair unmistakable, even in the dim light.

She's putting groceries into the back seat. Now I slip along the line of cars and approach from her right. A push, and I have her face-down in the back seat of her own car, legs kicking at me with surprising force. She's wriggling forward, but it's too dark in the car for me to see what her purpose may be.

I bend and catch her around the waist with my left arm, reaching for her face with the hand holding the chloroformed pad. With a snakelike twist, she turns in my arm—something is glinting in her hand.

There is a terrible noise....

WIDOW OF MURDERED MAN KILLS ATTACKER

Celeste Maines Craddock, 57, whose husband Benjamin fell victim to murder almost a year ago, was attacked in the parking lot of John's Cash Grocery on Tuesday, November Nineteenth, at seven o'clock P.M. The attacker, Clarence Venstetter, of 1033 Gary Drive, Clarkman, Texas, was employed as a clerk at Painters' Prize Art Shop in Clarkman.

An automobile parked near that of Craddock was identified as belonging to Venstetter, and in its trunk were cans of paint similar to that used in the bizarre murder-dismemberment of Benjamin Craddock. A search of Venstetter's duplex in Clarkman revealed clothing and personal items belonging to Craddock, as well as to four other people, all deceased and now believed to be Venstetter's victims.

Mrs. Craddock revealed that she had given a challenging statement to reporters at the funeral of her husband, hoping it would tempt his killer into attacking her. She had concealed handguns in her automobile and on her person, and only that saved her from suffering a fate similar to that of her late spouse.

Police say that no charges will be filed in the death of Venstetter. A letter of commendation has been offered to the feisty widow for bringing the deadly career of this killer to an end.

After her initial interview with reporters, Craddock refused further comment; media representatives report she has turned down a multi-million-dollar offer for rights to film her story.

No next of kin can be located for Venstetter; his parents died in a house fire two years ago. He has no siblings.

Serial killers make me angry. This is something I wish could happen to at least one of them.

THE ANTHOLOGIST

He loved to walk in the park at twilight, watching his potential prey. In summer, the scents of the trees and flowers almost overpowered him, and the glimpses of young men and women walking hand in hand beyond the shrubbery made him feel young and vigorous again. Even the children playing or protesting at being called to supper and to bed made him smile.

In such places, at such times, he added to his collection.

In a strange way, he considered himself an anthologist, though only at the onset of his periodic dilemma did his scholarly background lend itself to such whimsy. Then he would murmur to himself, "I am one who gathers flowers, indeed, as the roots of that word imply. *Anthos legein*—to gather flowers—most appropriate." And his smile would be a frightening thing to see.

He loved tender blossoms, and since early spring he had gathered a bouquet of eleven. They were not such blooms as could be pressed between the leaves of books or preserved under glass, of course. Yet eleven slender, fragrant flowers had joined his collection, and he lacked only one to make his perfect dozen.

He sighed with pleasure, remembering, and the park patrolman, checking the last of the home-bound children, smiled as they passed on the walk. They often saw each other in the twilight, for the anthologist had visited this area for a month. He took care to appear well dressed and innocuous, and he roused no suspicion in anyone, he knew.

This was a night perfect for collecting, he mused, as he strolled. And, leaving through the scrolled iron gateway, he saw a perfect American Beauty ripe for the plucking, just on the verge of opening fully to dew and moonlight.

He followed her at some distance, moving casually down the quiet residential street. This routine was a familiar one, and for half of his adult life it had never failed him.

Ahead of him, the girl paused to gaze into a shop window. He slowed, pretending interest in a display of garden implements. Could she suspect that she was being followed? Surely not! But he remembered the sunny gleam of the dress in that window. That had to be the thing that caught her eye and held her there.

He had perfected his imitation of a man trying to kill time until a reasonable hour for going home. He knew that fellow well, for he had invented a persona—a life and a job and a location for him. His family were all dead, and his respectable job paid him fairly well. He had never married, and he lived a lonely existence. He knew that man and felt vague contempt for him.

She was moving again, turning up a side street. A dead end, if he remembered it correctly. He glided more quickly, yet without seeming to hurry, to cross the street. At the corner he was just in time to see her go up the steps of an apartment house at the end of the cul-de-sac.

His head went up warily, as he paused. The place was familiar—he had hunted here before, to garner a daisy from the house nearest the corner. It had been several months—was it dangerous, now, to cross his own track?

He frowned into the dusk. It had been a long while, and he had been cautious. He never left a clue to his identity with his parting gifts to his victims.

He quickened his pace, for she was now inside the apartment house. He arrived at the steps in time to see her silhouette through the pebbled glass panel beside the door.

She remained in the vestibule for a moment—checking her mail, he thought. He waited patiently, glad of the thickening darkness, as she turned to go up the stairway.

There was nobody in the street. He listened, but could hear no one stirring in the house. It was early, and most of the tenants were probably out for the evening. He picked the lock with expert ease and went into the narrow hall.

There was only the sound of the girl's heels, tapping their way up the stairs. He flowed up after her, catlike, keeping just beyond each angle as she moved past the floors.

On the fourth landing, she left the stair and moved away down the corridor to the right. He risked an eye's width around the corner and watched as she stopped at the third door on her left. Her keys jingled; the door opened and closed behind her.

Now she was at home, safe and sound for the night. He grinned until his cheeks pulled taut. But the outer door opened below, the sound carrying up the stairwell.

He looked about, saw a door leading into a fire stair, and slipped into it. From its cobwebs and staleness, he knew that it was seldom used. He could hide until the proper time arrived.

He relaxed against the wall, his fingers losing their tension, his heart slowing to a regular thud. He was never nervous when he stalked his prey. Not even when others were about, interfering with his hunt. He had learned patience over the years, and as the minutes ticked past he dozed lightly.

The house stirred subtly about him, as its tenants came and went and came, at last, to remain for the night. After hours, he stirred and looked at the illuminated face of his watch. Midnight. Still too early. He dozed once again.

At eleven minutes past two he woke again. The house was silent when he opened the door to listen. Except for the creakings that all old houses held, there was nothing to be heard.

He crept down the hall and stood before her door, his crepe-soled shoes soundless on the worn wood. He put his ear to her door, but there was only the sound of a big clock that ticked loudly.

In the distance, a siren shrilled. A dog barked frantically in the street beyond the cul-de-sac. Something clinked and rattled in the street below the hall window. All were normal night sounds, and he disregarded them as he bent to work with his lock-pick.

In five minutes, he circumvented three locks to open the door separating him from his last blossom. In his buttonhole was the rose that he had brought, knowing tonight's hunt would be successful.

The apartment was tiny and immaculate, full of the fresh scent of growing plants, which made lacy designs of the light coming through the window where they filled a wicker stand. He could sense bookshelves along the walls, and the indefinable scent of well-loved volumes touched his sensitive nostrils.

He nodded to himself. A woman of taste, this one. Stimulating. He paused as a soft breath sounded from the bedroom. She must have turned in her sleep.

He drifted toward the door, his hand freeing the knife from its sling at his back, beneath his jacket. He dropped his clothing as he went, his shorts landing silently beside the door into the bedroom. When he stood at her bedside, he was nude, and the knife shone softly in the dimness.

He reached to touch her, to wake her to terror and to his own ecstasy—but he found that her eyes were open, regarding him, though she remained motionless.

Frozen with terror, he thought, disappointed. It was far more enjoyable when his victims struggled and fought and tried to scream. He touched her neck with the chilly blade.

"Be very quiet," he breathed into her ear, as he moved to position himself over her.

He sighed, anticipating the wonderful release, the ecstasy of the next few moments—but her arms were suddenly around his torso, jerking him down so quickly that he could not thrust with the knife. When he tried to strike her with the blade, he could not reach her, for she was protected by his own flesh, which covered her from head to heels.

The arms tightened about him even more, and he loosed the knife and gasped, beginning to struggle. There was a tearing pain at his neck, a trickle of warmth, and he realized with horror that her teeth were in his throat.

He tried to wrench himself free, but she clung like a leech, her legs twined about his, her arms holding him fast, her incisors fastened onto his jugular. His hand scrabbled for the knife, found its narrow shape. He stabbed at the sheets, the mattress, but it was no good. To kill her, he had to roll her over, and that seemed impossible.

Her cheek was hard against his neck, and her hair was clogging his eyes and his mouth. With utter horror, he realized that he could not move her at all.

For the first time, he knew what it was that his flowers had felt as he plucked them from life. It had been this way for them when they, too, were helpless, bleeding, dying in the darkness.

The blade slid from his hand. He was growing weak—how could he lose so much blood so quickly? He made a great effort to move once more, but no part of his body responded to his will.

And at last she moved, slipping from beneath him as if he were a featherweight. The knife was now in her hand, but she did not use it. She sat on the side of the bed, naked alabaster in the tenuous light of the street lamp outside. His blood patterned her mouth and her skin with dark streaks and blotches.

He gasped, tried again to move. Her eyes shone faintly in the dim light, as she sat quietly, waiting for him to die.

Now even his fingers refused to twitch at his command. Who and what was this person who could use him so? He was the predator, not the prey! She should have been his victim!

Exerting his will, he managed to gasp, "Who?" He kept his gaze fixed on her narrow face, which looked...much like that of the daisy he had gathered here early in the year!

She smiled, leaning over him, her black eyes gleaming. "You are a lover of flowers. I have followed your career, since you took my sister. I have read the poetic notes and seen the blossoms you left with their bodies. A delicate touch, naming each after a flower." Her teeth shone briefly.

"But you did not dream that there might be another of your kind, I suspect. I too am a collector...of predators." Her laugh whispered through the dim room.

"You have never before tried collecting a tiger lily, have you?"

Now she laughed aloud, the sound echoing through his head and away into the distance that was forming inside him, as he felt the darkness coming into him in an irresistible tide.

He had found his twelfth flower, on this mild summer evening. And she was a blossom entirely too terrible to gather.

On our research trips through the West, my husband and I fre-
quently passed a wonderful butte on our way to and from the Tetons.
The historical marker named it Crowheart Butte—and it spawned a
story.

CROWHEART

Wears-Many-Feathers looked with satisfaction across the long
reach of the valley lying along the river. On each side were mountains, which fed the river watering the land, and along its silt-rich
course grew many useful plants and enough grass to support numbers of deer and elk, as well as small herds of buffalo. While the
meat was a fine addition to the diet, the women of his band valued
the roots and plants, the withes for making baskets, the birds and
their eggs, even more, for those kept the people from sickening in
winter.

Although his people sheltered in the mountains in winter and
hunted there often, this was their principal summer camping ground.
Even now, he could see the distant dots that were women and children, who were busy gathering foodstuff that would be dried for
winter use.

A group of very young hunters was almost at the southern end
of the valley, out of eyeshot now. His son Raking-Tree Bear had
joined them today for the very first time.

He sat before the tipi and chipped carefully at flint, making
small, neat arrowheads with which to shoot birds and rabbits. Several that were roughed out lay in the coals of his small fire, and from
time to time he sucked water into a quill and dripped it onto the hot
shape of one of them, making the stone split along its flaws.

The heavier arrowheads for deer and the great long ones for
buffalo were always chipped first and set aside for his sons to bind
into shafts or fletch with feathers. He made these more delicate ones

for the children to use learning necessary hunting skills. Besides, the birds they brought down added flavor to the pot.

He laid the last of the fluted chips in the deer hide bag kept for such matters and stood to stretch his long legs. Before he was upright, he heard wild yells from the direction in which the boys had gone.

Those were not cries of excitement or pursuit. Those were warning yells, and almost before the realization struck him he was running for his horse, which was confined in a pole pen behind the tipi.

"Hi-yi-yiiiii!" he shouted, vaulting onto the paint and turning him with his knees to jump the low fence.

Other warriors had heard already. Even those who had not, now grabbed their lances and their bows and leaped onto their own mounts. Before he was beyond the loose circle of the summer village, forty men, all mature warriors whose skills had been honed in battle, were behind him.

The people working in the valley were already heading for the village and their own duties in time of attack. Grandmothers herded small children toward the rough line of bluffs and ravines edging the valley, where they would conceal them and wait for whatever might come. Mothers and daughters and very young sons headed for home to grab their weapons and melt into the brush. If this was an attack, they would fight to protect themselves. Absaroka did not run from battle.

More warriors joined him, coming from the group fishing in the river that ran along the middle of the valley. When the excited youngsters came yipping toward them in a cloud of dust, Wears-Many-Feathers's keen ears caught the rumble of hooves behind them.

"Ai!" he called. "Raking-Tree Bear! Who comes?"

There was no reply, and Skins-Deer, the oldest of the group, pulled his roan to a halt and kneed him over to the leader of his band. "Shoshonni!" he gasped. "They took Raking-Tree Bear. He may live. We could not see, though we heard his cry of warning. Then we rode to warn the people."

"Go back and help the others," the chief told him. "You have done well. Now ride!"

Without waiting to see their instant obedience to this sensible order, he kneed his paint again and swept, with his warriors close behind, away from the cloud of dust that marked the progress of the Shoshonni. To allow another tribe to hunt in this valley was unthinkable, for in a poor year it could spell the death of his own people by starvation. But to attack with insufficient numbers would be foolish.

The Shoshonni were a constant worry. They often came through the cut where the river ran down from the mountains and raided for horses and women and children. Although his own people did the same, that did not weigh in the mind of Wears-Many-Feathers. This was the way he had known and his fathers had known since the horse came to his people, generations ago. And now the Shoshonni had his son!

Gritting his teeth to keep from crying out, he rode desperately, his knuckles white from his grip on his lance, his knees pressed into the sides of the paint so hard that he felt the ribs digging into his flesh. Finding a hillock, he pulled up the paint and looked back toward his pursuers, still distant but now distinguishable. Once he saw the number of warriors pounding toward him from the south he knew that he had been wise to retreat; now was not the time to regain his son.

There were many hands of Shoshonni, at least twice the number of his own band. Riding into death meant that his people would be enslaved, taken from their own place into the dark country beyond the mountains.

This would not be a short skirmish between equal groups, it became plain at once. If he were to find his son again and to save his people and their horses, he must be wiser than the North Wind and more secret than the water beneath the earth.

His hand went up, and he pointed right and left. Those behind him, though their blood was hot for battle, understood. Their families were at risk, and they peeled off and scattered into the cottonwood and willow thickets along the river, riding for the village and their hidden women and children.

They would make lightning sweeps at the attackers as the opportunity presented itself. Scattered as they would be, the Shoshonni could not come at them in a body but must search out the thickets as they moved up the valley. This would buy time for the people.

The hunters in the mountains could be summoned with smoke. The battleground could be chosen, the enemy led into conflict with care and intelligence. Then, even outnumbered, the Mule Deer Band of the Absaroka might survive this raid.

As his paint tore through the brush toward the high stub of stone beyond the village, Wears-Many-Feathers was considering his options and deciding to scatter his villagers widely, so that few would be captured and carried away. When he arrived at the top of the butte, after leaving his horse below and climbing frantically, he found himself followed immediately by his four best friends and most trusted warriors.

"Signal with smoke," he said to Panther-Stalker. "Tell the people to hide in the mountains until we signal again."

While the fire was being kindled, he surveyed the valley, so peaceful earlier, now filled with confusion. Of his original group that had followed him southward, some triple handful was riding at full speed up the valley, taking with them any stragglers they found from the gatherers who had been there.

Most of his people had disappeared into the brush, and he knew that the women, the very old, and the small children would disappear into the rough country along the valley, surviving on what they could hunt or trap or dig from the ground until it was safe to come out again. He did not need to worry about them.

From his high lookout, he counted the line of Shoshonni that was dispersing to search through the valley for horses and women. A tight group of warriors—two hands of them, he thought—was gathered about a large man riding a black and white horse. He was gesturing, and Wears-Many-Feathers knew he was proposing a plan of attack against him, fully visible as he was on his stub of rock.

But the Absaroka had lived in the mountains about this valley for generations, and he knew its secrets. There had been other intrusions by Blackfoot and Shoshonni and Kiowa, and always he and his fathers had used the land itself as an ally.

Now he held his arm outstretched, palm down, and the dozen warriors who had followed him and now waited behind the butte moved into a long ravine that cut into the grassland, its edges screened by bushes. They could dart from that covert and bring down raiders, when the time came.

Wears-Many-Feathers slipped down the back of his elevated stone perch and mounted the paint again. The smoke that had told his people to hide still rose in an unbroken column, and he knew it was bringing enemies to his side.

But he did not ride out into the open. Instead, he joined Panther Stalker, Coyote-Tail, Leaps-Like-A-Rabbit, and Badger in the small canyon behind the stony height.

They urged their horses around it, through a cut so narrow that it seemed impossible for a horse to negotiate it, and pushed into a thick growth of alder whose roots grew in a hidden channel. Once beyond that, he found himself in a familiar place where slabs and arches of stone overhung the runnel.

The chief reached high and caught a rocky ledge that loomed over his head. With one smooth motion, he pulled himself up to lie flat on the stone.

His companions rode forward, and one by one he knew that they would find similar spots from which to ambush anyone following them along the difficult route. The horses would go on until stopped by the sheer rock face where the stream fell down from above, and in going they would leave a clear trail in the dust and debris of their path.

His breathing steady and slow, his gaze fixed on the narrow span of path below him, Wears-Many-Feathers waited for his prey.

The sounds of hooves scrabbling among stones alerted him at last, and the chieftain tensed, his flint knife ready, his bow strung and bound to his back, along with arrows.

When the first rider passed beneath him he allowed him to go on, for he wanted those who followed to be caught in a trap. Another moved into sight and out again, and another.

His ears noting everything, counting the number of horses, Wears-Many-Feathers knew when the last of the line came into view, and as soon as the rider was beneath him he dropped, silent as a serpent, onto the back of the horse, slipped one muscular arm about the young man's neck, and cut his throat. The horse did not miss a step as his rider was lifted clear and dropped quietly into the cleft.

Now mounted again, the Crow followed his enemies along the channel, whose angles hid each rider from the next for most of its length. He turned one such bend to see Badger drop onto a pony and repeat his own performance with silent dexterity. Now two of them rode at the tail of this line that had begun as ten enemies.

By the time the leaders reached the end of the channel, where the spring that had worn it dropped down from a hole high in the cliff, the odds were only six to four. Wears-Many-Feathers felt certain of the outcome of this skirmish in his new-sprung war.

When the leader, his face-paint denoting a raid, turned to speak to his people, the right number was there, but he was a wise old man and he knew his own. "Ai-i-i-i-i!" he yelled, pointing toward the four at the end of the line.

Instantly his followers turned, weapons ready, but in this cramped space it was impossible to risk arrows because a comrade was as likely to be struck as an enemy. The Absaroka had no such problem for they were behind all the rest, and in ten heartbeats three of the Shoshonni had fallen to their arrows.

Coyote-Tail obeyed a gesture from his chief and moved back into the cleft. His horse gave a strange sound as an arrow took him in the barrel, striking through to his heart, and dropped beneath him, sending the warrior over his head and onto the pebbles of the streambed. That saved his life, for an arrow whipped through the place where his chest had been an instant before.

Wears-Many-Feathers, surprised, turned toward this new threat, but before he could assess it a feathered shaft caught him in the throat and sent the leader of his people down into blackness. His heart was angry and bewildered, for he had not expected this Shoshonni, however old and wise in the way of war, to bring warriors on foot a long way behind his riders. That was the thing that defeated him.

He could hear sounds of fighting, grunts and the grate of flint knives on bones, but he was struggling to breathe through the blood that filled his mouth. A foot came down beside his head, and a pair of fighters grappled and gasped, but he could not tell who won and who lost. He drifted, now, on a tide of blackness, only occasionally coming to enough to know he was still alive.

When he woke to himself, hands were carrying him. A familiar face bent over his and Badger looked into his eyes. Wears-Many-Feathers could not speak. He knew that death was standing beside him, waiting to take him Beyond, but he had to know.

He made the sign for Boy, barely able to move his hand. Badger nodded. "We found him. He is safe. But we have lost this battle and are running into the mountains. There were too many of the Shoshonni."

The effort was almost too much, but the chief signed again. Heart. Heart.

Badger looked puzzled. Then his face cleared and he said, "We will take out your heart and hide it on the high rock. You will watch over our valley until we come again. It will be done."

Then Wears-Many-Feathers smiled through the blood and let his spirit spin free of his flesh. His heart would wait and watch, and his son would ride again in this valley. It was a good day to die.

I was reared with guns in the house and was taught to shoot as soon as I was physically large enough to hold one up. I used to be a good shot, when I could see better. I also love unusual western stories....

THE PISTOLEER

Even the gamblers tipped their hats when Marcus Gilliam ambled past, leaning only lightly on his cane, although his back was now held straight with noticeable difficulty. He didn't glance aside at them, and not one expected him to, but that did not disturb anyone. It was enough to have a living myth as a part of Cooper's Grove.

As usual, he took his place in the hickory-splint chair in front of Mrs. Barnwell's Boarding House and leaned it back against the weathered wall. The spring sun lit his worn Prince Albert coat to dusty gold and purple-black as he closed his eyes and dozed, as old men will often do.

Clive, watching carefully from the window of his room at the boarding house, had taken careful note of the gunfighter's schedule. Every day for the past four, Gilliam had left the boarding house, crossed the street, and walked slowly and carefully past the hardware, the millinery, and the feed store to the café that was patronized by all the old-timers in Cooper's Grove. And he always returned to sit in that chair.

Clive had never seen anyone presume to approach him, once he was in his place, and often he would remain there until noon took him again to the café. Still, the young man went cautiously.

Killing the greatest gunfighter of his generation, even if he was in his late sixties, was not going to be easy, he knew. It would make his reputation, there was no doubt of that: the old man still wore his gun, and that made him fair game.

Who was going to count backward and find that Clive had killed him when he was old? People weren't like that, he had found as he made his painful way through the world.

This was Friday. On Saturday mornings the street teemed with wagons of farmers coming to town for their weekly supplies. Ranch-hands came to get polluted and patronize Miss Sally's Entertainment Center, across from the sheriff's office.

There would be a big crowd to see him make his mark, and that was what Clive Keller wanted more than anything else. Once he was known as Killer Clive, he would have the respect that had so far eluded his pursuit. He need only wait another night, and then his name would become a household word, like those of the Clantons and the Earps.

He closed the blind and lay on the bedspread, after taking off his boots. No matter how he tried, he couldn't kick the habit, for his mother had drilled that into him with a switch when he was too young to resist.

He envied his occasional comrades, with their tales of tearing up a whore's bed with their spurs as they bucked and snorted. He'd never been able to do that.

Now he grinned at the fly-specked ceiling. He'd be Killer Clive the Bootless Bastard, that's what he'd be. Ned Wilkerson and his bunch of ham-handed, would-be bank robbers would beg to get into his gang.

When he woke, it was dark, but he had dreamed satisfyingly of his future career as a desperado whose name spread terror among gunmen old and young. A quick trip to the dining room and its plentiful supply of food did little to wake him from his fantasy.

Only when he stood in front of the peeling veneer of the bureau taking off his shirt, did he thump back to reality. In the spotted mirror, the round face, marked harshly with the pits of acne, the washed-out blue eyes, the tangle of nondescript hair, did not jibe with his visions of himself in that rosy future to be bought with the death of Marcus Gilliam.

Skinning down to his long-johns, he got into bed again. Dreams were far preferable to his waking life. But tomorrow things would be different. He would become Killer Clive....

He woke very early, with dawn just touching the sky outside his dusty window. But he had slept too much and could not lie still any longer. He had to be up and doing.

Dressed in his shabby best, he tiptoed down the hall, his spurs tinkling faintly, and paused outside the door assigned to Gilliam. No snore, no sound of any sort came from the room beyond it, but he thought with pleasure that tonight the famous man would sleep in Ike Carter's Undertaking Parlor.

The boarding house was quiet, though there was a hint of motion from the back where the cook was building the fire on which he would prepare breakfast for the tenants. Clive made no sound as he crossed the parlor, for he had removed his spurs and put them into his pocket.

He wanted to ride out onto the rolling country, letting the constant wind and the sand-blasting grit convince him that his day had come at last. That, however, was impossible, for his horse had died the week before, leaving him afoot.

He walked the dusty street, listening to the quiet whine of the wind around the inaccurate angles of the buildings. He passed the edge of town and turned, staring back at the huddle of low buildings, still dark against the pale dawn sky.

His heart was thudding wildly as he went back toward the boarding house. Today was his day!

* * * * * * *

Clive was careful not to be noticeable as he waited for the morning routine to be acted out. Gilliam drank coffee at the café with two men as old as he. They said little, but every word they exchanged seemed loaded with hidden meanings, for Clive, drinking coffee at a table in the corner, would see them chuckle or frown together.

Some code common to their mutual past communicated much in a single word. He had never known that kind of closeness with anyone, and Clive envied that effortless comradeship. From today forward, he would build up a group who would interact with him just as these three oldsters did. That was a part of the brilliant future he wanted so badly.

When Gilliam rose, pushing back his chair, the others rose too, taking their places on either side and escorting him to the door. They remained there, watching him as he went away toward his usual morning perch, and Clive watched them, wondering why they took the trouble. He was no older than they, no more feeble.

Giving the gunfighter time to take his place, Clive paid for his coffee with one of his few remaining coins and ambled toward the boarding house. When he was directly in front of the spot where the old man was already dozing in the morning sun, he stopped, dead in the center of the street.

"Gilliam!" he called, his voice, for once, not cracking. It held all the authority and the challenge that he had dreamed it might, when the time came.

The front legs of the chair thudded to the floor, and the old man was on his feet. Staring into his face, Clive saw with horror that his eyes, shaded before by the brim of his wide hat, were milky and blind. But his hand went snaking for his gun with speed that left Clive stunned.

Before Killer Clive could raise his own revolver, the slug from Gilliam's caught him above the eye, glancing off the bone and sending him into darkness.

* * * * * * *

He woke to more darkness, though it seemed to swirl with bright patterns, at times, as if someone shot off fireworks behind his eyelids. A voice beside his bed said, "He is awake."

Then a hand touched his chest, moved up to feel lightly the contours of his face.

"Just a damn kid!" That was Gilliam's voice. "Doc, I didn't know. I just shot at the sound—I know when somebody's about to shoot me, if nothing much else. I couldn't see who it was. He sounded a lot older and tougher."

"Oh, he intended to kill you, Marcus. No doubt about that. He's been around for a week now, though nobody knew what he was up to. Probably thought to make his reputation by killing you. If you'd only let us make it known that you're blind, it might stop such things from happening."

"No. I'll not have every penny-ante gunslinger in the country knowing that I'm helpless, Doc." There was a pause. "How many is this?"

"Well, this is the first that you've just blinded. The rest are planted on Boot Hill. But this makes seven, far as I can recall."

Again the hand touched Clive's face. "Son, I'm sorry. Doc says you may be blind, but I intend to make it right with you. No matter that you wanted to kill me—that's the way I made my own reputation. I killed Otto Schoendienst back when I was not much older than you. Nobody ever heard of him, nowadays, but he was *the* gunfighter when I was young."

There came a heavy sigh. "I'll pay your rent, along with mine. I'll put you right there on the porch beside me, and we can talk about things, when we're in the mood. I'll teach you how to get about, when you can't see. And if, one day, you heal and get back your sight, I'll be as glad as you will."

"Why?" Clive struggled to believe that he would be blind, like the man beside his bed, but such things didn't happen to young men—not to him! He strained to see, opening his eyes as wide as the lids would stretch, but no trace of light came through.

He felt of the bandage about his head. Pain shot through his skull, and he snatched his hands away. "Why would you take care of me?"

Nobody ever had, in all his life, since his mother died. Why would a man he had wanted to kill take on such a burden?

"An old man needs company. You're young. You haven't heard all my tales, though everybody else in town is sick of them. I can help you, and you can listen to me. Seems a fair exchange to me," said Marcus Gilliam.

* * * * * * *

Clive sat in his chair, leaned back against the wall of the boarding house. The sun was now hot against him, for spring had given way to summer.

He had gained weight, for his benefactor was, in a small way, very well-to-do. His room was comfortable, though he could no longer look from its window or into its looking-glass. He had a companion who cared for him, talked with him, took him everywhere, just about, that he went.

The town had accepted him without reservation, knowing that he would never threaten their Legend again. He even had a couple of friends his own age who envied him his association with the great Marcus Gilliam.

Beside him, the interminable voice droned on and on. "And old Otto turned, quicker than a cat, and saw me coming. He slowed a little, and I slowed a little, and for a minute we just stared at each other, eye to eye. Then he went for his gun, and I went for mine. Turned out he had slowed just enough to let me beat him to it.

"And that's how I got to be the greatest gunfighter in the West."

Forty times, if once, he had heard that tale. He'd hear it a thousand times more, if the old coot lived that long.

Mother had told him that everything has a price. That he'd pay, one way or another, for everything he ever got in all his life. Clive Keller sighed. He had something of what he had wanted, though not in the way he intended.

But he was going to pay a hell of a price.

At heart, I think I may have a touch of the outlaw....

POWDER RIVER HIDEOUT

Angus Tallfeather chased me out of Julesburg, Colorado, threatening to nail up my scalp on his front porch. It's no sin to beat a man in a horse trade; he had no call to get so angry about it, but Tallfeather, for all his Indian ancestry, had the temper of his Scottish mother.

I didn't really think he'd scalp me—he's civilized, after all, even if his grandfather was a Minneconjou Sioux. Still, I value my scalp as much as anybody, and I rode out in a hurry, making for Deadwood, where I have kin who will lie, cheat, or kill for family— even me.

I rode up into the Black Hills at last, taking care not to leave any sign Tallfeather might follow. I went so far as to remove my mare's shoes, so her tracks would look just like those of the unshod mounts of the Lakota bands that ranged there. Tallfeather's mare, Maud, snorted and grumbled, but she carried me up and down those steep hills, following the courses of streams that made wrinkles between heights, until she stepped into a stump-hole and broke her leg. Sometimes I think I have the worst luck of anybody.

I had to leave my saddle, of course, though I hid it in a rocky notch behind an upthrust of boulders. At that point, I knew I'd better leave the easy course I had followed and take to the high ground. They'd driven a road around the toes of the steeps into Deadwood, though in the beginning they'd winched down the cliffs all the materials and equipment needed for working the gold mines.

Luckily, I'd hunted and trapped that country before it got so damn civilized, so I knew a route to take that would avoid any possibility of my being noticed. Not everybody is willing to lie to protect Will Henley, though I've done my share of favors for a lot of people. Cheating on horse deals isn't the only thing I do. No, I'd best make it to Deadwood afoot and without being seen.

It took days, sweating my way up heights that would boggle a bighorn sheep and down their other sides. I slithered like a lizard down a sheer cliff into Deadwood on a Tuesday night, knowing that would be a quiet time in town. Of course, this wasn't one of the steeps over the middle of town, what there was of it, but the height above a knee of rock on which my cousin Lee had built his cabin. I damn near wore my fingers and toes down to the bone too, doing it by moonlight.

It wasn't easy. Those cliffs are sheer, and if I hadn't clambered all over them when I was younger, I might've broke my neck. As it was, I tumbled down the last couple of yards, banged my elbows on Lee's rear wall, and heaved a sigh of relief.

When I rapped three, two, three on his back shutter, I heard someone move quickly to the peephole. "Who's that?" came the question, though Lee should have known. That had been our signal when we were boys together back in Kansas.

"It's Will, you idiot! Open the door, when I get around to that side. I need to borrow a horse and get out before anybody's around."

"Figures!" he grunted. "Got a sorrel gelding you can borrow. If you stay alive, you bring him back, you hear?" I could hear his woman fussing as he shuffled toward the front door. She, I realized, might not lie, cheat, or steal to promote my welfare.

Lee might be grumpy and disapproving, but within an hour he had me supplied with a gelding, Mose, his second best saddle, more ammunition for my rifle, and enough food to take me a long way. He also provided a water skin that turned out to be more important than anything else.

I led the horse quietly along the zigzag path from his cabin to the rough track below. Then I followed the winding track until we were well out of the range of the nearest cabin. It was slow going, up and down wooded heights, until we were clear of the hills, but once out on the prairie I rode fast, resting Mose only when he began to wheeze.

It might seem strange, but I worked my way out of the Black Hills as fast as possible, leaving behind the relatively plentiful water supply there. Tallfeather wouldn't expect anybody to head out into the dry lands, particularly if he found the remainders of Maud and thought I was afoot. But I'd been up and down the country, back and forth through high and low, wet and dry, and I understood just what I was doing.

I was headed toward the Powder River country. There's a maze of dry washes, arroyos, and canyons there that could hide ten armies, if you could supply them with food. You can ride for weeks without coming to the end of the place. With the river looping crazily back and forth, I knew I would never be far beyond the reach of water, and at this time in the summer there was always game: pronghorn or even jackrabbit, if you were willing to risk a shot.

Now you may wonder why I was going to so much trouble to escape from a pretty far-fetched threat by Angus Tallfeather, and well you might. It wasn't just that, of course. I'd used that as my excuse to Lee, but actually I'd also sold the army a batch of stolen horses that they were certain to identify. Some Cheyenne friends of mine had liberated them while they were being driven for branding and training to another army post in Wyoming.

If Angus wasn't after me, Sergeant Butler was, as sure as death and taxes. I'd rather see my scalp decorating Angus's porch than my tail at the mercy of the sergeant. So I used every trick I ever learned from Crow and Kiowa, Arapaho and Sioux and Blackfoot.

I took Mose down into a dry wash—not the first or the third, but one with a nice hard path worn by buffalo and antelope, so as to show no track of a horse. We followed it until it ran into a deep arroyo, and we went along that into a canyon lined with every kind of rock God ever decided to make.

Every now and again I'd shoot a grouse or something and build a tiny fire back in some nook in the wall of whatever canyon I followed at the time. There was grass, it being early summer, and Mose managed pretty well, though he got a bit thirsty between visits to the river. Even a full water skin won't supply a man and a horse for very long, if you let the horse drink his fill.

From time to time I'd climb up whatever high spot was nearby and reconnoiter, lying on my belly and surveying the land. A good thing, too, for about a week after I went to earth I saw a column of dust way out among the swells and ridges.

It was not Indians—the dust lay in a neat line, rising from a disciplined column of riders and blown away east on the wind. I could tell the difference between that and sign of a band of Indians with my eyes closed. So I'd been right, and it was Butler, come to take his pound of flesh. I had known better than to make that deal, and Broken Hand had told me it would probably get me hung, but I'd wanted to skin the Army for years. Stiff-necked bastards! It was a cavalry lieutenant who begot me on my mother, and she said he never so much as said thank you for the favor.

Her kin should have done something about it—but maybe that's why Lee and Uncle Jebediah and his brothers always came up to taw for me. They must have felt guilty, now that I think about it.

Anyway, now I'd skinned the Army and it looked like the Army was all set to skin me in turn. I might have asked for it, but I didn't intend to take it, if there was any way to help it. So I watched until I was sure the column was just quartering the territory, looking for tracks, and then I dropped back down into my canyon and led Mose away toward the river for a long drink. If we had to hide for very long, he'd need it. That Butler and the scouts had noses like timber wolves.

* * * * * * *

The Powder River is lined along much of its course with cottonwoods, which makes very good cover for somebody who wants to stay hidden. They also make good cover for a wounded man, which is what I found on about my third trip after water. He was unconscious, which was why he groaned. Otherwise there wouldn't have been a whimper out of him. I knew that, for I knew the man.

Corporal Treen was just about the only soldier I ever had any use for. He'd been a drinking buddy of mine, and I don't drink with just anybody. What he was doing here I couldn't imagine, even if he'd been with the column I had seen earlier. He might have been sent to scout out this direction; no way to know, but there was no mistaking the arrow wounds, though he'd broken off the shafts and I couldn't see the feathers to identify what tribe he'd run afoul of.

And now I was in a pickle sure enough. I had no way to treat him, except for cleaning the wounds with some of my water and dribbling as much into his slack lips as I could without choking him. He had a lot of fever and was talking some wild stuff that made no sense. He needed an army doctor who understood what to do, or he needed Broken Hand's healer woman who would dose him with herbs and make him more comfortable, though he still might die.

But Broken Hand's summer hunting camp was a long way from the Powder River country, and Colonel Forrester's troop was someplace near at hand, though how that that bastard Butler figured out where I was going was one for the books, unless, some way, Lee's wife let the cat out of the bag. I had covered my trail mighty well, and I was sure Lee would never betray me.

I lifted Treen onto Mose and led the horse away into the tangle of canyons until I found a spot with a big cottonwood tree for shade. There I stretched Treen out and loosened all his buttons, getting him as easy as I could. I even spared some water to wash his face, which seemed to cool him off a bit.

Then I moved up the canyon to a spot where an upthrust of rock promised to give me a good view of the surrounding countryside. Sure enough, there was a line of dust over to the southwest.

If I knew Butler, he was still hunting high and low, and he'd never let Lieutenant Dodds stop until they got me. I'd seen him make young officers think Butler's plans were their own, over the years.

Talk about being between a rock and a hard place! If I sent up a smoke to call the troop in, I needed to be a long way distant before they could get here. But Treen seemed to improve a bit, as I kept dribbling water into him and bathing his wounds. If I quit doing that, I was afraid he might go downhill fast.

I slithered down the rocky bluff to the canyon where Treen was sheltered. Two rattlers buzzed irritably as I passed their dens, and a bunch of lizards took off in high dudgeon. I felt as nasty as they did, I thought. I stood to lose a friend or my freedom—and the friend might die, whatever I did.

Still, there was no way I'd run off and leave Treen alone. He'd come to a couple of times, not much, just enough to swallow a gulp of water and to stare up at me as if I were his Mama. If he waked alone—I didn't want to think about his brown eyes staring about, trying to find a friendly face and failing.

I moved cautiously down the canyon, around a couple of elbow bends, and slipped beneath the low branches of the bushes by the cottonwood that shaded him from the sun. Treen's eyes were open, and this time he recognized me.

"Will?" he croaked. "Where'd you...."—He coughed—"...come from?"

"Don't you talk, Jimmy. You're hurt bad, but there's a patrol pretty close by. I'm going to build a signal fire and call 'em in."

He tried to shake his head, but he groaned instead. "Will, I was out looking for you. Butler's got blood in his eye this time. You made him look like a fool, and because of that last deal the Colonel looked closely into other horse trades he'd made. Found he'd been taking kickbacks from horse dealers and reprimanded him. If he wasn't so valuable to the regiment, they'd have busted him to corporal."

I almost laughed aloud. That was better than I'd hoped, but it meant that once I was in Butler's hands I'd never live to face an inquiry. I wasn't in the military; he'd have to follow protocol with one of their own, but a shifty civilian horse trader and sometime volunteer scout was another story. He could shoot me and get away with it.

Yet Jimmy Treen was awake and aware, and I was damned if I'd run off and leave him to die. Without answering him, I began pushing together a pile of dead cottonwood branches. In ten minutes, I had a smolder going in the dead wood. Then I broke off some green branches and poked them into the blaze. The smoke darkened, rising out of the canyon in a thick column.

Then I sat down on a melon-shaped rock beside Jimmy Treen and grinned at him. "I don't have so many friends that I can spare any," I told him. "We'll handle Butler some way, when the time comes."

He grunted, and his eyes closed again. Then time passed very slowly. It was almost dark when I heard the click of a hoof on rock.

They were coming, and Jimmy was asleep. Now was the time to get away, if I was going to. I set the water bag beside his hand and moved away down the canyon to the notch where Mose was munching dry grass. I led him away up the maze of arroyos, keeping to stony ground and erasing any track left in a patch of dust.

We traveled long after dark, for there was half a moon to give some light. Only when we were miles away, the trail so confused that I couldn't have found my way back myself, did I stop. Mose gave a long sigh and went to sleep standing beside me. I dropped onto the ground and was asleep at once.

The next day I hightailed it out of there heading west. Not until I got well into the Bitterroots did I stop looking back, and that was weeks later. Ran into an old friend, Jeff Milner, near Missoula, and we decided to do a last bit of trapping for old times' sake. We pooled our money, bought supplies, and went up into the high country.

We had very little luck, except for little stuff. The beaver were trapped out, pure and simple. Still, there was plenty of game for eating, more water than anybody could ever use, and a stout cabin, after a while, to keep the winters off our hides.

Jeff finally gave up and decided to go down and find him a woman. "A man gets cold in winter, when he gets older," he told me. "If I can't find a white woman, I'll see if I can talk a Nez Perce lady into hitching up with me. I can't take this batching no more, Will. You stay if you want, but I'm ready for some civilized livin'."

I'd told him about my little problem with the Army, so he didn't take it hard that I stayed behind. We said goodbye and he led his mule down the mountain, and I thought that was the last I'd see of him.

I was wrong. The next spring there come a whistle that had been our signal through the four years we trapped together. I was pretty damn glad to hear it, because talkin' to nobody but Mose, pine squirrels, and jaybirds was getting to be mighty lonesome.

When he came into sight, he waved both arms so hard he mighty near spooked his mule back down the trail. "Will!" he yelled. "Will, you old son-of-a-gun, you're a damn hero, would you believe it?"

I poked a finger in one ear and gave it a twist. I'd never thought I was getting deaf before, but I knew I couldn't have heard what I heard.

Then he was there, lifting me in that bear hug of his that made me feel like a boy beside his seven-foot bulk. "You little bastard, the Army's been lookin' for you for a long time. Wants to give you some sort of award for saving the life of that boy Treen."

"Jeff," I said, "I've been alone so long I keep having dreams that seem real at the time. You give me a poke to make sure I'm awake. Then maybe I'll believe you."

But it was true. Treen had lived, and once they had him back at the fort he told Colonel Forrester all about the way I took care of him and stayed right up to the end, risking getting caught to make sure he was found safe. Sergeant Butler had blustered, but they'd found more bits and pieces of his thieving ways by then; even the army couldn't stomach him any more, and they paid no mind to what he said.

They had a letter of commendation signed by the commanding general. Forrester had added a cash reward out of his own pocket (or that of his rich wife, actually) that had been waiting for me while I cooled my heels up on the mountain.

One thing about Will Henley. Seems as if when I fall into a privy, I come out holding a gold piece. Though this time I handed that reward to my cousin Lee, whose wife had took off with one of Butler's men when they came to Deadwood looking for me.

It's a strange old world, but seems as if things even out, in the end. Now I can live among people, though I chose the remnant of my old friend Broken Hand's band. Got me a wife too. Seems my luck has changed.

Here's another mean one—never think that because I am a little old lady there is anything sweet about me.

TRAPLINE

Herzog tore a strip of jerky off the wolf haunch hanging behind the door and chewed it savagely. No chance to run the traps today. None yesterday, either, for the blizzards had come, trapping him in the cabin, when his season should have been in full swing.

Even before the snow had piled deep, the catch had been scanty, sometimes nonexistent. He had seen few tracks, as he made his rounds between snowstorms, and those had not been of the animals whose fur sold best.

There should be something moving soon, if the weather cleared, but he hadn't even heard a yowl or a screech, except for the wolves, for days. He needed wolverine, fox and lynx, mink and ermine to trade for cash and whiskey, when next he left the mountains.

And, dammit, a man oughtn't to have to eat wolf meat anyway. He hated the critters, alive or dead, and particularly he hated them jerked. He hankered for deer or bear or at least a good tender rabbit. The traps weren't catching anything, and his sporadic hunts, when the snow lifted, had netted nothing.

Now he lifted his head and listened to the wind. There came a long howl down the gale, and he shivered. He and the wolves had been competing for the scarce supply of animals, as this strange year went forward.

Instead of being able to make his three-day circle, checking his traps, he had been trapped here, this time, for a week. The jerky was the last of his meat, and meal and coffee and beans would not give a man enough energy to survive in this bitter cold. If the blizzard didn't die down soon, he would be too weak to run the trap line.

He rolled another big chunk of wood onto the fire and settled onto the bearskin that served as his bed. Tomorrow, surely, the wind would die down, allowing him to run the trap line!

* * * * * *

When the shutters were outlined with pale light, he rose and poked up the coals, building a new fire from the remains of the old. He wanted to check the morning, but his routine, when cabin-bound, was inflexible. Only when he had drained the iron coffeepot and eaten his can of beans would he open the door to see what this new day had brought.

When the door swung inward, letting in a mound of new snow, the sparkle of sunlight on the burdened branches of the firs almost blinded him. He began to grin. Today, he would start off on the run. Tonight, at his first campsite, he would eat meat. He only hoped that he would also have wolverine pelts, for the miners in the lower ranges wanted those in particular.

His snowshoes schuffed over the soft snow, leaving deep prints behind him. The shadows pooled blue on the warm-lit drifts, and the depths of the forest were purple and blue-green, concealing his usual track beneath its carpet of white. But he knew that trap line the way his mother knew her kitchen. He went unerringly to his first trap.

It held, praise be, a fat porcupine, which would roast well and whose quills would be trade-goods, when he met with any of the Utes who sometimes traveled this way. He wrapped it well in burlap and stuffed it into his game-bag.

The next trap had held a fox, but only a stiff paw still remained between the steel jaws. Damn! Then he ran out of luck entirely. By the time he hit his campsite, he had found nothing but empty traps. But at least he had food. That would help him along his way.

* * * * * *

The fat sputtered into the fire, as he turned the spit on which he had skewered the porcupine. He heard the snuffle and snarl of wolves beyond the circle of firelight. They hesitated, no matter how hungry they might be, to come near the blaze, but he knew that if he slept long enough to allow the flames to die down, he would wake in the belly of one of the big gray beasts. Often, he thought that they had begun to trail him as he went about his rounds. Sometimes they came up to the cabin and marked it as if it were wolf territory. He was game for their eating, he sometimes thought, which was only fair. He had eaten more than his share of their kind!

Full of hot porcupine, he rolled into his blanket, propped against a fir tree in such a way that if he sagged, he would fall over and wake. He dozed, rousing only when he needed to replenish the fire. The wolves gave up in the wee hours and went to hunt easier game, but he did not sleep fully, and when the sky lightened he was up, stirring the fire, heating the now frozen meat, opening a can of beans.

Still there were no wolverines in the traps. Damn! A silver fox, a small lynx, and a polecat were his morning's catch. His bait was not right, he decided, and he tried resetting the traps with meat from the fox, even though he knew that had failed before.

He should have been burdened with the weight of the pelts in his pack by now, but he plodded into Camp Two with a very light pack. One more day, and he would be back at the cabin, his work gone for nothing. He could only hope that something with a valuable fur had stumbled into one of his waiting traps on this last leg of the run.

The tally began badly—one wolverine paw. But his next trap had been sprung and carried away into the brush. Had he caught a bear? His equipment was usually too light to hold one of the big beasts, but perhaps he had caught a young one or a small female. He moved along the furrowed snow-track until it disappeared into a frozen runnel filled with light snow.

He hung his pack on a branch, removed his snowshoes, and plunged down into the shifting layers. The catch had been buried, probably in the storm of the day before, for the track was only half filled behind it. He smoothed away the snow and stared into the blind eyes of the Frenchman from the other side of the mountain. This was the bastard who liked wolves! He'd had the nerve to jump Herzog for killing the beasts and letting them rot in their hides.

What in hell was he doing over here? In a blizzard? Getting into Herzog's trap? The man felt a hot surge of fury, as he dragged the stiff body up the embankment and stretched it on the snow.

The other trapper had not been driven into the storm by starvation—he was still well fleshed. His buffalo-fur robe was new, and his double moccasins were little worn. Why had he risked everything in that blizzard? Had his cabin burned? Herzog had known men, suddenly without shelter, to freeze in these mountain storms. Probably that was it, but it made no difference. The puzzle was why the wolves hadn't eaten him, as he lay in the snow, helpless for a while and dead for a lot longer.

Now a powerful notion was taking hold of Wilhelm Herzog. If nothing he tried for bait worked, in this strange year, why not try something new, something strange, something that might attract wolf and wolverine alike? Why not use this damned Frenchman? Otherwise he would be wasted.

He skinned off the fur robe, the tanned deer hide shirt and leggings. Those were quilled, and he wondered what had happened to Villeneuve's Ute wife. Had she burned too? Or had he beaten her once too often and found himself driven out of his cabin at knifepoint? Herzog chuckled at the thought. He made it a point to take his Indian women first and kill them afterward. There was no risk that way.

When he had the body naked, blue-chilled on the icy stream bank, he tried his knife on the marble-like flesh. But it was hard as stone. He would have to be thawed before he could be cut properly for trap-bait.

It was not the time or the place to camp, but Herzog forced himself to build a fire, thawing out a circle to the bare needles of the forest floor. There he butchered his new-found animal with care, setting the chunks of meat carefully into his pack and putting the raw skeleton back into its former bed for the wolves to gnaw. That done, he covered the fire and set off again, baiting the empty traps with bits of Frenchman.

He came back to the cabin filled with satisfaction. Something told him that this was the turning point. His luck was about to change; he could feel it in his bones. He turned in that night warmed with more than his ritual slug of whiskey.

The blizzards set in again in the night. But in two days it cleared, and he was able to start out to run his traps.

There was an ermine in the first trap set with Villeneuve. A silver fox was in the second. Wolverines filled three, five, and seven. The rest ranged from rabbits to lynx, and a pair of wolves were still snarling and chewing on their paws in the last two. He dispatched them with his rifle and loaded up his bulging pack of pelts, grinning widely.

He had stashed the rest of the Frenchman in his cold-room at the cabin, and as long as the man lasted, his catch was superb. He had stretchers of hides stacked against the walls, and he knew that his bales of furs would bring him all the supplies, all the whiskey, and all the women he could handle when he went back down the mountain in the spring.

Unfortunately, he ran out of Villeneuve all too soon. He'd been a big man, but there was only so much of him after all. And once he returned to baiting with fox or wolf-meat, the catches dwindled abruptly. Wolverine, in particular, had loved the man-flesh, and he caught no more of the wily creatures.

So his spring selling trip netted him less by far than he had hoped. Yet, as he wandered around the trading post, he watched the other people there with new eyes. They were not men for the bragging with or women for the taking. They were not Indians who might turn into enemies or Frenchmen who were contemptible simply because they were French.

No. They were bait!

He left early, climbing into the summer forests and meadows, where hunting parties and prospectors ranged during the fine weather. He didn't go very far, and when he stopped he hid in the thickest of the woods and watched to see where men went, and how long they stayed.

Many approached the snowline, tapping at the rocks with little hammers or hunting the mountain goats. He considered their habits for some time. Then he set his traps.

By late fall, he had nineteen bodies stashed safely in the snows on the heights, and when winter set in again, he brought them down, one by one, to be butchered for bait.

His fresh crop of furs was incredible, and he went out, late in January, to run his traps with his hopes running high. He already had about as many as he could carry to trade. He could save the rest of the bait, safe up there in the deep snows, for the next year.

He staggered under the weight of his pack, as he came to the spot, no longer the site of a trap, from which he had tracked that providential Frenchman, whose bones, he was sure, had long since been gnawed to splinters by his friends the wolves. He sighed with satisfaction and went on, killing living catch and skinning out everything, until he came again to his cabin. When he shoved his show shoes off on the porch and stepped to the door, he paused, listening. Something was inside. A bear, wakened unseasonably from his winter sleep? A wolverine, seeking shelter?

He slipped off his pack and pulled his rifle from its wrappings, working the action to make sure it was not too cold to move. Then he shoved the door open with his foot and stepped inside.

Something was there. He could feel it. He could see a vague movement in the darkness, as something came toward him.

He fired convulsively, but the rifle ball did not slow the approach of Villeneuve, the Frenchman. He was a rack of bones, with strips of flesh hanging like fringe, dried now, and useless. The bones were pale now, and hard. His grin was broad and humorless, the long teeth wolf-like in the dimness.

CRAZY QUILT, BY ARDATH MAYHAR * 221

Behind him came the partially stripped body of the Cree who had been brought down from the heights most recently. Other shapes moved there as well, and he didn't want to see what they might be, though he caught the click of toenails on the rough wood of the floor. The wolves he had eaten—where they there too?

Herzog stepped backward, dropping the empty rifle. His hands went up to cover his eyes. He could not believe that this was happening. Dead men did not rise up and walk!

Something fastened into his calf from behind, and he went down on his back on the porch, landing hard. As he gasped for breath, he moved his arm to see what new enemy threatened him.

The muzzle of a skeletal wolf, grinning as broadly as the Frenchman had done, loomed over his face. Hot saliva dripped from the lolling tongue onto his cheek.

"No!" There was no breath to propel the word. It came out as a gasp, but it brought a reply.

"Yesss...," came the hissing reply between those alarming teeth in Villeneuve's skull.

And then both sets of fangs descended upon his cringing body. And Herzog knew at last what it was to fear and to suffer and to die.

I love stories of the frontier—especially those with a twist!

A COLD WAY HOME

The norther gusted through the big pines, carrying with it a spatter of sleet. A strand of auburn hair flapped against Callie's cheek, and she tucked it under her head scarf with an icy finger. Behind her, in the wagon, she could hear Jason's small feet thunk-thunking against the pine box on which he sat.

She turned to look back at the small, cold figure. "Don't do that, son. It's not respectful to Papa."

The boy's cheeks were mottled with cold, his eyes full of tears. Some probably were from the chill, but she suspected the others might be for his father beneath him in the rude coffin. She reached back one-handed, tucked the red scarf more tightly about his neck, and checked the buttons of his outgrown coat.

"Is it very far, Mama?" he asked, his thin piping almost inaudible in the roar of the wind among the pines.

She turned back to look ahead at the flanks of the shivering horse, head-down against the cold, the sky still barely touched with a scarlet sunset. "Not very long now, son. Grandpa will have a good fire, and Luke will probably have something good fixed to eat. Be patient. We'll get there."

He huddled into his coat, red hands in its skimpy pockets, and said no more. She sighed and fumbled out the lantern and a sulfur match. It was dark now along the tunnel-like road through the forest.

It grew darker, even colder. She was shivering, there on the high seat of the wagon. She hoped that her body and that small barrier of the seat sheltered Jason a bit from the blast out of the northwest. The horse was grunting with each step. The light wagon and its small burden couldn't work him that hard; she suspected that he too was suffering from the chill.

The sky went entirely dark. Only their tiny circle of lantern light bobbed through a world of rushing blackness. She was wishing so desperately to see the lights of home that when they did twinkle into view she half doubted her vision. But it was.... They rounded a bend, and the square of a window glowed steadily with warm lamp-light.

She stood and shouted into the wind, "Papa! Luke! Papa!"

She sat to flick the horse with the end of a rein. Her voice, she knew, had been carried away by the wind. How could her father and his old servant have heard her amid the uproar of the night?

Now only a scant half mile separated her from her home. She shouted again, her throat raw with chill and stress. And this time something changed at the house ahead. After a short while, a lantern bobbed into view on the back porch. She gave a sound that was as much a sob as a laugh.

"We're home, Jason! We're home!"

The boy made no sound. She could hear his teeth chattering like castanets behind her. She whipped up the horse, and the beast, no less ready than she for shelter, stepped out at a trot, the wagon banging and jouncing behind him.

Waiting in the small yard behind the house was an ancient black man holding high his light. "Miss Callie?" His voice was quavery.

He caught the horse's head as she pulled to a halt. The old man was staring into the dimness of the wagon. He nodded when he saw the child, but he was looking for someone else. "Where Marse Will?" he asked.

A tall old man had come onto the porch, wrapped in a blanket and scarf. She jumped down from the wagon and reached for the child. Then she answered the servant.

"He's in the wagon. In the box. He'll keep. Thank God it turned cold. We'll tend to him tomorrow, Luke."

The old man had staggered down the steps to meet her. "Callie, girl! Come in...come in. We've got a good fire. Luke can fix some ham and biscuits real fast. Here, bring the boy inside out of the cold. You both look frozen."

She carried her son in and set him down before the huge fire-place, where hickory logs crackled, emitting fragrant smoke. She peeled away the layers of coat and scarf and sweater as the child shivered under her hands.

Her father was staring at her. "Callie—what has happened? Where's Will? Why are you home...alone?"

She glanced up, her amber eyes crackling a command. "Not now. Later, when Jason is asleep."

The old man sank painfully into a rocking hair and kept looking from his daughter to his grandson. His puzzled eyes followed every move, but when Luke had the food warmed on the iron cook stove, he knew it at once.

"Come and eat," he said.

Jason looked up. "Grampa Anderson!" he said with pleased recognition. "I 'member you!"

Callie fed the boy, who was too weary to manage his own meal. He nodded off against her shoulder before he was quite finished, but she lifted him and took him to the trundle bed Luke had pulled from beneath the big four-poster. He didn't stir as she tucked the bright patchwork quilt about him.

Her father waited while she ate her own supper. Then he drew her over to the fire and sat again in his rocker. "What has happened, Callie? And where's Will?"

She sighed, backing up to the flames and lifting her skirt in back to warm her chilled legs. "I loved Will Lightwood, Pa. You know that. I'd have followed him to Hell if he'd asked me to." She laughed harshly. "I never thought he would ask me to, though.

"When he wanted to go down and live on the coast, I hated it. You know that...I love the woods and this farm and everything about home. But I went. I bundled up Jason, and we followed Will to Galveston. Lived in hotels. The only thing down there worth seeing is the Gulf of Mexico, and we saw too much of that."

She drew up a small splint chair and sat facing her father. "Will took to gambling. After he saw everything there was to see, he seemed to change. He got in with people—not the sort of people my son's father should associate with, Pa.

"The Lightwoods have always been respectable people. Not just because they had land and money—because they were good, decent people. But Will took in and lost all the money. Sold the woods his Pa left him and lost that money. He lost and he lost, and it changed him more."

Her father reached to pat her hand. "Surely it wasn't that bad," he said.

"It was worse. It got so he'd come home drunk and hit me. Worse than that, he'd hit Jason! The more money he lost, the meaner he got. That last night...he came in wanting me to sign away this place, Pa. That was left to me by my mother's folks! I wouldn't, and he threatened to rent me out to the drummers at the hotel so he'd have money to gamble with. And he beat me, though I fought him the best I could. So I decided that it couldn't go on.

"I took Grampa Lightwood's pistol out of the drawer, and I shot him dead."

Anderson sat up straight, his face slack with shock. "Callie...but how...is the law...?"

She shook her head. "The people in the hotel heard him, what he threatened to do. The sheriff asked me if he could help me get home, but I'd already bought a horse and wagon and hid it out, knowing that I might have to head home alone."

She unbraided her long auburn hair and began to comb out the curling strands. It crackled in the firelight, clinging to her fingers as the comb moved.

She looked up again at her father. "I wanted Jason to be proud of his papa. Looked as if the only way to do that was if Will was dead. All the land's gone. Only thing left was Grandpa Lightwood's pistol and my own place here."

She smiled then, her face suddenly radiant in the firelight. "But Jason will be proud of his papa. No matter what, Jason will be proud."

My maternal ancestors came to Texas when it was true wilderness. My grandmother would have taken a whip to a cougar in a minute, and the cougar would have been the one to run. The women in my family have never been wimps, and I have no patience with anyone who is one.

NIGHT OF THE COUGAR

She watched Jody as long as she could see the glint of his red shirt through the leaves along the brushy trail. The dim thuds of old Sam's hooves came to her ears for a little while longer. Then they were both gone, and the bird calls in the woods around the cabin didn't seem to interrupt the silence at all.

Julie sighed as she turned toward her garden plot. With little Jody and the baby both napping, her house was quiet too. She had always liked the woodsy spot they'd picked to homestead—East Texas was much like her southern Mississippi birthplace—but when Jody went off to work with the loggers it got mighty lonesome.

Her sunbonnet was hot against her neck, and its curving brim cut off her view of anything around her when she stooped over the rows, her hoe busy among the tender sprouts of cabbage and turnip greens and onions. She didn't really like sunbonnets—never had. It had taken the full weight of her father's authority to make her toe the line and wear one to keep the sun from browning her fair skin.

"'Tain't ladylike!" had been his most devastating indictment of any female. But she had never liked the girls he pointed out as ideals of femininity. It was just as well that Jody had come along and carried her away from Laurel and its cadre of ladylike prototypes.

There was motion—she turned her head to watch a coachwhip snake go slipping along the fence line by the cowshed. No danger there, she knew. But she kept a wary eye on any serpent about the house. Little Jody was at an age when anything new got chased and usually caught. She had no intention of letting him get bit by a copperhead or a moccasin.

The late spring sun was warm on her back. Sweat began sliding down her beneath her wool serge clothing. It was time to get out the summer-weight stuff, to cut Jody out of his winter underwear. She'd shed her own three weeks ago, amid her husband's dire warnings about late cold snaps and pneumonia.

Then the sweat all but congealed on her skin. A long wail cut across the morning woods-noises. A cougar, hunting late maybe. She hated the sound of them, the long lonesome cry like a woman in pain. And once she'd been warned about the beast, she had hated it even more. A critter that craved human babies was something downright evil.

There were tales among the old women she saw occasionally at camp meetings of the church in the summertime; they could tell you tales that would curl your hair and kink your bones. One of those women had lost her own babe some forty years gone, when a cougar had come right into the yard and taken it out of the basket where it was sleeping while she washed. Julie shivered, remembering.

Though she knew better, she put away her hoe and went into the house to check on the children. Little Jody slept in total relaxation, boneless, his small mouth open, his eyes partway open too. Lissa was beginning to squirm in her hickory splint basket the way she always did when she was getting ready to wake up. It was just as well she'd quit in the garden. The baby would be ready to nurse any minute now. And Jody would wake up hungry. He always did.

The infant whimpered. Julie bent over the crib, felt the dampish forehead. Lissa hadn't been feeling too pert for some time now. Likely some spring ailment—she'd make up some herb tea and spoon it down the child. Everybody needed a tonic in the spring, seemed like.

She lifted the plump baby and sat in the small rocker she'd brought from Mississippi in the wagon with the rest of their few bits of furniture and Jody's plow tools.

Unbuttoning her bodice let in a grateful bit of cool air as the baby suckled. Before they were done, Jody began to grunt and thrash, the way he did sometimes. Seemed as if a body needed to be twins, when you had so much to do.

She didn't put the children in the little pen their daddy had built in the front yard, when both were fed. She'd heard that cougar, and she was no fool. She kept them in sight all afternoon, though it meant taking off her ladylike sunbonnet and putting on her husband's old stray hat while she finished up in the garden.

Jody was fine, just playing with pine cones and marking in the dust with sticks and watching Coaly, the fiery black horse, pace 'round and 'round the lot where he was penned. But Lissa wasn't herself. She whimpered a lot, gave little bubbling cries from time to time. Julie began to feel uneasy about her. Something was amiss, and Jody had always been so healthy that she hadn't learned much about baby sickness in dealing with him.

There was a quiver of uneasiness inside her at the thought. With her husband gone and the nearest neighbor twelve miles east, through woods so thick you couldn't see ten feet in any direction, it was scary to contemplate what she'd do if one of the children got really badly sick. She had tackled a lot of hard things since leaving home and her mother. She shook herself, took a deep breath.

Nobody had ever promised it'd be easy, Jody least of all. In fact he'd stressed everything he could think of that might have made her change her mind. He'd wanted her to marry him, no doubt of that, but he'd had no intention of taking her off to something that wasn't what she thought it'd be. She couldn't fault him for the fact that there'd been things that neither of them had been able to guess at.

Like the lack of doctors. There wasn't one nearer than Nicholson, twenty-five miles to the west. It was pure luck that had put them as near as they were to Gramma Dooley, though twelve miles was a long way and took a half day to cover, with the road nothing more than a rough track through the woods. On horseback it was quicker, but if she were forced to make it there on her own she'd have to take the buckboard. You just couldn't manage a baby and a three-year-old on horseback. Particularly when the horse was Coaly.

She finished in the garden and took the children inside. It was mid-afternoon, already hot and steamy, though it was only April. She took the cotton clothing out of the long chest and shook it out, then hung it on the clothes line to air. The heavier woolens they'd worn all winter had already been washed or aired and gone into storage. By the time she finished it was twilight.

When she was fixing Jody's supper, nibbling as she did it, as she usually did for her own meals, she heard a sound from the sleeping room where she'd put Lissa back into her basket. A choking sound.

Her heart thumping in her throat, Julie ran across the dog-run hall and caught up the baby. The child's face was scarlet, and she was struggling for breath. As she lifted her, Lissa began coughing harshly, wheezing for breath between spasms. A dose of honey and vinegar didn't relieve the baby's coughing. The struggles to breathe made the baby try to cry, and that made everything even worse. The herb tea didn't seem to help at all, nor did goose grease rubbed onto her chest. By full dark, Julie knew that she needed help.

She hitched Coaly by lantern light. Crickets were chittering all around in the grass. Frogs of all sizes were chorusing down at the creek. A screech owl's shivering cry punctuated the rest, making her shiver. But she didn't hear the cougar. That was something she was thankful for.

She put blankets in the wagon bed for Little Jody. He was almost asleep when she laid him on them, and by the time she came back with Lissa in her basket, he was sound asleep. The baby was still making those strange barking sounds. She seemed to have a fever too, though Julie was so hot with haste and work that it was hard to tell.

She hung the lantern on the hook let into the pole at the front of the wagon, led Coaly out into the track that went roughly eastward past their front porch, and climbed into the buckboard.

"Hup! Coaly, giddap!" she said, and the horse snorted, tried to dance sideways between the shafts, then reluctantly moved forward. The night air was so much cooler than the afternoon had been that it felt almost cold to her hands. She tugged the spare quilt she'd brought for Jody about her shoulders and smacked the horse's rump with the end of a rein.

The forest was in darkness—deeper than the moonless sky. Leaves shone fitfully as the lantern passed, but the feeble gleam couldn't penetrate far into the dense wood on either side of the track. And the track itself took much of her attention. Coaly's neat hooves could pass easily over ruts and roots that jounced the wagon so hard it endangered its wheels.

Her eyes soon ached with the effort to see ahead, to guide the horse around the worst of the bad spots in the road. She was tired to the bone too, for her day had been work from beginning to end. But she wasn't sleepy, no matter how her eyes protested or her body ached. She heard every effortful breath her baby drew, flinched at every wheeze or coughing spasm.

The night seemed to pass as slowly as the miles. She had no clock, but the stars moved in a narrow ribbon above the cut where the track ran, and she could tell, when she looked, that the constellations were progressing westward. But so slowly!

She figured that she was somewhere about halfway to her destination when she heard the cry again. Like a woman screaming. The cougar! Had the beast been following her all that distance? Silently, creeping behind the slow-paced wagon, drawn by the scent of her child?

Coaly was tired now, though she had stopped twice to let him drink at creeks they'd crossed, and once to let him rest a bit. But she sat straighter and flicked him with the reins. He snorted with irritation, but he picked up his hooves a bit faster.

Julie felt beneath the rough plank-board seat and found the handle of the bullwhip Jody kept for running the stock out of her garden. Coaly had never in his life felt the weight of that four-ply lash—but she knew that the time might well be coming when he would.

Behind them there was another sound—not the scream now, but a rough, coughing growl. As if in answer, the baby went into a fit of coughing that seemed as if it would tear out her tender lungs. She found no relief until Julie reached down, one-handed, and lifted Lissa into her lap. Lying on her stomach, head down, the child gave a last choking wheeze and got a lung full of air.

Having to secure Lissa on her knees added one more burden to Julie's load. Coaly was moving faster, bouncing the wagon over obstacles she hadn't the time to pick out and steer around. Behind her in the wagon bed Jody was whimpering, still half asleep but disturbed by the rough jostling of the wagon.

"Go back to sleep, baby," she said over her shoulder. "We'll be there soon."

The little boy reached up to catch a handful of her shirt that hung over the back of the seat board. "I don't like it, Mama," he said. "Don't like to sleep in the wagon. Don't like goin' in the dark. Less go home. Please?"

"We'll be at Gramma Dooley's in a little while. You like Gramma—remember when we went to the revival and she gave you the horehound candy? She'll likely have some more for you. And sugar cookies. You know how you like her cookies!"

The wagon lurched over part of a stump left in the track, and Jody forgot about cookies and began to howl in earnest. As Julie speared a glance back, she thought she saw something in the track. It was too dark to tell what, and it was a long way back, but there was a deeper darkness there. Moving.

"Jody!" she grated, her voice harsher than he had ever heard it. "Shut your mouth! Lie down and roll up in the blanket! And be still. There's a cougar back there, I'm pretty sure. We've got to move fast, and it's going to be mighty rough. Now you do like I tell you!"

When he had rolled into a dark lump, she reached down and lifted the lantern from its hook. Then, holding the baby against her with both knees, keeping the reins in her left hand, she turned, holding the light high, and looked fully backward.

Two reddish sparks glinted with reflected light. Then they blinked once and were gone. So was the shadow, but she knew that the animal had taken to the trees. It could travel as quickly through the tangle as Coaly could along the roadway. There was no way a horse could outrun a cougar while pulling a buckboard, even if it had a good surface to run on. But she had to try to make Coaly do the impossible.

She put the lantern back in its place. One-handed, jouncing and bumping as she worked, she put the baby into the basket on the seat beside her and tied that securely to the braces holding the seat in place. Then she swung the bull-whip in a long arc overhead and cracked its wicked tip just above the black horse's nervous ears.

"Go, Coaly! Whup!"

Coaly went. Faster than she'd have thought he could, burdened as he was. The wagon seemed to leap into the air as it cleared a big bump, and it hit with a tooth-rattling jar. Jody cried out, and she heard him scrambling for a handhold.

Around blind curves, through masses of foliage that had leaned forward into the track the horse flew, and the wagon bounced along behind as best it could. Julie had her feet hooked into the seat-brace beneath her, reins clenched uselessly in her left hand, while her right steadied the basket and the baby.

When the scream sounded again it was entirely too close. Behind the wagon—but not by much. She risked a glimpse back, and a shadow was flowing along with the wild shapes cast by the swinging lantern. When the wagon-shade bounced and jumped, that other moved smoothly and steadily. Not ten feet from the tailboard!

Julie was thinking faster than ever before. The creature wanted Lissa. That was what all the folktales suggested—unless it wanted Coaly. They liked horsemeat too. But she felt sure it would prefer something tender...and human. What if she could distract it? Throw something out that it could smell baby-scent on?

She took the reins in her teeth and dug into the basket, pulled out a soiled diaper, and flung it over the side of the careening buckboard. Then she cracked the whip again.

But by now Coaly had caught scent of the big cat, and the horse's instinct told him what words could not. The stocky black had leaned his chest into his work and was making his former pace look slow. It was all Julie could do to keep from being flung out into the darkness, and nothing but the basket straps had kept Lissa from being dislodged from her place. Jody was rolling around in the wagon bed, too frightened to whimper.

They flew along the track for a half-mile before Julie pulled Coaly down a bit—enough so that she could risk another look to their rear. The other shadow was gone. She had no illusion that the cat would waste much time on the diaper, once it was sure it was empty.

With the horse under some control, she tore through the woods. And now she was able to see some landmarks that told her she was getting nearer her goal. The immense oak tree that leaned over the track—that was less than three miles from the Dooleys' house. With any luck at all, they just might make it. She cracked the whip again, but not quite so close to Coaly's sensitive ears. He kept moving, but he wasn't bolting now.

"Jody—how are you making it?" she asked.

"M...M...Mama, there was a great big something back there!"

She made her voice matter-of-fact. "Yes. That was the cougar. Remember—I told you before we went so fast."

"Oh. I didn't know they were so big. It was like Aunt Tilly's tomcat, but lots and lots bigger. It was scary, Mama."

"Well, it didn't get us...yet. And it won't, I think. I believe I've figured out the combination, Jody. You just get a good grip on the seat-braces, and you watch for it for me. Its eyes will shine in the light that gets back there from the lantern. You sing out if you see it coming after us again."

"Yes'm." His voice sounded as frightened as Julie felt. The wagon went swaying and jangling and creaking around more bends in the track, and Julie had begun to hope they'd left the beast far behind when Jody's warning came.

"It's there, Mama!" he shouted.

Once more the thing neared the tailboard, its shadow mingling with those of the wagon and its passengers. Again she picked a bit of cloth from the basket and pitched it into the road. And they gained another half-mile or so.

There was the skillet nailed to the ash tree, set there as a marker of the trail by some long-dead explorer of the region. It gleamed rust-red in the lantern light for an instant. Only a mile left to go. And then the wagon hit something with an ominous c-r-a-ack! The right front wheel went, and the bed pitched forward at an angle.

Even as Julie went over the side, she was trying to see behind to see if the cougar was there again. She was up almost before she hit the ground, rescuing the lantern from its hook, unhooking Coaly from the harness.

"Jody! Climb down, son. That's right—come here to me. You're going to ride Coaly, you know that? Do you think you can ride him?"

"But Daddy said he's too uppity for me!"

"Ordinarily, that's true. But this is something out of the ordinary. You're not only going to ride him, you're going to see to Lissa too. See? I'm tying her basket right into here—that's right. Whoa, Coaly. Easy, boy." She settled the two children into her makeshift rig of hamstrings and bits of harness, checked it out for security, then stepped back.

"You head right up the track, Jody. You can see where it is by the stars, and Coaly isn't going out into the brush, and he certainly isn't coming back here where the cat is. I'll be right behind you with the lantern. But you make him RUN, you hear me? Kick him with your heels. Slap him with the reins. Go now!" and she struck the horse sharply with the stock of the whip she had taken from the wreck of the wagon.

As the hoofbeats rattled away up the red dirt track, she turned where she stood and held the lantern high. No eyes parked at her...yet. She backed slowly up the way, watching sharply. Then she turned and ran as hard as she could for a couple of hundred yards. When she turned again there were red points of light there in the road.

Julie's heart thumped high in her throat. Beads of sweat sprang out along her hairline as she watched the tawny shape that she saw clearly now for the first time.

The cat was cautious. An adult human being wasn't its usual prey, and the fire in the lantern filled its eyes disturbingly. But its gut growled with hunger. Julie could see the creature weighing its hunger against the unknown threat she might pose.

Before it could make up its mind, she was upon it, the whip swinging down in a wicked arc, the metal tip cracking viciously as it drew blood that showed bright against its tan coat. The cougar crouched, snarling, its ears flat against its head, its eyes glaring. But Julie was past caution. To buy time for her children, she was prepared to risk everything. She danced to one side and cracked the whip again. Another trickle of blood gleamed against the creature's neck.

The lantern that she had hung on a stub of branch beside the track gave her enough light for maneuvering, and she struck again as the best backed away, keeping its head toward her, its eyes focused on her as the pressing danger it knew it faced.

Then a rain of whip strokes drove the creature backward into the edge of the wood...deeper. And then it was gone, a frustrated cough of anger coming back to Julie's ears as the last twitch of brush marked its passage.

Julie listened hard. The only sounds were tree frogs, a whip-poor-will in the distance, a hoot owl somewhere nearby, and the many small noises of a wood at night. There was no scream to be heard, nor any other sound that might mark the hunt of a big cat.

She turned in her track, the lash of the whip marking the red dust of the road. She took the lantern from the stub.

Now she could hear sounds from the road ahead. Men's voices, calling—but she was suddenly too exhausted to make a sound. The children were safe—that was all that mattered. If they hadn't reached Dooleys', nobody would be calling in the forest in the early morning hours.

Letting the lantern dangle wearily from her hand, dragging the whip, she started up the trail toward the east. The early morning constellations hung above the cut. A mockingbird was tuning up his song in the woods.

Another macabre tale of the Old West....

LIKE MOTHER USED TO MAKE

He rode into town lank as a winter wolf and mean-tempered to boot. When he stalked into the saloon (the inevitable Silver Dollar), he dropped three neat whiskeys into his empty belly and turned to the bartender.

"I been eating my own cooking until I'm ready to quit eating entirely," he growled. "I don't want no restaurant nonsense. I don't want no fly-specked bar goodies. I want real FOOD, like Mama used to make. Is there one single person in this flea-bit town that takes in boarders and feeds 'em as if they was people instead of hogs?"

The man behind the sticky bar gave a half-hearted swipe with a dirty rag and pursed his mouth. "There's Miz Peabody—but her cookin' ain't just the thing. Miz Grueber takes in a roomer, now her man's dead and gone, but she's already got the schoolteacher there. Hmmm." His brow wrinkled painfully, as if it hurt him to think.

Then his eyes cocked up at Mark Shaftoe as if sizing him up. "Course, there's Emmy Whittle. But she's...she's real special. Don't like nobody rowdy or that cusses a lot. Don't take many drifters"— he stared hard at the dust on Shaftoe's shoulders and pants legs.

"She treats her folks like they was kin. She sort of mothers 'em, y'see? Course, she really likes her boarders to like their vittles too. She hates a skinny man. Can't wait to fat him up, when one comes along. If you intend to stay around for a while, you'd be just her cup of tea. She'd have that big old iron stove of hers goin' like a steam engine, gettin' stuff fixed to fill out them bones of yours."

Shaftoe was leaning forward over the bar. "Aim me at her," he said. "I need just that sort of place for a month or two."

As he followed the man's directions, leading Yellowbone, he watched the street closely. Nobody there gave him a second look—

men at loose ends were nothing extra here in Packsaddle Stop, it seemed.

There was no sign on Emmy Whittle's boardinghouse. Evidently she took only those boarders sent to her by word of mouth. That told Shaftoe a lot—she probably had all the business she could manage. And if she was the sort of cook the bartender hinted at—he sighed with anticipation. It would purely hurt him to have to rob and kill her, once he got ready to go on. Still, that was the way he did things, and he didn't break his own rules.

The house was tall and narrow, with a porch that ran all the way around it front to back. A line of rocking chairs sat there, and it was late enough for most of them to be filled.

Shaftoe nodded as he clinked up the steps onto the porch. Banker, the steadier sorts of cowhands, drummers, four old ladies in black dresses and little shoulder shawls, a really obese Chinese in yellow silk, waving a little fan before his perspiring face—a motley bunch. Ripe for the picking, it looked as if.

He smiled politely at the skinny young woman who elbowed the door open as she came out with a tray loaded with cups. He slid past her into the cool dimness of a wide central hall. He could smell something heavenly—roast beef, perhaps. And apple pie with cinnamon. And fresh-baked bread—his mouth began to water.

Someone called from the back—the kitchen, he thought, "Who's there? Come here so's I can see you!"

He stalked down the polished boards of the hall and stood in the door of a big room that was dominated by a cook stove of Herculean proportions. From it came an array of odors that almost made him faint with hunger.

The woman who stood there was large and fair, her body sturdy without being fat. She had wiped her hair back with a floury wrist, for there was a streak of white across her forehead. Her round cheeks were flushed, and her cornflower eyes surveyed him shrewdly.

"New boarder?" she asked, her tone neutral.

"The man from The Silver Dollar advised me to come here. Just in case you might have room for me," he said. He made his eyes shine, as he had trained them to do, and his expression showed nothing but trustworthiness. "He said that you're the best cook this side of the Mississippi." Which was a lie, but couldn't do any harm.

She looked him up and she looked him down. She frowned for a moment as if trying to find a spot in which to put his skinny frame. Then she smiled and held out her floury hand.

"Emmy Whittle," she said. "Welcome to my house. You look as if you could stand a little home cooking. Staying long? I don't like to take in short-timers. Less'n a week, and I can't be bothered."

Mark Shaftoe sighed and grinned. "I intend to stay until you run me off, if I can find me some kind of a job to keep me goin'. At least a month, if I can't. That all right with you?"

Emmy turned back to the oven, which was filling the kitchen with heartbreaking smells of bread and cake and pie. She opened the door, revealing a space in which she could have baked half an ox, and pulled out a rack of pie-pans with an iron hook. Sliding them onto a marble-topped cook table, she closed the door and turned back to Mark.

"Get washed up for dinner. The folks on the porch is havin' coffee right now, but it'll be time to eat pretty soon. First door on the left at the very top of the stairs. Top, mind you—that's the onliest place I've got left, and it's pretty small."

Mark went back to Yellowbone and took down his packs. A small boy was pretending to play marbles in the dust of the road, but he was really watching the newcomer. Mark flipped him a dime.

"Take my horse over to the livery?" he asked. "Tell the man I'm staying here at Miz Whittle's and I'll be over after supper."

The child grabbed the coin and the reins almost at once. He tugged the tired beast across the dusty street and into the dark maw of the stable. Shaftoe watched them go, feeling oddly restful. It had been years since he had found a place where he could put up his feet and really relax, and this one seemed just that sort. A shame—but he shrugged away the thought and went to find his room.

* * * * * * *

Fall came in with gusting winds and a flurry of early snow. Shaftoe rode in from his piddling little handyman job huddled in his heavy jacket. He was feeling smug—this was the first winter in years that he would be warm and well fed. His plan to finish his business in Packsaddle kept getting put off and put off, for he never had been so comfortable in his life.

Not to mention the fact that his belly had moved away from his backbone. While he didn't have a paunch, exactly, he was getting a bit of flesh 'round the middle. Have to watch that—but Emmy's cooking made it mighty hard. He even, once in a while, toyed with the thought of marrying her instead of murdering her. But he shook that away as unworthy of him. He had, after all, his professional standards, and they were strict.

He washed up on the back porch, and Prue, Emmy's handy-girl, had hot water waiting in a can for him. He slicked back his hair and went into the hall, smelling the food that was already being put onto the long table in the dining room.

"Oh, Mr. Shaftoe," fluttered Miss Filligan, the youngest of the old ladies, "You're late tonight. We were worried about you." Her faded eyes brightened as he took her arm gallantly and ushered her into the dining room to join her two sisters and cousin at their usual end of the table.

Wang, the Chinaman, bent his head slightly in greeting. His little fan lay on the table beside his plate, and his pudgy fingers kept playing with the silk cord on its handle as they waited for their hostess to join them. He had grown fatter in the months Shaftoe had lived in the Whittle house. It was a wonder that even the stout mahogany chairs could hold his weight.

The banker and the single drummer entered and sat, and at last Emmy Whittle made her entrance. She always dressed fresh for dinner, and she looked cheery and bright in a dress patterned with scarlet poppies. But she looked sad, and her gaze kept turning toward Wang as she served the plates.

Before they rose from the table, at last, she tapped on her glass with a teaspoon. "My friends," she said in her light soprano, "I have some saddening news. Our friend Mr. Wang will be leaving us this week. We will miss him, but he says that his business here is finished and he must return to San Francisco. I can only hope that he and our Mr. Wingate have prospered, and that he will come again, one day, to stay in our home."

Wang was beaming. His small black eyes shone as he struggled to his feet and bowed as well as a perfectly round figure can manage to do.

"Is great pleasure to say, will return when can," he said. Instead of sitting again, he went out with Wingate to the parlor, leaving Shaftoe to finish his dessert and follow more slowly.

Emmy caught him as he left the dining room. "You are looking so well, Mr. Shaftoe," she said, her tone arch. "I feel that I have been able to improve your health during your stay. Do you think you will continue until Christmas with us? We do have such a jolly time, then, with a feast that will astonish you."

He bent over her hand in a courtly manner he hadn't used in a decade. "My dear lady, I wouldn't miss it for the world!"

He went up to his room and lay on his narrow bed, boots carefully propped on the foot rail. He was becoming puzzled as to his best move. Rules were all very well, but when it meant hurting yourself to go by your principles—he was more and more tempted to marry Emmy and let the whole business go.

* * * * * * *

The week passed slowly, with nasty weather delaying Wang's departure. At last one morning Emmy greeted those at breakfast with the news that he had left very early.

"He said that he was already late, and there was a wagon going to Denver that could take him and all his things. He said to tell you all goodbye and that he hopes to see you again." She looked chipper, her eyes bright and her cheeks flushed.

There was a murmur around the table, and Mark found that he was going to miss the colorful shape of Wang about the house. He was a note of Oriental splendor you didn't often see in a town like Packsaddle.

If he'd had any idea of leaving before Christmas, it dissipated in the next several weeks. The food, which had been good, became superlative. Emmy seemed excited and pleased, and the house was filled with cheerful voices and bright faces. A sort of Paradise, Mark thought as he went in and out about his small job.

Then he found the fan. It was purely accidental—the thing had been kicked beneath the heavy settee in the parlor, where Wang's imprint still marked the plush upholstery. Mark's lucky dollar rolled under, as he flipped it, and he got onto his hands and knees to retrieve the thing. It had been given him by his aunt, who was the first of his victims, and he had a sentimental attachment to it.

The room was empty, for everyone had gone to the church for a carol-singing. Mark took the fan upstairs to his room and sat for a long time on the bed. Wang might well have dropped it and been unable to find it. He couldn't, obviously, crawl under after it as he had done.

The Chinaman might well have had more than one, in fact. But somehow Mark felt that he would never have gone away and left that bauble behind. He pushed away the thought that kept trying to creep into his mind. Emmy...was Emmy. The thought was absurd.

But he went downstairs before day the next morning, and went cautiously into the back yard. He wanted a look at the smokehouse, where Emmy hung the meat she butchered herself. He wanted to know, surely and certainly, if he had been eating Chinaman for the past several weeks, though he had to admit that if so, it was the best meat he had ever put a tooth into.

The door was padlocked, but that didn't slow him more than a minute.

There was a side of meat hanging in the chill darkness. The scent of smoke was thick in the little room, but the smolder under the meat didn't give any light at all. Mark found a sulfur match and struck it. He found himself looking into Wang's eyes—upside down and open.

His stomach heaved. Something that felt ridiculously like righteous indignation filled him. What a horrible thing he had discovered! He must go to the sheriff, get a warrant, have Emmy Whittle arrested for murder. For cannibalism. For—but what about him and the others? Did they share in her guilt? What would the law say about that?

As he stood in the darkness, pondering the situation, the solution came to him in a flash. He need only go through with his original plan. To kill Emmy now would be a just and necessary thing. To rob her was only what she deserved.

He turned toward the door, but there was a shape there. Something glittered in its hand.

"Oh, dear," said Emmy Whittle. "I wanted to save you for New Year's, and now I'll have to go ahead. But the weather's plenty cold—you shouldn't spoil."

She moved toward him, and Shaftoe stepped back and back, until he felt Wang's cold nose against his neck. Then she swung the cleaver, and he never worried about anything again.

This is one of my favorite stories, and I cannot imagine why it has never been published. Somehow editors just didn't seem to get it!

WHISTLE IN THE WIND

It was a long old way from Barron's Landing to Twining, and I cursed every mile of it as I traveled. Hell, I cursed every inch of it, with extra thrown in for each gust of wind that filled my eyes with dust. Old Henry, my mule, didn't like the trip much either, and when Henry ain't happy he never intends for his rider to be happy either.

Which accounts for the fact that he sat down with me just short of halfway, which was two weeks out from Barron's in the middle of no place in particular, and looked around with that mule expression that tells you it'll be a cold day in hell before he gets up. I'd lit on my back, as usual, when he buckled his hind legs, and I wasn't in the best of moods myself.

That don't excuse what I did next, and I've got to admit I'm a mite ashamed of myself for losing control that way. A mule's not easy to get along with, and I knew that when I bought him off Petroff, the Jew peddler back in Missouri. I traded off speed and obedience for a lot of bottom, which Henry had, but it didn't do either of us much good once I'd blowed his innards all over the trail.

He kicked once or twice and let out a long toot and that was that. By then I'd cooled down a little and realized I'd done a real fool thing, but it was too late to mend. Toting all that stuff I'd been taking with me on my way west was going to be impossible, and I'd just cut my visible assets in half, being as Henry represented fifty percent.

It was getting on for dark when I shot old Henry, and as you couldn't say that track saw more than one traveler in any given month, I figured to camp right there, cook a strip of Henry for supper, and leave the rest for the buzzards when I went on. Bad decision. He was the toughest bastard I ever set tooth to, and I ended up eating beans.

Next morning I made me a kind of travois out of some of the skinny little cottonwoods that grew along a creek I'd passed a mile or two back and packed on all I could drag of my plunder. My clothes wasn't no problem. I had what I wore, which wasn't fancy, and a good outfit I kept for funerals.

There was my survival stuff, which I had to take along. But the main weight and bulk was my tools. A carpenter has to have those, and I wasn't going to leave mine behind if I drug my guts out.

So I set off the next morning pulling like a mule, and many's the time I cussed myself out for shooting the only transportation I had to my name. Sometimes Dan'l Blackwith could be pronounced Dan'l Lackwit.

* * * * * * *

That was one long sonofabitch trail, but when I came in eyeshot of Kaylowe Junction, which was a long way from my original goal, I still had my tools. I could see the shapeless clump of buildings, huddled together under that endless sky, for a long distance.

As I got nearer I could tell that a carpenter was not only needed now, he'd been needed back at the beginning. A bunch of ham-handed incompetents had put up the most godawful batch of shacks it'd ever been my misfortune to set eyes on.

There wasn't a corner in the entire place that was or ever had been square.

The roofs looked as if they'd take off in a big gust of wind, and the porches and steps were a reminder of the shortness of life and the frailty of human bones. When I settled my plunder beside the collection of loose boards marked HOTEL (in letters so faded you had to guess at them), I didn't risk the steps. I trod mighty lightly on that porch too.

The inside floor creaked and shimmied, and I had a vision of cracked and dry-rotted joists trying to hold up two stories of junk. It made me shiver, but not as much as the wind and chill of sleeping out in the open did.

An old fellow almost as creaky as the floor came sidling out of a back office when I rang the bell on the dusty counter. "Help you?" he asked. His voice matched the rest of the place, a sort of rusty whisper.

"I need a room. Don't know how long I'll be here, but maybe a week. You want pay in advance?"

CRAZY QUILT, BY ARDATH MAYHAR * 243

He almost went into shock. "No, no, you can wait till the end of the week, if you want. Nobody pays up front. Nobody. You certain sure you got that kind of money? A room costs a dollar a day, and you'll have to eat at Aunt Belle's, down the street."

"I think I'd better pay up front, just to give you the experience," I said. I pulled out my leather purse and counted out seven dollars in silver. When I got cash payment for the house back home I turned it all into silver coin. It's heavier to carry than gold, but it's not nearly as tempting to thieves.

I saw the old man slide his eyes sideways to judge the heft of that bag, but I keep only about fifteen dollars in it. The rest is in the money belt around my waist. I don't look rich, and I ain't, but I don't intend to get any poorer than necessary.

I handed him those coins as if I squeezed 'em out of my veins; he looked disappointed and put them into a cash box somewhere under the counter. Then I signed the register, which hadn't been used in two weeks, and went up to my room.

"Where can I put my carpenter's tools?" I asked him when I'd washed and come back downstairs. "I can't afford to lose 'em. They're all I have in the world." Which wasn't too far wrong, at that.

"You're a carpenter?" he asked, his colorless eyes widening. "A real live carpenter that can build something that won't fall down?"

"Been one all my life, and my Pa and Grandpa before me," I told him. "Back East I worked for a contractor that built the Missouri State Capitol Building. I can put up a pigsty or a palace, if you give me the materials."

"What about a...gallows?" he asked. "We need one real bad."

I felt something like a shock go through me. I'd never built a gallows in my life, but the principle was simple. "I expect I could. Why?"

"Cause we got us a man we got to hang, and the last time we tried it, the damn gallows fell down and kilt the hangman. The killer just got a broke leg. If you think you could do the job, the marshal and the mayor would likely pay you well; you might even set up business here. Things don't hang together very well in Kaylowe Junction."

I thought wryly that it sounded as if they didn't hang at all, but I kept that to myself. This place needed a topnotch carpenter more than most anyplace I ever saw, and if these folks could afford to pay me to do a gallows, surely they could pay me to set their houses right. There was no reason I had to keep on to Twining. It had just been a spot to shoot at when I started out.

Towed along by Rufus Feldmaster, I crossed the wide street, dust boiling around my ankles as we moved and blowing away toward the tottery gray church at the crossroads. The sheriff's office was slightly less shaky than the hotel. Its sign, however, hung from rusty hinges and creaked like a graveyard ghost as it swung slowly back and forth.

That porch almost held us up without threatening to fall through, and I suspected the marshal of doing some sneaky nightwork with a hammer and nails. The door was open, letting in the heat and an army of flies generated by the horse dung in the street; we stomped through and faced the little man sitting at the desk.

I assumed he was a deputy or clerk. He wasn't the size of a washing of soap, and he had the biggest, softest brown eyes I ever saw in all my life. Looked like a sweet little old fellow that couldn't hurt a cockroach.

"Marshal Pinner, this here's Daniel Blackwith, and he's a carpenter. A genuine builder that can fix a gallows that will hang Ole Tollersen. I think you're going to be tickled."

The old man shambled back across the street amid gusts of red-dust-laden wind, leaving me face to face with this unlikely marshal. He smiled gently and rose to his full five-foot-nothing.

"Welcome, Mr. Blackwith. We badly need your services, and we will pay well. Let me show you where the gallows must be placed—we cleared away the debris of the other after the catastrophe earlier this month." He tip-tapped out onto the porch in his shiny size-three boots.

The wind had picked up as the sun went low in the west, and dust hid a lot of what he tried to show me, though I did locate the post-holes that had footed the frame. No wonder it fell—they weren't more than six inches deep.

"We need to hang poor Ole before the end of the month, if it's possible. We have to borrow the hangman from Calito, and he can only come between the twenty-fifth and the thirtieth. Do you think you might get it built that quick?"

I ruminated for a bit. This was the twelfth. I could put up a one-man gallows with one hand in about three days, if I had the beams and boards and somebody able to help saw them to my measurements. But it was best not to make this look too easy, so I squinched up my eyes and looked serious.

"Ye-es, I think I could do it. But I'll need some help with the cutting, and I have to have materials. I don't have the time or money to go off and buy them and haul them in." Even as I spoke, I wondered where in tarnation in this flat, treeless country you were going to find lumber.

"That's no problem at all. Ole is a bachelor, and his house will be empty after the hanging. We'll just take the lumber from his home and build his scaffold with it." He beamed at me.

It sounded heartless, hanging a man on his own house, but I didn't say anything. Probably this Ole fellow deserved to die.

"Sounds good to me," I said. "I'll start tomorrow, if we can come to terms on the pay for this job. What're you offerin'?"

He pulled a small black notebook from a coat pocket and riffled through the pages. "Last man got paid forty-five dollars for the entire thing, but it fell down, and we ran him out of town. I figure we got about what we paid for. So this time, to get it done right, we're offering a hundred dollars, and we supply all the materials."

That was a handsome price, and I grinned my agreement. "I may just set up shop here, Marshal, if it's all right with you," I said. "I guess the fellow who built your gallows also put up the other... buildings...in town?"

The Marshal looked glum. "He did indeed. They're all about to fall down too, as you probably noticed. We can use your skills, Mr. Blackwith. I hope you decide to stay."

As I ambled back across the street to the hotel I thought about this crazy place. It just might be that I'd found my natural home, because everything I'd ever done was out of kilter, with the lone exception of my buildings. I run my folks half crazy with my schemes. I run my wife into the grave worrying about the money I kept losing on bad investments. Kaylowe Junction might be the place for me.

When I got back to the hotel, Feldmaster had my tools all neatly stored in a back room behind his counter, and he was beaming as if I was the best thing he'd seen in months. Looking around the Junction, I decided that, homely as I am, that just might be the case.

The café where I ate supper was a surprise. Aunt Belle wasn't plump and smiling as I had expected, but the wiry little woman wearing a permanent frown dished up as tasty a stew and as flaky a crust under her dried apple pie as I ever put in my mouth. But what took my eye was her niece, Lily, who swished around the cramped dining room like a dancer, her trays never wavering, not a drop spilling. She was no beauty, having more freckles than a dog has fleas, but her smile warmed up the whole room.

All in all, when I got back to my dusty room that night I felt as if I'd somehow come into my own. Next morning I was sure of it.

When I left the hotel for breakfast, there was already a pile of timbers in the middle of the square, and a bunch of fellows were busy hauling in more in a couple of wagons. I could have built a house—and then I thought. It was a house! Ole Tollersen's house. Damn! The idea bothered me for some reason.

The job was a snap. My only problem was making it seem like a lot more work than it was, and that was made easier by the fact that all my helpers, enthusiastic as they were, turned out to be accident prone and stumble-footed. For some reason that didn't surprise me at all.

But I went about that gallows-building as if I was building the Royal Palace in London. I measured Ole Tollersen, so the crossbar would be high enough to give the rope some play, the noose hanging just at the right height. The trap had to be big enough to let his size sixteen boots through the hole. I fitted that thing to him like a wedding suit, and if he didn't appreciate it, I didn't much blame him.

He wasn't a bad old bird, once I got to know him. He was the size of a house, of course, which had to be why there was so much timber in the stack growing beside the gallows, but he seemed nice and gentle, if you didn't rile him. Which, of course, three folks had done, in the past few years.

When he smashed the last one with one of those pile-driver fists, the citizens of the Junction decided he was too dangerous a neighbor to keep around and finally tried him for murder. Wasn't a doubt of his guilt, of course, and the judge agreed.

I stretched out the job until a week before the borrowed hangman was due to arrive. The Marshal seemed happy as a pig in clover, and everybody else likewise. Lily smiled at me when I went into Aunt Belle's, and when I asked her to sit down and eat supper with me one evening, she plopped right down and her aunt didn't say a word. Even Belle's frown eased up about three wrinkles worth.

The day of the hanging I didn't go. I was busy moving from house to house, store to store, trying to gauge how much work was necessary to keep the entire town from falling flat.

The wind was blowing harder than usual. Fat black clouds were piling up on the horizon, and I was glad I wasn't standing there in the open square, waiting to see poor Ole get his neck stretched.

Noon came, and I ate dinner with Feldmaster's brother-in-law, whose house I had just inspected. He and his mousy wife seemed tickled to have me stay, and we was sitting around the table, belching and making small talk, when I heard a train, way off in the distance.

I wasn't from Missouri for nothing. I dived under the heavy oak table, and Mr. and Mrs. Jenks joined me without wasting time. A good thing, too, because the walls went everywhichaway and a chunk of the roof fell right on top of that table, which was a stout piece of work, all the way from England.

The rain came down like Noah's flood, and when we finally peeped out into the rubble that had been the house, it was almost impossible to find a way out. The Jenks's house had been the solidest one I'd looked at yet. As I crawled out, I wondered what the rest of Kaylowe's Junction looked like.

Did my gallows stand? With a sigh I rose to my feet, pulling up by a chifforobe with a lace curtain spiraled around it, and reached down to help the Jenkses out from under the table.

The sky was getting lighter, though it was still raining fit to drown a cat. We picked our way out, Mrs. Jenks crying softly every time she spotted something busted or missing, and by the time we got into the front yard we could see that where the town had stood there was not much left. Scatters of junk, mostly.

I ran toward Aunt Belle's. Lily! Was she all right? I found her under the horse trough, which was rolled against a cottonwood tree. She looked dizzy, but once I lifted the thing (must have weighed a ton) so she could crawl out, she looked up and saw me and smiled, and the sun came out for me, right then and there.

The hotel was leaning over like a drunk at midnight. I carried her over and set her on her feet just in time to see Mr. Feldmaster stagger up from a ditch, holding his head and looking dazed. I helped him sit down on what was left of a step and turned, wondering what I would find of my gallows.

It stood there, rock solid, the trap visible where it had flapped down under poor Tollersen's boots. A foot of rope, dangling from the crossbar, moved in the wind and dripped rain.

There wasn't a sign of Tollersen. "Where is he?" I asked Lily.

Somehow I had put my arm around her shoulders, and I felt her begin to shiver. "Lord, Dan, that funnel come swooping down and carried him away with the rest of that rope whipping behind him like the tail of a kite. The stores and the hotel and the houses just seemed to collapse, and I think the Marshal's buried under that pile of lumber over there."

She pointed to another mess of trash beyond the gallows, and I ran to dig into it. That little fellow was probably as flat as Ole's enemies. But when I come to one of his boots, not so shiny now but still size three, I heard a string of cussing to equal anything I ever ran across.

I pulled him out and we set about finding the scattered remnants of the population of Kaylowe's Junction. It was a good thing they'd mostly been out in the open, watching Ole dangle and catching up on gossip. If they'd been at home, there would have been a lot of deaths that day.

As it was, they'd dived into ditches and behind rocks, of which there was a nice selection, and most come out all right. But not a single house in that entire town was left with a roof and walls enough to keep off a shower.

I never much believed in Providence, but I've changed my mind. Since these folks needed a builder the worst way, and since I'd proved my stuff to them, hands down, I've been busy as a tick in a tar bucket ever since. Lily helps me too. She hated working in the café, but she's a master hand with hammer and saw, and I've discovered that there can be marriages made in heaven.

The gallows is still there, though since Ole left us there's nobody mean enough to need hanging. The folks seem to like having it there, knowing it weathered that twister and never stirred a peg. Come another, I hope their houses will do the same.

We never found Ole. I wonder if some Injun village, someplace, had him thump down among 'em and never did figure out where he come from. But that's neither here nor there. The main thing is that the Junction is going back up, solid as granite, and business is booming since the main trail westward has livened up some. Cattle are scrounging grass out on the plain now, and even our little Marshal has gained a pound or two.

So has Lily. When Young Dan'l comes along next summer, we'll have another carpenter to raise to keep the town in shape when I'm gone.

From time to time I think of old Henry. Does Providence make a plan, the way I do when I build a house, and mark out how everything a man does affects everything else? It seems sensible to think so.

But if that's the way it is, how on God's green earth was it planned that I had to shoot a mule to set my life on track? Seems almighty cruel to me, and I figure old Henry would be the first to agree.

I love the mountains of eastern Oregon. They are harsh and comfortless and demand much of those who would live there.

HEAVY, HEAVY HANGS OVER YOUR HEAD

He could hear it humming in the wind. Not that anyone else could hear it—he'd asked some of his infrequent visitors and all had denied noticing it. But he knew. He heard it not only when the wind blew over the hanging rock, he could feel it at any time of the day or night, suspended over his house on that unsteady ledge, waiting for its chance.

The feud had begun the moment he picked this spot to build his cabin. This sunny niche on the south-facing wall of the narrow valley was ideal for his purposes, with a spring gushing from the rock not twenty feet from his door. It even had trees—six thick-bodied junipers had defied the elements to live to ripe old ages. He enjoyed hearing their husky voices when the wind blew. They almost drowned out the voices of the stone.

No sooner had he leveled a spot in the soil for his foundations than the mountain began throwing things at him. Gravels, at first, followed by rocks the size of footballs.

More harassment! He had left the world of his fellow men because of such things.

But he had retreated as far as he intended to go. He would make his stand in this spot, and if it meant a feud with a mountain, then so be it. He had lumber hauled up at ruinous prices. He sawed, measured, hammered in nails until he had a stout shelter in which to try to heal the wounds he had suffered "out there."

While he was building, he felt the mountain staring over his shoulder, like some oversized cat surveying its prey. That only made him more determined. On the day when he hung the front door, a heavy affair of oak boards secured with metal bands, the mountain made its first serious move.

It tossed down the boulder.

He heard the thing crashing and booming all the way. Not being a fool, he took shelter behind the spur of stone just beyond his porch, and risked half an eye to watch the behemoth from on high heading straight for his newly completed home.

Another spur of rock, higher up the slope, stopped the thing—just barely. Now it hung there, teetering insecurely on the ledge, waiting.

It was a threatening housewarming gift. It remained just above his roof, balanced precariously. But when Henry Hammond committed himself, that commitment was total. He had bought this valley, built his house. Now, by God, he was going to live there and write. All the mountains in the world could just go and take a hike, along with critics and editors.

He added the triple-damned publishers to his list while he was at it. He still seethed over their demands for the impossible, even while they reneged on contracts and payments. He'd escaped from that trap, and he was going to make it stick.

Once the house was finished, firewood gathered from the juniper forest in the next valley (he cut only dead wood, for he valued trees a good bit more than people), all ready to weather whatever the winter might send, he lined up his three portable typewriters and said, "Eeny-meeny-minie-mo!" That decided which we would begin using, though he intended to wear all of them out over the next few years.

At the end of about three years, he intended to descend from the high places like some latter-day Moses, bearing with him a body of work so arresting in its originality and strength that it would electrify the publishing world. He would do no more writing to moronic outlines, filling shelves with action/adventure tailored to a bloodthirsty audience. No more choose-your-own-ending books for children who would grow up thinking that sort of idiocy was storytelling.

His grandfather's bequest made it possible for him to tell his agent to shove it, his editors what he thought of their projects (as well as their ancestry), and his publishers what he thought of their financial chicanery. Having made every enemy he could manage to, he had taken off on his personal quest for the Holy Grail.

One way or the other, he would make it on his own. If his Revealed Truth didn't make any sort of impact, he would just come up the mountain again and go on writing. He was full of stories that demanded to be told. He had enough money to live for years and years. He'd write just what he wanted to write, and if it never caught on (he sighed at the thought), he'd pump gas when the money ran out. Never again would he write another potboiler.

Now he sat on his front porch, staring out over his own valley, listening to the magpies quarreling (or gossiping) in the willow by the spring. His plans were bright before him. His fingers itched to get to work. He leaned forward, rising, just as the mountain spoke.

A hollow booming filled the air. Another boulder?

It was, but this one caught in a channel of rock and went bounding harmlessly down the slope to raise a line of dust before splashing into the stream that flowed away from his spring. He grinned tightly at the peak above him.

"Yah! Yah! Missed me!" he taunted.

Then he went into the house, filled with glee, and started to work.

Summer waned. Fall, at these altitudes, was early and short. Winter was upon him before he knew what was happening. The ancient fellow who delivered his infrequent loads of necessities arrived with a warning. "If you get sick or run out of food, you're in trouble," he said, running his finger along the greasy brim of his weathered hat. "Be almighty careful not to fall. The only way in and out, up here, is by helicopter, if you can get to your radio, which can be doubtful. Then it costs an arm and a leg. You sure and certain you don't want to go out with me?"

Carl seemed genuinely concerned, but Henry shook his head. "Here is where I stay. I can call out on the radio, if anything goes badly wrong. I was raised in Colorado. That isn't much different from this country. I'll make it—thanks, though."

Carl rolled away up the rollercoaster track over the ridge. His Jeep grew smaller and smaller until it popped over the rise and out of sight. Then Henry listened—there was no sound but the wind. And, of course, the hum of the rock, in its many voices. Every knob on it had its own note, and he had learned them all. By itself, it was a tiny symphony.

The first snow silenced its song. The quiet heightened his intense concentration on his work, for, with firewood stored in the shed attached to his home, he was set for winter.

He worked as if the devil were behind him with a whip. Pages of manuscript piled up in the boxes from which the reams of paper had come. He found himself glad that he had brought so much ribbon and carbon paper, for at the rate he was going he would need more by spring. He went out every morning into a world of snow that was so cold and clean it intoxicated him. He learned again to use the snowshoes he'd brought with him, recalling his boyhood in the Rockies. But he was careful—he had lost, somewhere along the way, his conviction of immortality.

The rock still hung above the house, its cap of snow at a rakish angle. It seemed twice as menacing in its silence now. He wondered how much snow it might take to overcome its precarious balance, but he didn't worry about it. From now on, he would work. Money or fame or professional respect, not to mention danger, could go chase itself.

The first winter went by fits and starts, dragging when his work slowed, whizzing past when it went well. Spring surprised him with an avalanche down the steep slope to the west of his house. He had chosen his location deliberately, setting his house below the spur that held the rock. The formation also shunted aside snow slides.

The warning sent him into even longer sessions at the type-writer, and the boxes filled even faster. April came, and Carl arrived as soon as the slushy snow was passable for his Jeep, which had studded snow tires. There was a garbage bag full of mail, along with fresh supplies of food, toilet paper, candy, and luxuries like fresh milk and green vegetables. Carl brought cigarettes, but Henry had gone without since he ran out in December, and he didn't need them any longer. He decided not to start smoking again. He did accept the chocolate with gusto, and later he and Carl tied one on, using the Scotch the old fellow brought with him.

They spent the next day tidying up the winter's damage. When Carl left, Henry sat down to begin opening his mountain of mail.

The first letter was from his agent. A check for eleven thousand dollars! Royalties, by heaven, for a book the publisher had claimed for years was losing money! Henry sighed, thinking of how much it would have helped only last year, when his wife Celia was so ill. There had been no money for the treatment that might have pro-longed her life. Chalk up another one against the System, he thought. Too little and too late again.

The second letter was from Slocum and Lewis. The envelope, a thick manila one, contained fifteen fan letters from children. The juvenile that everyone in the publishing house had tried to dissuade him from writing was making a hit with its intended audience. It was on the William Allen White Award List in Kansas for the past school term! It was up for the Newbery.

Henry laughed. Still chuckling, he dug into the rest. Fan letters, ads, junk—and a note from Celia's mother. He didn't even open that, but laid it on the fire and watched it curl to ash. There would be nothing there except vituperation, he knew. She blamed him for being a writer, for letting her daughter die, when he might have just as well have been a businessman and had the money to make her live. She'd never understood that Celia had wanted him to write as much as he did. The thought made him sad.

There were no letters from those who had proclaimed themselves his friends. He was out of sight and mind, that was clear. He sorted out the junk and added it to his fire. He made out a deposit slip to send to the bank with Carl, the next time he came. He tacked the fifteen fan letters up over his rough mantel. Fifteen kids had been excited by his work. That would make a nice epitaph, when the time came.

When he had tidied up, he went through the boxes of manuscript he had finished over the winter. There were two novels there that were, without a doubt, the best work he had ever done. He wrote a short letter to his agent and wrapped it in the package with the manuscripts. Might as well send them out into the world to begin getting their feet wet. Carl could take them, when he came.

He turned to stare out of his lone window. The willow tips were turning pink. Before long, the magpies would return. Then he might go down again to see a few people, go through some bookstores, remind himself that he was still at least marginally human.

He would come back here. That was certain. He had learned a lot over the winter, even aside from the fact that a bit of money could buy a lot of freedom.

He had pursued fame and money, and they had fled before him like foxes before hounds. Now that he had turned his back and walked away, they were slinking after him, begging for attention. It was a valuable lesson, though now he found that this made no great difference to him. Perhaps that was a necessary part, that indifference.

Never again would he appear anxious and apologetic, ready to agree to anything in order to get his toe into the tight door of publishing. Now he'd do as he damn well pleased. The people down there in the world could do as they liked about him—with this fresh supply of cash, he could live comfortably as along as he was likely to last, and there might even be more later.

He found that he didn't give a damn, one way or the other. He stared up at the rock. Its snowy cap had slipped aside, revealing its knobby shape. With that thing up there, waiting its chance, he would never get cocksure and arrogant.

Any day, any hour, he could be squashed like a bug. Until that time came and the mountain won its battle, he would be his own man doing his own thing.

He grinned up at the ugly chunk of rock.

It hummed back in menacing tones, under the warming wind of spring.

Although the families mentioned here are fictional, this basic situation occurred in East Texas at the point when Anglo families moved into Mexican territory. The town of Chireno, Texas, was seized in a similar manner, and the Spanish/Mexican inhabitants were forced to move westward from their original homes into less desirable country. Their descendants still live in Nacogdoches County, and many of them are prominent in business, farming, or other areas.

WELCOME THE ANGLOS

Antonia Lucía Morales y Batista stood at the door of her father's home, staring out over the long stretch of pine and hardwood forest that sloped down to the southern curve of the river. Not a curl of smoke interrupted the endless blue of the sky. No sound of axe or bark of a neighbor's dog rang through the morning calm.

Sighing, she turned and went into the house her father had built for her mother, ten years past. Mama had loved it, loved Papa, loved this empty Tejas country and the endless forests. She had even loved the occasional Indio visitors, although both Papa and Antonia disapproved of her gifts of food and tools to the red-skinned people.

But Mama was dead. One of those terrible fevers that lived in the swamps along the river had taken her almost between one breath and the next. Antonia had nursed her desperately, trying to preserve not only her beloved mother but the only other pale-skinned woman nearer than the settlement at Nacogdoches, a hard day's ride to the west.

Tears filled her eyes, but Antonia wiped them away fiercely. She had not the pioneer spirit her mother possessed. She disliked the mosquitoes that swarmed by day and night, the snakes that slipped unnoticed even into the house, the predators that decimated her poultry. More than anything on earth, Antonia would have loved to return to San Luis Potosí, where her grandmother would have welcomed her into her house and her heart.

The young woman pushed that thought from her mind. Papa was here. He had claimed many hectares of land from the King, and he had Indio slaves working in the older fields, clearing away the great trees from new ones, grubbing out roots, making the land ready for planting. Cotton, tobacco, and corn grew here abundantly, and in time he would be among the wealthiest of the patrones in this new country.

In the meanwhile, his daughter wore away her life at household tasks or embroidering endless bright nothings, as the nuns had taught her back in San Luis Potosí. No woman friend existed with whom to exchange confidences. No acceptable suitor had appeared, and she was nearing twenty-five. *Una soltera* already, she knew that it was inevitable that she remain unmarried until it was too late to think of marrying at all.

Her chickens squawked amid a flutter and a swirl of dust in the two-track road beyond the front gate. Was that her father returning? She hurried out again and stood shading her eyes against the glare of the sun, which was still low in the east, lighting the mists that hung above the river.

Yes, that was Estrella, the mare he had brought from Spain, still stepping daintily, despite her age, under the slight burden of Don Enrique's wiry frame. Ordinarily, the chickens never paid the slightest heed to the horse. What was coming behind?

She stepped off the low veranda and peered into the haze of dust and sunlight. The sound of wheels, of jostling metal and leather and wood, came to her ears. Her father was leading a wagon to their door. Sudden excitement sent Antonia toward the gate with unseemly haste. She paused, recovered her control, and moved graciously to welcome the unexpected visitors.

Behind the first wagon trailed three more, each loaded with canvas-covered burdens. Alongside walked three trail-worn women, two young girls, and a gaggle of children, all of them sunburned, bitten, and exhausted. They were not, she thought, people of the best sort, yet they were so obviously in need of rest, food, and washing that she felt her heart go out to them.

"*¡Bienvenida!*" she called. "*¡Señoras, niñitos!* Do come into the shade and rest while the men dispose of your wagons. There is cool water from the well, and I have small cakes that I make because my father loves them. Perhaps the small ones would like them, yes?"

The tallest of the women, her skirts flapping in dusty folds about her ankles, looked up beneath the limp brim of her bonnet. Seeing the sprawling house, the shaded walk, and the welcoming woman, she smiled and turned toward Antonia.

Was this woman to be a friend? Antonia wondered. But then she knew that these people were headed farther west. They always were, thinking to find better land beyond the spot where they stood.

The women gathered beneath the white oak tree, gulping water from the tin dipper. Scented by the cedar bucket in which it had been drawn from the well, the water was, Antonia knew, incredibly cold and refreshing. She could see new life pour into children and women alike as they drank their fill.

Luisa, who had served her mother from childhood, came onto the porch, and the young woman turned to her. "Have Rosa prepare more food. Chickens, vegetables from the garden, some of the fresh venison perhaps. These people are hungry, I know. We must feed them before they go on."

Papa was coming now, with the oldest of the men. She knew they had sent the younger men to unhitch the oxen and mules from the wagons and to water all the livestock that accompanied this small train. The well in the pasture would be busy for a time.

She smiled and curtseyed as the gray-bearded newcomer approached. *"Bienvenida, Señor,"* she whispered. "We are preparing food for your people. You are more than welcome to our home."

The man smiled, but his small gray eyes remained chilly. "Thank you, young lady. Don Enrique, we appreciate your help. It's been a long old way, and I can't say we're not tired to death. A bit of rest, some water so the women can wash, and a bite to eat will be mighty welcome."

Antonia felt odd. Courtesy among her people required more than this, but perhaps these newcomers had different customs. She turned and hurried around to the back, where the servant women had laid planks across trestles to make a long table, which would soon be filled with food.

As she worked, Antonia watched the Anglo women. They pitched in, tired as they were, to help with preparations for feeding this unexpected number of guests. The tallest one, Melinda, seemed to see what needed doing very quickly, and she had the children fetching and carrying without getting in the way of the rest.

An admirable woman in some ways, Antonia thought, despite her draggled appearance and obvious lack of education. It was possible she could not even read, though she was obviously quick-witted.

Once the meal was served and the litter cleared, Rosa and Luisa shooed everyone away and took over washing up pots and what plates had been available for use. The precious china from Spain had not been risked with this ragtag group.

She led the women to the wide space at the rear of the house, where the *niños* belonging to their servants kept the grass cut with a scythe. There two great red-oaks and a pine reared their heads at the edge of the ridge on which the house stood, and there was always a grateful breeze, no matter how hot the day.

The women sank onto the grass, their skirts about their ankles, while the children went off to pester chickens or play tag. "You are going west, then?" Antonia asked in her best English. "To make farms, perhaps?"

Melinda shook her head. "Walter's a carpenter. He'll build houses and shops, I guess, for other folks that come. Ought to be good business, time they get to be a good many."

In surprise, Antonia asked, "There are other Anglos coming? I did not know that."

"Oh, yes," the woman said. "Since Mr. Austin done the treaty with Mexico, a lot of folks'll be comin' to Texas. We get land grants, so much for each couple and more for every child. That'll give Walt and me a big spread."

Though the talk turned to other things, Antonia found herself thinking about Melinda's words. A subtle unease formed in the pit of her stomach. What would happen to the country with all these uncouth people arriving and setting up their own towns? Even Mamá would not approve, she felt.

* * * * * * *

Don Enrique gave his visitors directions toward a good camping place for the night. It was some miles along the road leading to Nacogdoches, and by the middle of the afternoon the wagons pulled out again. The women walked with brisker steps, and the children, full and happy, scampered about like puppies.

As Melinda's husband led their team away, the tall woman turned to Antonia. "Thank you," she said, her voice filled with an emotion the younger one couldn't quite identify. "If I can, I'll pay this back."

Now what had she meant by that? Antonia wondered. It was unlikely they would ever meet again. And if they should, Melinda had what was in that wagon and the clothing on her back. It was highly improbable that she might ever supply anything Antonia Lucía Morales y Batista might need.

As everyone knew you must, despite the heat, Antonia slept with her shutter barred against the night air, though it meant squirming and sweating in her bed through the humid hours of darkness. The mosquito netting drooped against her and stuck. Her nightgown grew unbearably hot.

At last she rose and crept down the hall to the kitchen. A cedar bucket of water stood ready on a shelf along the wall, and she stopped to dip a cupful and pour it over her face and hands. The sudden coolness made her shiver, but she moved along past the kitchen, down the steps, and out into that area beneath the trees, where she had sat with those odd women.

The damp stuff of the high-necked gown now clung to her, and she pulled it away, fanning with the fabric. As she stood in the milky moonlight she saw something move at the side of the house. Turning, she gathered herself to run for the kitchen, for many dangers lurked in the forests about Don Enrique's home.

Then she realized that it was a child. The little boy Melinda had called Dennis was beyond the fence.

Antonia felt a quiver of intuition. Melinda had promised to return favor for favor. Might this be the fulfillment of that promise? She had felt while they talked that there was something the woman wanted to say but dared not mention while they were surrounded by the others.

She stepped out of the tree-shadow, and the boy turned swiftly and saw her. He darted through the gate, past the house, and came up to her, his wide eyes shining in the moonlight.

"Lady," he panted softly, "My Momma sent this for you. She told me to git it here and not to git et by no critter. Here it is, and I got to go." He took off through the bushes along the garden fence and disappeared from her view, leaving Antonia holding a slip of crumpled paper, still warm from the boy's pocket.

She shivered again, this time with a mixture of dread and excitement. What was so important and yet so secret that this stranger risked her son to deliver it to one she had just met?

Antonia moved out into the full glare of the moon, which had now risen high. She held the dirty scrap into the light so she could decipher the scrawl of lines.

"Deer Miz", she made out,

> Yu was kind, and I preshate that. The men they like yore Pa's place. They alreddy sed they'd tak the 1st good land they seen. They goin to cum bak tonite

and take it. Go and hide. They mite kil yu and yore
fokes.

Melinda Roper

Antonia turned, her full nightgown flying, and sped to the
house. "*¡Padre mío!*" she cried. "Hurry! Get your things, your guns,
your books. Luisa, Rosa, Emilio, Pedro! Wake, wake! We must go
now! Wake the children!"

Her father came to his door, his aquiline face stern. "Have you
gone mad, Antonia?" he asked.

She thrust the soiled paper, which she now realized had been
torn from the end pages of a Protestant Bible, into his hands. He
stared down, recognizing the source of the paper, trying to make out
the meaning of the ill-spelled words. When he looked up again, she
saw the reluctant conviction dawning in his eyes.

When he moved it was like a whirlwind. While Antonia packed
up her sturdiest clothing, the heavy skirts and shirts she wore working in the garden, the stout shoes and boots, her journal, her sewing
gear, her mother's letters and picture, she heard the servants packing
necessities for this sudden move.

She met the rest of the household on the front lawn. The children had been sent to the pasture, and now the horses came snorting
into the garden. There was no time to load a wagon. Everything they
wanted to keep was packed onto horseback. When that was done the
servants headed for the small Mexican village farther along the trail,
while Antonia and her father went down into the river bottoms, leading the laden horses.

Even in the deep shadow of the forest they did not dare light
torches; as they moved, Antonia heard a clamor up on the ridge. Her
chickens squawked and the yard dogs began barking wildly. Six
shots ended that bedlam, and she knew that the faithful watchdogs
were dead.

She drew a quivering breath, and her father's hand touched her
shoulder. "We must be grateful to that *señora*, Antonia. We might
well lie dead beside the dogs, if she had not given warning. I
hope"—his voice thinned before continuing—"I hope that her warning will not be known. I hope she does not suffer for saving us."

Antonia had not thought of the possible punishment Walter
might mete out to his wife for betraying this plot. Now she shivered
in earnest.

She followed the dark bulk of the mare; behind, she heard the
hooves of the pack horses plopping into the soft soil that floored the

bottomlands. Don Enrique knew these trails as only a devoted hunter could. He led her surely across branches running into creeks that ran, in turn, into the larger stream. From time to time they turned to follow running water, hiding the marks of the passing horses.

Her feet were wet, mud squishing between her toes. But she followed without complaint, wondering, now that hardship had overtaken her, if she could face it as well as her mother would have, even though Mamá would have been furious at such abuse of her hospitality.

Antonia could almost hear that clear voice. "My Indios never would be so ungrateful," she would have said. "These *perros* are without pride and honor, and we must, in time, go back and punish them for their perfidy."

She felt heat rise in her throat. Anger? When had she ever been truly angry before? Antonia kept her gaze fixed on the dim blur that was her father's mare, but she was thinking hard.

Would they ever be able to return and drive out those usurpers? Melinda had spoken of more Anglos who would come into this country. If there were too many of them, it would be mad to try fighting them. Yet it was unbearable to think of running and running, without a place to rest.

A sob caught in her throat, and the horse ahead stopped. Don Enrique, invisible in the murk, was a moving darkness as he came and caught her against him. *"Hija mía,"* he murmured, "do not grieve. We are alive. We have the horses, our clothing, and weapons and tools. Even some books. We will survive, Antonia. In time, we may find another place in which to settle and another bit of land to farm. Our people will come to us, when it is safe."

She nodded against his chest and straightened. Before she could speak, there came a rustle so faint that she thought for a moment it was imaginary.

Then a gruff voice spoke from the darkness, using the guttural Spanish the Indios had learned from her mother. "Come, *Señor*, *Señorita*. We take you to good place. Back there, only death. *La Señora* give much to us. Now we give back, take you away. Then you be safe."

Antonia felt her father's astonishment through his circling arm. It equaled her own.

Mamá had sown her seed and been scolded for it. Now the two of them were reaping the harvest of her kindness.

"Gracias," Antonia whispered into the darkness. Unlike those who had thanked her the day before, she meant that with all her being. These savage saviors would never have reason to regret their kindness. As she moved after Don Enrique, she swore to the Virgin that she would devote her time and even her life to helping them.

They followed their invisible guide deeper into the swampy country along the river, and Antonia knew that those they had left behind would never find them. With sudden joy, she felt that her life had changed forever. She had found a purpose for her existence, and in time she might find herself useful to these quiet people.

"Gracias, Mamá," she murmured into the dank swamp. "Even in death, you watch over us still."

She heard her father clear his throat. Then his voice came to her through the darkness. "So she does, Antonia. So she does."

There was a painting hanging in our bookshop of just such a barn, and it told this tale to me.

COLD TEARS, COLD STONE

We played in the stone barn as children, half fearful in the dim light and the unnatural coolness contrasting with the brilliant summer days. Breath-stopping games of hide and seek went on there. Spies crept and Indians ambushed. Elaborate charades, most of them involving haunted castles with dungeons and torture chambers, were acted out there. It was, literally, the haunt of our youth—not constantly, but when we were in a certain half-daring mood.

As with all the other things from those long-ago days it was almost forgotten, like the farm, our grandmother, dead these many years, and the ancient pony on whose back we all learned to ride. Seven cousins, their ages ranging from six and a half to ten, lived only in occasional fits of nostalgia. The self I had been was packed away into my mental attic, along with the rest.

I was a busy woman, commuting to a job I loved from a marriage I didn't quite know how to end without hurting a person I had thought I loved and still had tenderness for. Arthur suspected, I thought, but he didn't say anything to me, and I certainly didn't know how to broach the subject to him. We were jogging along together like an ill-matched team of horses pulling a wagon whose spokes were loose and whose frame was shaky. Neither of us quite dared to suggest unhitching—or at least repairing the wagon, to carry the analogy altogether too far.

The call from the lawyers interrupted the comfortable set of habits we had formed to substitute for something warmer. The estate had been settled at long last. Every one of grandmother's offspring had rejected the bother of accepting the farm and putting it into order to sell. Situated as it was, it would bring a paltry sum. All of us were busy. Nobody wanted the old place. Would I be interested?

The will had been odd. Chester, the oldest cousin, had called each of us to let us know its content, and we agreed it was strange and let it go at that. For Grandmother had left the entire estate to whichever of us would take the farm. She knew, I suppose, how people change as they grow older. If she had offered it to us when we were ten or so we would have fought to the death over it.

They had all turned it down. I was ready to do the same when Arthur talked me out of it.

"Why not go look at it? You have some comp-time coming, and I have to go to California next week. Why don't you take off and go up to see the place before you make up your mind? You never know—taxes aren't all that much in that part of the state, and we might use it for a vacation home, or rent it, or something useful. A free farm doesn't just fall into your hands every day of the week."

He was right, of course. And, once I opened the door of that mental attic, many things fell out into my memory that filled me with pleasure to think about. Grandmother for one, with her strong brown arms and ever-damp apron, feeding the calves in the pen beside that barn. Chester and his younger siblings shutting me and my brother into the hayloft by taking away the ladder. Games and long talk and wild notions hatched in its dim recesses. It was the barn that drew me back, not the house.

I drove up on Saturday morning, taking half the day just to get there. Arthur had insisted that I take my sleeping bag and provisions, for we knew there hadn't been anyone living there since Chester's last tenant left and Chester died. There would be no utilities, no food, probably no furniture.

Once I made up my mind I was excited at the prospect of getting entirely away from my usual round. As I drove through the rounded hills that got steeper as they approached the turnoff, I found myself inexplicably cheerful. I kept telling myself that there would be nobody there. That you can't go home again. That the child I had been was irretrievably gone. But something inside kept bubbling away. I came around the downward curve of the drive, around the clump of birches that had now grown into fine big trees, and the house was before me. Off to the left, almost hidden by a maple grove, was the stone barn. The yard and the lot were overgrown with weeds. The rose vine that had always rimmed the front door with disciplined blossom had rambled all over the front of the house, even onto the roof.

I pulled up before the front steps and looked about. Trees that had been saplings now were as thick as my body. Had it been thirty years since I stood on this ground? The years had peeled away, and I felt no older than I had the last time I sat in Dad's car, straining through the window for a last hug at Grandmother. And now they were all gone, even Charles, my brother. It gave me an eerie feeling of disorientation. They should have been all around me.

An old house, shut over a winter, has a distinctive smell that contains elements of generations of mice and mold, ghosts of ancient meals, dry rot and furniture polish and wood smoke—and something else I have never defined. Grandmother's house smelled like that, and I almost felt tears come to my eyes. She had kept it smelling of lemon oil and rose potpourri and hot soup simmering on the back of the stove. How she would have hated to smell her house now!

But I opened the door wide, unfastened and opened all the windows on the ground floor, and kindled a small fire in the fireplace to dry out the damp. I'd camp down here for the time I stayed. How long that would be, I didn't know. It was so quiet—I was used, nowadays, to the hum of traffic and the varied clicks and throbs of household appliances doing their automatic duty. A house that held only the scurryings of mice and the scrapings of the rose vine against the clapboard was entirely too still for comfort.

I went through the rooms. To my surprise some of Grandmother's furniture was there, not too much damaged by damp and lack of care. The huge bureau, the eight-foot bed with the carven posts, the Victorian dresser with the candle sconces on either side—those were valuable pieces, and I had thought someone would have sold them long before now. Or that some tenant would have absconded with them. I was glad to see them—it was almost like having some of the family there to greet me.

The sun was low, though there were hours of daylight left. I unpacked my foodstuff, made a fire in the wood cook stove that Grandmother had kept, even after she got her good electric one, and made a stew that helped restore the smell of the place to something like its old state.

Once fed, I strolled about the fenced yard, re-creating in my mind the rose garden, in which a few hardy varieties still clung to life, the vegetable garden in the back, the rockery. Only the rockery kept its character—nothing but aeons of time would wear away those blue granite boulders Grandfather had brought down from the upper fields for his bride. Dill and Jerusalem artichoke still survived like the weeds they were in the vegetable plot.

I had the feeling I'd had when seeing films of war-ravaged cities. Where there had been order, there was now the wildest chaos. It filled me with something that wasn't quite gloom, but it didn't miss it by much. I went indoors as the sun sank behind the trees to the west and rebuilt my fire. It was just barely cool enough to have one, but its cheer was a thing I needed.

It wasn't long until I rolled into my sleeping bag. The drive had been long and tiring, and the arrival worse. I didn't sleep well—the silence kept me awake, for the few sounds of night birds and insects were alien to my ears now.

I woke early. The sun wasn't over the wood to the east when I staggered into the kitchen and used the kindling and wood I had gathered the night before to make another fire for coffee. Only when I had a cup inside me did I feel up to cooking a good breakfast. After that I looked toward the barn. I knew that had been my goal since my decision to come. Something drew me to it.

Pulling on my boots and heavy pants, I readied myself as if for a hard journey. Perhaps it was one—the journey back into childhood. I had no idea what I expected to find within those cold stone walls. Not even the ghost of the child I had been could lurk there still, I knew quite well. But I had to go, and now. I had put it off last night, but it could be delayed no longer

The meadow grass was long, ungrazed, and unmowed. Tangles of brier knitted it together, and I was soon glad I had worn the boots. The maple grove had grown out of recognition—the trees were now huge, whereas they had been merely large when I last walked this way.

The barn hadn't changed a bit. The dark stone still shone warm red-brown in its surrounding of pale mortar. Greenish moss had grown in some of the cracks, but the overall effect was the same as always. Solidity. Security. Continuation in the face of time and weather and whatever else the world might throw at it.

I stopped before the structure and stared at it. Its back was to the rising sun. The front was in shadow, the single many-paned window opening into darkness. The oak door was solidly closed, but I knew that it had never had a lock.

Now that I was here, I hardly knew why. The compulsion that had brought me so far left me, and I stood for a good long while, waiting for some inspiration to come to mind. But I had come, and I might as well go inside. Into that cool, other-worldly place where my cousins and I had solved all our problems when we were young. Now I had no problems—I stopped myself. That was a lie. I had problems to make those long-ago ones look trivial. Perhaps that was why I had come.

I pushed the latch, and the door moved a bit. It stuck against the stone floor, and I lifted and pushed against the old wood, feeling its splintery texture, familiar as my own skin. Then I was inside, staring up into the high peak of the roof.

The floor of the hayloft had fallen, and the entire expanse was open. The cool light from door and window left deep shadows behind the supporting pillars and in the corners, but there was no feeling of fear there. It was as it had always been, strangely comforting in its darkness and coolness.

There was a sawhorse at one side that held the remnants of leather harness, the ruin of a saddle. I didn't remember any of that—it must have belonged to a tenant. I perched on its end and breathed the dusty straw scent. This smell, at least, had not changed at all.

There was a rustle overhead, and I looked up. The snowy owls were still nesting high in the rafters. Somehow I had expected them to be gone, though these must be the many-times-great-grandchildren of those I had known. When I looked back down, I almost expected to see my cousins sitting about on the straw covered floor, waiting for me to begin a game.

What I saw, in my mind's eye, was Arthur's face, quite distinct against the dimness. He looked sad. Sad and older than I remembered. He was gazing at me, and in his eyes I could see something I had never allowed myself to notice.

"He's miserable too," I said to myself. "As much as I, or more."

There was another rustle from overhead. A mouse scurried somewhere in the piles of straw.

"I've been thinking about how I feel, and I never did consider how he feels. Isn't that true?" I spoke aloud, and the muffled echo was still there, muttering my words back to me.

I sank into a kind of reverie, staring blankly at the dark-shadowed wall. The barn sighed and rustled around me, and its sounds were part of me.

The cousins were there. I could almost see them. Grandmother was outside, tending to the calves. I was ten again, full of importance because I was the one who had the imagination. I was the one who made up the games, solved the problems, told the stories. I, I, I. Always.

Now I moved outside myself and looked hard at Elizabeth Sanderson. It had never occurred to me to do that before, not at home, not at work. I was always too busy talking or examining my feelings or agonizing over my woes.

How long had Arthur looked like that? Trapped? Desperate, almost? Probably for as long as I had felt that way. Or maybe longer—I had been too full of self to notice.

He was a gentle person, Arthur. Never would he hurt anyone if he could help it. How long had he wanted his freedom? How long had I ignored his needs in fooling myself about my own nobility?

Grandmother had sat here, in this very barn, I recalled suddenly, and told me something like that. "Nobody loves a martyr," she had said. "I don't want to find out that you've turned out to be one. Elizabeth the Martyr isn't my idea of a useful person. Be Elizabeth the helpful, Elizabeth the interesting. Anything, oh Lord, but the Martyr."

The old woman had cocked her head and fixed her pale gray eyes on her granddaughter. "Martyrs think I, I, I. When they think they're dying for a Cause, they're really polishing their egos."

I could almost see her. And I felt a blush spreading over me from forehead to toes. I had forgotten her words, forgotten everything she had taught me in her self-disciplined, caring life.

I rose from the sawhorse and looked up at the owls. "Thank you," I said softly.

I hurried back to the house and flung the camping stuff together. I could be back home before night. Arthur wouldn't leave before tomorrow at noon. I could make it with time to spare.

Cranking the car, I pulled away from the farm, knowing that I would accept it as my heritage. I needed it to remind me of the things I might forget again. It would be a good place to live—afterward.

For I was on my way, as fast as I legally could make it, to set us both free.

ACKNOWLEDGMENTS

"Fido Is a Loving Beast" was first published in *Sorcerer's Apprentice* in 1984.

"A Harping of Waters" was first published in *Dark Regions* #4 in 1991.

"A Painterly Effect" was first published in *Marion Zimmer Bradley's Fantasy Magazine*, Autumn 1996.

"The Weapon" was first published in *Excalibur*, ed. by Richard Gilliam, Martin H. Greenberg, and Edward E. Kramer, Warner Aspect, 1993.

"Gryphon's Nest" was first published in *Dragon Magazine* #183, July 1992.

"The Forging of Fear" was first published in *Dragon Magazine* in 1985.

"Who Accuses This Woman?" was first published in *Owlflight* in 1981.

"A Shimmer of Blackness" was first published in *Dark Regions* #4 in 1991.

"The Next Generation" was first published in *Fantastic Collectibles* #117, July 1993.

"Indulgences" was first published in *Midnight Zoo*, Vol. 3, #5, 1993.

"Hunting Truce" was first published in *Fiction Magazine* in 1974.

"Fungi" was first published in *Redshift*, edited by Al Sarrantonio, Roc, 2001.

"The Power That Preserves" was first published in *New Pathways in SF* #16, July 1990.

"Ratings War" was first published in *Espionage Magazine*, 1987.

"Solo Performance" was first published in *Bloodrake* #8, 1982.

"The Children Beneath the Stones" was first published in *Eldritch Tales* #27, 1992.

"Concerto" was first published in *Weirdbook* #30, Spring 1997.

"The Dig" was first published in *Borderland* #3 in 1985.

"A Night in Possum Holler" was first published in *After Midnight*, edited by Charles L. Grant, Tor, 1986.

"The Tuck at the Foot of the Bed" was first published in *The Twilight Zone*, May/June, 1983.

"The Eagle Claw Rattle" was first published in *Mummy!* edited by Bill Pronzini, Arbor House, 1980.

"Through the Padded Door" was first published in *Night Voyages* in 1984.

"The Affair of the Midnight Midget" was first published in *The Misadventures of Sherlock Holmes* in 1989.

"Crawfish" was first published in *Psychological Perspectives* in 1971, and reprinted in *Alfred Hitchcock's Stories to Be Read with the Lights On* in 1973.

"Aunt Dolly" was first published in *Dark at Heart*, edited by Joe R. Lansdale and Karel Lansdale, Dark Harvest, 1992.

"The Creek, It Done Riz" was first published in *Cold Blood*, edited by Richard T. Chizmar, Mark V. Ziesing, 1991.

"Jigsaw" was first published in *Hardboiled Magazine* in 1996.

"The Anthologist" was first published in *Blood Review* in 1990.

"Crowheart" was first published in *Western Digest* in 1998.

"The Pistoleer" was first produced as a dramatic radio reading by PEN Syndicated Fiction Project in 1990.

"Powder River Hideout" was first published in *Western Digest* in 1998.

"Trapline" was first published in *Razored Saddles*, edited by Joe R. Lansdale and Pat LoBrutto, Doubleday, 1989.

"A Cold Way Home" was first published in *The New Frontier*, edited by Joe R. Lansdale, Doubleday, 1989.

"Night of the Cougar" was first published in *Best of the West*, edited by Joe R. Lansdale, Doubleday, 1986.

"Like Mother Used to Make" was first published in *Horizons West*, August 1990.

"Whistle in the Wind" is published here for the first time.

"Heavy, Heavy Hangs Over Your Head" was first published in *Recording Arts and Letters* (magazine of Stephen F. Austin State University), 1992.

"Welcome the Anglos" was first published in a Spanish language anthology in 1994.

"Cold Tears, Cold Stone" was first published in *Impressions* in 1988.